A WOMAN AS PROUD, FIERCE AND FREE AS THE UNTAMED LAND

Anne Langford: She shone like diamond-fire amidst the glittering salons of Georgian London. Men dueled and died for her incomparable beauty but her heart remained untouched. Until she met the only man who could set her soul ablaze ...

A MAN POSSESSED BY THE SPLENDOROUS WILD LAND AND THE WOMAN WHOSE HEART WAS WILDER STILL

Henry Gladwyn: He was the handsome, legendary hero of Quebec, a courageous soldier who thought his wars were over. Until, with a daring mastered on fields of battle, he captured her hand—and set out to conquer her heart ...

A SEARING PASSION THAT FLAMES ACROSS THE PAGES OF HISTORY FROM THE OLD WORLD TO THE NEW

LOVE'S WILDEST FIRES

The timeless, tempestuous saga of a beautiful woman who burned with love's unquenched desires and the man who must make her his own. A rapturous love that soars beyond daring, beyond desire ... beyond forgetting.

LOVE'S WILDEST FIRES

Christina Savage

A DELL BOOK

Published by
Dell Publishing Co., Inc.
1 Dag Hammarskjold Plaza
New York, New York 10017

Dell ® TM 681510, Dell Publishing Co., Inc.

ISBN: 0-440-12895-1

Printed in the United States of America
First printing—August 1977
Second printing—September 1977
Third printing—September 1977
Fourth printing—September 1977
Fifth printing—October 1977
Sixth printing—October 1977
Seventh printing—November 1977
Eighth printing—February 1981

BOOK I

CHAPTER 1

No one particularly cared if His Majesty had retired early. They had seen him often enough as it was and his continued presence would have only dampened the highly spirited festivities. The Great Hall of Kensington Palace was ablaze with a thousand candles reflected in ten thousand jewels and tinkling beads of glass. The musicians were superb, even if most of the guests ignored them. The food was everything but ignored, disappearing rapidly in the face of score upon score of ravening appetites. There to see and be seen, England's finest swirled and strutted, posed and paraded, clothed, coiffed and periwigged as fashionably as the day allowed, which was fashionable indeed.

Laughter, masked by the haze of swirling candlesmoke, rose in sumptuous clouds, gathered in great clumps high over the chandeliers, fell back to the crowded floor in a shower of merriment. Wit crackled about the room from corner to corner, subjecting to acidulous tongues the rumor and gossip of the hour, spewing them out again in brightly constructed puns and aphorisms which themselves made the rounds and came back, polished and sharpened, to their sources. Lord Pitt, eyes flashing and the madness upon him, had come and gone. Newcastle reigned supreme in the center of an enchanted, sycophantic circle. Lord Hervey listened sympathetically to a cluster of young courtiers, his arm encircling the waist of one pretty youth he had singled out for more intimate discourse later in the privacy of his chambers. Horace Walpole, already promising the same enormous girth as his prestigious father, sat to one side, observant and assigning to memory that which he would later commit to paper. Cumberland, Marlborough, Talbot, Harcourt, Ancaster, Hamilton . . . the guest list was long and illustrious.

The music stopped and dancing partners bowed, the signal for the intricate pattern to break apart into couples who headed for seats or one of the great tables where freshly filled wine decanters stood waiting to be emptied.

Anne Langford slipped her arm through Stephen Berkely's, allowed him to lead her to one side before excusing herself, and, with a gaggle of her peers, retiring to a side room to repair her face. Laughter still light on her lips, she appraised the image in the mirror, noting neither modestly nor immodestly, but with the casual aplomb of those born well, that she matched in beauty the power and influence of the Langford name. Long hair flowed down her back and spilled over her shoulders to offset the creamy skin above the revealing décolletage. Quickly, her fingers rearranged the curls at her temples, twisted the strand at her left breast so it rested more flatteringly. Few young ladies kept their hair its natural color, and Anne didn't like hers in the least. It was auburn and mousy drab to her way of thinking, an opinion unshared by her father, who spoke in glowing terms of the deep, natural lustre of fine woods, fawn colored in one light, bay in the next. Once married and out of her father's house, she would be free to powder and shape her coif as she pleased, dazzling white and piled high in the proper fashion.

A tiny pout, and a sigh of resignation. Sir Spencer was a dear man but a whimsical tyrant of a father. As with her hair, he permitted only a modicum of make-up, leaving her face a natural hue, a light cream too dark for the current mode, marked with but a single natural—though not, she judged, unpleasantly shaped —beauty spot high on her left cheek. Still, she was forced to concede a degree of wisdom to her father's outrageous edicts: her skin *was* devoid of sores and clearer than her acquaintances', who already were forced to wear heavier and heavier layers of the pore-filling ceruse to conceal more and more blemishes. Looking more closely, she checked for wrinkles. None yet. Her face was satin-smooth and girlish. Her eyes— brighter and clearer than most, since not constantly irritated by gouts of powder—were the gray-blue of mid-winter ice and tempered the brightness of youth with haunting depth.

The barest hint of red—only enough to simulate a blush, for any more and Sir Spencer would chastise her—added to cheeks and lips, and she was ready. Stephen was waiting. Dear Stephen. He looked so fine and she was so proud, so lucky to be his beloved. Anne paused inside the door and watched him.

He was not tall, but well proportioned. The dark blue velvet flared with white lace, glittered with silver and gold embroidery. There was a certain stubborn set to his jaw after all, and while his lips were a little thin, his nose and brow were long and sloping, shaped well and indicative of good breeding and intelligence. She loved him so, felt a keen joy in just watching him as he conversed with Lord Grafton, now serious, now laughing politely. Lord Stephen Berkely's future was secure, and with her at his side, he could not fail at anything he attempted. And did he not love her as she him? He must, for as if catching his beloved's thought, as if plucking a dream from the very air, he turned and gestured. Anne made her way across the crowded floor.

"Mistress Anne! Your beauty never fails to amaze me. Were I younger, I would do my utmost to steal you from Lord Stephen." Lord Grafton was in fine mettle, drunk enough to lose the slight lisp he usually affected.

"Then 'twould be a complicated piece of thievery, sir, for you would have to take Stephen, too. I would not stir with him far from my side."

"And hence an awkward damned affair at best, milord, for I fear I'd be ill-suited for such a triangle," Stephen added, taking Anne's arm and patting her hand familiarly.

"Why, triangles are very much the mode," the Duke quipped. "The most august set us the example. Should we not then follow?"

Anne laughed with the men. Poor Prince George! His mother, the Dowager Princess Augusta, and the Earl of Bute had been laughed at for ten long years, and still they were grist for rumor's mill, especially since the Prince had taken to hanging on the Earl's coattails.

The conversation ran to more mundane topics and Anne, secure on Stephen's arm, let her attention wander. It was near midnight and she was tired. Such a long exciting day.

A crash of dishes attracted her attention. As she turned her head to see what had happened, two figures entered through the great doors. Admiral Saunders and . . . who? She'd never seen the man before. Curiosity piqued, she looked more closely. He was handsome, at least from a distance, and a large man . . .

Grafton was calling. The Admiral looked around, caught sight of the trio and steered his companion toward them, working his way among the other chattering groups, greeting one or another casually, only rarely effusively. "Damned capable seaman, Lord Stephen. Might give you some ideas," Grafton teased.

Stephen snickered. "I doubt it. In any case, I'm too old. All those young midshipmen . . . I should feel like an old uncle and I'm much, much too young to play an avuncular role with anyone. Who is the chap with him?"

Grafton peered about a little near-sightedly and shrugged his shoulders. "Haven't the foggiest. A *protégé*, no doubt."

"In that absurd get-up? Really."

Anne smiled, agreeing. The Admiral had stopped a dozen paces away and the enigmatic guest was in a three-quarter profile. He was adequately dressed, but looked awkward in his finery, as if he were unused to the cut and weight. Not that the weight should bother him, she thought. His shoulders were as broad as any man's—perhaps broader by a shade—and while the coat had been tailored to give him ample room, still one got the impression his massive shoulders would burst through the seams at any moment. The total impression was of power, of great strength at rest, barely contained, waiting . . .

". . . wager five pounds to your two he's a soldier," she heard Stephen whisper.

The Admiral and the newcomer left Lord and Lady Blevinsham and headed their way. Anne shifted her attention to Stephen and Lord Grafton in time to see Grafton nod in agreement. She snapped open her fan and wished she'd applied a bit more rouge and perfume.

"Ah, Admiral!" Grafton greeted him with genuine enthusiasm. "Good to see you. You know young Stephen Berkely?"

"Indeed. Know his father better. Has Samuel improved any?" the Admiral asked bluntly, his years at sea having washed away many of the niceties.

"Passing well, sir. The gout has settled in his stomach, but the doctors choose to be optimistic."

"And Mistress Anne Langford . . ."

"Sir Spencer's daughter then?"

"None other."

The Admiral held her hands, openly inspecting her before beaming his approval. "Well, young lady, your father and I spent some little time together in Rome, I recall, though I shall not recount for your tender ears exactly what we were about, eh? The last I saw you, you were only so high." His hand extended at waist level and he laughed deeply. "But you've grown. Magnificently. I should think Sir Spencer is proud indeed."

"I hope so, milord."

"Hope? Hope?" he queried the world in general, bouncing on the balls of his feet. "Come now, my dear. I'll wager a fair wind he is. But . . ." He paused, placed one hand on his companion's elbow, "would you meet a friend, please. Lord Grafton, may I present Lieutenant Henry Gladwyn. Henry Gladwyn, Lord Grafton. Henry's with the King's First. Served with James Wolfe in Canada, and by God won the General's interest before the damned French mowed poor Jimmy down."

"A lieutenant, eh?" Grafton asked.

"Yes, milord. I'm pleased . . ."

"A lieutenant! Damn. You've lost me two pounds.

Young Stephen here spotted you for an officer and conned me into a silly wager. Should have known better. Don't hold it against you, of course, still . . . Here, meet Lord Stephen Berkely. Son of the Duke of Arenton and soon to take his seat, less I miss my bet."

Henry Gladwyn extended his hand, politely shook Stephen's. Unaffected by the allusion to his father's imminent death, Stephen smiled faintly, as if amused.

"And Anne Langford. She's desperately in love with the pup, by which you may translate unavailable, in case you're wondering."

Anne met the Lieutenant's gaze, felt a tiny shock run up her arm as their hands met. His eyes were warm, brown, and fixed on hers, steady and unwavering.

The Lieutenant concealed his surprise. Langford was every bit as prestigious a name as Grafton. Saunders hadn't been exaggerating when he said he'd introduce him to the very best. That the best were the most beautiful he wouldn't hold against them.

"Gladwyn, eh?" Grafton rolled the word around sonorously, placing the name and recalling the pertinent information. The spell broken, Anne withdrew her hand. Unconsciously, she made a tight fist to retain the heat of his touch. "The son of Anthony Gladwyn?" Grafton asked.

"Aye, sir."

"Mines, the Chiltern Hills Canal, shipping. An astute man, sir."

Henry smiled for the first time. Grafton undoubtedly knew much more, used this little bit as a pleasantry. "As are you, milord."

"Thank you. Pride myself in knowing these things. Prosperous dealings out there in the Chilterns. Took a man with some vision to see it." His eyes narrowed.

"And all yours one day. Like Stephen here, perhaps soon, eh?"

The smile faded and the jaw line hardened. "I have an older brother."

Lord Grafton's eyebrows raised almost imperceptibly. "Ah, yes," he noted, his cordiality dropping a degree as he glanced a question at Saunders. "A common affliction, sadly enough."

"General Wolfe was a dear friend of our family, Lieutenant," Stephen broke in smoothly. "So you served with him?"

Henry's tone matched the younger man's in coolness. "Closely, sir. I was at his side when he fell, thrice wounded. He was a gentleman and a fine officer."

"Damned fine!" Saunders approved. "But I'm thirsty, and Jimmy Wolfe won't hold it against us if we drink to his memory instead of recounting his exploits, eh? Come, milord, lead me to drink. Stephen, come along and tell me about your father." With that the trio made their way across the floor, leaving Anne alone with Henry.

Anne smiled impishly. "Well, sir. It appears we've been cruelly abandoned."

The hard line of jaw softened and the eyes twinkled. "In this world, madam, I can think of ten thousand worse fates. May I call you Anne?"

Her hand gripped the fan tightly. Too forward? From somewhere, her own voice answered. "Why, yes. And I shall call you Henry."

The musicians began to play again. The crowd stirred, shifted, separated to make room for the dancers. "We soldiers are more used to the drum of marching feet and the harsh existence of camp life than the touch of a beautiful lady's hand on the dance floor,"

Henry said, extending his arm, "but if you will consent to be my tutor, I would be most honored."

He waited, steady and confident. Shyly, she knew not why for shyness was not her way, Anne closed the fan, let it drop on its slim golden chain and placed her hand in his.

The hours of the evening met, swirled about and coalesced into a single magical moment which stretched as long as the measured time of the music. Forgotten was Stephen Berkely, forgotten Lord Grafton. Forgotten the knots of lords and ladies, sons, daughters and admirers. Before her now, passing behind her then to reappear again at her side were those eyes which somehow had captivated her, caught her up and swept her away. She was lost in their depths, at their mercy. How tender for a soldier, how well taught and subtle in his steps. He moved with assured grace, attentive yet at ease. Anne found herself inspecting him closely, noting fine details. There were crinkles around his eyes, put there by sun and laughter. His nose was a touch too large, but still elegantly shaped, with a slight hook at the end which, in a certain light, gave him an excitingly sinister look. His lips were full—no, not full, mature—and the right hand corner of his mouth twisted slightly upward in a tight, ever-present hint of hidden humor, waiting only for the permission of those eyes . . . which relaxed and smiled, at last.

Deftly, he controlled her movement, his right hand leading, left hand resting on his hip. The nail on his ring finger was cracked, the blood underneath no longer red but dark blue, almost black. She was sorry, worried about the pain he must have endured. The knuckles were large, his wrist wide and strong, leading to a forearm, arm and shoulder she could only try to imagine. He was not much taller than Stephen, yet how like a doll she felt beside him now as they moved from the crowded dance floor to the promenade. The mystery lay in his smoothness of motion, the unstudied command he exercised over muscles that seemed designed for grosser gestures, for picking up great weights or wielding horrid weapons.

The music stopped and for a long moment she did not remark its passing. How long had they danced? Minutes no longer mattered. In a daze, she paused, let him hand her a cup of wine, felt its warmth match that of her cheeks. Her father approached, eyes glinting with curiosity. Anne introduced him by rote, listened vaguely to their speech and found herself dancing again. Try as she might, she couldn't remember a word that had passed between them, even though she knew they must have talked—of something.

The deep roar of men's laughter rolled around the drawing room. Attendants brought wine and spirits, tobacco for pipes. Stephen sat with his feet propped on an ottoman, his mind hazy as the smoke-filled air. The fellow had bothered him and he wanted to ask more, but talk centered on the continent, the French General, the Duke of Choiseul and the war, or what passed for a war, at sea. The major question was of Spain. Would France succeed in pulling her in? Grafton hoped not, but Saunders thirsted for the chance: prizes galore were waiting, not the least of which was Cuba, inviolable now due to Spain's neutrality. Stephen couldn't have cared less. "What about this Gladwyn fellow?" he finally interjected during a lull.

Lord Grafton made a face and Saunders grew serious. "A damned good man. With Wolfe, as I said. Unsung 'til then. Jimmy wrote me before the assault on Quebec. Had a premonition and wanted to be sure the lad—he's not a lad, but thirty or so—had his chance. Wrote the same to General Anson, as it turned out. Neither of us paid much attention until we learned it was his regiment that broke the French attack. Wounded twice himself, once in the arm, again in the side. Didn't faze him. Kept going, and after Wolfe suffered his grievous injuries, turned and fought at his side until the General expired. Then Gladwyn rallied his men and routed the French. Without the chap, as I've been told by those who should know, there was a damned good chance we'd never have taken the God-forsaken place. Wolfe was ill, you know, before the battle, and there's a rumor Gladwyn himself suggested going up those cliffs and was responsible for half the planning, though he modestly denies it."

He paused, accepting a glass. "My decision was made the moment I met him. He's the kind we need, by God. Strong as an ox, smart—a first-class military mind—and as devilishly adept as any I've seen. Anson agrees," he noted pointedly to Grafton. "The lad deserves a chance. We're taking a great interest in him."

Grafton growled, unconvinced. Stephen sighed to himself: why in the world some people thought just because a man could get shot and live he was capable of anything more, puzzled and irritated him. He himself had never been shot, of course, but damn it all, there was more to life than being a target. He said as much and received a silent stare in return. "Well, I'm right, aren't I?" he persisted. "It's perfectly obvious the man's a lout. Look at him. No breeding whatsoever, can't get out a decent sentence. I'm surprised he has the gall to walk in here and . . ."

"Be careful how you choose your words, lad, save

they be applied to yourself," Admiral Saunders said
sternly. He turned to Grafton. "The Gladwyn fortune
is greater than most expect, as you may know. Anthony Gladwyn was—is—no man's fool. Nor is Henry,
who is worth £7,000 a year now—five more per annum when the old man dies, which will probably be
soon. He's second in line, true, but I've met his elder
brother, Charles, and doubt if he'll last more than a
year or two at the most. No one lightly mentions how
much Henry Gladwyn will be worth then."

Stephen rose abruptly. The very mention of a
merchant's money was simply too fatiguing. He didn't
wait to see Grafton nod his head, for the first time,
in approval.

The hall had become a blur, the only point of clarity his eyes, still gazing into hers. When at last Anne
could no longer bear the stifling influence of the con-
gested room, she begged for respite and a breath of
fresh air. Without waiting, she escaped through a side
room and ventured alone into the exquisitely sculpted
gardens. A moment later, as she had known he must,
Henry joined her. Trembling with the eternity of the
moment, Anne allowed him to take her hand and
caress her fingers with a kiss.

At the touch of his lips, her soul took flight. Her arm
in his, they wandered alone through the green-and-
flagstoned maze.

Had he been in many battles? Yes. She was as beautiful as the night. The fragile blossoms scenting the
breeze were unworthy of her.

Had he been wounded? Several times, but only in
the flesh. His heart had gone untouched.

Had he suffered cruelly? Every soldier does, as does
every lover, should his love pass unrequited.

She took his kiss and the strength of his embrace was like nothing she'd known. Not some mooning, calf-eyed, pampered youth, but a man whose arms could be filled by nothing less than a woman. The idea was acutely thrilling, a daring departure from what she now saw as the childhood games of love with which she'd been so enamored. Stephen? My God, she thought. I'd almost forgotten him. How far in her past he seemed. Had she thought she loved him? An infatuation, really, the product of youth and immaturity.

They continued their stroll. Unbelieving, Henry gazed down at the incredible creature at his side. The preceding months had been filled with battle, with incessant tramping along muddy trails, sleepless nights, bad food, boredom, blood and death. Now, by some stroke of fortune, he found himself walking in a fairy-land. He felt too large, too awkward, a rough-hewn boulder beside a delicately cut, flashing diamond. Her lips had hinted of the dew of a summer's eve—soft, cool, a healing balm against the heat of day. A wisp of hair crept over the side of her face, hiding one eye and softening the line of her cheekbone and a jaw strong enough to promise strength in spite of a sheltered existence. A hint of flesh at her shoulder drew his eyes to the highlighted mounds of her breasts, the dark crevice between them a mystery he longed to solve. Pressed closely together by the binding bodice, he imagined them free, standing apart, their tips dark in the night . . .

"Madam!"

Henry and Anne stopped in their tracks. Ahead, in the dim light from a quarter moon, a slim figure stood at the corner of a hedge, half hidden in the shadow of a giant yew. Instinctively, Henry gauged the space around him, considered and then rejected action.

There was no danger in the gardens of Kensington Palace.

"Is that you, Stephen?" Anne called. The figure emerged from the shadows and approached. "Will I see you again, sir?" Anne whispered quickly.

"You have my word on't," came the quick answer. "Unless, of course, you wish me to stay."

"No. Don't cause a scene. Father would be furious." She squeezed his arm gently, stepped forward to meet Stephen. "Wherever have you been, Stephen? We looked for you but you'd vanished into thin air. Isn't the night lovely?"

The young man glared at Henry, who waited silently. "I trust you've enjoyed your little stroll with my fiancée, sir?"

"Very much." It was neither an apology nor a challenge.

Stephen bristled at the insufferably simple answer. How was one to respond adequately to an inane 'Very much'? Smoldering, he took Anne's arm, turned roughly and led her away. "It's late. Everyone is leaving."

Henry sat on a marble bench. Stephen's last audible words—". . . highly inappropriate and embarrassing. How could you?"—floated through a gap in the hedges, borne by a light gust.

She was gone. There one minute and disappeared the next, almost as if she'd never been, never held his arm, gazed into his eyes, kissed him. . . . Damn it! What kind of a fool was he to moon over a woman? He'd come to this ball because Saunders said he needed to be seen, needed to meet some men who would be important to his future. After ten years of knocking about he had finally gained the interest of those in prominent places, and if he played his part well, his career was assured. He needn't be a lieutenant all his life. Not if he kept his head. There was no future in losing one's senses over a wisp of a woman, no advantage in nighttime garden strolls.

Well, what was done . . . was done, he thought. Nothing to do but get back, find the Admiral, apologize and keep his wits about him from then on. Henry rose, started back accompanied by the indelible taste of her lips and the memory of the touch of her hand on his arm. Anne Langford. A pretty enough name. Beautiful, too, in an aristocratic sort of way. By God, when she pressed close to kiss him, he had felt . . .

No! What was that fellow's name? Something or other Grafton. Close to the King. What was it Saunders had said about him? Ah, yes . . .

And the ice-blue eyes . . . how cool her lips . . . how soft . . .

CHAPTER 2

The hours with Henry passed so swiftly as to take her breath away: the days between each rendezvous dragged on with such excruciating slowness as to smother her. Admiral Saunders saw to it his charge was busy here, meeting there, visiting with a duke and dining with an earl. Anne languished, the ennui broken only by snatches of fantasy in which she explained, coolly and calmly, to Stephen why she could not marry him and to her father why she would not. Reason explained to romance why Henry must be kept from her side: his career, only now budding, was at stake; the cultivation of friendships in the right circle was more than merely desirable, it was mandatory. She had no right to expect him to wait on her every whim. Were he less circumspect, as a matter of fact, they might arouse Stephen, and possibly Sir Spencer as well, to ugly extremes. As it was, Stephen had become a constant thorn in her side. At first she was guilt-ridden, later angry. Always, she was afraid. A jealous Stephen was perfectly capable of mounting a campaign designed to thwart Henry's rise.

But anger, guilt and fear left her during those precious moments she did share with Henry, for then she forgot not only Stephen and her father, but Henry's commitment to his own advancement. On a Tuesday in late May, they travelled by coach to the country for a picnic of cold venison, thinly sliced cucumbers, light-as-down biscuits flavored with freshly shredded oranges and smothered with wild-plum jam, all washed down with a light white wine smuggled from her father's cellars. Henry even brought some chocolate, which he heated over a tiny fire he built himself, much to Anne's delight. The day was warm and cloudless, the air pure and vibrant with the songs of birds and the chuckle of the tiny stream beside which they spread their blanket.

When their meal was finished and Anne lay at length on the sweet grass, he had bent over and kissed her. At first, she offered no resistance, but when his tongue entered her mouth she was stirred by the first pangs of alarm. Frantically, she twisted her head to one side. "Henry . . ."

He didn't understand. His hand stroked her stomach, slid boldly up to cup one breast as he pulled her to him and his lips met hers again. Torn, she surged to the electric awareness of his touch. Her breast swelled and her breath quickened. Yet she was afraid!

Henry drew back. "What is the matter?" Anne could only shake her head from side to side, embarrassed at the tears that rolled down her cheeks. "Why?"

"I don't know," she finally managed, sitting up and clasping her arms about her knees. "Everyone else does it, but I . . . want to . . . want to but . . ." She gulped, unable to formulate into words a deeply held belief in chastity and fidelity. "Won't you please try to understand?"

Inexplicably, unexpectedly, he laughed—neither harshly nor meanly, but with warmth and kindness. Gently, he unwrapped her arms from around her knees, laid her back on the grass. He propped his head on one hand, rested the other lightly on her stomach.

A smile softened his face. "My darling Anne. I will do far better than understand. I will cherish your chastity and hold it dear." He bent, brushed forehead, eyes, nose and lips with barely felt kisses. "Sleep, if you will. I will watch over you."

Sleep she did, more relaxed than if she had been in her own bed. When the afternoon breeze sang through the ancient oaks on the knoll above them, he awakened her. They rode back in silence, hand in hand, as twilight deepened.

It was the first Friday in June before they met again. Masqued to protect her complexion from the sun, Anne accompanied Henry to a bearbaiting, squealing with delight and clinging to his arm as the bear dispatched six hounds before eventually succumbing to the seventh. The next Sunday was a real adventure. They went in disguise to the fair at Bald Downs, strolled through the crowds, ate hot buttered corn until the juice ran down their chins. In the afternoon, the locals had arranged a contest of ride-the-goose. The whole throng was limp with laughter at the young men trying to grasp the greased and frantically bobbing neck of the bird. When Henry himself, with a borrowed horse at a dead run, finally succeeded in parting the squawling fowl's head from its body, the crowd roared with approval and hoisted him to their shoulders. Later, nodding gently to the rhythm of the carriage, Anne rode home half asleep from the excitement, her head resting against his chest. She could hear his heart beat and feel the warm protection of his great arm around her.

On only three nights could she escape the watchful eye of fiancé and father. Stephen was insistent and distrustful, aware of Anne's escapades and adventures with Henry but too proud to mention them aloud,

while Sir Spencer, only too aware of his daughter's
proclivity for social intrigue, admonished her sternly
and hoped for the best. Still, Anne dared to be escorted by Henry, knowing full well the idyll could not
last, that a hundred awkward and exaggerated versions
would get back to irate parent and outraged fiancé.
These nights were a fairyland of feasting, dancing,
cards and gaming. Anne positively glowed, and contrary to her father's wishes, for he was not present,
was brave enough to wager and most luckily win a
hundred pounds on the correct assumption that the
Bishop's wife would consume at least three bottles of
port before the stroke of midnight.

Best of all were the stolen moments spent in quiet
tête-à-tête with Henry in a half-dozen hastily arranged
locations when he had an hour or two to spend and
could get a message to her in time. After these brief
minutes together, Anne analyzed in infinitesimal detail Henry's every nuance, seeking meaning behind his
most mundane utterance. Later, sleepless, feeling sorry
for herself and a little silly, she would chide herself
for dreaming of marriage. If only they could!

But a host of reasons forbade such a match. A marriage had already been arranged to the satisfaction of
both the Duke of Arenton, Stephen's father, and Sir
Spencer. To break a marriage contract and then wed
a man without title—a commoner, though he was far
from common—would be an unheard of scandal. The
Langford fortune, through haphazard management
and untimely ill luck, was near depletion: marriage to
Henry would severely diminish the only true capital
her father still held—his prestige and name. Since
Henry was second in line and hence without a fortune of his own, they would surely starve. Worst of
all, he had not asked her—or even broached the sub-

ject. Sleepy at last, reasons fled and she dozed. With sleep came dreams, and with dreams came, once and ever again, the touch of his hands and lips in sweet caresses.

But dreams lost their power by day, and Anne was forced to cope with the real world, all too often without Henry. For the last two weeks of June, Lord Stephen, with Anne in tow, hied off to the Berkely summer estate at Arenton, separating the would-be lovers and plunging Anne into gloom. Nothing cheered her. Long walks in the garden served only to remind her of the night Henry had entered her life and stolen her heart. A dance suggested his bow, his sure elegance. A picnic became no more than a day in the beastly sun, plagued by insects and the cloying concern of a betrothed she no longer loved. There was only one consolation: they would return to London for her birthday on the ninth of July. She counted the days, ticking them off on the calendar of her heart.

"Very well, sir!" Anne admitted, near tears. "You are right. I invited him. Have I not the right to ask . . ."

"You enjoy those rights which I choose to allow, as well you know. I will not have that man in my house."

"But it's *my* birthday, Father. I'm nineteen, and surely . . ."

". . . old enough to assume the responsibilities of your position, those demanded by the name of Langford. That you should act so abominably is simply appalling, Anne. Worse, to hide from me . . ."

"I hid nothing!"

"I do not wish to argue. The fact remains, you did not tell me. I had to learn of your rash behavior from Stephen. As long as you are in my household, daughter, I refuse to tolerate such subterfuge." Sir Spencer's voice had risen with each word he spoke. In the pause that followed, a maid had the temerity to enter unbidden. "Out!" It was a roar. "Now!" The startled girl fled.

Anne wept, tears flowing in scalding paths. She had never seen her father so angry. "Don't you understand, Papa?" she sobbed. "I love him."

"Love? Henry Gladwyn? The son of a common merchant who has profited obscenely with a ditch and a hole in the ground?" The thought was preposterous. Sir Spencer wagged a finger in her face. "Love has nothing to do with it, young lady. Love! He's a commoner, and by all that's holy, I'll not have my daughter . . . rudely consorting . . . with a commoner."

"Father! How could you . . ." Infuriated, she stamped her feet and whirled away from him. The strength with which she spoke brought Sir Spencer up short.

Trying another tack, he pulled the chair close and sat before her. "Anne." His voice was softer, more gentle, as he pleaded for reason in the face of misguided obstinance. "This match with Lord Stephen is a good match. Do you know how much the lad is worth? Don't you realize what his position will be when his father . . . that is, upon his succession? Well?"

"Yes, sir. I do. But . . ."

"Then what else could you possibly want?"

"I don't love him, Father."

"Two months ago you could speak of nothing *but* love for the lad."

"That was two months ago. I don't love him now," she insisted.

"It doesn't matter if you don't love him. Damn it, girl, he's in love with you! Absolutely calf-eyed, to see him. After you've married the man, you may continue your affair with this . . ."

"Papa, please. We haven't . . . I mean, you don't think . . ."

Sir Spencer raised a hand in conciliation. "Very well. I concede the point. You may *have* an affair with this Gladwyn fellow, if you must. But before God, Anne, the match is made. All London knows you are going to marry Stephen. You must go through with it."

Anne didn't answer. The tears had stopped and her back was stiff. "As far as I'm concerned, Henry has been invited and will attend my birthday party. I won't make a spectacle of myself, if that will make you feel better, but I do insist upon his presence."

Sir Spencer rose. "You are determined?"

"I am, sir."

He inhaled deeply. The attempt to reason had failed. "Very well, daughter. We shall see . . . what we shall see." A tight smile played across his face, disappeared. "You'd best begin your toilette. The guests will be arriving soon. You've but two hours to prepare." A tired man, he strode from the room and called for a messenger. Stephen would need all the time he could get.

"Ye're daft, man!"

"You've yer whole life ahead," complained Sergeant Fulton.

"And wars to be fought. Glory to be won," added Private Breen. "On the battlefield, not the bed."

The other men chuckled good-naturedly, but Lieutenant Henry Gladwyn was not to be swayed by the concern of his common fellows who, in most rare camaraderie, sat with their commanding officer and drank to his health. No reformer, the Lieutenant was not one to spend his days with the rank and file, and yet these very men were as responsible for his rapid rise in influence and the newly bestowed personal commendation from the King as was his own gallantry under fire, so bravely and fiercely had they followed his lead. But privates and corporals and sergeants, of whom blind duty and little else was expected, never received the thanks of the Crown. To show his gratitude, Henry had called together the remaining twenty of his command and summoned them to this obscure tavern on the south side of London. In the revelry that followed, the rafters rang with laughter and bawdy ballads echoed down Old Street to the Thames. Henry bawled for another round of the tavern-keeper's hardy rum. Tankards were lifted in toast and the men cheered. Sergeant Fulton, a coarse, beefy, good-natured man who would never see forty-five again, sidled closer to his commander.

"Now, seriously, sir. There's yet battles to be fought, and good men such as yourself needed to lead. What will our crew of lads do without you? March behind a bag-wigged prig of an ensign who don't yet know how to wipe his arse? No, sir. We'll not have it! You've spoiled us after the example you've set."

A score of voices around the table murmured deep-throated assent. "So it's marriage ye're after. And then what, pray? You'll move to yer father-in-law's estate and become a squire, more than likely, with yer feet in front of the fire and a brace of little ones at yer knee. Gout, ague and ill humors will plague yer days and nights, leaving the drums of war little more than an echo in yer blood. Nay, sir. A bit of bed warmin' is what you yearn for, and that simple enough for a lieutenant like yerself to be obtainin', with a fine, strong-bodied lass, too, free of the pox. By m'oath, but a pale, blue-blooded lass yet new from the cradle is the last thing you need."

The tavern exploded once more into a chorus of whoops and laughter. Henry managed a grin, his resolve unshaken. "Cradle indeed, Sergeant. She's a fair, fine-trimmed lady and nineteen today, as near an old maid as you'll find and yet as pretty as a sunrise over the Chilterns, which you, in your terrible ugly ignorance, have never seen. A man could search far and wide and never find a beauty to match the likes of Anne Langford."

"But you hardly know the girl, sir," Fulton persisted a touch waspishly, the rum giving boldness to his tongue. "You've said that yerself."

"Have you become my father that you counsel me so, Sergeant Fulton?" Henry asked sternly. Ribaldry was fine, but the last remark sounded suspiciously insubordinate. The tavern quieted immediately and an embarrassed hush darkened the proceedings. Henry's voice softened, his tone quiet and meant for friends' ears alone. "I've told you about the woman, but you can't imagine how she looks without having seen her with your own eyes. There I was, marching into Kensington Palace as if I owned the place. You'd not believe the glitter, the majesty. Admiral Saunders led me across the floor and there she stood, as if waiting for me . . ."

His eyes closed and he could see her as plainly as on that first night. The men gazed raptly, caught in the story. The hiss of candles and the meager, flickering light cast an enchanted spell over the rough company as they shared their lieutenant's dream. Henry went on, his voice hushed. "Clothed in jewels and bathed in candlelight, I thought she must be a goddess set there to lure a lonely English soldier. When next I came to my senses"—he peered into the intent faces, pausing for the effect—"we were dancing. Floating, I should say, for I cannot remember touching the floor. And she moved with such lightness and grace I thought my heart would burst to watch.

"The music ended. We ate. We drank. We talked, then danced again." Henry's face clouded and his listeners tensed. "Suddenly, she turned and walked away from me and made her way out the doors to the garden. I, a puppet dangling on a string, followed . . ."

"And?" Fulton's voice was ripe with suspense.

Henry laughed, breaking the spell. "And what transpired there is for no man to know but myself, you bold old rooster." The Lieutenant stood and drained his mug. "It's late and I must be off and see my lady. Wish me well, lads. 'Tis an end to your lieutenant's wanderlust."

"And to a fine soldier, I fear," lamented the sergeant. "They'll be none more like ye, sir." The company assented vigorously. "But if you're off, you're off, and who are we to stay our friend's pleasure? The least we can do, lads, is give him a cheer in memory of fine times past. Let's hear it, then!" Rising to their feet as one, the last twenty raised their cups, Private Breen the most unsteady of the lot, and bellowed three cheers, each more boisterous than the last until the rafters rattled with their approbation.

Henry held his hand high. "A final toast then, lads, and I'll be gone." The crowd hushed as the tavern-keeper filled the mugs all around. "To the finest England has to offer. May your women be many, and though their eyes be crossed, never their legs!"

A hearty cheer rang out as their commanding officer drained his mug. Slamming the pewter tankard on

the table, he produced a small but well-packed purse
and tossed it to the tavern-keeper. "Give them what
they will, man. When the gold is gone—and see you
don't short-change them or I'll have your ears—shoo
the lot from your door. *If* they can walk. If they
can't, pitch 'em into the Thames and let 'em swim."

A chorus of laughter and a final three rousing cheers
followed him into the night where a lurking, unseen
figure scurried into the darkness, mounted a horse and
hurried off unseen.

The barge struggled against the sluggish current
and passed the Tower. The dark walls looming strong
and sinister against the night sky were a symbol of the
strength of England, the power of her monarchs to
make or break men's fortunes. Staring at the massive
stone, Henry imagined the bars and rings of steel, en-
gines of torture and scurrying, chittering beasts of filth
and darkness. What would his own fortunes be? he
wondered. Life had been simpler and less troubled
ten years before when, with no particular aspirations
in mind, the youngest Gladwyn son had willingly followed his father's advice and accepted the commission
of ensign as bought and paid for. The next two years
had seen little action beyond bar and club rooms, for his
country was at peace. In 1752 he'd been sent to India
as a courier. Returning home, he wasted another pair
of years and then watched helplessly as Prussia went to
war with Austria and France. Bored and looking for
action, Henry volunteered to be sent as a secret observer to Saxony in time to watch Prince Frederick
turn the tide of war at Rossbach. Three weeks later,
under overwhelming public pressure, the Great Commoner Pitt reversed the prior policy of peace in a
spectacular *volte-face*. England went to war.

War is good for young ensigns if they are lucky enough to survive. At twenty-eight Henry had pleaded for greener fields and was sent to the American frontier to join General James Wolfe. On June 26, 1759, the first shot was fired in the battle that was to signal the collapse of the French in America and become Henry Gladwyn's one great chance for advancement. Wolfe was determined to take Quebec and break Montcalm's back, but by the sixty-seventh day of the siege, the English had lost over eight hundred men and fifty officers. Henry, by virtue of vacuum, received his lieutenant's commission. On September 13 the heights were scaled and Henry stood with Wolfe on the Plains of Abraham, awaiting that final battle which would claim the life of England's most honored general.

How quickly, in retrospect, the time had flown. Now, ten months later, he was back in England, had been fitted with an entire new wardrobe and admitted to circles of which he'd once only dreamed. At first, as he played about on the periphery of London society, he was only dimly aware of its dangers and pitfalls, but as each day and week passed, they became more evident. Now the time had come to plunge into the very center of things. The suit he would press this night would commit him to a new course and he had no plan other than to press on boldly. Within the hour, Henry Gladwyn would ask for Anne Langford's hand in marriage.

There were problems, not the least of which was Anne herself. Their hours together convinced him of her love. Accustomed to wealth and power, Anne was not unused to making her own decisions, yet would she go so far as to break her commitment to Stephen Berkely? Would her father permit it?

Henry had known the name of Langford, but only over the past weeks had he come to realize the prestige Sir Spencer wielded. The man was of an old family. His word and honor were valued beyond wealth. How would he react to a change in his daughter's plans? How would he react to the idea of his daughter marrying into an untitled family, even if they were wealthy? Badly, Henry feared, yet he continued to hope.

As for Stephen Berkely, there was little question. Soon to be Duke of Arenton, the young man would hardly tolerate being crossed, especially by a commoner. Henry was an acute embarrassment Stephen could not afford to ignore, and the young nobleman would attack with neither scruple nor quarter. Henry's position was painfully obvious: his fortunes had risen, so could they fall—precipitously and irretrievably.

Henry drew a deep breath, pulled the heavy cloak tighter. The river air felt good, tasted fresh and tangy after the smoky pub. Bright lights reflected in the water, shimmered along the path leading to the future. The way was clear. He'd come this far and was damned if he'd turn back. The world and all it held was for the strong, for those who dared to strike out, to grasp and hold. Determination, confidence and optimism were the weapons available to every man: this was one man to wield them with all the power at his command, and win. Falling in love with Anne Langford was pure serendipity through which a fortune would be molded and a career assured.

Aye. Taking a wife was serious business, Henry reflected. No more those delightful explorations of London's boudoirs that a handsome man was free to enjoy. Anne would have nothing of it, he was sure. Wistfully, he recalled the latest. Mary Delany was a buxom

lass made for tumbling and pleasurable exercise, a fine
piece in tawdry finery, her notorious character un-
complicated by morals. He sighed. Marriage would
see an end to sporting with Mary.

The barge rasped onto the gravel shallows a little
below White Hall where his carriage waited. A blanket
of fog had followed them upriver and now swept
over the boat. Henry, grateful for the heavy fabric of
his scarlet cloak, bundled it about his shoulders, paid
for his passage and mounted the stone steps leading
away from the narrow bank. A moment later he was
safely into his carriage and on the way to the Gladwyns' London residence in Grosvenor Square. The fog
thickened in pockets, making progress difficult through
the gloom and forcing his driver to halt from time to
time to get his bearings. At one such pause, Henry
distinctly heard a shuffle of footsteps approaching the
carriage, but though the sound was ominous, he took
little heed. London was dangerous at night, but the
heaviest danger lay in the dark side streets and the
teeming slums to the south and east, not here where
the nobility was wont to walk.

The noise receded. The carriage jolted forward and
Henry relaxed, lulled by the rum he'd drunk with the
sergeant and his men, half dreaming of war and battles, and of Anne, who even then waited for him. He
woke with a start. The carriage had stopped and he
could hear muffled voices followed by the dull sound
of a blow and a thud as his driver fell unconscious.
Cautiously, he peered out the window. They were at
the corner of Dean and South Audley streets for he
recognized the apothecary. With one clean move, he
was out of the carriage and melding into a shadow,
his weapon drawn.

The fog was thinner there, but he did not need to

see. The sense of danger born of battle spurred him into action even as the first assailant lunged from the mist. The soldier leapt back and the form of a man sailed past, helped on his way by a well-placed fist laid across the back of his neck. A rustle of steps to his left. Henry danced aside and planted a booted foot to a stout behind, speeding a second attacker across the cobblestones and into the stone wall of the apothecary, where he crumbled like a stunned ox. "The art of cut-pursery has fallen on hard times indeed, if this is the best you can do," Henry laughed, spinning at a sound to his rear. "Aha! Another Robin Goodfellow up to mischief, is it?" he continued, peering into the fog's shroud. His curiosity grew. Such bumbling idiots could hardly be professional agents of the night come to claim his gold or his life.

"Hold, sir, or die!"

Henry's eyes widened with amazement as he recognized the third assailant, who stood legs aquiver, aiming a horse pistol at him. "By the mark! Young Stephen Berkely, is it?"

Startled, the youth clutched at the hood hidden in the folds of his cloak, then, realizing the time for disguise was long past, attempted a vicious glare in the officer's direction. But the wavering pistol betrayed any real threat.

" 'Tis a pretty pass you've come to, Berkely."

"Nay. Stay where you are, or by my faith, I'll shoot," the youth answered.

"Your faith? If your faith is no stronger than what you've shown me so far, you'll roast in hell, boy."

"Save your jests, sir, and substitute with prayers." His companion, the lad who had met the apothecary shop with such a healthy swat, groaned as his hungry lungs gulped at the night air. "Get up, Charlie. Disarm him." But Charlie, legs awobble, scuttled away into the gloom. "Charlie!" Stephen called plaintively, but the retreating figure paid no heed.

"Walter?" he called hoarsely to the foggy depths beyond, his voice a wistful plea. No answer came. Both confederates had fled, honor not worth a bruised stomach nor split skull. Stephen stepped back as Henry approached. "Keep away, sir. I shall settle this matter alone, if I must."

"What matter?"

"The matter, sir, of Anne Langford."

"A pretty matter, indeed."

"You shall leave off pestering her or I shall . . . Keep back, I say."

But Henry was already advancing. "Give me your hand like a good fellow and wish me well, for I'll not want to see you before our wedding."

Stephen blanched and his eyes widened. "Wedding? By my word, you shan't! Keep away, I say, or I'll kill you!"

"The French could not, Stephen. Can a frightened, jealous boy prevail where far more dangerous foes have failed?"

"Yes!" Stephen jerked on the trigger, but to his horror, nothing happened. Then something hit his chest and his legs struck the curb. He threw his arms wide in a futile attempt to regain his balance and shrieked as he tumbled over backward and fell flat into a small sea of mud.

"I think not," sighed Henry, leaning over the stones and extending a hand to help Stephen to his feet. Instead, the youth scrambled out of the mud and took to his heels. "The Hawkins is a fine weapon, lad,"

Henry called into the fog. "But even the finest will fail to strike flint when not cocked and set. You'd best remember that."

The soldier chuckled, not without a trace of sympathy for the vagaries and misfortunes of young love. He would have done no less were he Stephen and in love with Anne. Still . . . His laughter faded. Not fifteen minutes ago he'd pondered the very question. Berkely had struck sooner than expected, and though awkwardly, with enough courage to kill if necessary. Had Henry not been versed in warfare, he might now be lying on the cobblestones, life's blood draining in the open gutter. And though Stephen Berkely may have been a bungler, he wasn't one to give up. He'd try again. Henry would have to be ready at all times. There would be no telling when or how the next blow would come.

Bolstered by the ease with which he'd handled one confrontation and the perverse delight he took in anticipating the next one, Henry roused the unconscious driver and salved the servant's wounds with a shilling. Soon the carriage was on its way to the handsome house on Grosvenor Square.

By ten o'clock, Henry was standing before the mirror in his room and inspecting himself closely. The new coat fit well, accenting his strong physique. A simple bagwig gleamed bright white in contrast to the deep russet velvet. The *frac* waistcoat, a deep, deep maroon pricked with silver embroidery and fastened with black mother-of-pearl buttons lent him a studied elegance sure to please Anne.

The image in the mirror frowned. If Stephen Berkely had spies and knew where to find him, Henry, too, was well informed. Though Anne had invited him to

this birthday fete, her father hadn't. He would be unwelcome in the house of Sir Spencer Langford, and
suspected that the servants had been instructed to
deny him entry.

What, he wondered, would Sir Spencer do if presented with a *fait accompli?* Cause a scene and have
him thrown out bodily? He doubted it. London would
love such a tale. Once inside, he was safe. But how
to get inside . . .

Damn! They'd taken Montcalm from behind, hadn't
they? A moment later, he'd slipped out the servants'
door and headed up the dark alley.

The rear of the Langford household was similar to
that of the Gladwyns, and for the first time since he
could remember, Henry thanked his brother Charles
for insisting on situating the family's London home at
Grosvenor Square. Henry adjusted his wig, brushed
off his sleeves and marched up the stairs.

The kitchen was a beehive of activity. Maids and
butlers scurried back and forth, pausing only to wipe
the sweat from their brows before heading down the
hall to the august galleries where the party was in
progress. Putting on a stern face, which had he seen
himself would have appeared more a pained and uncomfortable grin, Henry paraded in as if an entrance
through the kitchen were the most ordinary occurrence. All activity halted immediately. Cooks, maids
and butlers fell silent. "Please. Please continue as you
were. Just passing through," the out-of-place visitor
said to the array of startled faces.

"Gaw . . . !" came a stifled exclamation from by the
stove. The offender doubled over, a butler's elbow in
his side.

The hall, thank God, was empty. Behind, he could
hear the excited buzz of the servants; ahead, music

and gay laughter. He dodged into a side drawing room, withdrew quickly at the sight of one of the guests busily adjusting her panier and underskirts. Another door across the hall led to a parlor. Here there was darkness and quiet, a moment to set himself to rights and reconnoiter. Two doors led off the small-ish room, one to a smoking parlor, the other to a main room where gaming was in progress. Henry cracked the door, peered out into the back of an enormous coiffure on which a flock of stuffed songbirds perched. Damn, but she looked set for the rest of the evening. "Move, damn your hide!" he hissed, quickly closing the door as the matron jumped in alarm. He would have given a guinea to see her face. The door rattled but would not open for the foot and shoulder holding it tightly closed. He waited a few minutes and tried again. "Move, damn your hide!" Her head whirled, but too late. The door had closed.

When he tried ten minutes later the view was un-obstructed. The coiffure, whoever she was, had moved from the haunted door to station herself at the punch bowl. Henry cast his eye across the room and found Anne immediately, sitting at the faro table. There was no sign of Sir Spencer. In the smoking room? Possibly. No sign of Stephen either. Still combing the mud from his wig, no doubt.

Boldly. Just like Quebec . . . As nonchalantly as possible, Henry slipped out the door and strolled across the room, greeting raised eyebrows with brief nods and polite smiles.

Anne had just won a hand and had turned to share a brief tidbit of gossip and a tinkling laugh with a girl standing behind her. The loser was rising to vacate his place. Henry slipped into the seat and picked up the deck. "When mademoiselle is ready . . ."

Anne spun about, her eyes wide. It was late and she had abandoned hope. Something out of the ordinary was up, for Stephen hadn't appeared either. Had there been a confrontation? Was she now free to . . . She dared not finish the unspoken question. Years of training came into play to control the emotions which set her heart beating at an unnatural pace. "Monsieur . . ." she replied, her voice calm, her hand steady.

Henry plucked the single rose from his coat, laid it with great care before her on the table. "I play for high stakes, mademoiselle."

Anne's answer was a slow, sensual smile followed by a deft movement to her hair. Then a single bud, white and gleaming in the candlelight, lay next to his bloom.

Henry nodded and Anne reached for her cards, chose one and lay it face down on the table, discarding the rest of the deck. The onlookers shifted, murmured speculatively. A throaty laugh was quickly stifled.

His deck shuffled, Henry handed it back of him for cutting, then held it lightly in his left hand while his right peeled off the cards. The first was a trey. "My win." He placed the card to his left. The second was a nine. "Your win." The card went to start a second pile to his right.

More guests crowded around, silently expectant, their eyes shifting from one pile to the other as the deck slowly slimmed. Anne sat, apparently placid, glancing up briefly only when Sir Spencer, his face red with the news, forced his way through to the end of the table and stood, glaring, at the game. Henry didn't look up, but kept his eyes locked on Anne's while the litany continued.

"My win . . ." The snap of a card as it left the deck and turned over.

"Your win . . ." The quiet slap as it joined its brothers on the table.

"My win . . ." The queen of hearts on Henry's pile.

Anne's hand moved and Henry's froze in mid-air as she showed the card she had chosen. The queen of hearts. Ice-blue eyes looked boldly into his. She moistened her lips with the tip of her tongue and said, so softly only the nearest could hear, "Thine."

CHAPTER 3

Henry awakened only moments before the brass knocker sent shivers through the floor to his room. He had known Sir Spencer would come and had erred only in predicting the time. The old man must have been fit to be tied to show up at such an hour. "Let him in, William. Put him in the study," he shouted to the valet, swinging bare legs over the edge of the bed and grabbing for his gown. A half-filled cup of chocolate sat on the night stand. After dashing cold water on his face, he gulped down the last of the still-steaming fluid and made a face at the bitter dregs.

After leaving the Langfords' the night before, he had passed the early morning hours marshalling arguments and choosing a method of presentation. By the time sleep overtook him, he had finally decided on a blend of conciliation and strength. Henry scowled as he thought of the somber, responsible-looking clothes he'd laid out for the interview. But now there was no time.

"No question about it. I should have expected something like this," he muttered to himself. Sir Spencer was an old campaigner and a far cagier opponent than Stephen Berkely.

Which was the answer, of course. He'd simply have to beat the old fox at his own game. Henry checked himself in the mirror. Horrible. His hair, matted from wig and morning abed, lay flat and tangled. The robe, a dull blue and ragged from years of wear, almost scraped the floor. It would obviously have to go, favorite or not. The linen nightshirt poked out at the neck. Off with it, of course. And the old slippers were a disgrace. He ran a hand through his hair, stripped off robe and nightshirt, kicked away the slippers. Sir Spencer expected to embarrass him, eh? "Two can play that game, milord." The whisker-stubbled jaw in the mirror grinned in agreement.

Sir Spencer Langford stood with his back to the room, staring with exaggerated intensity at the tapestry on the wall over the fireplace. Some damned thing from the East, probably picked up for a song and hung there with the hope of impressing the uninitiated. Impatient, he struck the floor with his cane, struck again for good measure. The door in the opposite wall opened softly.

William entered without a sound. "The Lieutenant will join you in a moment, milord," he said to the visitor's back. "If you please, there is coffee or chocolate . . ."

Sir Spencer rocked forward, shifted the cane to the front and leaned on it, glowering at the servant, who left with a whispered, "As milord pleases."

"As milord pleases," the irate father growled. "You're damned right, as milord pleases." He turned and paced, taking in the darkened room. A library, he supposed, or a study, though in unpardonable disarray. A stack of books and papers lay tumbled about on the desk, holding down a large, worn map.

Would the fellow never show up? Sir Spencer passed in front of a mirror, glanced at himself. The dark gray morning clothes gave just the right effect. Somber. Angry. Serious. Impeccable. He permitted himself the luxury of a tight smile. Henry Gladwyn was in for a surprise all right. Hastily shaved, dressed, bewigged and trying his best to make a good impression, he'd fail. Oh, he'd squirm, all right. Pay for his impertinence. And pay again, for once having been taught one lesson, the insolent pup would be thrown to Stephen, and under more propitious circumstances for the lad, be taught another. Satisfied with his plans, Sir Spencer chuckled as he leafed through the books on the desk, only to leave them at the sound of Gladwyn's voice and assume his stance at the fireplace. The very picture of dignity, the old fox put on his sternest face, squared his back and waited.

"Good morning, Sir Spencer. So sorry to keep you waiting. William tells me he's already brought coffee and chocolate. . . . Ah, you've not had any?"

Sir Spencer finally turned, deigning at last to note the young man who had ruined so many of his plans. "I have not come, sir, to drink . . ." He stopped, speechless with shock, his mouth gaping. "By God!" he choked.

"A bit gloomy in here, wouldn't you say? If you'll permit me . . . ?" Three strides and Henry was at the window pulling open the drapes. The room flooded with morning light. "There. That's better, don't you think?" Without pausing he reached out and took the older man's cane. "Here. I'll take this for you."

"Perhaps I'll have a touch of chocolate after all," Sir Spencer allowed in a near whisper.

Henry clapped his hands, rubbed them together briskly. "Good. Have a seat."

Sir Spencer sat heavily in the indicated chair, stared

in dismay. The barbarian . . . No wig at all. His hair, long and tousled, rose straight up like a nest of snakes, twisting every which way. He was unshaven, a dark shadow of stubble covered jowl, cheek and neck, and rasped clearly as Henry ran his palm across his chin. Before God! The man had nothing on his feet! Worst of all was the robe. Sir Spencer averted his gaze, but found his eyes drawn back to the tasteless monstrosity. An impossibly decadent design in garish greens and reds on black. Cinched at the waist, the thing was open at the chest and reached only halfway down his thighs, exposing great hairy legs with knotted calves. Had the man not a shred of decency?

"You've caught me at an awkward moment, Sir Spencer, I must admit. It's only a little after eleven, you know."

"What?" He jerked up his head guiltily. "Oh, yes. Of course. Didn't realize you'd be . . . that is . . ." Damn, he thought. I'm apologizing! A cup of chocolate materialized in front of him and he accepted it, trying with difficulty not to stare at the hairy chest behind the cup. Never in a lifetime of unusual scope had he been served by a bare-chested Englishman. The experience was unsettling in the extreme. "Thank you."

"Honey?"

"Ah . . . what?"

"Do you want honey? The chocolate's a touch bitter."

"Ah . . ."—a tentative sip—"it's fine, thank you."

"Good." Henry went back to the tray, poured another cup, halting in mid-stride to irritably pick up the book Sir Spencer had inspected, leaf through it until he found the right page, then tear off a scrap from a newspaper and mark the place. "That's the trouble with an educated servant. Damned if he won't play about with your books. I'd be better off with a man who didn't read."

Sir Spencer flushed, hardly wanting to admit he had been going through another man's desk. "Yes. Don't allow it myself. More trouble than they're worth."

"I'll be damned if I know why William wants to read about the Punic Wars anyway," Henry went on, not allowing his prospective father-in-law to get in a word on the subject. "Know much about them?"

"No, I'm afraid I don't." Sir Spencer was recovering, beginning to understand he'd been conned. "Now see here, young man. I didn't come here to discuss the Punic Wars."

"I daresay not, but they're most instructive. Hannibal, you know . . ."

"Lieutenant Gladwyn!"

". . . was a damned fine general. Anyone who has any pretensions to command would do well to read him. Those elephants, for example. A lesson to be learned there. Phenomenal power, of course, and the capability of scaring hell out of the enemy. By all logic, the superior power they represented should have . . ." He paused, lost in thought, then went on. "They didn't, of course. In the first place, elephants tended to run amok. All that power, once released, couldn't be controlled, and often as not turned on the very forces for which they were meant to pave the way."

Henry stopped and stared intently at Sir Spencer. "Shall I tell you, sir, why Carthage lost in the end? It's important, you know," he continued, not waiting for a response. "As I say, there's a lesson to be learned here. Carthage was old, entrenched, well established.

Rome was young, bold, scrappy and on the way up—
and wanted the Mediterranean for her own trade. The
first time out she won, but not decisively. The second
time out, by far the more interesting of the two,
Rome won also, but quite effectively. No matter that
Hannibal did have a superior cavalry—or elephants,
for that matter. Rome had an indomitable will to win,
superior economic resources and some first-rate gen-
erals. Carthage was finished. The Third Punic War is
a bit of a bore, a mopping-up operation. Carthage itself was razed, the inhabitants slaughtered and sold
into slavery, the ground plowed up and put to grass.
A sad tale."

The room was silent. Sir Spencer had sunk back in
his chair and crossed his legs. He took a desultory sip
of the chocolate and set aside the cup. "So you are
Rome, eh?"

Henry raised an eyebrow, surprised at the response.
"I believe I am."

"I like that. Like it very much. Now tell me. It
follows that I am poor, pitied Carthage." His tone
hardened. "Do you then see Anne as the Mediterranean, ravaged, plundered, exploited and ruled by
your mercenary self?"

"Of course not. I wasn't . . . that is, I didn't . . ."
Henry hesitated, caught in his own analogy. The old
fox wasn't so easily taken after all. "I must admit the
analogy breaks down there, sir. No. I do not see her
that way."

"How do you see her?"

"As the woman I love."

"Ah, yes. Love. My daughter's favorite word. She
uses it frequently—every time she falls into it, which
is often enough. I trust you won't be surprised to

learn I've heard the word a number of times in the last few hours."

"I hope so. . . . That is, I'm not surprised."

"Sit down." Sir Spencer waved languidly toward a chair, for all the world as if he were in his own study. A very, very serious look gave no indication of hidden amusement.

"I beg your pardon?"

"Sit down. Relax." Henry started to sit, realized there was no way he could decently do so, dressed in the short robe and nothing else. Sir Spencer rose, went to the tray and poured another cup of chocolate. "No need to worry. Spent some time in the service myself. A peek at a lieutenant's privates won't shock me. Damned good chocolate, by the way," he went on, "you'll have to tell me where you got it."

"If it's all the same, I'll stand."

"Very well, if you insist on modesty. It's your house, after all. More chocolate?"

"No, thank you. If you don't mind, I think we have some business to discuss."

Sir Spencer sobered, returned to his seat, and leaned back, finally allowing himself the long-repressed chuckle. "The Punic Wars! By God, that's good. I like it."

"I hoped you would, sir," Henry answered drily.

"You did, eh? And that get-up, if that's what you call it? Had me going there for a minute, I confess."

Henry grinned. "I was shooting for contrast. Hoped I might . . . you know . . ."

"Turn the tables on me? You succeeded. But the Punic Wars?" The old man's laughter was infectious and Henry found himself joining in until Sir Spencer suddenly stopped. A new voice cracked, whiplike.

"That was a damned scandalous bit of impertinence last night, young man, and I'd like to know by what right you insinuated yourself uninvited into my house and made a damned fool of me in front of my friends and guests."

Henry stiffened. Laughter, followed by the attack. Once again he'd been taken off guard. "I'll explain that, sir, after you've been kind enough to explain by what right you conspired with Stephen Berkely against my person."

They glared at each other silently, neither wishing to give way first. Henry finally yielded, sinking into the chair with a sigh. "Very well, Sir Spencer. How else was I to break through the layers of distrust and hostility with which I was faced? I love your daughter and want to marry her. But I would hate to do it without your consent and blessing."

"Why didn't you just come and speak with me? I am, after all, a reasonable man."

"You would not have heard a word I said, Sir Spencer. You were . . . entrenched."

It was Sir Spencer's turn to sigh. "I acknowledge the point. Very well. Since Stephen has sent me a rather virulent note breaking our contract—what else could he do after last night?—you have my attention. But I warn you, I'd arranged a good match for the girl, one I'm damned sorry to lose. You'll need some strong arguments to win me over."

"I ask no more than the chance to argue, sir." Henry rose, paced the room twice and stopped abruptly. "I shall be concise. First, although I repeat myself, I love Anne and offer her a good home. I am not a vagabond. After ten years of the world at large, I am ready to assume the duties of husband and father.

"Second, the Punic Wars—insofar as the analogy

holds—are still valid. I am young, hungry, capable and on my way up. I shall let nothing stand in my way. I don't claim to be another Pitt, but from his success you may see that one not nobly born may advance— and spectacularly.

"Third, the Gladwyn fortune is not inconsiderable. Since the death of my brother Byron, I am second in line. My older brother is undisciplined and, though it pains me to say so, dissipated to the point of incompetence. Without being overly mercenary, I am confident I shall succeed to my father's fortune within the next five years. I'm sure you've discovered my income by now, as I have yours. Judiciously stated, the house of Langford could stand an infusion of funds, specifically, in light of certain disastrous losses in the Harkness Gardens fire. Those funds shall be forthcoming. On the evening our vows are said I shall hand you my check for £5,000 to defray those expenses."

Sir Spencer sat up. How had Gladwyn known? His estimation of the lad rose a notch.

"Fourth, your young champion came after me with two friends. All were armed and they should have succeeded. They didn't. I tell you now, the boy is surrounded by an aura of failure. He's soft, weak, pampered and effete. He's overbred and underworked. He has no conception of the strength of those pushing from beneath to take his place, which he cannot hope to hold. He and my brother have much in common.

"And fifth and finally," he paused momentarily to stand again, "is yourself. The last hour has been nerve-wracking but instructive. You need someone with whom you may contend—keep you on your toes, so to speak. Stephen Berkely is no fit contest for you, as you well know."

Sir Spencer swirled the dregs of chocolate, brow

furrowed against the weight of all five arguments. "Your suit has merit, I admit. I have only one question. Why? And don't tell me it's just because you love her."

Henry leaned forward. "Very well." His eyes glittered as he glimpsed success. "Your name and your good will. I have told you I intend to advance, and so I do. But I am not so naïve, so brash as to think the path devoid of difficulty or danger. I will need help. Powerful help. I need the aura of tradition and breeding that belongs to Sir Spencer Langford. I do not wish to batter down doors which at a word or gesture might willingly be opened. Success is my goal, not contention for contention's sake. I seek respectability which is yours to offer, if you but will."

"You are blunt."

"Would you have me any less?"

Sir Spencer squinted up into the confident, determined face. Well spoken. Bold, hungry and blunt to boot. By God, he realized, I like the lad. "No," he answered, rising. "I'll take no less for a son-in-law."

"Then may I have your hand, Sir Spencer?" Henry asked, extending his.

"On one condition."

Henry retracted the hand. "Which is?" he asked suspiciously.

"I'd rather not be Carthage, if you don't mind."

Henry laughed as the two shook hands. "I'll see to it."

"Rome. I'd rather stay Rome for a while. You shall be Scipio, the general."

"Done and done again. William? Let's have something to drink here. A marriage has been arranged!"

❖   ❖   ❖

Henry ordered the driver to rein in, then leaned from the carriage to better see the coach and team tied before the Gladwyn London house. "Damn!" he swore, slamming the door closed again.

"Looks like Master Charles," the driver said from above.

"Yes. Yes. I know my brother's coach when I see it," Henry replied irritably. He had not expected Charles so soon, and derived little comfort from the fact that his brother probably carried the check for Sir Spencer. Anne rested her fingertips on Henry's arm. He squirmed inwardly. Not having told her of the monetary arrangement with her father, he had no wish for her to discover the facts from Charles. "I wonder what brought him to town?" Henry asked a little lamely.

"News of our betrothal, of course," Anne said. "I look forward to seeing if all those naughty things you've said about him are true," she added impishly.

The carriage jolted to a halt and Henry climbed out without waiting for the driver to help with the door. "You'll soon see for yourself," he answered, handing her down. "You'll soon see."

The very thought of Henry's arrival set Charles' teeth aching, and teeth, he thought, lifting his upper lip, were a damned rotten nuisance. He rocked forward on the balls of his feet and looked closely in the mirror. The one on the upper right was the offender, he was sure. Nothing to do but have the barber pull it. He cringed at the thought, and followed it with a curse as a carriage pulled up outside.

At forty years of age, Charles Gladwyn looked fifty. Girthed with an enormous excess of fat that rippled in watery rolls beneath his velvet coat, no one would have guessed he was a relative to Henry, save for a vague, ill-defined facial resemblance hidden beneath layers of ceruse and over-indulgence. A small constellation of black marks applied to cheek and jaw concealed two growing sores which, under the none-too-benign influence of ceruse and oil of vitriol, irritated him more than he cared to admit. Only two personal servants—who for a price had been known to hide a colleague where he or she might catch a glimpse of a comically naked master—knew that the lord of Gladwyn Manor was entirely bald, for his head was at all times swaddled in a vast, powdered wig.

Heir apparent to a still-growing Gladwyn fortune, Charles had been stricken in youth with an inflated and unshakable sense of self-importance. His present uneasiness was based on the single overriding fact of his lack of an heir, for fate had, after all, been unkind. He, his first wife and only child had contracted the mumps during the second year of marriage, and while his wife and infant son had died, Charles was cruelly spared and left sterile. A second wife died childless and no suitable third could be found, for while Charles refused to accept his condition, the truth was painfully obvious to the titled world to which, in spite of protests to the contrary, he sought entry. After ten years of enforced bachelorhood and more than a score of attempts with one available maid after another, he had finally bowed to the inevitable and admitted the Gladwyn name and fortune would not pass through him, but fall instead to his younger brother's sons, if any. The prospect was deeply mortifying and, for an individual given over to overweening vanity, unbearable.

The door at the other end of the drawing room

opened and Charles turned to see Henry enter with a woman on his arm. She didn't look bad from a distance, he thought, as they started toward him, but then, Henry always was the lucky one. "Well, brother," he said, a hearty joviality disguising his rancor. "I'm glad to see you."

"Hello, Charles." Henry's voice echoed emptily in the high-ceilinged room.

"And this must be the lovely Anne Langford," Charles continued, grasping her hand and bringing it to his lips.

"I didn't expect you until next week. I'm afraid you've surprised us," Henry said.

Charles glanced shrewdly at him. "Family matters. Many of which concern you." He raised an eyebrow. "William tells me you're engaged tonight?"

"I'm engaged every night," Henry answered, glancing fondly at Anne. "Perhaps we could talk now?"

Charles nodded assent. Henry took Anne's arm and escorted her toward the east door where William waited. "Forgive me, darling. I fear Charles and I have a moment's dull business to tend to. We'll join you in the morning room. You will forgive me, won't you?"

"I shall if it is only a moment and no more," Anne said, pouting playfully.

"Good. William, will you see about something to eat? A little tea, perhaps, and a cake or two will do nicely."

On her departure, Charles abandoned even the façade of good humor. His face took on the aspects of one of the stern portraits hung along the west wall. "She really is lovely," he commented as Henry returned.

"Thank you," Henry replied. "But you said we had

business. Did you bring the money from Father?"

Charles sighed. "How quickly we drop the pleas-antries, Henry. But you rush about so. Certain things must needs take longer. I shall present the draft in good time. Fiscal matters should never be hurried."

"Then why are you here?"

Charles swung about, gestured expansively. "This is the Gladwyn house, is it not? And I should say, little brother, far more mine than yours. But never mind that. I've brought you a present."

"Oh?"

"You're not curious?"

"Charles, your affection for me is as deep as a pud-dle of spittle. I can only suspect you bring me mis-chief."

Inexplicably, Charles laughed. "Mischief? You have a fine sense of humor. Mischief, indeed." The laughter died as Charles reached into his coat and withdrew a sealed envelope. "Instructions from a weary father. Surely you do not doubt his love?"

"And what am I to take that to mean?"

Charles handed the envelope to Henry. "Why, mis-chief, of course," he chuckled, handing over the letter. "As you may read for yourself."

William served the cakes, poured the tea and left as silently as he'd come in. Anne relaxed and sat back to nibble on a seed cake. The pleasantries between Henry and Charles had not deceived her in the slight-est. Beneath their cordiality ran a vein of icy ill will that would, she feared, never melt.

Quite suddenly, she became aware she was being watched. Anne looked up. A girl stood there, un-abashedly staring at her. How incredibly beautiful she is, was Anne's first reaction. Long scarlet locks framed a face as naturally soft and white as a rose petal. One slim hand rested on the top of a pedestal holding a marble fawn. The girl continued to stare. Anne smiled. "Hello," she said, the cool gray of her eyes thawing. "I'm afraid we haven't met."

"Yes," came the answer.

"What?" Anne asked, a little confused.

"Yes, you're very beautiful. Everyone said you were. I hope you are kind and even-tempered as well."

"I beg your pardon?" Anne almost laughed. The child—she could be no more than thirteen or fourteen —was testing her for some obscure reason.

The girl abruptly started across the room. "If you were not kind and even-tempered, I should never approve. I could never countenance Uncle Henry married to someone awful."

"Why, you're Elizabeth!" Anne said triumphantly. The daughter of Henry's older brother, she recalled, left alone after her father had died in some dismal corner of Europe.

"I prefer Beth," the girl replied. "I'm terribly jealous, you know."

"Really?" Anne gestured to a seat across the table. As Beth moved closer, she noted a hint of freckles and bright, green eyes. Closer, too, the child was not nearly so beautiful, but still pretty enough.

"Oh, yes," Beth answered, sitting and helping herself to a cake. "You see, next to Papa, I love Uncle Henry more than anyone. He had only just arrived from the colonies when I was sent to Grandfather's. Now that Grandfather is so ill, I've been shuffled off to here."

Anne smiled. Beth was quite likable, really, once one got over the initial shock. "I hope you will not be too jealous. I should like us to become friends."

"I'm sure we shall," Beth agreed enthusiastically, popping another tiny cake in her mouth. "For a time."

Anne frowned. "For a time?"

"Because when you are old and ugly, I shall still be young and beautiful, and will steal Uncle Henry away from you."

Anne sat up, unsure whether to continue being amused or to be angry. She was saved from having to decide by Henry's entrance and Beth's cry of joy as she bolted from the chair and all but flew into her uncle's arms. "Uncle Henry!"

"Elizabeth!" Henry laughed, sweeping her off her feet and swinging her in a great circle. Anne watched, bemused as Henry put Beth down and wrapped an arm about her. "So you're here. I see you two have met."

"But of course," Beth answered brightly. "She's beautiful. We're going to be friends."

"Then you approve of the match, eh?"

Beth curtsied mischievously. Anne still couldn't tell if she was serious or not. "Yes, Uncle, I do."

Henry detached himself from his niece, circled the table and bussed Anne on the cheek. "Then we are in luck, my dear. There are no more obstacles to be overcome."

"I'm so relieved," Anne replied tonelessly.

"And I'm hungry," Beth proclaimed. "Ladylike or no, I'm going to the kitchen." Without another word, she was off.

Henry shook his head and sat on the arm of Anne's chair. "Well, what do you think of her?" he asked.

The question took Anne by surprise and she hesitated, not at all sure what she did think. The child was either a perfect brat—or a delightful breath of fresh air. "She's very . . . outspoken," Anne finally managed.

Henry chuckled. "Yes. As was her father, which was his downfall." He tilted her chin and kissed her full on the lips. Anne loved the delicious strength of his hand on her throat, and wanted more than anything to please him.

"I hope she'll visit us often when we're settled in."

Henry reddened, rose from the chair. "Yes," he said. "But I'm afraid she'll do more than that." Anne's silent, questioning expression prompted him further. Henry pulled from his pocket the letter Charles had given him and gave it to Anne. "A letter from my father instructing Beth to my—our—care. As soon as we are wed, she's to live with us."

CHAPTER 4

August 19, 1760, the day of the wedding, was sunlit and gay. The window outside Anne's room was alive with the ebullient chatter of birds. A bouquet of pastel butterflies, looking like a host of blossoms come to life, fluttered past the window. Bees, tiny buds of gold and brown, hovered, then lazily dipped to glide among petals and gorge themselves on drops of nectar.

Alone at last for a moment, Anne toyed unnecessarily with her hair. When would the musicians begin, she wondered, irritated at how slowly the time passed. She had looked forward to this day forever, it seemed, and now that it was here, she was forced to wait even longer. It would be hours yet before she was alone with Henry.

Alone? But how alone? Beth had come by earlier to see if she needed anything, and Anne had declined pointedly. She had accepted the fact the newly acquired niece was to be their houseguest and charge, but didn't need to be saddled with her at this most important moment. Or for the next two or three years, for that matter, she thought irritably. And yet, what else was she to do but accept the arrangement with good grace?

The door opened and her maid, Sabrina, came in without asking. "Child? They're ready."

Excited all over again, Anne turned about in a full circle. "Do I look all right, Sabrina?"

The maid suddenly broke out in a fit of weeping. "You're beautiful, child. Simply beautiful."

Anne tenderly embraced the woman who had practically raised her. "I'm so happy, Sabrina," she whispered.

"Good evening, Henry. Gentlemen . . ."

The greeting was answered with an assortment of nods and grunts. Henry looked up, relieved to see his brother Charles at last. "Gentlemen, if you'll excuse me a moment . . . ?" The question was rhetorical. "I think we can talk in here," he continued, leading Charles through the connecting door into the small parlor where he'd hidden only scant weeks earlier.

"Lovely bunch. So responsive," Charles commented even before the door closed.

"Perfectly delightful when you get to know them, Charles. Have you brought the . . ."

"My my my. Impatient, aren't we?"

Henry shrugged. Charles had turned unpleasant already, and not two dozen words between them.

Charles sneered. "Little brother buying a title for £5,000."

"You'd pay thrice that and jump at the chance."

"The Gladwyns have done perfectly well without titles to date."

"Jealousy becomes you, Charles," Henry laughed, taking the check and reading the amount and signature carefully. "I wish Father could be here."

"No doubt you do."

"I shall miss Byron today as well," Henry said, unable to resist needling just a little.

"Well, you have his daughter, so all is not lost. And

welcome you are to the vixen. I feared Father would burden me with her. He might have, had I not pointed out that the child needed a mother. In this sense, your marriage is most propitious."

Henry did not doubt that Charles spoke the truth. "I have read through Byron's papers. He left little . . ."

"Debts only," Charles sniffed.

"Speaking of which, I trust you'll see to the draft before long."

Charles' lips pursed. £3,000 per annum went to Byron's daughter. It galled him that the product of Byron's indiscretion should drain so munificent a sum from the Gladwyn coffers. "The first year's stipend has been arranged. The papers requiring your signature are on my desk. I doubt you'll be anything less than hasty in tending them."

Henry sighed in exasperation. His older brother could be most trying. "Charles, it might surprise you, but my main concern in life is not to pilfer your purse. I press in this matter only for Beth's sake."

"In a pig's eye, you do!" The older Gladwyn swung about and lurched toward the door.

"Charles!" The command filled the room and stopped Charles, hand on door. "I really am sorry you feel that way."

Charles turned slowly, eyes bulging and hands trembling, mouth unaccountably slack. "Don't mock me," he whispered. "Don't . . ."

"Are you in here, then, Henry?" The door opened, sending Charles off balance. Admiral Saunders entered. "Aha! The bride and guests are ready and the brothers chat in a side room. Come, sirs, I shall escort you."

Charles could do little else. Trailing along, he followed groom and escort into the west drawing room.

Seven o'clock in the evening. The sun streamed
through laced curtains and set the room aglow with
amber light. Admiral Saunders, Henry and Charles
entered, made their way to the front, Charles to one
side. Henry and the Admiral turned to face the buzzing assembly, a sea of faces silhouetted with the sun
at their backs. Henry surveyed the jagged line of wigs
and towering coiffures, and for the first time felt nervous. This was nothing like the screaming savages he'd
faced, nor the brittle, battering regiments of French
soldiers broken on the Plains of Abraham. He'd
weathered storms at sea, aye and bravely, too. Then
why had his knees turned to custard now? Under the
amused scrutiny of Anne's and Sir Spencer's guests, he
wavered. Unsteady fingers strayed to a coat pocket,
sought comfort and renewed strength from the slim,
rectangular keepsake there. The queen of hearts.

The crowd hushed in expectation as a single flute,
haunting and wistful, sent a simple country marriage
tune afloat through the gossamer light. Henry stiffened
and glanced apprehensively at Saunders, who winked
back.

A stir of motion at one side and the crowd parted.
Simultaneously, two violins joined the flute in bright,
joyous harmony. Henry held his breath. Thomas Sher-
lock, Bishop of London, entered, paused and continued regally down the aisle, the bride behind him.

Anne! The guests inhaled as one in obeisance to her
breathtaking beauty. Anne Langford, in white, stood
before them, her hand on Sir Spencer's arm. A veil of
the most delicate Bruges lace covered her head and

flowed behind in a steadily widening train borne by two children. Rich auburn hair entwined with silver thread spilled from under the veil and over creamy white shoulders. A single narrow width of white velvet on which lay a brooch of gleaming diamonds circled a long and exquisitely sculpted neck. Full breasts, barely caught by the low line of the lace-trimmed bodice, sloped to a dainty waistline. An intricacy of embroidered flowers, white on white, exploded majestically on the wide panier, fell straight to the tips of slippers almost too fragile for walking, flowed back in a great train under the billowing lace veil.

The music swelled, transforming the simple peasant tune into a stately proclamation of joy. Henry watched in a trance as his bride neared, step by measured step.

As if in a dream, the onlookers, the blushing twilight sun, bishop and brother faded. Only you, he thought. And you, she echoed, their unspoken thoughts mingling. Words, from a great distance . . . hand in hand . . . a ring floating from the shadowy distance . . . I do . . . Oh, Henry, I do, my darling . . . and the answer . . . And I . . . now and forever, Anne, 'til death do us part, under God, man, the sky, stars, sun, wind, the universe itself, I do. . . .

"With the authority vested in me by God and King, I now pronounce you man and wife. You may kiss the bride."

His hands raised slowly. Calloused fingers caught the edge of the veil and lifted it, revealing ice-gray eyes melting now at last. Lips, barely moving, formed his name, to be answered with a kiss.

Sir Spencer, Anne and Henry stood at the door to greet each guest, most of whom had met Henry by this time. There was a moment's awkwardness when

Stephen Berkely arrived uninvited, but the lad behaved graciously enough. "What the hell is he doing here?" Henry asked during a lull.

"Stephen? Showing how brave and unaffected he is, I should imagine. From what I hear, his pride received more of a blow than his heart."

No more was said on the matter.

Dinner was finished by nine and the dancing began. Anne and Henry led the first pavane and for the second, Sir Spencer and Anne took the floor, followed by Henry and his niece Elizabeth.

Beth's flaming red hair, faint and alluring freckles which would never quite disappear, green eyes from her mother and budding figure compared favorably with the rest of the guests and she knew it. Now, beneath the watchful eye of a dashing handsome uncle who towered protectively over her, she positively glowed. "Do you know what?"

"What?"

"I'm dreadfully sorry Papa died, of course, but this is so grand! You can't imagine how happy I am to be sent to you instead of Charles."

"Why, thank you, Beth."

"You're so much more like Papa—except he was better looking."

"You're a poor flatterer, Niece. A more proper sentiment would be that I'm the most handsome, dashing fellow about."

Beth smiled impishly, her eyes sparkling. "Then so you shall be, sir, and I shall tell everyone."

"And receive a caning for your trouble. You're not too old, you know, and I *am* your guardian." The music ended and he bowed to her curtsy. "Now, mistress, hie you off. You're far too pretty and attentive, and I won't have tongues wagging on my wedding night."

Still glowing, Beth left the floor. Anne could not help but feel relieved when a host of young courtiers stepped forward to assume the place left by Henry.

Henry Gladwyn stood to one side, in a contemplative mood and with a cold eye to the future. Piece by piece, all the parts of a new life were falling into place. The wedding had gone well. Most of the best families in town were represented and their good wishes had sounded genuinely warm. He had long prepared for this night and impressed most, he felt, having memorized their names and two or three salient facts about each. Politics was basically no different from warfare —a new game, but one in which planning, intelligence and innovation, were what counted. The rest was easy —to keep one's eyes peeled and roll with the blows, ready to call up the reserves and counterattack decisively.

A strident note cut through the layers of thought. The laugh was Charles'. Drunk already? No. Henry caught a glimpse of his brother, glass in hand, gesturing in conversation with Stephen Berkely, of all people. The words were unintelligible but their faces told the tale. Henry scowled. There was an alliance the world could do without. A prudent man would take precautions. How quickly a man gained enemies!

To one side, Sir Spencer beckoned. Henry patted a hidden pocket. The check was still there. Now would be as good a time as any.

Anne applied one final touch of rouge then hurried from her bedroom, following the lilting music to its source. She paused at the top of the wide staircase leading to the grand hall where dancers circled and bowed in choreographed splendor. Caroline Chisworth, with whom she had shared many an adolescent adventure, disappeared through a doorway down the hall into a nearby parlor. Caroline, a plump maid of twenty, had hardly spoken to her all evening. Anne had decided she was jealous. As she watched, a plain, angular-faced woman she thought was some admiral's wife paused in the doorway, apparently oblivious to Anne. Then the woman entered the parlor.

Curiosity overwhelming her, Anne hurried down the corridor and entered a side gallery which opened onto the parlor. Discreetly, she tried the latch and pulled the door slightly ajar. Laughter surged through the room.

"She'll learn now, my dear, why one shouldn't save herself for so many years. When I think of what she's missed . . ." That was the admiral's wife.

"I swear, he'll die of a stroke when he finds her of one piece," Caroline giggled.

"Think something's wrong, he will."

"My Harry would be glad to correct the matter before she leaves," an unseen guest quipped. "He's fast enough."

"Nay, too fast," came the retort from another corner. "Besides, a virgin should lose her maidenhead in bed, not standing up nor on the run."

"Which is a lesson in its own, my dears. Unlike some, I'll wager she keeps time for her own husband, lest he be free to run around looking for them that has time." Harry's wife laughed as loudly as the rest.

" 'Twere Henry Gladwyn, I'd gladly have time for him," the admiral's wife announced.

"Aye, and at your age you'd have time for anyone who'd consent to endanger himself," Caroline snickered, her soft flesh jiggling.

"Standing up or lying down, at that," a second girl added.

"Alice Fletcher," Anne muttered beneath her breath. "The harridans . . ."

"Standing, for sure, for he'd have to stand the wrinkles!"

Laughter pealed through the room and the unfortunate admiral's wife turned bright red underneath the thick cosmetics.

"Silly goose. She's let out it's love brought them together," Alice Fletcher remarked, delighted at being able to introduce a new piece of information.

"Love? La! A country wench's conceit."

The room swelled with laughter. "Love it shall be, then," Harry's wife said. "Love and a hard-nosed contract, I hear. It's amazing what a few thousand pounds will buy these days."

Anne paled, pressed closer to the door. Contracts?

"Nay, ladies. You jest overly." The room quieted as the admiral's wife took the floor. "It's an even match: his purse for her father's name and good will. The man is ambitious. Mark my word. You'll see a rapid climb there. Saunders, Grafton and now Langford. An audience with His Majesty and just the other day with Newcastle—*tête-à-tête* at that. The Gladwyns may be commoners, but they're no fools."

"There's worse matches been made, for a truth," Caroline sighed.

"Mary Delany doesn't agree," Harry's wife snipped viciously. "She'll be missing her lover too much, I'm afraid."

"Serve her right," a new voice declared. "She's had enough of the man in the last two fortnights to last a year, they say."

"'Tis her own fault, for having the wrong father. Were the old man titled, like as not Henry Gladwyn would have wed Mary as quickly as he has our Anne.

The Lieutenant knows full well wherein lies the path to power, my dears."

Henry and Mary Delany. Horrified, Anne pushed open the door another inch.

"Still, Mary needn't worry. She'll have Henry back before long."

Alice adjusted her bosom, loosening her bodice the better to entice some young suitor. "On her way back, you mean," she sneered.

"Aye. There's an affair won't die on the bush."

"No doubt about it," the new voice declared. "Once Mary Delany's caught a man by his longest part, she's not one to let 'im go easily."

"Then *you've* naught to worry of my dear," Harry's wife broke in. "When it comes to longest parts, unlike Henry Gladwyn, your James is sadly lack . . . Oh, dear. What *ever* have I said?"

The room exploded in raucous laughter at the intentional faux pas. Anne blanched, leaned against the wall for support. Mary Delany? My God, she thought. She's no better than a courtesan. But then to *my* bed? Shuddering, she forced back the tears and, quietly, lest they hear, shut the door and groped for a chair.

Had she been a fool not to give herself to Henry? After all, even Sir Spencer had assumed she had. Perhaps he wouldn't have gone with Mary Delany if . . . No! She had been right.

But how could he have so counterfeited love? Tender caresses, sweet words—and in the next breath creep away to Mary Delany! Those remarks concerning Henry's alliance with the Langfords—surely the Gladwyns would gain, but only as a felicitous concomitant to marriage. And Sir Spencer. Was this marriage no more than the selling of a daughter? He couldn't. He simply couldn't.

Determined to separate gossip from fact, Anne rose and made her way from the room, carefully checking the hall before running down the corridor toward her father's study. Not too long ago she had seen Henry leave in that direction with her father.

". . . do you think?" Anne stopped suddenly and shrunk back into a shadowy alcove as the door to her father's study opened and the two men emerged.

"I wonder," Henry said in answer. "Perhaps we would be better off meeting them here. With a few more thousand, we could brighten up the place—no offense, of course."

"Nay. 'Tis not needed. Newcastle will come because he's my friend. And Pitt? Who is to say? In any case, another pound or another five thousand won't make a difference. Not at this stage of the game."

"You know best," Henry conceded. "Shall we?"

"After you."

Their footsteps receded down the hall in the opposite direction and Anne was left alone, face white as chalk, mouth gaping open in disbelief. "No," she whispered pitifully. "No no no no . . . " Their words echoed down the empty corridor, reverberated painfully, mockingly. "A few thousand more . . ." "Another five thousand . . ."

Under the spell Anne approached the study, opened the door and entered. The lamp on the desk burned low, flinging shadows against the furniture and book-lined walls. She hurried to the desk, slid the main drawer open. In the center of the tray lay a rectangle of paper on top of some nondescript-looking documents. Slowly, against her will, a pale hand touched the paper, turned and drew it toward her. The words leaped from the check:

"Please be so kind as to debit my account to the sum of £5,000 and pay to Sir Spencer Langford. (signed) Anthony Gladwyn, Esq."

The nightmare evening dragged on. Anne played her part well, portrayed a beaming bride and accepted with grace the worn, well-wishing phrases, the congratulations from friends who but scarcely an hour past had revealed their true natures in secret, one to the other. Most difficult of all was the final galliard with Henry. Somehow Anne managed to hide from her beloved—now her betrayer—the seething turmoil that caught her heart in an iron glove of despair. Ebullience that radiated from her new husband became a painful glare. The intertwining of their hands seemed but a hollow temple where before had been a cathedral for love's votive mysteries.

Suddenly everyone was gone. Sir Spencer kissed Anne on the cheek and led her to the carriage for the short trip to the Gladwyn mansion, a scant hundred yards down the street, where the carriage stopped and Henry led a reluctant bride up the stairs and through the door, up more stairs and down a corridor to a darkened chamber. Each step on the cold marble echoed through the hall, transforming tender memories to bitterness and disgust. He had lied! Yesterday's kisses were dross. Cold, empty, heartless. Love? She scorned to laugh. Calculation and ambition would be apter words: a piece of property had been bought for £5,000. All was mockery. The gowns, the pageantry, the oaths sworn, the tender embrace before the bored throng in front of which a foolish girl had played the part of an enchanted princess. Of what value now were all the cherished hopes and dreams? None. Anne

Langford was no more than any other, a stitch in the tapestry of power and statecraft, a poor knot tying her husband to position and prestige.

Anne spun in the doorway with every intention of a final kiss and then escape to an empty room, but Henry moved too quickly, stepping inside, and the moment was lost. "No, my dear. This day has seen the end of my aching loins. Never more need I depart famished from your door."

Composure and control disintegrated, dissolved in mindless panic. Blindly, Anne tried to flee the man who had tricked her into marriage under false pretenses, but Henry caught her in his strong arms and carried her to an ornate bed with turned-down covers. Smiling, he dropped his bloused shirt on top of the already-discarded scarlet coat. A huge expanse of white skin covered with dark brown hair gleamed in the pale amber candlelight.

"Sir, you forget yourself," blushed Anne, somehow holding back the tears.

Henry paused, amused, kicked off his boots. "Nay. You forget yourself, Mrs. Gladwyn."

The name struck like a cold slap. Sudden rage replaced fear, timidity bowed to anger. Emboldened, she resisted fiercely as Henry crushed her in his arms, tongue seeking and darting hotly between her lips. Anne broke free but a muscular finger caught her bodice, grasped the fragile lace and ripped it apart. Anne gasped and tried to cover herself, even as the laces of her corset loosened under knowing fingers. Leaping from the bed, she took refuge in the corner, and turned to see a look of hurt curiosity cross Henry's face. "The time for coyness has passed, Anne. This is our wedding night," he said softly.

"Liar! Pernicious, self-seeking, opportunistic liar!"

Henry paused, pale and colorless, temper barely under control. "I am much chagrined to find you so waspish, mistress," he said a touch too formally, restraining the growing anger. "Nor do I understand what could have transformed the cooing dove of yesterday to the termagant hawk of tonight."

"I merely listened to the other birds chatter of how my dear, dear lord dissimulated."

"You wrong me, Anne. You know why I married you. For love, it was, though out of time. I could as easily accuse you of base motives, for your father's fortunes are in disarray. We've both profited, as have our families. But come, now. This is silly chatter. I love you. You love me. We've a bed before us, and there we shall proceed to important matters."

"You may, sir, take your important matters to hand, for all of me," Anne spat. "I'll have none of you." Crossing her arms over her naked breasts, she stalked from the corner and made for the door connecting to the next room.

Henry moved rapidly. "A chase is it, then? All right, I'll give chase and convince you of my love." He bounded across the floor, catching her in two great strides, the force of his momentum carrying them both to the bed. Anne struggled but found her wrists firmly imprisoned in one large hand. Lips brushed cheek and neck and descended with kisses and tender nibbles until her breasts swelled in anticipation, glorious pink crowns hard and erect.

Anne fought valiantly. Still he teased, touched, played and fondled, lips and fingers caressing every newly revealed inch of luscious geography. She lay half under him, held down and helpless, tense and quivering. His right hand ran the length of her thigh and then fumbled with his breeches, fought them off inch by inch and finally kicked them free. Warm skin and coarse hair pressed against soft, downy flanks. Anne was acutely aware of the hot flesh rising along her thigh, and though she tried to get away, Henry held her tightly, captured her legs with his own, deftly lifted her hips and whisked the skirts from the bed.

The struggle went on in silence. Anne squirmed to the left; Henry followed, fingertips ranging each curve and angle, exploring her virgin form. Anne rolled to the right; Henry, not to be denied, grasped her from the rear, one hand cupping her breast, the other forcing itself between her legs from behind and massaging the swelling, soon to be violated flesh that moistened at his caress. Anne clawed the hand from her breast, bit deeply into his wrist; Henry jerked free, swatted her bare rump sharply and rolled her over, kneeled straddling her, fire in his eyes.

Unwilling yet unable to stop, Anne risked a glance down. There, springing from close, tightly curled locks, stood the fearful monster of love, swollen and hard, rampant with lust. "No. Please," she whispered, terror in her plea.

Henry paused, gazing down. "Then it's true? You are a virgin?"

"Yes." It was a whisper.

"Then I shall love thee all the more, little doe."

She tried to thrust her tormentor from the bed, failed, and with new horror looked again at the pulsating organ as one and then the other knee forced apart her thighs. "No!" she cried again, but Henry was deafened by ever growing passion. His hips lowered and the tip of his manhood touched, moistened, and slowly, evenly, irresistibly spread open the tender lips. Barely inside, he paused, full insertion restrained by the membranous proof of virginity.

"'Tis true, indeed," he said, looking down.

Anne couldn't help but follow his gaze, there to see the tumescent, veined shaft, the swollen head concealed, male attached to female. Disbelief clouding her vision, she watched as the engorged tip, hard and warm, rubbed gently, lubricating and readying her. Unwillingly, she responded, eyes glued to the sight, breath coming faster and faster.

Suddenly he thrust, rendering asunder the thin veil of maidenhood. Anne cried out with the sharp pain, resisting him. Henry only moved more furiously against her.

Suddenly, he stopped, held himself still deep inside her and, as the pain subsided, all she could feel was warmth and fullness. Anne's eyes glazed and she turned her face to the side to hide the tears which even then started to flow. Henry let go her wrists and she didn't try to fight. Gently, his hands stroked her hair, forced her to look into his eyes. They were both fierce and gentle.

"My lady Anne," he whispered huskily. "My beauty, my love. The pain is over. Now is the time for pleasure."

He moved slowly at first, slipping in and out, twisting from side to side. Pain gave way to pleasure. Instinct and raw passion defeated her reluctance, as slowly, Henry's ardor became her own. Then she was arched against the bed to more closely embrace the searing shaft of love, matching the blood-pounding rhythm stride for shuddering stride. Swelling, she tightened, felt and relished each inch a fathom as he drove himself over and over again until exquisite spasms gripped her in great, heaving waves of ecstasy.

* * *

Satiated, Henry slept, unmoving, his breathing even and untroubled. Anne stirred beneath the weight of his arm, slid from the musky bedding and walked to the window to stand in the moonlight, naked and shivering, staring forlornly at the late summer's night sky. She touched where he had entered, still sore but no longer painful. Far more painful was the shame and humiliation, for in the last moments she had joined him in rapture. A deep anger suffused her. Never, never again. Rather, she would . . .

What? The world was different, now. The moonlit cobblestones, silvery and still, had changed in some inexplicable manner. How foolish to think she stood apart from life as lived by everyone else. How galling to admit the truth, that a silly, addle-pated, lovesick Anne Langford had paraded, wide-eyed and innocent, into the arms of a man who lusted after her father's power. How naïve to have thought their love was unique!

Henry rolled over and the bed creaked in protest. Anne turned, gazed about the room. Their clothes lay strewn on the floor in rumpled disarray. On the bed, her new husband sprawled, relaxed and unconscious of her inspection. In sleep there was a clean innocence about him. The covers lay to his waist, leaving his chest naked to the night air. He *was* handsome, she thought wistfully. Damn, but he was handsome. And that moment when they had been joined, a single pulsing animal, had been more wondrous than she had ever imagined love could be. Again, she touched the aching flesh and felt desire spring.

No. Thought rebelled. She did not—would not— love Henry Gladwyn. Could never love him now. There had to be a way out, a solution. One day she would have retribution for this terrible hoax. One day. Until then she would play the dutiful wife and perform as expected, but with neither love nor tenderness.

Somewhere, a clock tolled the time, spoke the dreary hour of darkest night. Silently, carefully, a disillusioned bride crept back to bed and lay stiffly next to the stranger she had married.

CHAPTER 5

The King is dead. The thought ran sluggishly through her head as Anne stared into the fire. Long live the King.

Who knew what would happen next? How quickly time flew. Only two months ago, a naïve and trusting girl had exchanged wedding vows with her beloved, only to learn she'd been bought and sold like so much chattel. All her dreams were shattered, and though she was careful to put on a coquettish and charming face in public, privately she continued to avoid her father and reject her husband's overtures and protestations of sincerity.

Exasperated and utterly perplexed, Henry quickly buried himself in the work at hand—advancement. His rugged good looks and facile tongue endeared him to the ladies. His quick grasp of the rudiments of politics and his seemingly unerring ability to say the right thing at the right time impressed the men. The climate was favorable: with Pitt, the Great Commoner, in office, society was more inclined to accept others with a common birthright. In short, Henry was doing well. He had met everyone important and was on the verge of intimacy with several of them. Acting on the advice of friends, he invested in some shipping interests and could look forward to a handsome return. It wouldn't be long, Anne could tell with some resentment, before he would be knighted, if not more.

In October, Henry arranged a week of hunting at the Gladwyn estates. The trip was a fiasco as far as Anne was concerned, for nothing went right and no one was happy. Anne hated the loneliness and sense of isolation and wished devoutly to return to London. Beth resented Henry's preoccupation with his own career and became truculent as she more clearly perceived he was becoming everything her father had hated. The Chilterns were an abomination: cold, wet and windy. Charles was a surly host, given to complaints and grumbling over trivia. Anthony, Henry's father, was ill in bed and the pall of disease hung over the household. Henry was impossible. Tense and on edge, constantly aware of his guests, he had no time for a brooding, unsympathetic wife. Each day he and the men went out to follow the hounds, leaving the women alone in a wintry, draughty building. As a result, Anne and Beth found unforeseen allies in each other. For two months they had been at odds. Now, within two days, they became close friends, more near sisters than aunt and niece. At the same time, the relationship between husband and wife deteriorated almost irretrievably.

The death of the King changed everything. Word reached the Chilterns on October 26, the day after the royal death. By the twenty-ninth, the whole entourage was back in town. George II had not been in the best of health, but neither had he been particularly ill. Everyone was taken by surprise, and the stroke that carried him off instigated a widespread, complicated and merciless power struggle. George III was young, ignorant, weak and controlled by the Dowager Princess and the Earl of Bute. As the new regime took over, the Great Commoner Pitt and Lord Newcastle watched helplessly as the winds of change plucked at their political cloaks and tore away great swags of power, for the new King and his mother both hated and distrusted them. Caught in the maelstrom, Henry's rapid rise was in jeopardy and he was forced into a new and vastly more sophisticated game for which he was totally unprepared.

Anne sat at home alone and observed the beginning of her husband's fall in much the same way as she stared into the fire—with virtually no reaction. The process was too painful to watch with anything less than complete, numbed detachment. So absorbed was she in the flames, the opening of the door passed unnoticed. "Anne?"

"Hello, Father," she said, rising and dutifully kissing him on the cheek.

"Why so pensive?"

Anne smiled automatically and sank back into the chair. "It's a pensive sort of a day."

"When do you expect Henry?"

"I'm not informed of his hours, sir," she answered sourly.

Pensive himself, now, Sir Spencer helped himself at the sideboard and poured a glass of wine for each of them. "I notice a chill in your voice and manner," he said, handing Anne one of the glasses. "Toward me, I presume?"

"You are very direct, sir."

"Bluntness is a father's prerogative. You haven't answered." Anne busied herself with the goblet. "Come, child. Am I to be resented and not know why?"

Anne's eyes flashed briefly. "Do you really not know why, Father?"

Sir Spencer sat heavily. "No, I don't. You have

been in ill-humor since the wedding. I'm beginning to suspect that gossip is truth and all is not well between you and Henry. Why this extends to me, I'm unsure."

"I don't appreciate finding my private concerns flying like dirty linen in the wind."

"A dreadful situation, I warrant," Sir Spencer laughed, "but never one to bother you before."

"I know of your financial arrangement with Henry," Anne countered, irritated by his levity. "Is it wrong to resent being used as a pawn?"

"A pawn, is it?" her father asked, a little taken aback that she knew. If Henry had only told him, he could have solved this problem long ago. "A pawn, indeed. My daughter all but ruins her name by breaking our contract with the future Duke of Arenton and accepting the favors of a commoner. When I protest, she moans of her lovelorn state and cries to the heavens how her father is a heartless man. When I accede to this same daughter's demands and allow the marriage, I am accused of bartering her away in a game of my own device simply because I had the good sense to procure compensation for my magnanimity!" Worked into a fine state, he rose and stood over her. "Very well, madam. Now it is my turn for resentment! Good day!"

"Father?" she called, like a child scolded and reaching for a return to grace. Sir Spencer obligingly halted and turned, careful to keep his face appropriately stern and unyielding until Anne rushed to embrace him, weeping.

They sat together near the window, Sir Spencer now the comforting father. "What am I to do?" Anne finally asked.

Sir Spencer considered. "Why, be happy, of course."

"I don't know if I can."

"Nonsense. The man loves you. What else can a woman ask?"

"I feel as if I hardly know him."

"The marriage bed is certainly the place to get acquainted."

"Father!"

"Don't lose your temper with me, young lady. You've asked for advice and advice is what you'll get." He retrieved his wine, gaining time to choose the next words carefully. "The King is dead and all our fortunes are at stake. Henry is bright and incisive, but inexperienced, if not naïve in some respects. He has at least one highly placed enemy, probably more. No man is immune to that sort of thing, especially with Stephen against him." He paused, shushing her. "Don't look so surprised. Did you expect the lad to take such a great insult and not respond?

"Now, what Henry needs is advice and direction. You were an apt pupil, and can now be an invaluable teacher and partner. Don't waste all you've been taught. Bute must be courted. The Dowager, too, but Bute is the key. Henry's boldness and your finesse can salvage success from what initially appears a setback. It will take time, of course, but no goal of great worth comes quickly or easily."

He sat, took Anne's hands. "Once Henry is established and you both bask in the perquisites of power, then come to me and tell me if you are indeed unhappy." He squeezed her hands gently, then rose again. "I must be off."

Anne took her father's arm as they crossed the room. "I'm glad you came by."

"So am I. Have Henry stop by tomorrow, will you?"

"Of course."

"And Anne. Do not squander this opportunity."

A renewed sense of determination and importance lit Anne's eyes. "I won't, Father. Thank you."

Sir Spencer received her second kiss, and it was far more earnest than the first. Only when he was safely at his carriage did he allow an impish smile to transform an otherwise dignified appearance. He looked back at the Gladwyn apartments to see Anne wave from a window. "Carthage, indeed," he grumbled, returning the wave and taking his seat. "I'd like to see the day!"

Rejuvenated by the session with Sir Spencer, Anne came out of her shell. That night, Henry returned home to find a new wife, one who greeted him with a warm kiss, and later, surprising ardor. Though she was less than candid the next morning, he was acutely aware her attitude had changed, and attacked the day with new vigor and confidence. From that moment, London was a brighter place, the heights more accessible. The Gladwyn money, resented by Charles but supplied by the ailing Anthony, and the Langford name and social expertise, made a powerful and effective combination. Dinners, parties, dances: with great dexterity, the shift was being made from Pitt to Bute, from the second George to the third.

Anne found the process exhilarating, and became more and more attuned to the Henry she had first fallen in love with. In fact, she was sure, she was falling in love all over again. Husband and wife working in harmony, their days became a continuing whirl of planning and preparation. One social maneuver designed to cement a constantly improving position followed another. Their nights, often enough, were filled

with tender caresses and passionate lovemaking that
left them exhausted but recharged, ready to begin the
common quest anew.

And then disaster. Anthony Gladwyn died on New
Year's Day of 1761 and a triumphant Charles beat his
way through nearly impassable roads to rush the news
to London. Appalled, Henry read the papers, read
them again. He had been left £20,000 in addition to
his £12,000 per annum. There was no need to ask for
any more. Charles' gloating look was answer enough:
they needn't expect another penny.

One disaster wasn't enough. Not yet satisfied,
Charles found a partner in Stephen Berkely, who
snapped at the chance to even an old score. Within a
fortnight, Stephen had put together a combination to
compete directly with Henry's shipping interests.
Through the action of friends of friends, credit was
tightened. By the end of February, Henry was a partner in a collapsing venture.

Henry and Anne's position melted like snow on
still-warm cobblestones. Bute, an old friend of Berkely's, was given stock in Stephen's new company, and
reacted as predicted: the King and Dowager Princess
were convinced the upstart Henry Gladwyn had never
cut his ties with Newcastle and Pitt, and was working
secretly to continue the onerous war with France.
Credit became difficult; friendships cooled abruptly.

The beginning of March brought a personal crisis.
Henry had been despondent for a week, and with
despondency came the realization that a life measured
in flattery, bribes and fatuous parties followed by a
storm of bills was ridiculous. Politics! A nasty, venal
charade. A game played by avaricious, power-hungry
connivers. He had snapped up the bait and now he
was trapped. What kind of a life was that for a man

to lead? Dull and dispirited, Henry stood before a mirror and appraised the dark circles beneath his eyes, the softness brought on by too much food and drink and too little exercise. He did not like what he saw.

But where was the way out? Bullheaded, he turned back to his desk and the mound of bills. The largest and most shocking lay on the top. Maintaining a company of the King's soldiers was no miniscule burden, yet if he was ever to gain entry into the highest ranks, the expense must be met. Rubbing his forehead, he ran down the column of figures. Little was left of the twenty thousand. The twelve thousand for the year was already committed. Damn, but he couldn't help wondering if the game was worth the price.

Spring dragged into summer. Henry's despondency increased and he stamped about in a dull rage. Uncertain of her position, Beth withdrew into her father's fantasy world of charity and good works. Her constant talk of impoverished beggars and needy children drove her uncle to distraction. The debts piled up. Charles and Stephen were behind every slight or setback, real or imagined, and Henry turned livid invective against them. Sir Spencer was useless save for spouting platitudes. Even Anne drew his ire, for she was an indefatigable font of optimism, and worse, he was sure, spent every available moment flirting with whomever she thought might help their cause. That the charge was untrue and a result of his own frustration and anger, he could not see.

Anne watched Henry's demoralization with increasing trepidation. Did he not understand that political life had always been this way? As surely as their fortunes had risen once, they would rise again. Of course there were problems, but tenacity was required. And determination. Their current predicament was temporary, and if they but kept trying, they would soon emerge stronger than ever.

She loved him more than ever during the dark days. Grieving silently to see him so stymied at every turn, she worked harder than ever to help him regain his confidence. Her best chance came in July. Oliver Page, an old childhood friend and now the fourth Duke of Cloughbrent, had just returned from an extended stay in Italy. They met, quite by accident, at Covent Gardens during an afternoon stroll. Oliver was three years Anne's senior—a large, burly man who was in love with the world. He was also wealthy, having succeeded to the third Duke's vast domain in the north, and extensive shipping and trading rights in the Far East. Best of all, Oliver hated Stephen Berkely.

As the afternoon wore on, Oliver agreed to buy Henry's interest in the shipping company, and would pay cash to boot. By evening's end, Anne and Oliver had renewed their friendship and Henry had made a new friend. That night, for the first time in weeks, Henry made love with the abandon of a twenty-year-old.

The next weeks were a beehive of activity. Henry had lost a great deal on his original investment, but the cash received was still a handsome sum. Word of his new relationship with Oliver got around quickly, and for the first time since his father's death, Henry cheered up. Anne, too, seemed more alive. Cloughbrent and his influence had given them both hope. Anne's optimism, it appeared, had been well-founded.

Almost a year ago, Henry mused, heading up the main staircase of the Langford home to better overlook the dancers. Only two weeks, and he and Anne will have been married a full year. The chatter fell away as he climbed. The room looked different from the vantage point of the balustrade. It was gayer, brighter. He kept a calculating eye on the servants, making sure glasses were kept full and empty platters were replenished. The party was not large, but all the guests were important. He and Anne were counting on this affair.

Anne. She'd been through a great deal with him in that short year. Unable to relax, he searched for her, easily picked her out of the crowd. As ravishing as ever, she was dancing with Oliver. A tiny frown, quickly erased, crossed his face. "Damned lucky, I should say."

"Yes."

Henry turned to see Beth. "Yes, what?"

"Yes, lucky I found you, of course."

"Snuck up on me, don't you mean?"

"I've little choice if I want to catch you. You move about so. And talk to yourself."

Henry laughed good-heartedly. "Am I really that inaccessible?"

"Yes." The look on Beth's face was serious. "You work so hard to join that mad crowd, there's no time left for a niece." Henry followed her gesture to the party-goers. "Papa would tell me to give up on you, but I shan't."

"That's nice of you," Henry remarked drily, still watching the floor. Anne and Oliver were leaving the room, heading out a side door. The frown returned. "And what would your papa recommend I do instead?" he asked abruptly.

"Why, dance, of course," Beth answered flippantly. "Are you going to ask me to or not?"

Henry gazed speculatively at her. She was growing up, quickly learning the little tricks a woman used.

Yet Beth would never use them well, he thought. She was too honest. What she truly wanted showed in her eyes too clearly to be mistaken. "Byron would have found the perfect solution, then," he finally said. "Come on. Dance it shall be." Arm in arm, as the strings retuned, they descended to join the dancers.

Lord Oliver Page, the fourth Duke of Cloughbrent, was a bear in finery. Coat and breeches of deep burgundy, and *frac* coat of the same, were tailored to soften a hefty physique more suited to playing fields than palaces. A boyish face radiated joviality beneath a fashionable mask of powder and lightly applied rouge. The deviltry in his eyes only added to his charm with what the ladies called sweet contrast.

This night, Oliver was playing the platonic friend as he and Anne stood on the balcony overlooking the mall. There, under the few stars visible through the eternal haze, London seemed deceptively lazy, almost as if it slept. They had danced, then sought fresh air and wandered through the halls and up the stairs, chatting innocently of this and that and nothing in particular. But on the balcony, a subtle change tinged their words, and Anne realized she was trembling with anticipation.

Somehow, Oliver's hands were on her waist, pulling her to him. Anne hadn't meant for this to happen, and yet she was in his arms, responding hungrily and without protest as his tongue ran lightly over her lips. When his hand found her breasts, she stepped back quickly, suddenly aware of the rising heat that coursed between them. "Sir, I dare not."

Oliver was contrite, the picture of enthusiasm gone awry. "I did not mean to offend you, Anne."

"Nor have you."

"But your beauty overwhelms my judgment." He took her hands in his. "And judgment flies in the face of bewitchment. Is it always thus with those you choose to capture?"

"Capture?" Anne laughed, enjoying the adroit turn which set the blame on her. "Indeed, sir, I . . ."

"You protest needlessly. I am your prisoner. Do you pity me?"

"You make me sound the tyrant," she retorted easily, enjoying the attention and standing on tiptoe to grace him with a fleeting kiss. "There. That's for my pity."

"Anne . . ."

"Come. The music ends. My husband will be looking for me."

She turned to reenter the gallery, but Oliver caught her in an inflexible grip and spun her into his arms. "See? Your diffidence transforms me."

Anne placed her fingertips across his lips. "Transformed, indeed. From colt to stallion," she said amused. "Yet you will release me."

Oliver paused, searching her eyes. When she did not look aside, he loosened his grip, clasped both of her hands and kissed the steeple of her joined fingers. "And so I do. But I am filled with an awesome aching, mistress."

"Then 'twere best you secure a less dangerous linament, sir," a low voice answered from the door.

Oliver and Anne turned in sudden embarrassment. Henry stepped onto the balcony. "I would have a word with you, madam." He glanced at Oliver. "My lord?"

"By all means." Oliver bowed stiffly. "If you'll excuse me?" He left quickly, retreating from the transparent hate in Henry's eyes.

Anne retreated too, but only so far as the railing at

her back. Henry's voice was soft. "What has happened to us, Anne?"

"I don't know what you mean." Henry didn't respond, only glanced back the way Oliver had gone. "Surely you don't insinuate I am in any way wrong," she continued a little too sharply. "I chose a partner for a brief respite from the din. I sought the refreshment of a summer night's breeze. I need not defend myself, sir. Think what you will."

"Stephen Berkely."

Anne looked confused. "What?"

"Stephen Berkely came upon us the night we met. He was incensed to find we had escaped for the refreshment of a summer night's breeze." He paused. Anne was avoiding his gaze, and he placed his fingers under her chin to bring her eyes to his. "Have I become a Stephen Berkely, Anne?"

Anne shuddered at the pain in his voice and eyes. "No," she whispered, on the verge of tears and seeking the reassurance of his arms. "No."

Henry held her, felt her shoulders tremble. "I love you, Anne," he vowed.

She looked up, eyes bright. "And I you, Henry. I love you very, very much."

For a long moment neither spoke. Finally Henry smiled, almost wistfully. "We'd better go back in," he said gently. "Our guests are waiting." One finger touched where a tear had run down her cheek. "You'll want to see to your face." Arm in arm, they left the balcony. There would be time, later, for more.

The hansom clattered along the sleeping cobblestones. It was three in the morning and the party was over. Anne rested her head on Henry's shoulder and dozed lightly. "We're here."

"Mmm?"

"We're here. Wake up."

Anne sat up, rubbed her eyes. The coach jolted to a stop and the horse snorted. Henry waited for the driver to get the door, got out and helped Anne down. The night was cool and the city quiet. When the carriage drove off, they were left alone. "Ready for bed?" Henry asked.

"Mmmm."

"Talkative, aren't you," he said, leading her up the stairs.

"Mmm."

The door opened. William had waited up. Henry looked at him questioningly. "Someone to see you, sir," he said tensely. "In the library."

"You'd better go on up," Henry said, suddenly alert. He kissed Anne on the cheek, started her toward the stairs. "I'll be along." He waited until she was out of earshot before turning to William. "What's going on?"

"Your brother, sir. And Lord Stephen Berkely."

"What the hell are they doing here at this hour?"

"They didn't say, sir. They arrived at midnight and insisted I let them wait."

"Damn!" He paused, tried to foresee what they wanted and failed. "Thank you, William. Go on to bed if you wish."

"I'll stay up, sir."

Henry grinned. "Thanks." Straightening his coat, he entered the library.

Stephen and Charles had heard the carriage drive up and were waiting. Charles waved a goblet in a wobbly salute as Henry entered. "You'll forgive me if I don't stand, dear brother?" Henry nodded, went to the sideboard to pour a glass for himself. "You do remember my friend, Lord Stephen Berkely?"

Stephen stepped into the light. Henry ignored him until his drink was poured. "Of course," he finally said, acknowledging the unasked-for guest with a perfunctory nod. "Your health, gentlemen."

"My poor health, don't you mean?" Charles asked nastily.

"No, Charles. Simply to your health."

"With me lying next to Father, it would all be yours to squander on your own overriding ambition."

"Oh, for pity's sake, Charles. It's three in the morning," Henry exclaimed.

"Yes. Pity. More's the pity for you," Charles wheezed.

Henry waited, looking from Charles to Stephen and back again. "Very well, gentlemen. You've come for some reason. Let's get it over with."

"You're very perceptive, Gladwyn," Stephen spoke at last. "Why don't you tell us why we're here." Charles snickered. Henry glared at him. "We were glad to hear you have a wealthy new friend, and have come to congratulate you."

"I'm glad you're glad," Henry answered sarcastically. The image of Oliver pawing at Anne returned to plague him.

"No doubt. Wealth is useful when one has debts."

"I don't believe my debts are any of your business, Stephen."

"Really?" Stephen asked, incensed at the use of the first name but refusing to be baited. He pulled an envelope from his pocket. "You'll be interested to know Charles and I have been busy making them our business," he said, tossing a packet onto the desk. "Go on. Read them. Gunsmith, dressmaker, wigmaker, caterers, etc., etc."

Henry glanced down, scanned the list and paled as

he realized they'd all been sold to Stephen. "What is this?" he asked hoarsely.

"It adds up to fifteen thousand pounds, approximately. A rather large sum."

Charles lurched to his feet. "Rather larger than you can cover, eh, Henry?"

Henry stood between them. "You really hate me that much, then?"

Stephen laughed. "Hate? Heaven forbid. But you stole something from me once. I am simply repaying the favor."

Head forward and shoulders hunched, Henry stared at Stephen. "What do you want?" he asked, barely retaining control.

"It only requires your signature." Henry turned. Charles held out a piece of paper. Snatching it from his hand, Henry read quickly. "It's not as complicated as it sounds," Charles added, pleased with himself. "In short, upon your signature you accept a captain's commission as a member of His Majesty's forces in the colonies. All your debts—with the exception of those Stephen has bought—which you may repay with interest at a later date—will be liquidated. Of course, your wife will be provided for until you wish to send for her. Preferably soon."

"And if I refuse?" Henry asked.

"Refuse? Why ever would you? You seek advancement, we offer the same. From lieutenant to captain. Come, come, Henry. Even you admit you tire of this senseless struggle."

Henry folded the paper, tossed it on the desk. "I hate to disillusion you, but what happens if I simply pay these bills?"

Stephen laughed again. "How? Who will lend you any more funds? Cloughbrent? He's already bought a useless investment. Will you return, hat in hand and on your knees, while all London looks on and laughs? Will you really?"

"I should kill you," Henry said in an ominous tone.

"I don't think so," Stephen drawled, nevertheless stepping back out of Henry's reach.

"You've come a long way in a year, Stephen," Henry hissed.

"Yes, I have. And now, if you'll sign please."

"No." Henry drew himself up. "Not yet. I'll give you my answer tomorrow. You may call at three. In the afternoon. And now, gentlemen, I'm tired. If you'll forgive me?"

Charles and Stephen hesitated, unsure of their course in the face of Henry's unanticipated refusal. Finally Stephen nodded. "Very well. Three o'clock. But no longer. You have a great deal to do between now and Saturday week—when your ship sails. Charles? It's late." Without a further word, the two conspirators marched out, slamming the door behind them.

A moment later, Henry heard the front door close, then William pause outside the library door before leaving for the back of the house. Alone at last, he wandered around the room, snuffing out all the candles but one, then slumped in the chair vacated by Charles. The single candle guttered and the house grew quiet, the silence disturbed by nothing more than troubled thoughts. Charles and Stephen were apt conspirators, as the pile of unpaid debts vouchsafed. They certainly wanted to be rid of him. A captain's commission: all debts discharged. "It's what you want," Charles had said.

Was it? Henry wondered. Perhaps. Vivid still was the morning in February when he had stood naked in

front of the mirror and passed judgment on himself
and the life he was living. A nasty, venal charade, he
had decided. It still was. Even worse, if that were
possible. Anne loved him, he was sure, but the episode
with Oliver had been a humiliating harbinger. A year
ago he would have killed the man, duke or no. Tonight he had merely interrupted them. What would
he do the next time? Sneak away and let his wife play
the whore for his ambition? As for running to Cloughbrent for more money, Berkely was right: all London
would laugh.

Laugh at him? Damn them all, then. Choked with
rage, he rose, stalked to the desk and picked up a
sharpened quill. Next Saturday wouldn't be a minute
too soon.

"Mistress Anne?" Sabrina paused in the door. "He's
ready."

It was raining. Water ran down the window panes
in erratic tracks. Their first anniversary would be in
four days, but Henry was leaving today. "Tell him I'll
be down shortly," she said hollowly.

The door closed gently. Only then did Anne turn
from the rain.

Everything was ready. His trunks had been sent
ahead and lay waiting aboard the *Black Prince,* which
lay at anchor in the Pool of London. He had called
upon those who had befriended him, sent letters of
gratitude to others. Little good they would do, but
at least he had expressed his gratitude. Henry brushed
the sleeve of his coat, glanced in the mirror. He had
gained more weight, felt soft and less than competent.
The pounds would slough off in the colonies, though,
and confidence would return. It galled him to be

beaten, and yet, in a peculiar fashion, he owed the conspirators something. Deep in his heart, he was glad to be going.

"Uncle Henry?" He turned to embrace Beth, who hesitated only a moment before rushing into his arms. "I'm glad you're going," she whispered fiercely. "But I'll miss you horribly. What am I to do?"

"Why, be Anne's trusted companion, I hope. I shall miss you, too." The door opened and Anne entered. "Kiss me goodbye, Beth, then wait in the drawing room. No, no tears. We'll be together again." Weeping in spite of the admonition, Elizabeth hugged Henry and kissed him for the last time, then rushed out the door.

Anne's face was pale and drawn. The ten days since she had read Henry's signatures affixed to the final agreements had been a nightmare of futile entreaty. She had committed herself to Henry's rise, worked long and hard to help him succeed. By giving up, he was repudiating all she had done and rejecting her as well. Bewildered and hurt, she had withdrawn, sharing little with him as he went about the chores of quitting civilian life and England for the military and the colonies. Only the night before had she allowed him to her bed, and then their lovemaking had been empty and hollow, a passionless imitation of earlier times.

Henry leaned to kiss her but she turned away. "Do you hate me so?" he asked quietly, touching her shoulder.

"You have stolen my question, sir."

"What do you mean?"

"It is you who have abandoned me," she said, going to the window.

"If I stayed, Anne, I'd be abandoning myself as well,

to a life I'm not meant for. This isn't a morbid ending, but a new beginning. Before long I'll send for you and . . ."

"I've told you I . . ."

"Anne! We've been through this before."

"And I'm supposed to pack up and leave just like that?" she asked, whirling angrily. "For some perfectly horrid wilderness? To beggar away my life in squalid surroundings because you . . . you . . . Oh!" She covered her face with her hands. "I won't go, Henry. I won't!"

"You are my wife," Henry retorted, his own anger growing. "You will do as I order."

"Your uniform becomes your manner, sir. Insufferable and peremptory."

"Damn it, Anne!"

"Yes!" she spat. "It is that type of situation, isn't it?"

Henry stared at her, forced himself to calm down. "I have but a moment. I don't want us to part this way, Anne. Please try to understand."

"I do," she answered, icy calm again. "Perfectly. You are a quitter, a coward and a commoner who doesn't deserve the heights."

"Heights? What use a summit inhabited by mean and false gods?"

"You presume to say my ambition and life are mean and false?"

"Yes."

"In what way?"

Henry's face seemed carved of stone. "In every way, madam. Goodbye!" He bowed stiffly and left the room.

William waited in the hall. "The help wants me to wish you their best, sir," the butler said, handing Henry his tricorn.

Henry smiled. "I'm very grateful, William. You may tell them I'll miss them all."

"Thank you, sir."

"And William? Watch out for Mrs. Gladwyn for me, will you?"

"I'll do my best, sir."

Henry looked around the hall, committing it to memory, then turned and left. Outside, the rain had tapered off to a drizzle. The carriage was waiting, and in it, to Henry's surprise, Sir Spencer. "Thought you ought to have someone friendly around to see you off, if you don't mind company down to the river."

Hesitating only to glance back at the house, Henry climbed in. "It's good of you, sir. I appreciate it." He tapped on the window and the driver cracked his whip. They were off.

Anne watched from behind the curtain. He strode out, hesitated, glanced back and was in and gone without a wave. "Henry?" she whispered, repeating his name as if the all but silent entreaty would bring him back, as if it might excise the bitter invective, leaving only the core of their love.

The carriage didn't turn back. She was alone, slumped in the window seat and weeping miserably. Suddenly the door opened and Beth entered, ran quickly to Anne's side and held her. She didn't know what to say; she only knew that she shared this woman's grief, and found kinship in the sharing.

"In four days we will have been married for a year," Anne sobbed.

One year. One, only.

CHAPTER 6

Spring's warming breath blew in serpentine coils through the rolling landscape, filled the shallow valley with whispers, stirred the flowers and set them dancing across the sweep of sculpted garden. The April breeze flowed on over the trim lawn to ruffle the reflecting pool and set the trimmed hedges aquiver, strike the terraced walks and spill up the neo-Palladian façade of Gladwyn Hall. Anchored in the bosom of a fertile green valley high among the Chilterns, the Gladwyn country estate was noted for elegance of design, sweetness of air, felicity of solitude and the delicate succulence of the trout which thrived in its crystal-clear streams.

Anne had awakened early, her sleep disturbed by unsettling dreams. Now she stood before the open window, hair tousled by restless sleep and tossed by the breeze. Slender fingers clasped her dressing gown tightly lest the folds of light material part and reveal to any prying eyes below the perfection of a body so sensuously outlined by wind and silk.

"You're about early, child. Are you ill?"

Child? Anne Langford Gladwyn smiled at the term. Wed and all of twenty years old, and still Sabrina called her a child. Sabrina, who had been in the service of the Langfords for as long as Anne could remember and had come to the Gladwyn household when her mistress was married, plucked a warm wrap from the wardrobe and hurried to protect Anne from the morning chill. Anne turned, waving aside the robe. Sabrina was such a fuss. But what was one to do with the fixture to whom, as a tearful young bride, she had confided in those first bitter weeks following the shock of an unpleasant wedding night? "No, not ill, Sabrina, just restless. I feel quite fine, thank you."

Sabrina paused, retreated a pace and waited. You'll catch your death, child. The wind is damp and will give you the ague."

Anne petulantly strode to the mirrored dressing table. The world spun about on its axis and circumstances had a way of changing, but Sabrina kept a dogged course, convinced that the mistress was still a little girl, might as well never have married, never left the sheltered simplicity in which she had been raised. "I'm quite warm enough, Sabrina."

Warm enough indeed! Since Henry Gladwyn had sailed for the Americas almost nine months ago, there had been warmth aplenty, once she relaxed and left the bitterness behind. Then she found herself capable of laughter and flirting outrageously, even of accepting invitations and favors she would never have entertained a few weeks earlier. She was still young, still beautiful. Everyone could see marriage had, rather than commit a girl to bondage, freed a woman to experiment with the delights of the flesh. Should she then suffer the deprivation of worldly pleasure when lusty young gentlemen were so temptingly available? Never!

Were it not for Sabrina's dour looks and the mandatory monthly letter Anne felt constrained to post, she might even imagine there had never been a wedding. Still, Sabrina had raised her, and to Sabrina she owed a certain allegiance, even though the old woman hung about her, clouding the joy of her newfound freedom. In the mirror, the crone advanced again, ready to help with her mistress' hair. The old woman's bonnet was askew and her wrinkled face bore the lines of a frown. "I should like to spend this time alone, Sabrina, if you don't mind."

Sabrina faltered, started to speak, then stopped. She loved Anne Langford Gladwyn and was loved, she was certain, in return. "Yes, mum." Quietly, she stole from the room and silently closed the door.

At the window again, Anne stared down at the grounds. The breeze off the Chilterns kicked up slightly, and she shivered and stared out to the north where a pungent hint of acrid woodsmoke drifted from early-waking cottages and cocks were beginning to crow. Another day was spinning toward dawn. She wished the far-flung ridges could part and reveal the rock-fringed knob of a hill called Brohan's Mound, almost five miles away, where Oliver Page, Duke of Cloughbrent, would soon put his devotion to the test of steel.

Anne smiled. Sweet, lusty Oliver. In the lonely weeks that followed Henry's departure, Anne had succumbed to his ardent advances. A boisterous bull abed, Oliver was quick to take offense should any ill-advised suitor so much as approach in pursuit of her favors. His opponent this day would be one Ensign Patrick Campbell, Charles' guest by the back door, so to speak. A brash young man whose sister was married to an acquaintance of Charles', he had prevailed upon this tenuous relationship to inveigle an invitation. Poor man. She might have found him interesting. The memory of his eyes left her chilled and she drew the wrap more closely about her.

She had never seen a formal duel, but the thought of one left her limp with excitement. What woman would not be flattered? And how many could boast of being the object of two such *affaires d'honneur* in the space of nine short months? Patrick Campbell should have taken her refusal in the spirit in which it was given. Instead, he had persisted, trailing after Anne and Oliver to interrupt an intimate garden dalliance. It was an unforgivable breach of etiquette, made worse by his strident insults. With a beneficent, lazy smile, Oliver had smoothly accepted the young man's challenge.

Anne glanced to the east. The moments were passing all too slowly. Had her suitors arrived yet? Discarded coats and touched blades? Did the sound of arms already ring out over the stubby hill where so many men had gone to die in honor's name? Flushed with excitement, she turned again to the distance and watched the drama unfolding in her mind's eye.

Slowly, her breath quickened. Blood was flowing—would flow—in her name. Soon, Oliver would return and they would meet in the garden house. She could see him already, the cruel light of danger and triumph still in his eyes. About him would linger the sharp odor of fear faced and overcome. She would know, then, that the blood lust was still on him, that he wanted and would take her, tempering brutality with tenderness until, spent, he lay at ease at last in her arms.

An ache spread through her loins, set her breasts tingling. How she craved Oliver's touch! They would picnic on the heights, later, and the sweet-smelling new grass would be their bed. She would snuggle against him and relish his strength, the warmth of his body against her, inside her.

As the first ray of morning sun shot over the surrounding hills, lighting the tops of the distant trees, a tremor ran through Anne. With sunrise, the duel would start. Quickly, she strode to the dressing table and jerked sharply on the bell rope to summon her maids. She must attend to her toilette immediately. She wanted to be beautiful when her beloved Oliver returned.

Oliver's carriage, ornately carved and pulled by magnificent matched black geldings, clattered along the rock-strewn path, careening precipitously along the hillside trail. Manes flying, nostrils flaring, the horses plunged forward under the cracking black whip that popped the air over their backs and between their ears. In the hurly-burly of approach, the coach tilted crazily from side to side, daring tragedy before righting itself and continuing up the incline to pull to a skidding halt a few feet from Ensign Campbell's mare. As Oliver had intended, the gray spooked and his rival was forced to leap to the reins and bring his animal under control again. Oliver alighted before his coach stopped rocking and glanced around imperiously, his dark eyes taking in the entire setting. Already the seconds were present and assisting in the preparation of the foils. Good, and good again. Oliver was the last to arrive, as befitted his high rank and good breeding.

The man he had come to kill, Patrick Campbell, calmed his horse and stiffly strode back to his original position some ten paces in front of Oliver, not deigning to turn for a discourteous length of time, then bowing a little too insolently to suit Oliver's taste. Nevertheless, the Duke observed the formalities punctiliously, noting as he bowed in return, the hint of fear in the youth's eyes. Turning to pass his cloak to his valet, Oliver doffed his coat and accepted a toddy of brandy.

Silence reigned on Brohan's Mound, broken only by the slow moaning of wind through the single oak on the western edge where the hill fell a hundred precipitous feet. A party of four, the seconds, a surgeon and Squire Martin, acting in Charles' behalf as an impartial third party, clustered in a group and conversed in muted whispers. The coachmen and Oliver's valets remained by the horses. The antagonists stood alone, eyeing each other.

The contrast in the two was evident. Oliver Page was barely six feet tall and just shy of corpulent. Sixteen stone plus spread on a heavy-boned frame, he carried his weight with little effort. From plain black pumps to shining white hose, from buff breeches to the new *frac* waistcoat only recently obtained in London and covered with an intricate gold-and-black silk design, from ruffled collar to immaculate yet simple wig, he was the picture of studied elegance. Underneath the layers of clothing was a massive torso against which his mistress Anne loved to snuggle, squirming deliciously. His face was calm, his attitude haughty.

The newcomer who challenged Oliver's place at Anne's side stared back and took an equal measure. Attired in the elegant green-trimmed officer's uniform of some silly regiment of which Oliver had never heard, Patrick Campbell stood five feet ten, his weight evenly distributed over a physique as slight as a girl's, yet firm and trim and unmistakably masculine. A lithe fellow, he stood in repose much like a cat, able to move from inaction to action in an instant. Under the simple wig and tricorn hat, his face was precisely rouged and powdered. Only his eyes burning brightly betrayed the inexperience which underlay his exaggerated show of breeding. Oliver Page eyed the set jaw and did not underestimate his opponent.

Below, in the distance, the sleeping village of Brohan's Keep darkened, obscured as a barrier of clouds drifted across the horizon to blot out the morning light. The airy obstruction passed slowly, moving from the village toward the duelling ground, trailing a purple patch on the green slope. When the shadow enveloped them, Oliver felt a distinct chill creep the length of his spine. Slowly, even as Patrick Campbell removed hat and coat, Oliver shed the tight waistcoat and loosened the collar of his shirt. The work ahead could be strenuous.

The sun peaked above the horizon as the cloud passed. The time for sizing up was over. Squire Martin asked if both wished to continue. One by one they nodded affirmatively and accepted the weapons held by their seconds, tested the heft and balance of their blades and waited for the squire to recite a brief summary of the reasons behind the meeting, not once mentioning the true cause. The oratory finished, Oliver and Patrick bowed curtly and limbered their arms, each slicing the air with a deadly, menacing slim yard of steel. They were ready.

The duellists studied each other across the two paces separating them, each plotting the best attack, trying to determine the other's weakness. "Gentlemen, *en garde*, please!" Blades rose in salute, dipped to meet with a rasping sound that set teeth on edge. The squire removed a strip of bright cloth from his sleeve, draped it across the slanted steel cross askew in the air where it fluttered, alive in the breeze, vibrant red, the color of blood.

Patrick Campbell's blade slid down, glanced off the ornate metallic cup protecting the hilt and his fingers. Oliver parried, and off balance, felt a slight tug as his opponent's blade snagged his shirt. Heaving, he threw the lighter man from him and backed away, breathing heavily. Patrick Campbell was a better swordsman than Oliver had anticipated. Marked and bleeding on shoulder and forearm, the fellow persevered, ignoring the cuts delineated by lines of crimson plastering a sweat-sodden shirt to his wounds. He had not tired yet, but fought coldly and without passion, technically, as if in exercise. But he couldn't last much longer. He hadn't the strength. Boldly, begrudging his smaller opponent even a brief rest, Oliver lunged unexpectedly, hoping to catch Patrick off guard and end the duel.

Patrick retreated slowly, letting Oliver wear himself down, parrying thrust after lunge, barely turning the blade and giving ground. The man was too fat to go on much longer. Breathless and weary, he had to break soon. Suddenly, Patrick's rear foot found a rounded pebble and he slipped to one side. Oliver took advantage, rushed and lunged. Patrick had no recourse but to let himself continue falling, felt with alarm a fire in his side as the blade drove home and as quickly pulled out. He hit the ground and rolled, came up immediately, clutching the biting pain where the sword had entered.

"A touch!" called Oliver's second.

Squire Martin cautiously stepped between the combatants, halting the duel. "Ensign Campbell. You're wounded. Thrice marked. Will you cease?"

The officer dropped his hand from the wound in his side. "Stand aside, sir. Three scratches is all. I'm fit."

"Nay, lad. 'Tis the rules. Thrice marked and my duty is to intercede. M'lord, he's touched thrice. Is your honor satisfied?"

Oliver shrugged. "I'm satisfied. My blade is bloodied and the boy is plainly beat as all may see. He's learned a lesson, no doubt, and is free to go and patch his wounds as best he may."

"To the devil with My lord Page." The youth's face had turned white with rage and a flame of hatred burned brightly in his eyes. His shoulders stiffened and he trembled at the unforgivable condescension. "We shall see who gleans the final satisfaction—an officer in His Majesty's service or a mere pot-bellied page boy dressed in fancy clothing. Step aside, good sir."

Squire Martin shook his head ruefully. He had tried. So be it.

The two men faced each other again, Oliver with renewed interest in light of the fresh insult. Wary, he faced the unbearable brat who would now most definitely die. Before, he had attacked. Now he would fight defensively, goad his inexperienced adversary to indiscriminate fury and wait for the inevitable mistake. Campbell's recklessness would be Oliver's advantage.

Blades touched in ritual salute, rasped downward, the metallic sound swallowed by the surrounding hills. As Oliver had anticipated, Patrick attacked rapidly, sword flashing right and left, coming on strong. Oliver parried easily, backing slowly, a thin smile on his face.

The smile drove the young ensign to a fury. Faster and faster he came, the sword a blur in the bright morning light. Suddenly he seemed to slip and his blade dipped to the right as he sought balance. Oliver saw his chance. The mistake, and the kill to follow! Too late for mercy now. Ensign Campbell would die. He shifted his weight and charged forward to knock the smaller man onto the ground.

Damn! Where was he? Oliver's rapier pierced empty air and he swirled back to feel a steel tongue slice his face. Too late, he screamed, dropped his weapon and threw up his hands, stumbled and tripped, rolling a few feet to the edge of a sharp incline. Crawling to his knees, he clutched at the twin cuts running the length of each cheek from eye to jawline. Overhead stood the white-faced Patrick Campbell, staring down, lips distorted in a twisted smile.

"My God!" Martin muttered. The seconds grimaced at Lord Page's disfigurement and the demonic smile on the Ensign's face.

Oliver's cheeks were laid open to the bone. Blood streamed down his neck and soaked his lace collar and linen shirt. The fight was lost: he was beaten by a whelp. His weapon was gone, lost somewhere on the ground. He stared up at the face hanging disembodied in the air, saw the lips move. "A pot-bellied page boy with a bloody running mouth. What say you now, sir?"

There was only one chance left, a brief glimpse of victory gleaming in the face of defeat. He'd strangle the pup, break his neck with bare hands.

Oliver came from the ground, energy and dwindling strength brought to bear for the final attempt. The bloodied blade was pointed to the ground. There would be no time for the tip to rise, no time before the insolent face was smashed to pulp and the windpipe crushed. His whole being focused on the face as he charged and quite suddenly slowed. Two feet away, the smile grew, a monstrous laugh parting the lips, drawing them back horridly to discover the double row of gleaming white teeth. Nausea. Searing agony in chest and lungs. Still he lurched forward, closing on his tormentor, so intent on his fury that he barely felt the pain as Patrick's sword exited from his back. Glancing down, he stared with disbelief at the ornate hilt attached to his chest, the red bloom spreading. They were face to face an inch apart. "No," he protested weakly. "No . . ."

"Yes," the drawn lips hissed.

Oliver sagged forward. Rough arms pushed him back, and he toppled to his knees. The face loomed evil and dispassionate, the smile gone now, the expression flat, almost curious.

Someone was bracing him, holding his head while he stared at a patch of sky over Squire Martin's shoulder. Above, a hawk circled. At least he thought it was a hawk. Yes, he was certain. He could hear the far rush of air through wings. "Anne . . ." he whispered, choking on the rising blood. "Anne . . ."

". . . is mine," Patrick Campbell finished.

Anne knelt by the edge of the pond. Water lilies floated just beyond reach. Slender fingers dipped into the frigid spring water and created a false, swirling current. One budding barquentine broke free from the others, abandoned the blossomed flotilla and bobbed toward shore. She laughed softly, plucked the lily from its bath and pressed the cool petals to her cheek before casting the bloom back into the water. There was barely time.

The winding path led to the garden house, an elaborate child's toy whose exterior mimicked in minutest detail the classical Palladian features of the main house. Inside, the single room was elegantly appointed in the old style as befitted the purse and taste of an earlier generation, a perfect spot for the most private *tête-à-tête*. The door was ajar and she paused. Was Oliver already there? But she had not heard his carriage, nor the usual call of greeting. Frowning, she hurried the last few steps and entered. The fire, laid the night before, crackled merrily but no Oliver stood at the mantel. She dropped her shawl and advanced cautiously. "The draft disturbs the flames. If you would be so kind as to close the door . . . ?"

"Oh!"

A figure rose from the chair facing the fire. Patrick Campbell, his face pale, turned to greet her. "Please forgive me, madam, for startling you. I did not hear you approach," he said, bowing ever so slightly.

Anne backed a step, and heart thundering in her breast, pushed the door closed. "Oliver . . . ?"

"I am sorry."

My God, she thought, her mind awhirl. In a trance, she moved to the fire, stared into the dancing flames. Oliver dead? Her own Oliver who loved her? "I . . . I don't understand."

"There is little to understand. We fought, as men will. He was the stronger, but I the more cunning. A pity, for him."

"Pity?" Anne bridled at the tone of condescension. "A pity! I think, sir, the emotion is foreign to you. Good day." So saying, she made for the door before he could see her tears.

"You are right, madam," he answered, cutting off her escape. "Pity is as foreign to me as maudlin, sentimental tears are to you. I pity no one."

"You are a monster with a heart of steel, sir, a man

I should like to see no more." The accusation stung and remorse turned to anger. "Let me pass."

He didn't move. "On the contrary. You are overly hasty in your assessment. In matters of the heart I am soft to a fault, more tender than a father with his babe."

"A tender murderer? How droll."

"Is it? Did you find it so amusing when the man I killed murdered another for your sake, three more prior to your time? Did you find pleasant diversion in the prospect of my death, my blood on your hands and immortal soul? Come, madam. I am not so easy a mark. Lord Oliver Page mistook me for a boy, a grievous error of which I did nothing to dissuade him and for which, I assure you, he paid dearly. I trust you will not make a similar mistake."

"You deceived him!"

"As you deceive Captain Henry Gladwyn? Yes."

"Malevolent animal!" Anne swung, furious. Her hand caught the side of his face, leaving livid marks.

Patrick stood stock still. "You know why we went to Brohan's Mound this morning, madam. But perhaps I have misjudged you. Please forgive me." With a self-effacing bow, he stepped aside.

Anne paused, taken by surprise. Was this the same harshly contentious suitor whom she had dismissed so flippantly as a callow youth? She gazed into his eyes. They were placid, but with a faint hint of mirth waiting for release. Of her own age, he was undeniably handsome. Perhaps she *had* misjudged. Perhaps she should apologize. But no! Oliver was dead. Coolly, she stalked to the door, turning at the last moment. "I hope you . . ." she began.

His hand dropped from his side and a distorted

grimace of pain flashed across his face then disappeared. "You're hurt!"

"Aye," Patrick answered slowly. "A touch or two." Patrick denied himself the pleasure of a smile. She had taken the bait.

Anne moved quickly, unfastening his coat and gasping at the sight. Great red-brown splotches of dried blood caked the sweat-darkened linen at his chest and side. She blanched. "Give me your coat."

"It is nothing. Truly."

"Your coat, sir." Seizing the lapels, she helped remove the heavy garment. Another stain reddened his right arm. "And yet a third? You are too modest." Her fingers flew to release the lace collar. "Undo your shirt, please."

"I'm afraid it's stuck to my skin. Is there brandy?"

"Yes. In the sideboard."

"Get some, please."

"But . . ."

Strong hands seized her wrists. The struggle drained from her and Anne wilted as Patrick's embrace tightened. Suddenly short of breath, she realized his fingers had moved to her chin, tilting up her face. The softest lips imaginable met hers in a kiss so fleeting and tender she was surprised to hear him speak again. "If madam will do as I instruct, my wounds will soon be taken care of. Then shall I do my utmost to physic any and all maladies brought on by emptiness or loneliness as my mistress might wish cured."

"I have a wound, sir, and a fever which could stand curing."

"Then quickly to mine," he answered hoarsely, "and the sooner you shall be my patient."

* * *

Anne woke to drowsy warmth, the bearskin rug luxuriant under her nakedness. An arm's length away, his back turned, Patrick squatted, poking at the fire. She suppressed a giggle. How awkward he looked with shrunken manhood all adangle and silhouetted against the flames. Impishly, she squirmed forward, stealthily reached between his legs and lightly touched the now familiar flesh.

Startled, Patrick dropped the poker. "Damn!" he swore, startled off balance and twisting to fall at her side.

The laughter died aborning as Anne looked up contritely. For the first time, there was time to look. How slender he was, the light of the fire surrounding him with a glowing aura. Undressed, his chest stood out, muscles taut and dropping to the flattened belly. Fair silken hair—so much less than had Oliver—started at his navel and ran in a thin line straight down to a thicker growth from which sprung a veined and glistening root. Again she reached out, took the arched and resting member in one hand and ran trembling fingers down its length. "A most marvelous restorative, sir," she said in a low and husky voice. "But a single treatment doth not effect a full cure."

"Then I shall," he murmured, already on the rise and filling her hand, "prescribe a daily regimen." His lips sought her breasts, full with desire and aching for his touch. Sighing with pleasure, he moistened first one and then the other, his tongue making unbearable the delay.

Moaning, Anne grasped him more firmly, pulled him to her. "Hurry."

"In time," came the muffled reply. His hand stroked her flattened stomach, dipped momentarily to stroke

the inside of her thighs and explore with probing
fingers the fragrant moistness between her parted legs.
Satisfied, he reared over her as the guiding hand led
him to the fevered portal wherein he was so welcomed.

Gently, gently he sank into the enfolding haven,
white flanks tightening against the exquisite pleasure.
Anne sucked in her breath as the warm flesh, turgid
and hard, entered, filled and plumbed her depths, and
locked her legs around his waist to force him deeper.
The first time had been too furious, too hurried. This
time they would prolong the moment. The eager
length plunged to the hilt then pulled out, poised,
barely held for a breathtaking moment, then slowly
descended once again, the motion repeated over . . .
and over . . . until the rising fire caught and lifted her,
breath hissing through clenched teeth. "Patrick . . .
Patrick . . . !"

He groaned against her neck, withdrew once more
until she held but the pulsing tip, unsheathed and
throbbing. At her cry, he thrust home through the
tight warmth, deeper and deeper until she could hold
no more. Locked together as one in passionate embrace, the rolling spasms enveloped them.

CHAPTER 7

Sir Charles—gout, jowls, new title and all—wore the name of Gladwyn the way other men wear crowns, that is, with suspicion and jealousy. In spite of favor and quick success, he had withdrawn into a shell of his own making. Laughed at in London, where everyone knew the sordid details of the vengeful conspiracy against Henry which had bought him a sullied knighthood, he ventured to town as seldom as possible, preferring to act the part of a squire and live exclusively in the country where he could indulge his whims without being subjected to acidulous tongues that were too quick to recall his birth and compare him to his father and young brother, both of whom he daily grew to hate more and more.

As the hate grew, so did Sir Charles' determination to squander as many of the funds and wreak as much havoc as possible before the dimming of light took him from the face of the earth. At the same time, he took refuge in religion and became as the Pharisees, extolling virtue at the top of his lungs while discreetly pandering to secret yet noteworthy saturnalian extravagances, investing heavily and unwisely in speculative land ventures in the New World and dabbling from afar in dangerously deep political waters. He was known throughout the region as a man who privately revelled in the gaiety of life while outwardly seeking the light of the Lord. No matter if they did think him a hypocrite, he was fond of saying, he was still the richest man in the Chilterns.

But being rich didn't solve every problem. This morning, Sir Charles Gladwyn was in a foul mood. He scowled through the window, squinting into the bright noon sun and then moving back where the light wouldn't hurt his eyes. Twenty feet below, a manservant hurried down the garden path to intercept Elizabeth on the walkway and deliver a message. The girl turned to the window, but her face was hidden by distance.

Charles stepped away from the glass. The illegitimate bitch, he thought. Damn her anyway, with that stare that always reminded him of the bold look in Byron's eye. She'd soon learn, though, that Charles Gladwyn was not a man to defy. The little bitch would learn better if he had to beat her, which just might be a toothsome responsibility, given the roundness of those girlish buttocks. It was bad enough she had to leech on the Gladwyn name and resources without becoming the soiled heroine of every beggar in London. And then to dispute his word in front of guests! Utterly wild, she was.

He sputtered in self-righteous indignation. Damn them all, his younger brother to begin with. Who else would have insisted on taking a useless girl from her common mother? Just like Byron. And then to get killed in a squalid little tavern and leave a bastard daughter around everyone's neck!

Charles, given a free hand, would have cut her off with nary a single shilling and let her descend to the natural level from which she came had it not been for Henry's acceptance of the girl's custody from his ailing father. Charles fumed at the inconsideration of fate and the inexplicable behavior of his surviving brother. No Gladwyn owed the girl so much as a seat at the family table. But Henry was an honorable man. Honorable, aye, with Charles' money of course.

And Anne. There was another sore spot. Having lost the internecine war and accepted his generosity, she should have, as any well-bred woman would have, passed the girl on to Charles. Then at least he could have exercised more stringent control over Beth's stipend. Failing that, the least Anne could have done was accept responsibility for the nasty thing and keep her from excessive philanthropy. But no. Henry's silly bride was all too happy to dip sticky fingers into the Gladwyn purse. Why shouldn't she? When the dark angel came to claim his due from Charles, title, money and land would pass to her husband. She had obviously decided to start enjoying them without waiting for that mournful day.

Charles shuddered at the morbid thought, summoned his last reserve of strength and poured another tankard of port in an attempt to dismiss death's fearful prospects. He'd fool them yet, by God. They could pick at him as a goose picked at strawberries, but he'd hold on. They'd bide a long time to gain Charlie Gladwyn's fortune. Smugly toasting himself in the mirror, he limped to his chair, cursing the savage affliction of gout that made the effort of walking so excruciating.

Elizabeth knocked and called at the door, entering without waiting for permission. Irritated by her temerity, Charles glanced in the mirror to see her sweep across the room. At fifteen, young Beth had already acquired many of the characteristics that had led her father to a scandalous, contention-ridden life and a mean and unnecessarily premature grave. Not quite pretty, her face was ever serious and too disapproving to attract a suitor of station, which to Charles' disgust and utter disbelief suited Beth just fine. A marriage—and she'd be ready in another year—would at least take her off his hands. But no. He had taken the trouble to include several promising young men in his house parties but did the imp appreciate his efforts? No. He had never seen such rude behavior in a child. She was a misfit and her behavior at table the evening before had infuriated him. How dared she spout those insane reformist notions and make him a laughingstock before his guests? Hospitals indeed. Charity wards! Consorting with ragamuffin beggars and the assorted flotsam of society.

"Do I disturb you, Sir Charles?" Beth inquired politely.

Charles glowered at the girl, her fiery hair pinned demurely away from her face and bound tightly against the back of her neck. Butter wouldn't melt in her mouth, but that didn't fool him one jot. Beth's angular face blushed beneath the lengthy inspection, cheeks red in remarkable contrast to alabaster flesh. "Of course you don't. What took you so long?"

"I came immediately, Uncle." The stiff brocaded gown of saffron velvet rustled as she drew near.

Charles toyed with a stack of papers on the desk and busied himself applying the elaborate signature which authorized a staggering variety of payments, half of which were directly attributable to Anne and her charge. Beth waited his pleasure. He blew on the ink, replaced the quill in its holder and peered at the girl in silence. Only when she met his gaze did he look down, gauging the finery she wore with practiced eye. "Gladwyn gold," he muttered.

"Uncle?"

"The gown. I should think such an elaborate gown cost more than a tuppence."

"Yes, sir. I had it second hand and altered."

"Mmm. How nice," Charles purred. "And a beauty it is, fit for a lady. Yes, a lady." Beth held her breath, guessing well his baiting game. "But not for the likes of you!" he exploded.

"Sir . . ." Beth valiantly attempted to defend herself but the man's rage was overpowering.

"Do not interrupt!" Charles struggled to his feet, sweat running from under his wig to groove impeccably powdered cheeks. "The Gladwyn name has ever been held in the highest esteem. This estate is the pride of western England. Many look to us, emulate us, respect our name and what we stand for. And now you . . ." He slumped into the chair, gasping for breath.

"Sir Charles . . . ?" Beth started around the desk, obviously concerned.

"No. No, leave me alone. Your fault, all of you. Like to see me dead so you can take my fortune. I know you plot against me."

"That's not true."

"You lie! That's why you carry on so. I've never seen behavior as rude as yours. Absolutely vile. I will not allow you to drive me to a stroke. Wasn't your father's ruinous reputation enough?"

Elizabeth bristled at the mention of her father. "My father . . ."

"Bah!" Charles sensed the sore spot and pressed his advantage. "Dear brother Byron was a foolish, vain, infernal sufferer—a victim of misplaced piety and pity for the rabble. I know his type. Second in line for a fortune they'll never get, they immerse themselves in damned foolish social reform movements and concern for all the other fools in the world. If he'd limited himself to wenching and gambling, I wouldn't have minded overly much, but any ass who would involve himself with saving rum-sodden, broken-down sailors or teaching paupers' brats to read deserves . . ."

"Stop!" Beth stamped her foot, leaned on the desk. Her face was bloodless, eyes widening in anger. "I owe to you, Uncle Charles, my bed and board. To your good graces I have attempted to address myself. I mean no disrespect, but will not allow you to slander my father's name. I will not, do you hear?"

Charles leaned back slowly, eyes closed, lips pursed. His voice was quiet and far away. "Very well, mistress. We will not speak of Byron, but of you instead." He paused, a smile flitting across his face. "You have presumed to scream in the shrill tone of a fishwife. From this I see you lack breeding as well as prudence. In addition, the lack of restraint you display in your behavior leads me to believe extraordinary measures are necessary if you are ever to achieve a modicum of civility."

He opened one eye and fixed her with a stare, loving the moment and holding it until Beth capitulated. "To this end, I have made an . . . unpleasant decision. On the day after tomorrow, Anne and the rest of our guests are scheduled to return to London for the final month of the season. You will stay here and practice the modesty and discipline befitting a fifteen-year-old child."

"Uncle, I . . ."

"Silence. I have not finished. You will also attend chapel each day, and so hopefully moderate the uncontrollable passions to which you are evidently prey. I have spoken to Master Pearson, who will make humility, self-control and obedience the subject of his sermons."

"Sir, I . . ."

Charles rose, his face turning beet red under the white lead ceruse. "You will remain silent until I have finished, mistress. Do you understand? You are impertinent, abusive, insolent, argumentative and willful, and I have reached the limit of toleration beyond which I will not, cannot . . ."

"Charles!"

The blustering tyrant jerked at the sound of his name. Beth, nearly in tears, was as startled. Anne stepped into the room and held open the door. "Elizabeth, the musicians are in the garden, but there cannot be a quintet without a fifth member."

Charles, mouth agape, watched as his quarry escaped once again. Beth paused in the doorway. "I will thank you not to speak of my father behind my back, sir."

"Your father was a troublesome malcontent," Charles grumbled, "and you will more than likely wind up no different."

"I should hope so," the girl retorted, confidence restored, and stalked from the room.

Anne met Charles' angry gaze with a smile. She had been at odds with her brother-in-law far too long to be upset by his outbursts. Faced with merely another in a long sequence of unpleasant encounters, she waited patiently with the cool calculation of an experienced general. But then, she had been born to parlor warfare and could more than hold her own on the exotic and glittering battlefields that made up the noise and furor of London's social world. Charles' bumbling efforts were child's play.

"I fail to appreciate your interruption," Charles finally managed. Anne closed the door, first casting a stern glance into the hall and scattering a flock of eavesdropping servants. Charles coughed nervously. He couldn't deny Henry's marvelous luck in acquiring the hand of such a beauty. A long, sculpted neck thrust high a goddess' face and head. Full, round breasts barely concealed by a thin layer of lace threatened to burst free at any moment. The sumptuous figure exquisitely encased in white and gold, promised excitement that overrode anger. A man might dare any length for such a lovely creature, suffer any trial to see the warming of those wintry gray-blue eyes.

Anne neared the window overlooking the side garden. From her vantage point she could see the musicians, deft fingers fluttering amid string, peg and bow. A faint, disharmonious chorus drifted upward as they tuned the instruments, reminding her of the warblings of gathered morning birds. Soon Beth appeared and sat at the harpsichord which had been carried out for the occasion.

Charles cleared his throat and Anne sighed. She yearned for London and the Gladwyn apartments at Grosvenor Square. Patrick had left the night before and would be waiting for her. How she longed to see him again, to visit with him. She persisted in the silence which always puzzled Charles because he wasn't sure what she was thinking, much less what she would say.

Behind her, a clink of crystal. "Sir Charles," Anne began, turning to the table and pouring a glass of port. "My husband promised Byron he would oversee Elizabeth's education and arrange a suitable marriage at the proper time. When Henry left for duty in America, he explicitly passed on those duties to me. If she is to be scolded or rebuked, I shall be the one to do it."

Charles snorted. "I fail to see how you are to chastise her when you are blind to her faults. The child needs discipline."

"Of what faults are we speaking, Sir Charles? Has Elizabeth done something of which I am unaware? Has she insulted some person of station? Acted badly?"

"You know damned well, madam, what faults. Her behavior last evening was shocking. I will not have those infernal notions spouted at my table."

Anne smiled, recalling Charles' fury. She had already spoken to Beth, urging her not to provoke him, but would never admit it to Charles. "I must insist she return with me to London. How else is she to learn? The child was brought up under unfortunate circumstances and lacks a proper concept of station. Given time I intend . . ."

"Time!" Charles could not contain himself. "Indeed, madam, you could take all eternity and still be left wanting. She has no station. She's a bastard—my brother's bastard daughter and nothing more. Child, ha! You're but a child yourself."

"Enough, Charles!" Anne's voice snapped like a carriage whip. "Elizabeth bears the Gladwyn name and is under Henry's patronage by her father's wishes. Whatever your opinion regarding the legitimacy of her birth, she remains a Gladwyn, though at times she makes a poor showing of it, I'll admit. But she's made of fine stuff, and until Henry returns, the problem is mine and mine alone. I will not have you intimidate her merely because of some abject dislike for your deceased brother."

Charles sat, grimacing at the pain in his foot. He would win after all, damn her. "My dear sister-in-law," he began silkily. "You are rash. I am not powerless, you know. I hold the purse strings here."

"To which, sir, I say . . ."

"You are as inconsiderate as Elizabeth, who has undoubtedly learned from you to interrupt while others are speaking. Allow me to make my point, which is of some importance to you." He went on sarcastically, "May I?"

Anne bit back angry words. "Of course."

"Very well, then. As I said, I am not powerless. Though I choose to remain in the country, I am neither deaf nor blind. Many interesting tidbits of information reach me, some of which, I am sure, would be of interest to not only your father but your husband as well."

Anne blanched. "Sir, blackmail is a . . ."

"Call it what you will, but understand I refuse to put up with your infamous behavior any longer. Oliver Page was, I suspect, more than a friend to you. Now he has fallen to one Patrick Campbell, who bedded you . . . No, please, do not interrupt again . . . bedded you no more than an hour after he killed Oliver. I do not begrudge your little infidelities, but I do dislike the peremptory manner in which you hop from bed to bed like a common harlot before the blood has so much as dried or the body is buried. Such conduct offends what little sensitivity I admit to, and I will, if need be, use the knowledge to my benefit. I will be contested no longer. Do you understand?"

Anne understood very well, but disagreed. He would be contested. She moved close to him, forcing Charles to turn away quickly from the alluring scent of bath water, long pale throat, smell of powder and sight of full breasts. Poor Charles. She knew she could drive him to rages of jealousy. The one woman he would never be allowed to experience stood before him, laid a hand on his arm. "Dear Charles, how wrong of me to underestimate you. I must admit you have taught me a lesson. You are right. You are not powerless and I would do well to listen to you. And so I have." She spun away sharply and crossed to the window, her haughty grace evident in seeming retreat. Charles' satisfaction would be short-lived.

She continued quietly, her back to him. "But perhaps I should teach you a little lesson, too."

"Ha. You may try, madam, but I doubt . . ."

"When, exactly, did you receive the messenger from Lord Pitt, Charles? Was it Tuesday or Wednesday? I forget."

Charles sat up quickly, startled. "I . . ."

"Oh, yes. Wednesday, was it not? I remember because Wednesday was the day Patrick left. I had just said goodbye and started back into the house when the messenger rode up and hurried in. "No," she said, holding up a hand, "don't interrupt until I've finished. How foolish to allow a man to come by day, even if the message was important. How unfortunate if Lord Bute and our dear, long-lipped monarch should learn Sir Charles has joined Pitt and his friends and secretly renounced his opposition to the war with France simply because peace will lose the Gladwyn enterprises a few thousand pounds. I am at a loss to assess how such information would affect the close relationship you now enjoy with the King. Could you help me?" She turned, smiling sweetly. "Well?"

Charles stuttered and fumed, unable to answer. Before he could collect his thoughts, Anne gathered her skirts and made for the door, turning to say, "Dear

Charles. I am sorry to have had to use such heavy
ammunition for such a slight skirmish. However, you
may be assured I have not played all my cards." She
smiled sweetly. "Do not take defeat too badly. The
Langfords were adept at such game-playing when
this estate was but a spot of trackless waste among the
Chiltern Hills, long before the Gladwyns had dug
their nasty ditch or mined a single lump of coal, much
less bought their first scow and treacherously conspired for an undeserved title. Good day, Sir Charles."

Sabrina lay a gown of light blue velvet worked with
a pink-and-violet flowered pattern across the bed-
stead, while Anne settled into the luxuriantly warm
depths of the bath. The surface of the water glistened
with a myriad of rainbows as the fragrant oils swirled
and eddied with the motion of her flesh. Somberly, she
cupped her breasts, recalling the touch of the last to
hold them and wishing Patrick were there. Two more
days and then London. On the third day . . . Patrick.
She lay back and closed her eyes, drawing sensual
pictures in her mind.

Sabrina patted the gown and shook her head. "This
has seen little use."

Anne sighed. "Yes. These dreary hostilities with
France wreak havoc on a wardrobe. At least peace is
close and a lady is free to wear what she will when she
will. Would you wash my back, Sabrina?"

The old servant knelt by the tub, scraped the brush
across the soap dish and set to scrubbing, remembering
at the same time the tiny child she had washed so
tenderly twenty years before. "With the coming of
peace, will Master Henry be returning, mum?"

Anne started, brows knotted together. For the first

time, she realized the possibility was very real. "I . . .
I don't know, Sabrina. I don't know."

Sabrina laid down the brush and creaked to her feet.
"It will be good to see him again, mum. He's a fine
man."

Anne sat unmoving. "Would you leave the towel on
the chair, Sabrina?" she said, more curtly than she'd
intended, "I'd like to be alone a while, if you don't
mind."

Sabrina slapped herself. Old fool, she thought. Now
you've made her unhappy. Quickly, she piled extra
towels by the tub and headed for the door. "I wish him
safe and sound for your sake, Anne dear," she said before closing the door.

Anne was unaware of the woman's departure,
wrapped as she was in a web of unsettling conjecture
and confusing memories.

The servants brought in the sweet, a confection
molded in the shape of a hare made from eggs, sugar,
orange-flower water, canary, nutmeg, hartshorn and
fresh cream. Charles sighed with satisfaction. There
were few things he enjoyed more than a good meal.
He beamed across the table to the guests, who groaned
with delight, satiated with veal, a side of mutton, a
giant ham, a turkey and a brace of roast goose; three
cheeses melted over the freshest of spring vegetables,
a fresh-caught trout for each and innumerable bottles
of burgundy and port. The hare, ringed with smaller
dishes piled with custard pudding and berry tarts
swimming in more heavy cream, was the crowning
glory of the feast.

Having started at five, the hour was seven and the
servants brought in the candelabras for the dessert

which was to be served with chocolate. Charles kept close watch on Anne for any sign—perhaps a clever innuendo to the wrong person—of trouble. Something was bothering her he was certain, for she had picked at the mountain of delectables with an unusual lack of relish. Beth, on the other hand, ate her usual prodigious amount which, Charles vowed, would burst her belly one day. Not that he cared, she had been too busy eating to talk.

Everyone was too full to eat much more, and within ten minutes those who wanted to had stuffed down the last of the hare, set back and washed their fingers and rinsed their mouths. Charles stood, tossed off the contents of his goblet and called for another bottle. "Ladies and gentlemen, there is more wine. The cellars are stocked against the next war when we shall have difficulty procuring such delightful beverage. If the ladies are ready . . . ?"

Servants bustled around the table. The cloth was removed and new glasses brought and filled. The ladies rose as one and filed out, leaving the gentlemen to drinks, pipes and talk. In the hall, Anne managed to escape the rest of the company, pleading a sick headache.

The door closed and she was alone at last. A strange mood had settled over her since Sabrina's innocent remark, a strange and disquieting premonition that had blossomed through the meal. Night had fallen completely and a fire glowed in the hearth to dissuade the creeping Chiltern damp. Though the afternoon had been warm and brilliant, toward sunset a storm had gusted up from the south and threatened a torrent. A single candle sat on the table and Anne slumped into a chair, staring into the flame across the room and trying hard not to think beyond the next few minutes.

Only when the door creaked open and closed and Beth took a place across the table did Anne turn and manage a polite smile.

The younger girl paused, bit her lower lip in thought. Five years her senior, Anne Gladwyn was so self-assured, a creature of such fragile loveliness she made Beth feel like an awkward pauper. "Thank you," she finally began. Anne's face frowned in question. "For interceding with Charles."

"Ah, yes. You will return to London after all."

"I knew you would . . ."

". . . but you will mind your manners," she said. Then, more kindly, "Charles is right, you know. We shall have a difficult time as it is arranging a suitable match for you. If you consent, I shall find a gentleman —or gentlemen—with whom you might reasonably be seen. A lady should have a proper escort."

"Like Patrick Campbell?"

Anne's face darkened. Her eyes measured the girl for hidden meaning. There had been far too many insinuations creeping into their conversation recently and this latest, after Anne's effort in her behalf, was inexcusable. Still, Beth's face remained innocent of subterfuge. "Don't try me, child. You're very quick and learning more every day, but don't try me. Yes. Like Patrick Campbell. You could do worse."

Beth giggled but her face was hidden in shadow. "Charles was a sight!"

Anne tried to figure out if the change in topic was ingenuous or a bold gambit. A smile replaced her frown: that she couldn't tell was indicative of Beth's adroitness. In some ways the child was old beyond her years. She decided to let the remark pass and laughed softly. "Charles is capable of being absolutely frightful at times. I like to think it is because of the

loss of his wife and child, and hope his crude traits do
not run in the family."

"Oh, no," Beth answered quickly. "Father was kind
and gentle. He wasn't anything like Charles. Nor is
Uncle Henry, but then you know that, of course."

Anne's face clouded momentarily. Once again the
talk had turned to Henry Gladwyn, a fact Anne found
more disturbing than was pleasant to admit. "It's late,
Beth, and I feel like being alone. You must have a great
deal to do in order to be ready to leave. If you don't
mind . . ."

"Please don't make me leave, Anne. Not tonight.
Please?" She leaned forward in the candlelight. "You're
the only one here who cares for me. All the rest think
I'm . . . I'm some sort of horrid creature too young to
talk to and too old to go to bed with the children." She
paused, face and voice pinched and tight, holding back
the tears. "That's why I acted as I did last night. For
the last nine months, since Uncle Henry left, you're
the only friend I've had."

Anne smiled, took the girl's hands and held them
tightly. "Stay if you will, then. We all need friends—
at least one friend."

Beth brightened. "Shall we play cards?"

Anne nodded. "If you will."

Beth sprang to her feet, gathered more candles and
the cards and brought them back to the table. While
Anne shuffled, Beth lit the candles. "Chemin de fer?"
Anne asked.

"Faro." Beth grinned in the orange glow. "Father
taught me. He said I was good luck. One time in
Naples he won fifteen thousand pounds in one night."

"Fifteen thousand pounds?" Anne asked, incred-
ulous. "Byron?"

"Yes. The next night I had a fever and was kept in bed. He lost it all, plus another two thousand kept for emergencies. I was very angry."

Anne examined the clear sweet face of the girl across the table and wondered at the strange mixture of child and woman. "But we have no money. And if we are to gamble, then there must be something of value. What shall our stakes be?"

"Truth," Beth said, her eyes sparkling.

"Truth? La! What unusual stakes!"

"Are you afraid?"

"Of course not. I simply wonder if either of us will recognize such an elusive creature."

"You've become a cynic, Aunt Anne."

Anne laughed, the weight falling from her shoulders. "You're far too precocious, dear. Very well, truth it shall be. How do we play?"

"If you win, you may ask me something and I shall answer with the absolute truth. And you must do the same if I win. It's a game Father taught me," she shrugged her shoulders, "after we ran out of money. Here is your deck. This is mine," instructed Beth, ignoring the possibility of contradiction. "You may choose first."

Anne looked warmly at the girl and tried to recall the distant, mist-filled time when she, too, believed the truth could be told. She fanned through the cards and picked the jack of spades, placing it face down on the table. Beth began to play at once, turning over the topmost card of her deck and placing it to her right. This would be Anne's pile; the one to the left, Beth's.

"Your win," Beth said, discovering the deuce of diamonds. "My win," she continued, turning over the jack of hearts. "Your win." The five of hearts for Anne. "My

win." The ten of diamonds for Beth. "Your win." The
jack of spades showed and was placed on Anne's
brief pile of cards.

Anne reached out and touched the card she had
chosen from her deck, turning over the matching
knave so Beth might see. "Indeed, my win."

Beth gathered her cards. "Ask what you will."

"There's nothing I wish to know," Anne answered,
replacing the jack in the deck.

"I should not waste the opportunity," Beth warned.

"Very well. Are you . . . are you happy here?"

Beth sighed. Anne wasn't taking her seriously. "You
know I'm not," she replied.

"If Sir Charles were to . . ."

"Only one question."

"But . . ."

"Only one."

Anne scowled and chose another card. Beth shuffled
the cards, took the topmost and turned up the nine of
clubs. "Your win . . . My . . ."

"Ha!" Anne reached over and triumphantly displayed the card she had chosen, the nine of clubs. "It
appears, dear Beth, I shall learn more than you expect to reveal, while not being asked anything about
myself."

"I need win but once to ask what I want to know."

Anne's eyes narrowed with a hint of anger. "And you
think I would not answer you truthfully without the
subterfuge of a card game?"

"Yes." Beth reached for the cards and began to
shuffle the deck.

"What are you doing?" Anne protested.

"I answered your question. You must win again to
ask another."

The older woman looked flustered, finally managed a reply. "Then play, mistress, but I promise to be gulled no more." The king of hearts, regal in robes of scarlet, caught her fancy. She played the card and Beth resumed the litany of the game. "Your win . . . my win . . . your win . . . my win . . ." And so it went as each stack grew taller and taller. "Your win . . . my win . . ."

Anne held up her hand, flipped over the card and revealed the king to match the one atop Beth's stack. "Your win," sighed Anne. At the same time a horse raced by under the windows and there came a call at the back entrance. "Ask what you will."

Beth nodded seriously, paused for effect. "Patrick Campbell notwithstanding, do you love Henry Gladwyn?"

Anne bolted upright, scattering the cards and almost knocking over the table. "Mistress, you forget yourself!"

The door flew open and one of the servants barged into the room. "Beggin' your pardon, mum, but an urgent dispatch has arrived for you. The messenger rode without stop from London."

With a final cold glance at Beth, Anne left the room. The messenger, a weary scarecrow of a fellow in crumpled and mud-stained livery, waited in the entranceway. There were two missives, one from London, the other—and her heart went still—was in Henry Gladwyn's handwriting.

My dearest Anne:

I have been assigned a permanent post here as commanding officer of His Majesty's Fort Detroit in the almost-unsettled tract of land we call the Lake Erie frontier. I vow this country is the most fascinating and thoroughly colorful, beautiful place I have seen in all my travels, as I am sure you will agree.

After deep consideration, Anne, I have decided to ask you to join me in my command. To that end I have arranged for you to sail from London to the township of New York. There, with transportation provided by Sir Jeffrey Amherst, our Commanding General here in America, you will make way to Fort Niagara where, God willing, I shall meet you.

Passage has been arranged on the *Sea King*, Captain Ardmore, commanding. Under no circumstances accept other arrangements. Life at sea is difficult at best and Captain Ardmore, an old and dear friend of my father, is one of the few men with whom I would trust your life. He will arrange for your victuals aboard, and I beg you pay him the honor of respecting and following his opinions and orders to the letter.

I write hastily, as a runner is even now waiting at the door.

Dearest Anne, I look forward to this reunion and remain, madam,

> Your most loving husband
> Major (temporary) Henry Gladwyn
> Commander, Fort Detroit

Anne closed the letter. The world spun slowly. Passage was arranged. She was to leave everything, everyone. Passage was arranged . . . to the colonies . . .

Unwilling to give Charles the satisfaction of gloating over her sudden change in fortune, Anne remained sequestered, spending the next day sitting in bed and alternating between stunned and bitter dejection and pitiful weeping. The second letter had been from Captain Ardmore: the *Sea King*, laying to in the Pool of London for refitting, was scheduled to leave as soon as newly provisioned, hopefully by the end of the month. Ten days . . . little more than a week. The tears brimmed in her eyes, scalded her cheeks once again. Leave England? The life she so enjoyed? No!

But what else might an unlucky woman do save comply? Run? Where? She could imagine Sir Spencer's stern lecture. The duty of a wife, he would admonish, commanded that she join her husband wherever he wished. A Langford breaking a marriage contract was unheard of, and he would counsel she leave with as much grace and dignity as she could muster.

And what of Henry? She glanced down at the letter in her lap. The words were barely legible in the dim light which seeped through the curtains. The penmanship was a scrawl, devoid of elegance and style. How crude, she thought, compared to Patrick's latest note. The fine parchment filled with rich, poetic imagery was almost a work of art. Feeling and emotion sprang from the page, so handsomely were phrases drafted and thoughts fashioned. Henry's smacked of brutal directness, of military formality. His "My dearest Anne" left her listless; his instructions made her weary and despondent.

Why had he sent for her, given the ugliness and rancor with which they had parted? Could not life have gone on for the better as presently arranged? Why must he foist on an unwilling wife the indignity of a mean and uncultured society, as everyone knew life in the Americas was? To be cruel? To revenge insults spoken and implied? Of course. Cruelty was the only reason. Why else? Why?

A gentle tapping sounded at the door. "Who is it?"

"Beth." Anne's ward entered, closed the door silently. "I had to come. Are you still displeased with me?" she asked, crossing the room to sit on the edge of the bed.

"What . . . ? Oh no. Not now." For the first time, Anne noticed the girl's red and swollen eyes. "You've been crying. Why?"

Beth collapsed on the bed, embracing Anne and burying her face in the quilt. "I shall miss you so. What shall I do with you gone?"

"It won't be that bad," Anne said, trying to console her.

"But it will. Once you've left, Sir Charles will have his way and I shall be left without a friend. There will be no one in this house to take my part."

Anne was suddenly and deeply moved by Beth's display. Twice in a period of twenty-four hours the girl had admitted dependence on her. "Dearest Beth, what can I do? You know what this letter says. I must leave. I have no choice."

Beth's tear-stained face rose, the light of an idea vibrant in her eyes. "Take me with you."

"I can't," Anne said, shocked.

"You'll need someone in your service. Leave Sabrina and take me. Please," she went on before Anne could protest, "I'll be your servant. I'll do anything you ask and never disobey. Please?"

"Henry . . ."

". . . is fond of me. I know he is, as he was of Father. He'll understand, and won't mind."

"Do you know what you're asking, child? To leave the country of your birth? Your home?"

Beth's eyes reflected a truth accepted long ago. The look on her wise child's face tore at Anne's heart. "I have no country, nor have I a home, save with you and Henry."

Anne grew thoughtful, then slowly nodded. "Pack what you wish to carry. We shall travel together, you and I." She brightened, trying to cheer Beth. "Charles will be stricken with apoplexy."

A smile of pure joy replaced Beth's tears. "Oh thank you, thank you . . ." She was gone before Anne could answer.

Anne Gladwyn looked about the darkening boundary of the quiet bedroom and sighed in the stillness. "Very well, then, Beth. We shall both be landless, homeless waifs." In truth, Beth's company would be a comfort. She extinguished the candle Beth had carried in and lay quietly, watching the rising moon through a silky string of smoke which spiralled upward and lost itself in the inky darkness.

CHAPTER 8

A veritable forest of masts sprung from the Pool of London, the ship-glutted stretch of the Thames between the Tower and London Bridge, beyond which no vessel of any size could pass. Here, where all shipping was required to load and unload, a thousand tiny boats struggled from ship to shore and back again, transforming the once-quiet river scene into a seething, bobbing mass of frantic activity. Screeching gulls and equally vituperative boatmen filled the air with a confused babble.

Anne Gladwyn watched from the tiny park on shore, searched for and found the *Sea King*, a ship-of-the-line standing out among the less magnificent merchantmen which, now that the war had abated, could more easily ply the world's trade routes.

"One hundred and ninety feet long, forty-eight on the beam. Eighteen hundred tons. She draws thirty-one feet, carries seventy guns and a crew of four hundred and fifty." The voice came from below. Captain Ardmore, distinguished in his uniform, stepped lightly onto the stone ledge and made his way up the moss-covered steps of the quay at which the ship's barge had docked. "Good morning, Mrs. Gladwyn. It's a fine day. God willing, we'll have another tomorrow for our departure. And what brings you down to the Pool, if I may be so bold to ask?"

"To see the *Sea King*," Anne replied lightly.

Ardmore took her at her word. "She's a fine ship, madam," he said with quiet pride. "Many a Frenchman she's sent to the bottom, and will again if need be."

"I trust the need won't arise during the next few weeks, Captain Ardmore. I'm afraid I shan't be in the mood for fighting."

Ardmore laughed shortly, the mark of a man unaccustomed to the company of ladies. "We shall do our best, madam. I think there'll be little trouble." He bowed, stepped back. "If madam will excuse me, there is business. I trust you've been informed we sail before dawn with the morning tide, which waits for no man —nor lady."

"I shan't delay you, Captain. My provisions are . . . ?"

". . . on board, with a special watch mounted to ensure their safety. All has been seen to, and you will be made as comfortable as possible."

"You are most gracious, Captain."

Ardmore blushed, unused to compliments from a lady. "The privilege is mine, I assure you. And now, if madam will excuse me, I must bid you good day." Without further ado, he turned and strode to a carriage marked with the admiralty crest. He was glad to be away. Only once before had he carried a lady of station aboard, and that had turned out badly. Ladies, dammit, made him nervous. A ship ran badly with them aboard. Something always went wrong. There was nothing to be done though, for Anthony Gladwyn had been a friend when a friend was needed and his son's request could not be denied.

Anne turned from the Thames and considered the

strangely taciturn Captain Ardmore. Twice now they had met, and twice conversed with not one more word than absolutely necessary. The Captain was courteous enough, in an old-fashioned way, but stiff, too, aloof and isolated in a shell of command. That she would be safe on board the *Sea King* there could be no doubt. Perhaps she would be able to draw him out later, but the prospects seemed dim, for the Captain was far different from other men who moved easily and comfortably in society. Like Patrick.

The coachman waited by the horses' heads, caught her glance and returned a quick, negative shake of the head. No one else was about. Perhaps Patrick would not show, even though his note had said he would be there. Foolish mistress, to expect he would waste time with her any longer. Once again she had been gulled. Patrick was probably well on the way to winning a new mistress, even as the old one waited in vain.

Disconsolate, she rested on the marble bench. The slice of river visible through the trees was alive with a puzzle of small craft working their way upstream and down, weaving intricate patterns among the anchored ships, finally disappearing behind the stern of the *Sea King*. *Sea King* . . . seeking . . . A simple pun, but intriguing. Seeking what? Or who? Odd, she thought. Captain Ardmore referred to the *Sea King* as "she" in spite of the masculine name. Anne wondered if he recognized the incongruity of such a title, decided he had most probably never given it a thought. Seafaring men were a strange lot, even the best of them.

The clatter of hooves on cobblestone, followed by the whinny of an animal eager to run yet held in check, drew her attention. She turned to see Patrick Campbell alight gracefully, tether a high-strung mare to a wrought-iron fence and hurry along the walkway. Anne glanced away as he sat and grasped her hand. "I was preparing to depart, Mister Campbell. I may still, since you seem to be not overly concerned about arriving on time."

"My lady is waspish," he admonished gently. "I assure you my tardiness was not a slight. In fact, I've spent the morning to your benefit. As for my late arrival, I can only respond that carts, cattle and commoners fill the streets even at this hour. Were I accorded carriage and means, madam would have found me here upon *her* arrival, bedraggled and dew-covered, for I should have waited the night through lest I failed to keep the hour. Unfortunately, I must make do with haphazard avenues, for I have not the station necessary."

"Neither the station nor the breeding and manners as befit a proper lover," she snapped spitefully, whirling. But anger could not last. "Oh, Patrick, what shall I do?" Sobbing softly, she leaned against his shoulder.

Patrick's arm encircled her. "God, but I thirst for you, Anne," he whispered, the words soft and sweet.

Filled with eager, heady desire, Anne met his lips. When they parted, both were aware of the driving warmth generated, one within the other. "I am leaving all that I know and love and hold dear," she lamented in a voice as quiet as the flowing Thames.

"Not all, Anne." Patrick's eyes glittered with mischievous knowledge, a secret of his own making.

"What do you mean?"

"I told you I was occupied to your benefit," he explained with apparent candor. "You will not be going alone. I have arranged for a friend of mine, a young lieutenant, to accompany you to America."

Anne stiffened. She had heard of such things, but to

find herself passed from one man to another like a piece of baggage . . . "I beg your pardon!"

"This . . . lieutenant, captured heart and soul by your great beauty and charm, was most desirous of being with you wherever you went, and was willing to pay an outrageous sum in order to . . ."

"I think I have heard enough, sir!" Anne rose, so infuriated she could barely contain herself. How could he have! Incredulously, Patrick laughed, compounding the affront. Anne's face turned dead white. "I have never been so insulted in my life, sir, nor am I accustomed to . . ."

Patrick reached into his breast pocket, pulled out and extended a parchment. "Here. Read this."

"Sir . . ."

"Please, Anne," he pleaded, voice gentle and soft. "Read it."

Reluctantly, she took the paper. Lord Bute's personal seal was embossed at the top and the opening words sprang from the page. "To Lieutenant Patrick Campbell . . ."

Anne sat heavily. The rest of the words swam in a mist, defying further reading. Patrick refolded the commission and took her hands. "Dear Anne. This tiny piece of paper cost more favors than I shall be able to repay in three lifetimes. Cloughbrent's friends, calling me murderer, hoped to have me sent to India. I bowed and scraped and pledged my name. I have not slept these last two nights, but I won that which I most desired. You will not go to America unaccompanied, because I am going with you."

Midnight. Elizabeth stood apart from the gathering of well-wishers congregating around Anne. Her fifteen years had seen numerous departures and arrivals, and once again there was no one to wish her goodbye or Godspeed. The past months with Anne had been the longest she had stayed in any one place, save for the year and a half with her father at the villa outside Naples. Four years ago, she realized with a pang. Not a long time, really, yet how far away seemed those days of warmth, those music-haunted nights. If there were other homes she had loved, they were too buried in memory to be recalled. She felt Patrick's presence before he emerged from the crowd and came to stand at her side. "You scowled," he noted. "I hoped we might have a truce since we are to be travelling companions."

Beth's face tightened. "You exceed the bounds of taste, sir. We will be making the voyage together, but hardly as companions." With a flip of scarlet curls, she stalked across the landing, stepped aboard the boat which would take them to the *Sea King* and allowed Mr. Simon, the third officer, to escort her to a seat. Once again she was alone, lost in thought and ignorant of the sidelong glances of the sailors manning the oars. So Patrick would accompany them—Patrick Campbell of the pleasant smile, courteous manners and elegant, charming demeanor. And, of course, the determination to possess Anne no matter what the cost. Anne was free to indulge in affairs: there was nothing wrong with a woman taking a lover when her husband had been gone for nearly a year. But to fall in love with a man like Patrick Campbell was not only reprehensible but dangerous as well. What would happen when, as was certain, Henry Gladwyn met his rival? Beth shuddered. Anne would be caught between two equally determined men, neither of whom would give ground gracefully, each of whom would jealously blame Anne for his rival's presence.

Beth glanced again at the cluster of people on the landing. Never anyone to whom Beth Gladwyn might wave farewell? Never anyone who cared? Never mind. Still, she wished the boat would hurry, that Anne would hurry, that they could be off and away before her façade of firm resolve and poise cracked and exposed the loneliness and fear beneath.

Sir Spencer held his daughter in loving embrace. When at last they drew apart, she glimpsed the unexpected moistness in the old man's eyes. "Papa?"

Sir Spencer shook his head. "I've had too little time for you, Anne. Too little, I say."

Anne smiled bravely so he might not see the terrible fears rampaging through her breast in this final moment. "Since I've married, you've enjoyed an untroubled household. I should think peace and quiet would be the crowning glory of your efforts, dear Papa. Just imagine—no babbling woman about to gossip and make absurd demands. You'll be free to scheme and plot to your heart's content."

"I thought so too, at first, but . . . Oh, never mind. A silly way for an old man to bid farewell to a daughter. You'd best go now, Anne, with my love. Join your husband. Be well."

"May I escort you to the boat, madam?" Patrick materialized at their side, offered Anne his arm. "Good evening, Sir Spencer."

Sir Spencer inspected this young man who, he'd learned quickly enough, was his daughter's new lover. All week the two had been involved in a quiet struggle in which Sir Spencer had failed to have the young ensign assigned to a command on the continent, safely out of the way. Now they'd met and his first sweeping glance confirmed what his natural inclination, and a few discreet inquiries, had taught him. It was well he had taken precautions, slight though they were.

Anne felt the tension and recognized the look in her father's eye. The absolute discretion Patrick had exercised in town had gone for naught. Sir Spencer had surely been approached with rumors of the affair and, if she knew him at all, had taken measures in Henry's behalf. He smiled and she was certain. "Ah, yes. The young man who has spent the week, as it were, bargaining away his soul. Pleased, sir. Most pleased. I trust you will keep my daughter from harm and see to her safety during your voyage."

"Sir, I have one hundred and fifty men of the King's First Regiment under my command. Neither she, nor you, need fear for anything."

"No one will bother her then, eh?"

"No, sir. You have my word."

Spencer held the young man in a penetrating gaze, finally smiled. "Sir, I have no doubt," he said, the hidden chuckle discernible only to Anne, who had no further time to wonder what her father had been up to. Sir Spencer touched Anne's hand again, giving her a brief pat. "And so we part. I hope not forever. I'm certain Ship's Captain Ardmore is anxious to have you aboard."

Anne nodded, kissed his cheek for the last time and without another word left for the boat, not looking back until the barge was cast off from the landing and headed down river. Behind, in the dim torchlight, the figure of an old man receded in the distance, his features rapidly becoming indistinguishable in the heavy shadows. A host of friends were there, too, waving and calling farewell, but her father was the one she would miss. The oars creaked and the barge hissed through the water. Suddenly, the night sounds on the river faded, to be replaced by the whisper of deep-running water, heavy with premonition: she might never again set eyes upon her father.

London, familiar, dear London, the center of the world, slipped by in the dark. White Hall, Savoy, Somerset House, St. Paul's Cathedral, Black Friar Street. From the shores on either side came calls and cries of the never-sleeping city. Ahead, a string of lights appeared to block the way. Soon London Bridge loomed overhead and the barge was safely through and into the thick mass of ships clogging the Pool. Mr. Simon leaned close. "Cover yourself with the capes. Do not make a noise." Anne and Beth hurried to obey, at the same time heard the whisper of curved steel drawn from scabbards and the dry click of metal signalling a pistol had been cocked. The river here was dangerous: all manner of thieves and river pirates roamed at will under cloak of dark shadows and towering hulls.

The barge slid under the prow of a ship, touched the side and came to a halt. Voices called muted whispers and a lantern was lit, others above held out to light their way. A gangway swung down from the rail and an officer identified himself and asked them aboard. The *Sea King*. Relieved, Anne took the arm offered and clambered up the thin stairs. There was no question about it. If the rest of the trip was to be as hazardous and filled with exhausting intrigue as the beginning, she'd return to shore before going another step.

Another officer with a lamp preceded Anne and Beth to the rear of the boat, leading them through a doorway, down a hall and into a single room with a row of dark windows lining the far wall. "Your quarters, ma'am. The Captain bids you a good night and will call on you in the morning."

He was gone. Anne and Beth were left alone, slightly frightened in a half-lit room filled with the never-ending creaks and groans of timbers and ropes aboard a ship. Neither spoke, only looked about to get their bearings. The cabin was narrow but well-appointed. A luxurious-looking fourposter bed occupied nearly a quarter of the available space. An armoire filled the opposite corner, leaving room for a table, three chairs and a narrow passageway where one might pace back and forth. The biggest surprise of all was yet to come. Anne sat on the edge of the bed, felt movement, squealed and leaped up again.

A tousled, familiar head rose from under a pile of extra blankets at the foot of the bed. "Sabrina!" Anne exclaimed.

The old woman extricated herself from the blankets. "Forgive me, mistress. I fell asleep waiting."

Anne embraced the older woman. "Captain Ardmore must be told to put you ashore. The voyage will be . . ."

"Beggin' your pardon, mum, but I been carin' for you since you was a babe. It's my place to go and none other. Besides, your father gave his approval. 'Keep an eye on her, Sabrina,' he said."

Her father! So that's what Sir Spencer had been up to. Two chaperones! Anne tried to look angry but couldn't. The old woman's presence would be a comfort, no matter what, and on a ship the size of the *Sea King*, Patrick would certainly be ingenious enough to find places and time for clandestine rendezvous. "Very well, Sabrina, but you must promise to allow Elizabeth to do her share."

Sabrina beamed and nodded assent, then climbed

out of the bed and turned back the covers for what
remained of the night. A half hour later, with Anne
and Beth tucked in and already fast asleep, Sabrina
took to her own bed, a pallet on the deck under the
fourposter. A splendid adventure, she thought sleepily.
And at my age. Who would have thought it?

Anne woke to the sound of running feet and the
hoarse cries of the ship's crew. The bed rocked to and
fro and the ship groaned mightily. "Lord!" she gasped,
sending Beth straight up beside her, clutching the
covers and staring wildly about. The room pitched
back and forth, rolled from side to side. Gray light
seeped through the line of small windows. They were
at sea!

An hour later, wrapped in warm cloaks, they stood
at Captain Ardmore's side on the quarterdeck. Not at
sea at all, the *Sea King* was running down the Thames
with the tide. Another hour and the ship began to
pitch violently as they hit the first choppy waves
where river met channel. Sailors ran about like apes,
climbing ropes and hanging from spars, setting sails
for the run to the west. They were on the way, necks
already stiff from watching the incredible dexterity of
the men aloft, who seemed to hang in the very sky
with not a care for life or limb.

The next day saw them clear Land's End, with nothing but the open ocean ahead. The *Sea King* was well
named, for she—or he, which pronoun Anne thought
the more apt—clove the chill gray waters of the North
Atlantic like a monarch, gliding effortlessly over the
high rolling swells. Avidly she questioned Captain
Ardmore and the first officer until a hundred new
terms were mixed and jumbled in her head. Full sail
was set, including the mainsails, topgallants, sprit and

staysails and a hundred indistinguishable others, none of which seemed to be blessed with so much as a single vowel. Floors were decks, walls were bulkheads, halls were passageways, stairs were ladders, right was starboard and left was port, unless she had them switched again, for how was a person to keep them straight?

The first few days spared little time for thought of Patrick, so rich and complicated was her new life. It was just as well: the new lieutenant was indisposed, thoroughly occupied with a bucket over which he bent with distressing frequency. The women were less unfortunate. Accompanied by Beth, Anne marvelled at the navigation charts, studied the log which only slowly took on meaning. By day the ocean and sky amazed the senses, a constantly changing palette above and below. By night the heavens were brilliant with an abundance of jewels beyond comprehension. Ahead, an orange moon-fruit laid a shimmering course through the watery vastness. Behind, the shadowy sea took life in a twinkling, glowing, phosphorescent wake. Between the two lighted avenues, ship and passengers hung suspended from the white cloud of living sails. Awed, Anne kept vigil on the poop deck in order to better behold the ineffable splendor of a boundless creation that defied the night and took her mind off the uncertainties and imagined hardships to come.

On the sixth day out the sky grew dark and the very air electric with an approaching storm. Ghostly balls of light played about the masts and rigging. They rode before the winds for three days, the white cloud above the ship diminished to only a few small and stiffly bellied sheets of stout canvas. The *Sea King* made good time, but Anne was imprisoned in the cramped quarters where there was little to do but play cards with Beth or pace back and forth in the tiny free area. Her nerves were ragged within a day. Every few minutes, it seemed, feet pounded on the deck above as men ran to change sails with each shift of wind and sea. The groaning of wood against wood turned in her mind to a nightmare shriek of a tortured animal. The ship rolled and pitched and tumbled crazily. Sabrina was sick, Beth pale and listless. None of the three felt like eating, and what little Anne did manage to choke down was cold and flat. The sky outside the windows was a monotonous gray by day and black by night. A constant wind filled the air with water and left clothes and hair soggy and clammy, flesh chilled to the bone.

Anne tried to recall home, but the misery of spring in the North Atlantic defied rational thought. She attempted to construct a picture of the colonies, drawing on books and papers she had read in London and the little she had gleaned from Henry's terse letters. Beth caught the fever and carried on, fantasizing about the vast continent of mysterious dense forests filled with exotic beasts and savage primitives. The more she talked the more enthralled she became with the adventure they were undertaking, a view Anne shared less and less with each frustrating minute.

Patrick called and announced he was going to live after all. The little cabin was full to overflowing, driving Anne even further into despondency. Even his witty conversation failed to alleviate the gloom. When Anne snapped at him he left, only to return the next morning with a copy of Pope, whose couplets soon became as boring as the wind. Swift proved as tedious. Anne was in no mood for political satire and watched angrily as Sabrina, of all people, giggled and cackled at Gulliver's mishaps among the Lilliputians. Through all the hours—as provided for by her father—Anne and Patrick were never alone, a situation that finally resulted in a belligerent outburst from Anne, a tirade against the rain, the ship and the voyage itself. When she finished, Beth and Sabrina sat in cowed silence and Patrick, vexed, bitter and unsympathetic, vacated the cabin for the more amiable company of the ship's officers. Anne, only a few minutes later, apologized to ward and servant, then slumped disconsolately on the bed and dissolved in tears.

The storm blew out during the night. With dawn came clear skies and though the ocean still threw waves in their path, relative calm. Anne woke to an eerie silence. She dressed rapidly and climbed the ladder to the deck, the sound of a drumroll quickening her steps. The ship's officers, Captain Ardmore to the fore, lined the quarterdeck and on the main deck the ship's complement was drawn up into ranks. Anne mounted the ladder quickly and found a place along a deserted section of the rail. The drum stopped and three manacled wretches were led from a hatch and stood before the mainmast, while the first officer read charges of stealing fresh water during the storm. Without further ado the miscreants were noosed and hanged from the yard.

Anne turned to find Captain Ardmore at her side. "Good morning, Captain. Hanged for stealing water?" Hangings were common enough in London, and though an astonishing number of seemingly minor offenses were capital crimes, one was not yet hanged for stealing water.

"A heinous crime at sea, madam, I assure you. Fresh water is as highly valued here as gold is on shore. The crew is allotted a gallon a day per man, and if someone takes more, the rest must go without." He paused, watching as the men were cut down and heaved overboard. "So. It is done. Have you had your breakfast? If not, I apologize for the delay. Now, if you'll excuse me?"

Patrick joined her as the Captain returned to his quarters. Officer and lady stood alone for the first time in days. "I hope my lady's temper has abated."

Anne smiled. "I'm sorry, Patrick. I acted horribly."

"For which you are forgiven. I hope I may . . ."

"You are welcome in my quarters as ever, dear Patrick."

"Would that I were housed so," he responded. "Firmly lodged, for both our benefit and delight."

"When Elizabeth and Sabrina wait to watch over me most carefully?"

"Aye. I know."

The two stood in silence, watching nothing more than the empty ocean disappear and meld into sky. Anne's hand touched Patrick's and a charge ran through them both, a charge fueled by two weeks of enforced abstinence in the face of tantalizing proximity. As they watched, the wind shifted and the helmsman shouted to the mate. Immediately the mate was bawling orders and men were swarming out from below decks and climbing the rigging. A door slammed below the poop deck and Sabrina scurried across the open deck and into the hatch leading below to the galley. A second later, Beth strolled forward on the arm of Mr. Simon, the young third officer, who had taken a fancy to her. Anne and Patrick exchanged quick glances. "Patrick, I think . . ."

"Your cabin is empty, and . . ."

". . . and so am I," Anne whispered breathlessly.

"Then I'll fill you, madam, as full as I may. But if we spend the morning talking . . ."

"Will you join me, sir?" Not waiting for an answer,

she slipped past him, her breast brushing his arm and her hand sliding unobtrusively over to tug at his sleeve. "Hurry, Patrick. I shall be waiting."

Patrick ambled to the other side of the deck and descended the port ladder to enter the passage leading to the cabins from the opposite direction, for it would not do for them to be seen journeying down together. Unable to delay longer, he ran to her door, quickly checked the passageway and entered.

Anne hurried into his arms, seeking comfort and release in his fierce embrace. His arms were around her, holding her close as their lips met in a bruising kiss. Too long she had waited. His tongue entered her mouth, driving her to distraction. Two weeks! "Patrick . . . Patrick . . ."

"Anne, the last few days have been torture." His head dipped and he kissed the tops of her breasts where they mounded over the tight bodice, groaned as he felt her fingers find him and fumble for buttons. His manhood swelled, outlined against the tight breeches, impatient to be free. Two weeks! Frantically, he pulled up her skirts and found the dark triangle of love, already moist in anticipation. "Anne . . ."

"Quickly, Patrick," she gasped. Breeches half undone, his flesh, hard and erect, leaped to her hand. Suddenly he picked her up and was in her, supporting her weight with his thighs as she settled down on him. Anne's head fell back and she sobbed shamelessly.

"Nay then, sir, until later. But I will dine with you."

"Damn!" Patrick swore bitterly at the voice in the passage. He and Anne exploded in a flurry of action, regaining footing and balance, smoothing skirts, buttoning buttons, trying to make themselves as presentable as possible. Already the latch was turning. They

sprang apart, flushed and out of breath. Anne dove
for the table, grabbed a deck of cards and tried to
slow her breathing. Patrick left off trying to fasten the
last button, instead drew his coat closed and leaned
against the armoire feigning nonchalance.

"Oh, pardon me," Beth said as she entered, far too
innocently to be believed. "I thought you were on
deck, Anne. Good morning, Lieutenant." Her face remained free of guilt in spite of Patrick's murderous
stare.

"Good morning, Elizabeth. We were about to engage
in a . . . game . . . of cards," he explained lamely, noting the deck Anne held so conspicuously. His loins
ached and he couldn't think straight. "Unfortunately,
we . . . that is, Anne seems to be feeling . . . out of
sorts. A touch of the ague, perhaps, or a rising of the
lights . . . Tonight, perhaps . . ."

Anne dropped the cards, slumped in the chair. "Yes,"
she added weakly. "Perhaps then . . ."

Patrick bowed before he had to find more words,
bid them both good day and backed out of the room,
awkwardly holding his coat closed. Anne watched as
Beth shut the door and commenced to chatter on
harmlessly about Mr. Simon—he hoped to be made
second officer before too many more crossings—and
set about preparing the table for Sabrina to serve
breakfast. Anne listened without hearing, aware only
that her breasts ached and she felt awkward, swollen
and unfulfilled. If only . . . Sabrina entered with the
first hot food in four days and Anne ate listlessly,
beyond anger. There was no one to blame but herself,
for Beth had come along with her permission. Dully,
she realized that the remainder of the interminable
voyage was bound to be just as frustrating.

It was. Beth and Sabrina kept close watch, appearing whenever the two lovers manufactured a moment to tend to more intimate concerns. Once, four weeks into the voyage, they plotted to meet below decks in a safe place Patrick had discovered. The very plan was a measure of desperation, for the ladies had been most sternly forbidden by Captain Ardmore to venture into any part of the ship other than the cabin area, galley or poop deck, where there would always be an officer or mate on watch. He would, he said, take no risks with the nearly six hundred untrusted animals who ran the ship and would, if given the chance, undoubtedly cause a most disagreeable incident.

Night had fallen and the ship was heeling to starboard, running easily before a quarter wind. Elizabeth was at dinner with Mr. Simon, and Anne and Sabrina were alone when Anne, on the pretext of an appointment with Captain Ardmore, slipped out of the cabin, down the hall and disappeared below decks, following Patrick's directions as best she could in the gloom. Three minutes later, absolutely terrified but still resolute, she crept down a dark passageway under the low ceiling, found the third station to the right and entered the large room described by Patrick. Everything was as he had said it would be. Along the outside wall—bulkhead, she tried to remember, using the nomenclature to ease her anxiety—sat a row of hulking cannon, gleaming dully in the light of the single candle she carried. In the far corner, a pile of canvas lay neatly folded. To right and left on the bulkhead hung a row of buckets and unfamiliar paraphernalia. The steady creak of the ship sounded ghostlike in the room, as if the very emptiness was alive and alien, somehow threatening.

"Patrick?" The whisper was swallowed by the groans of a thousand ghosts. The smell of powder mixed with blood and sweat lingered in the fetid air. She imagined a searing hell of smoke and flame, and in the din of battle, a blood-soaked deck. Men long dead screamed in pain and crawled through the gore, searching for lost legs and arms.

"Patrick?" Steeling herself, she stepped further into the room, let the flap of canvas drop over the entrance-way. Had she the right place? Had she followed the directions? A noise to the rear sent her skipping forward. A rat, huge and evil-eyed, sat on gaunt haunches and glared at her, eyes red in the candlelight. God knew what the rats on board ate. Garbage . . . offal . . . ? "Patrick, where are you?"

A groan from the pile of canvas froze her in place. "Patrick!" Someone had found him, knocked him over the head and left him to the rats! She ran forward and stopped suddenly, aghast.

A long-haired, dumpy figure of a woman rose from the canvas, rubbed her eyes and stared at Anne. "My Gawd, but it's the lady."

Anne screamed, clamped shut her mouth lest the noise be overheard. "Who are you?"

The woman rose from her makeshift bed, pulled her skirts down, stretched and yawned hugely. Barefooted, she stood almost as tall as Anne and outweighed her by a good forty pounds. Her skirts were gray and shapeless as was her face, which showed evidence of the pox and God only knew what other horrendous diseases. Her stench was overwhelming, overpowering even the strong perfume Anne wore against the pungent shipboard smells. "They call me . . . Well, what they call me ain't for dainty ears." She laughed. "Me name's Molly, if anyone cares to remember. I 'eard about you. They talked of nothin' else for the first week."

Anne stood stunned. "You're a woman!"

Molly chuckled. "That I am, dearie, as the men will all tell ye. They should know."

"But aboard a ship . . ."

Laughter cut her off. "Shows what you know, dearie. We're part of the navy, though you'll not find us on their rotten books. How else would the poor slobs make it from port to port without spendin' 'alf their time at the bunghole?" Her eyes screwed up, searched the room. "What're ye doin' down 'ere?"

"I . . . that is, the Captain . . ." Anne's mouth and throat worked but no more words came. The grotesque caricature advanced, a toothless grin splitting her pudding face. "Now see here . . ."

"Shouldn't be below decks, dearie. Down 'ere you're far from 'ome." On she came, closer and closer.

Anne backed away. Always before she had been insulated from creatures like this. She'd seen them, of course, but from the safety of a protected carriage. The woman was obviously mad and should be in Bedlam or gotten rid of. If Patrick were there he would . . .

"What's the matter, dearie? Don't be afeared of old Moll."

"Keep back!" A loathsome creature, worse than the rats and far more dangerous. "Stay away from me."

"Just want to touch, dearie. See 'ow a lady feels . . ."

"Keep back, I say. Don't you dare . . ." The woman lunged and Anne thrust the candle into her face. The room was plunged into darkness. A scream of pain and rage rent the air and Anne felt claw-like fingers plucking at her, trying to hold her. Panic-stricken, she struck back, turned, fell and scrambled backward, desperately trying to remember how to get out. Something touched her hand. The flap of canvas! She was

out and stumbling down the length of the ship toward
a patch of light, tripping over a misplaced piece of
rope and slamming into one wall and then the other.
An eternity later she reached the open passageway and
the ladder which led to the main deck and the hallway to her cabin. Breathless, she sagged against the
wall, and a moment later fell into Patrick's arms when
he emerged from the opposite hatch, frantic with concern and forlornly chastising her for once again confusing port for starboard.

Two weeks passed, during which she and Patrick
relinquished the quest. Days were given over to cards,
watching whitecaps, and endless, pointless conversation. Only once, when a seaman was found asleep
on watch and was given twenty lashes for the in-
fraction, was there any excitement and even that
faded rapidly into the half-remembered past by dinner time. Nights were little more than cards and conversation followed by a drugged half-sleep chased
about with confusing, jumbled dreams. Longing for
Patrick was replaced by a far more urgent wish to be
off the rolling, swaying world of the *Sea King* and out
of the prison of a cabin where tempers had risen to
the breaking point. Sabrina stayed out of the way as
much as possible, but Anne and Beth bickered and
clashed constantly.

One night after the sixth week had come and gone,
Beth lost her temper completely and stalked out of the
cabin. The night was calm and she made her way to
the stern where she leaned on the rail and stared at
their wake. A canopy of stars mimicked the flashes of
phosphorescence until sea and sky were joined in dark
marriage, one indiscernible from the other. Did they
sail upon the watery fabric of the heavens, or beneath

the airy currents of an enchanted ocean? Three weeks earlier it had been a romantic notion. Now she no longer cared.

Patrick spied her and crept soundlessly across the deck to stand behind her. "Are you not worried to leave your mistress alone?"

Beth managed not to jump, and much to Patrick's disappointment continued to stare into the night. He leaned on the railing at her side. "How so, Lieutenant?" she finally answered. "Are there not one hundred and fifty men of the King's First Regiment to see to my lady's safety? Certainly she is immune to harm. Besides," she gave him a taunting smile, "Sabrina is with her."

Patrick colored, thankful the night hid his distress. "Your concern for Anne is most commendable, though a trifle lax."

"Lax? I had not expected to be accused of laxity by *you*, Patrick."

"And yet, 'tis true. You misconstrue your duty, which is to attend to Anne's well-being. If you truly cared you would allow her to make her own decision."

"I will not see Uncle Henry come to harm!" Beth exclaimed.

Patrick laughed. "Harm? How harmed? Let us be honest, Beth. Your uncle is not here. And yet how touching for a niece to fear her uncle might lose his wife."

"You mistake, sir," Beth interrupted acidly. "I am afraid you might lose your life, for when you are discovered in your infamous adultery, my uncle will match you not with words but blade for blade. Good night to you, sir!"

Beth whirled from the rail but Patrick grabbed and held her arm, swung her around. "It's time you learned what blossoms your frosty temperament has destroyed in the bud." Patrick's face dipped as he pressed her to him in an imprisoning embrace. Beth had never been held so tightly, never found herself powerless in another's grasp, and though she struggled, she could not break his hold. A sinewed arm pulled her hips tight against his to feel the hard line of swollen flesh rubbing against her belly. The harder she fought, the more tightly he held, until finally he released her and laughed softly as she tripped and almost fell. "Step between us again, sweet Beth, and you will find yourself the recipient of my unchecked affections. No. I am not jesting. You've bled, and are certainly old enough to bed."

"You presume . . . too much, Lieutenant Campbell," Beth protested, almost in tears. "When I tell Anne you've . . ."

Patrick's hand curled around her wrist and tightened cruelly. His free hand lightly touched her cheek. "How pretty a face. No pox marks. No scars. Watch well your tongue, mistress. As for Henry Gladwyn, my sword has claimed his lady, and can as well claim his life." He dropped her wrist and turned to the rail with a curt dismissal.

Beth fled, the contemptuous good night ringing in her ears. Patrick had revealed a vicious, brutal streak she had not suspected, and in the process frightened her more than she thought possible. She rested at the bottom of the ladder, still feeling his powerful grasp and unable to dispel the haunting image of his sneer. Gradually, fright gave way to determination. Elizabeth Gladwyn was her father's daughter, and no gasconading, over-inflated fop of a lieutenant could keep her in check for too long. The Lieutenant! Fah. Repulsed, she purged the distasteful scene and ugly threats from memory. Yet, a twinge of worry lingered. To see Henry made the cuckold was more than a loving niece could bear, for he had been like a second father. If Patrick continued to push the matter there would be open conflict and blood would spill. Was Patrick Campbell as capable as he implied? Possibly. Very possibly so. Soberly, she hurried back to the cabin and reconciliation, for the hundredth time, with Anne.

"Not long, now." Anne fumed. How many times had Captain Ardmore repeated the tiresome phrase? "Not long, now." The voyage lasted nearly seven weeks and she was still cooped up in her own private Bedlam. She hoped fervently never again to journey on a sailing ship, revised the too-hasty wish immediately: never again unless headed east toward England.

Sabrina finished with the powder, stepped back to the armoire while Anne removed her mask and studied the results. The old woman had fared remarkably well so far and hummed a cheerful ballad while fussing with the gown her mistress would wear for the evening's dinner with Captain Ardmore. Beth wandered out on an errand, listlessly informing them she'd return in a moment and leaving without so much as a by-your-leave. "Sabrina?" Anne asked.

"Yes, dear?"

"Is Elizabeth ill, do you think?"

"Ill?" She considered at length. "No more than the rest of us, mum. Bored is more like it."

The door burst open, barely missing Sabrina and slamming against the armoire. Beth, her face flushed with excitement, rushed into the room. A rippling, thunderous explosion jarred the ship before she could speak.

"My God, are we under attack?" Anne screamed.

"No . . . No! A salute! We're here . . . there! Land!"
As quickly as she had entered, she disappeared.

Anne sprang from the table. "Help me, Sabrina,
quickly. I shan't be unclothed for my first sight of
land."

Men shouted and clapped one another on the back.
Land meant taverns, women, food other than weevilly
biscuits and salt pork and stewed peas. Fresh water!
By the gallon if they wanted. A chance to see what
sport the colonies offered before heading back to the
brutal reality of the sea.

Patrick led the King's First Regiment on deck. Anxious to be off the ship, he paced nervously on the quarterdeck until Captain Ardmore drove him from un-
derfoot with a string of oaths. There was nothing a
landlubber lieutenant could do to hasten matters,
nothing to cut the remaining hours until the anchors
were dropped. Impatient and restless, Patrick looked
to the distant shore. America! A chance to prove his
worth beyond a doubt. Here there was glory to be
won, position, rank and the fulfillment of all the elusive dreams that had haunted him for so many years.
He turned at the sound of women's slippers rushing
across the holystoned hardwood deck. And the lady
he loved above all else, above all others. Her hand
was on his arm and he swelled with pride. She was
beautiful, she loved and trusted him. Later, Henry
Gladwyn removed from the scene, he would sail back
to England, sail back in glory with her at his side.
What more could a man want?

A puff of smoke from the shore preceded the dull
thunder of an answering salute. Patrick doffed his tricorn, bowed to kiss Anne's hand. With great fanfare
and a wide, far-flung flourish, he gestured to the shoreline as if to say the sight was in some manner his doing.

But it was Beth who underscored the solemnity and emotion of the occasion. Behind them, she whispered the single word that signalled the dramatic end to one adventure and the beginning of the next.

"America!"

BOOK II

CHAPTER 9

"I shan't have this take all day, Mr. Price."

"Aye, sir."

"If you would be so kind, please, tell Sergeant Livingston to hurry up or I'll be down there myself."

"Yes, sir!" Ensign Price moved off smartly down the hill to the thin line of sweating men struggling to load the *batteaux*. Before nightfall, each of the great canoelike boats fitted with masts and sails and designed to navigate the North American waterways would be loaded to the gunwales, ready for the trip up the Hudson, across the Mohawk to Lake Oneida, down the Oneida and Oswego rivers to Lake Ontario and across to Fort Niagara. Twenty boats sufficed for the hundred and fifty men, their officers and nearly ten tons of supplies, all destined for Fort Detroit, the key outpost on the Lake Erie and Northwest Frontier.

Anne Gladwyn watched from a camp chair set a few paces from the waiting carriage and gazed with admiration on the coldly efficient Patrick Campbell as he sent Ensign Price scrambling to a dozen tasks. There were, indeed, seeds of greatness in her lover. How proudly he stood, how crisp his words! His dress and face were immaculate in spite of the difficult surroundings, a sign of rigid discipline and inflexible will.

A runner with a message approached the Lieutenant.

Anne sat back, raised her parasol, relaxed and studied the land and water, the bustle of activity that was the port of New York. One was forced to admit admiration for the view. There was so much room! So much empty, uncluttered room. The Hudson was unbelievably immense in comparison to the Thames. The Pool of London could have fit five times over in the immediate area, and there was incomparably more empty space both up and down the river. The air was unbelievably fresh. Clear and sparkling, it reminded one more of the countryside in western England than the metropolitan hub of a colonial empire that stretched for uncounted thousands of square miles. Everywhere, everything her eyes touched attested to the untold bounty of the New World. Not a hundred yards away lay a huge stack of great timbers, tree trunks straight as an arrow and no less than three feet at the base, ready for shipment to the navy yards back home. Earlier, General Amherst's driver had pointed out warehouses stuffed to the brim with saltpeter, charcoal, potash, fine hardwoods for furniture, pitch, hides and pelts of muskrat, beaver, fox and a half dozen other exotic beasts. Most exciting of all, perhaps, had been the quartet of Indians they had passed an hour ago, as they rode to the waterfront. Savages, her host had called them. Primitive savages. She shuddered.

America! One could not help but feel excitement after more than six weeks of enforced idleness. The night's sleep had helped, no doubt. To think she'd ever appreciate such a simple thing as a bed that didn't heave and pitch about like some giant beast gone mad. Ahead, a long, narrow craft driven by two skin-clad, bushy-haired and bearded men darted downriver. Thrilled, she realized this was a real canoe, come from the wilderness.

The wilderness . . . where they were bound. A frown of concern replaced the moment of excitement. The wilderness and Henry Gladwyn. Surely he wouldn't look like those men, so unkempt, no doubt infested with vermin and God only knew what else. Yet, if Henry were on the frontier, he must be associated with such men. She uttered a silent but fervent prayer that he had maintained some semblance of his heritage. But how could one maintain anything so far from civilization? Shaken, she tried for the thousandth time to picture the Godforsaken place that was to be her final destination. Fear of the unfamiliar engendered wild suppositions and fantasies in which she stood helpless at Henry's side, subject to privation, the whims of nature and the vagaries of a savage and unknown frontier. Would Henry care? Would he simply laugh at her terror and shove her out to face hostile elements and Indians? Was this his revenge for the aristocratic arrogance and spiteful accusations of cowardice she'd flung in his face? Sweat beaded her upper lip, trickled down her temples and between her breasts. Oh, she had been a fool to come . . . A fool!

"And so, madam, at last a moment."

Patrick stood before her, cool and collected, so in command of and acclimated to the strange surroundings, he inspired the fainthearted to take courage. There was hope after all, in the light of such confidence. She was safe with Patrick. "You impress me, sir," she answered quickly and with no hint of the disquiet that had been tearing at her breast only seconds before.

"How so?"

"I had not seen you at work before. Command suits you."

Patrick allowed himself a thin smile. "And you, too. Have you forgotten I am at your command?"

"Dear Patrick." Anne laughed gaily, spirits restored completely. "You have rejuvenated me. Are you then truly at my command?"

"You know I am, Anne."

"Good. I am glad." She rose and took his arm. "You are then commanded to escort me tonight to a small but very important ball to be held at Sir Jeffrey Amherst's quarters.

Patrick stiffened perceptibly. "The General's orders were quite clear, Anne. He has no use for mere lieutenants.

"The General, dear Patrick, has changed his mind and now insists you join us. He has further," she smiled, eyelashes fluttering in a parody of the tactics which had compelled a stubborn host to submit to a charming guest's pleas, "reconsidered the need for a hasty departure on our part. Sir Spencer Langford's daughter wishes to spend a day or two in New York and the General hastens to grant her such an insignificant favor. In short, we have a week, during which time I have no doubt we shall find ample opportunity . . ."

"A week be damned," Patrick whispered huskily. His hands held hers tightly and he stared into her eyes. "I care for tonight, Anne. Tonight, I . . . we . . ."

"I know. Tonight at last."

Sir Jeffrey Amherst, Commanding General of His Majesty's forces in the Americas, leaned his heavy bulk on the balcony railing and gazed fondly across the rolling landscape. A scattering of late-blooming apple trees kept pace with the ebb and swell of land, dotted the bucolic panorama stretching as far as the tenuous trail which became Saint Thomas Street and later, New York town itself. The balcony on which he stood ran nearly the length of both sides of the L-shaped, two-storied red-brick house which, as was his conceit, he chose to call a manor. The manicured fields had once been swampland, deeded to him by the King's Council in exchange for draining them and so ridding New York and the island of Manhattan of a dangerous breeding ground for miasmic vapors. Sir Jeffrey prided himself on the cleverness of the exchange, lauded himself for so caring for the health of the colonists and congratulated himself for the wealth his welfare had provided. One counted one's blessings—and saw to the multiplication of same.

Sir Jeffrey was a patient man with a definite objective, but at times like these, the crush of business dismissed and the western sun lying at long angles on the smooth fields, he was given to contemplation. One could do worse than be Commanding General. One could do better, too, of course, but until he had a posting to England and the honors he so richly deserved, there was little of which he might complain. He was relatively comfortable, his wealth increased each and every day, men jumped to obey his commands and he was beyond reproach politically—though, of course England was far away and one could never tell which way the all too capricious political winds were blowing until the next ship came in. He sighed. All one could do was play as adroitly as possible and then depend on luck. As for the people involved . . . Gates was one, knocking about up there in Boston, slyly pursuing a continued campaign designed to discredit Amherst and move into his position. A hundred others, each with his own resources and interests, waited in line behind Gates. The Gladwyn fellow was a good enough example. Why the devil had he let them send him away in the first place? Supposed to be climbing rapidly and then get posted to America? Didn't quite jibe: he must have some powerful enemies after all. Still, making him commander of Fort Detroit and throwing in a temporary commission as major was a shrewd move. It never hurt to play safe. At least Gladwyn knew how to handle Indians. A touch too outspoken from time to time of course, but who was to say? Perhaps this was a virtue in one of such a wealthy family, of one who had married so well. The woman was a stroke of fortune. A Langford. A name to be reckoned with, to be sure. Her friend would be her father's friend, and any friend of her father was well placed indeed.

The General's fingers drummed nervously on the balcony railing. A homely man, he worshipped beauty. Anne Gladwyn was an extraordinarily handsome woman, and a commanding general could be allowed a moment's foolishness. Hope sprang again in his breast and he went over the preparations for the evening. The manor was spotless, the orchestra hired. Guests had been invited and cooks set to work. She'd be dazzled, to see what America and a general could offer. By God, he'd managed that bit well, too. A silver tongue and the power to influence a woman's mind. A week in New York, eh? Hardly enough, if all went according to plan. He'd conjure up pictures of savages and deprivation beyond description. With luck, a week wouldn't be long enough.

The shadow of the giant elm touched the edge of the drive. Almost six and the carriage wasn't back. Sir Jeffrey Amherst waved a languid hand and the sergeant posted below snapped to attention and saluted. "Sir!"

"Find them, dammit, and be quick about it. Find out what's happened. They should be back by now."

"Yes, sir!" the sergeant barked, already moving. A

moment later a horse pounded down the south road.

Sir Jeffrey Amherst sniffed and wiped his beakish nose with a silk kerchief. Black, heavy eyebrows beetled upward to nearly touch the heavily powdered campaign wig that covered his bald pate. With a final sigh and a glance south in hopes of spotting the carriage, he reluctantly headed inside to finish getting dressed. There were advantages to being commanding general. And the General would be at his best to welcome the lady who had smitten his heart at first glimpse, whose regal beauty made poor the trappings of office and gentility, and who was so unfortunately married to that upstart of a Major Henry Gladwyn, damn it all to hell.

"A street, they call it," fumed Anne as she jounced against Beth, who in turn bruised a shoulder on the carriage wall. "More of a goat path, I call it," she continued, bracing for the next lurch. The carriage fell in a chuckhole, bounced out and sent Anne halfway to the roof. "I'll report your driving to the General," she called out shrilly, raising her hand to beat on the window. "Do you hear . . . !" The carriage hit another hole and threw her into Beth's arms. "Oh! Damn them all!"

"I think you condemn too quickly," Beth cautioned. "He's merely trying . . ." she gasped as the seat rose to jolt her, ". . . to get us there on time." She had spent most of the afternoon with Mr. Simon, sightseeing around the growing city before returning to meet Anne. "I found their temperament quite charming."

"Charming, indeed!" Anne snapped. They had been delayed for the last half hour in a dingy side street while a vicious argument between two draymen raged around the blocked carriage. "As charming as their roads. Uncouth and vulgar, I call them. We know how to treat such impossible creatures in London. Your silly theorizing and philosophizing was wasted, as you can plainly see. If anything, these provincials are much more common than those at home, who at least know how to behave around their betters."

At first, the afternoon with Patrick had been stimulating. Buoyed and euphoric, she had been lulled into a sense of security by the sights and excitement on the waterfront. New York had been English for more than a hundred years, after all, and wasn't completely uncivilized. The streets were wide, and though the air wasn't as fresh as on the river bank, one could at least breathe. The effects of the first forty years of Dutch rule could be seen in charming white picket fences and the quaint, austere architecture, a not unpleasant experience on the whole.

When she was forced to take a closer look, however, her cheerfulness disintegrated, chipped away by a host of petty but annoying incidents. The town was thronged with coarse men. There were few women. Tall, husky, bearded louts roamed the streets and showed no concern for her person or position. As befitted a guest, she had searched for a suitable gift for Sir Jeffrey, but could find nothing worthy or even minimally interesting. The last straw had been the dress shop. "Dress shop, indeed," she fumed, surprising Beth with the change of subject. "Dress shop? You call that a *dress* shop? If *that* was the best New York has to offer . . . I can't imagine. Not a single decent tailoress in this, the queen city of the colonies according to Sir Jeffrey. The women must have to make their own garments. Can you imagine? What kind of manner is that to obtain one's clothing?"

"Every dress must be made in some fashion, Anne," Beth countered, trying to calm her companion.

"But not by me," Anne retorted haughtily. "I can do without such egalitarian nonsense. Fortunately, I insisted on my extra trunks, else I should be forced into the dire situation of a beggar by the end of my first week in this Godforsaken place. No doubt I shall be reduced to homespun like all the other women we saw."

"Well, I find it exciting," Beth allowed. The coach lurched again and the girl yelped as she bruised her elbow on the window's hardwood sill.

"And painful," Anne added quickly, conspiring with carriage and road to make her point. "It is hardly exciting to be late for one's own ball. Personally, I should rather be bored and punctual."

The coach came to a sharp halt, throwing Anne forward. By the time she regained her seat the coachman was peering through the curtained window. "Mare threw a shoe, ma'am," he explained apologetically. "If you'd care to step out I won't take but a few minutes and we'll be on our way again. The church across the way is . . ."

Anne's face darkened. ". . . No doubt a bore. Drive on, please."

"Beggin' your pardon, ma'am, but this is Regina, the General's favorite. If she was to come up lame . . ." He paused, embarrassed. The lady was displeased, but the General would have his head. "We've but four miles to go, ma'am. Won't need but five minutes."

There was nothing to be done. Vexed beyond words, Anne reached across Beth, slapped open the door and stepped down, not waiting for help. The loam avenue offered only a few isolated dry spots on which one could place a frail slipper. On the verge of cursing openly, she picked a crooked path across the churned, half-hardened mud trail given the misleading name of Broadway.

The side gained, Beth and Anne gazed at the church. A poor country cousin when compared to the grand architecture of St. Paul's, there was yet a unique, pristine beauty to the chapel, for in truth that was all Anne could consider the small structure.

"Trinity Church," Beth read, lingering while Anne went ahead through a wrought iron gate in the low fence surrounding the church. The doors stood open but they did not enter, choosing instead to explore the surprisingly well-kept grounds. A lush carpet of rich green grass spread outward from the brown brick structure, and to the rear, neat lines of white stone markers gave mute testimony to the effort and sacrifice involved in securing the colony. Many of the markers were of the middle and late 1600's, some from the first years of Dutch rule. Almost a hundred and forty years had lapsed between the time the original settlers had been placed in the earth where the present daughter of one of England's more prestigious families now so casually strode. Men, women and children rested in even rows under names and dates too many to recall, a litany to an elusive dream that had called them from home and hearth to cross a wild ocean and brave the interminable hardships of pioneer life. Anne looked to the burgeoning village of New York. She had been compelled to come, duty bound, to play out the role her name and position demanded, and though the town hardly seemed significant, she could not help but realize what a tiny and unprepossessing village it must have been so many years earlier, how utterly lost and isolated those few frightened settlers must have been.

In that moment, standing before hardier souls, Anne felt more than a trifle humbled. A dress shop. She had complained of a dearth of dress shops. How useless a dress shop would have been a hundred years earlier when even food must have been at a premium. A gold-finch landed on a nearby shrub and poured from his tiny, golden throat a showering cascade of limpid notes. The sound startled Anne and she jumped, sending the bird aloft to spiral the bell tower which pointed with precise emphasis to heaven. Whispered voices from the past, gentle voices full of confidence, sure of themselves and the goal they had sought, followed with a song of their own.

The poignancy of the moment was shattered when the coachman called from the carriage. Anne, as if caught in a dream, stared about, waking to shrug off the last of the ephemeral vision and calling to Beth.

"Oh, Anne, just think what they must have gone without to bring stained glass all the way across the ocean," the girl marvelled.

"Yes, I'm sure," Anne answered, her irritation unaccountably returning. "Come along. The coachman evidently has corrected whatever problem caused us to stop. We must hurry. Sir Jeffrey will wonder what kind of guests he has, to be so unconscionably late."

Beth hurried ahead. Ironically, Anne tarried a moment more, her eye caught by a granite angel, sun bleached, veined and weather-cracked but standing cool and white, caught in delicate flight against green grass. Was it her imagination or had the statue smiled pityingly at her?

Disturbed, Anne hurried toward the coach, leaving

the suddenly eerie cemetery and its troublesome notions behind. Her opinion of the New World was
hardly about to change because of a silly headstone.
Silly? The adjective shamed her and she completed the
short journey to Amherst's manor in guilty silence.

The canoe glided effortlessly as a skimmed stone,
pushed by the river's current and making good time.
Two men dipped their paddles into the Hudson, the
fur-clad man in the bow doing the lion's share of the
work, the man astern—a soldier of the King by his
scarlet coat folded at his knees—using his paddle as
a rudder to keep them on course. From time to time
the man in the stern steered the frail bark-skinned
craft past snags or partially submerged boulders. The
danger past, he bent his back to match the rhythm of
his scruffy companion. "How much farther, Jehu?"
the officer called.

The scrawny, bearded woodsman at the bow thrust
his paddle into the water one final time, lifted the
dripping wood to his lap and rested. Night would fall
soon, but no matter. There was a moon and they were
close enough that there would be no halting the soldier
until they reached their destination. Of course, he
thought to himself, I could lie, but not enough to matter. Anything under twenty miles and the Major'll
keep on; anything over and he'll know I've been lyin'
an' be distressed. "Little less than twenty miles, for
sure," Jehu figured aloud. "Won't get in 'til well after
dark. Be a long day, I'm thinkin'. Sure you don't want
to . . ."

"Fall to, Mister Hays," came the reply. The ranger
muttered a curse beneath his breath but the soldier
heard him. "Come now, Jehu, don't begrudge me. I've
taken my turn forward."

"Ain't me, Major. It's me arms. An old tree bears brittle limbs."

"And remains standing after many a sapling has fallen before storm and fire," the soldier laughed. "Don't try to arouse my pity, 'old' man. I saw you throw three of my most hardy lads a fortnight ago."

Jehu grinned despite himself, relishing the memory of the match they'd said the frontiersman couldn't win. "Aye, but they were English-born lads, slight and pale and out of breath."

The soldier bristled at the ranger's good-natured derision. "Lest you forget, I tossed two stout boys of your own that same night."

The woodsman grimaced at the thought. "A bleak night, in truth," he answered, his voice thick with mock despair. Sighing, he resumed the rhythmic, by-now-unconscious effort and the canoe leaped forward with the current until the shore line slid speedily past.

Shadows lengthened rapidly across the river and obstacles became fewer and more defined. Major Henry Gladwyn retreated into a timeless haze of reverie, trying once again to identify those emotions that had driven him to summon Anne to America. Whether or not she had obeyed was impossible to tell, yet there was room for hope. Perhaps . . . perhaps she had changed, had cast aside the bitterness engendered by the unfortunate reversals at Charles' and Stephen's hands, by the change of heart and reversal of aspiration which had led to their separation.

As for himself, Henry did not regret the decision to return to the colonies. The year's separation from Anne had only proven the ties which bound his heart and destiny to Anne were indissoluble. He had fulfilled his duty to King and country, and none could accuse him of cowardice or the shirking of responsibility in the pursuit of personal gain. Best of all, in this wild, untamed vastness he had found his element, had waxed strong and bold under the immense freedom the frontier allowed. Though still a British officer and servant of His Majesty George III, Henry Gladwyn was a far different man from the one who had embarked on a political and social career antithetical to his very nature only a little over a year earlier.

Jehu, given the rank of captain and in charge of the thirty American Rangers attached to Gladwyn's command, had warned the new Major on his arrival in Detroit. "Quebec weren't nothin'. Where you're goin' now, well, the howling wilderness will work its magic on you, Major Gladwyn. Changes most men—some for the better, some for the worst. For the better, you'll survive and stay and be more the man for the experience. For the worse, you'll run back home or die." Henry well recalled the words. He was proud of his survival and realized more and more each day how much he wanted to stay, how important it was that Anne share the marvellous new life he had found, loved and wanted to keep.

For better . . . or for worse. The question was, how would Anne interpret the changes he'd undergone? Anne . . . He could still picture the long untamed wealth of auburn hair, the refined, high cheekbones and graceful neck. And more. Her trim, delicately rounded form that so provoked and stimulated him beyond measure. No, he had not been celibate during the months of separation. He had taken Catherine, an Ottawa maiden, to his bed and for his sometime companion. A pleasurable taking it had been for the both of them, yet even lusty release and the satisfaction of the moment always left his desire for Anne undimmed, almost as if the one woman, through some curious alchemy, had increased the slow-burning need for the other until finally the words had flowed onto the paper of their own accord and the letter, ink still damp and seal not yet hardened, was in the courier's bag and on the first leg of its long journey. During the dark months that followed, he refused to consider the possibility that she might choose to remain in England. Whatever their differences, Anne Langford Gladwyn understood duty as well as any. If not already in New York, she would be soon.

Jehu ceased paddling and with one swift movement exchanged paddle for rifle, automatically checking the pan and pulling the flint back to full cock. With a curt nod he indicated a spit of marshy land. Henry stiffened, immediately loosened the pistol thrust in his belt and held the rudder to the left to put as much distance between canoe and shore as possible. The current carried them near an out-thrust spit where the marsh grass grew tall, and set into action by a gentle breeze, waved them past. Jehu peered into the darkness of the forest beyond, then relaxed. "Nothin'." He replaced the rifle and once more began to paddle.

"Shouldn't be much to worry about. Still, ya can't relax jest because we're close. A fella learns to stay careful if'n he plans on livin' to see his beard gray."

"Just the same, there's been little trouble among the tribes."

Jehu snorted. "Don't mean nothin'. We shoulda come across Pontiac on his way upriver."

"So?"

"Didn't see him, did you?"

"Maybe he's still in New York."

The woodsman shook his head. "Not that redstick. Hates towns more'n I ever will. No, sir. Him an' them two other chiefs would've said their piece an' skeedaddled. An' beggin' the Major's pardon, but I can damn well guess what that fool Amherst told them."

"Sir Jeffrey has little tact with Indians, I'll grant you," Henry agreed. "But Pontiac is a good deal more eloquent than most of them. It was worth a try to have him talk to the General."

"All I know is, them Injuns should've been along an' we should've seen 'em. If we didn't, it's cause they didn't want us to, an' if they didn't want us to, then feathers is ruffled an' trouble's ahead. You mark my words."

With that prediction, the ranger said no more, only leaned into the job at hand and paddled. But the warning haunted Henry in spite of his efforts to disregard it. After all, a reunion with Anne in the face of an Indian war was a dismal notion. Weary from the rushed journey down from Niagara, Henry Gladwyn pressed to their course and buttressed waning stamina with the memory of his lady's gray-blue eyes and the recollection of her heated body. The exercise proved a sufficient palliative, and once again he was able to disguise the painful truth: what lay at river's end was a conundrum, the solution to which was hidden in the unpredictable nature of a woman's heart.

The scent of bayberry candles hung like a fragrant invisible drapery over the festive crowd, delighted the senses and imparted an atmosphere of gentle elegance to the almost-courtly trappings of Amherst's estate. Almost, Anne thought, was as descriptive as one could get, for try though Sir Jeffrey had, there was still a certain shabby rusticity to the proceedings. The ballroom was well enough appointed but with conspicuous gaps reminiscent of a poor country squire's gathering hall. Fresh-cut floral decorations flung willy-nilly in

every nook and cranny managed to cover most of the
rough spots, but at the same time screamed of homespun make-shiftery that occasional truly fine pieces of
furniture from England failed to disguise. Similar
criticism could be levelled against the dress, or lack
of same. Well-worn gowns were at least two years out
of fashion, but Anne, out of etiquette as well as sympathy for the plight of the colonists, pretended to
ignore the obvious inadequacies and chose to play the
role of vivacious bearer of all the latest gossip and
tidings, for which everyone was starved. The gentlemen and ladies would have been mortified to learn
that Gladwyn's lady considered them rustic, when
everyone in attendance knew that the real rustics inhabited the wilderness outside the city.

Anne found herself the center of attention and dignified the evening with sheer poise and charm, a calm
presence radiating the image to which the others as-
pired. Dinner was called promptly at eight and she
found herself at Sir Jeffrey's right side, chatting gaily
with him and Sir Harold Treman, a land speculator
with whom she was briefly acquainted through Sir
Spencer. Patrick languished, meanwhile, at the far end
of the table, stuck between Widow Lespenard, an old
friend of Sir Jeffrey's and their hostess for the evening,
and a Miss Tucker, daughter of a colonel posted
temporarily to Boston. The ladies differed in all respects save one. Both were bores.

Miss Tucker he dismissed with a glance, trying to
ignore her high-pitched giggle, which, had not Patrick's
wig covered his ears quite securely, would certainly
have driven him from the table. Widow Lespenard
was another matter. The wrong side of forty but singu-
larly well preserved, she—Marie, as she whispered
sotto voce to Patrick—was more than mere hostess.

The party was, in a very real way, her own, for she had planned the decorations and food and overseen the preparations. Patrick was duly impressed. The widow wiped her lips, shifted an amazingly proportioned and barely concealed bosom so she might be more comfortable. Patrick repaid the gesture with an appreciatively raised eyebrow. Madam Lespenard blushed faintly and offered Patrick a nibble of leg of lamb. At the same time, under the table, her knee found his and pressed ever so gently. Patrick smiled wanly. "Madam is most generous."

"It is my nature," the widow allowed, leaning forward to demonstrate exactly how generous she was. Her left hand reached out and a pointed, painted fingernail gently scratched the back of Patrick's right hand. "You are a handsome young man," she whispered lazily. Hooded serpent's eyes blinked an unmistakable invitation. "One who, no doubt, has much to give. And to whom one would be most happy to give in return."

Patrick realized he was blushing. He was accustomed to stalking feminine prey, but never had he been so blatantly propositioned. He wanted desperately to look somewhere other than into the widow's eyes, but feared seeming a coward.

"Ladies and gentlemen!" Sir Jeffrey's command saved him. Widow Lespenard smiled and looked away. Patrick's leg was free and the scratching finger withdrawn. He sighed with relief and turned to the head of the table. "I should like to propose a toast," the General went on. The men came to their feet and the company raised their glasses. "To our guest of honor, the most beautiful and gracious Anne Langford Gladwyn. Madam, welcome, from the bottom of our hearts, to New York and the colonies."

A chorus of "Hear, hear!" rang from around the table. Anne rose as the men sat down and held her own glass high. "Sir Jeffrey, ladies and gentlemen. You are more than hospitable. I must admit to a certain degree of . . . trepidation . . . upon my departure from England. I can only say that in such magnificent surroundings, under the protection of a most charming host and in the midst of equally engaging and stimulating company, I find my earlier fears unfounded. You have enchanted me, and I am most happy and pleased to be here with you. Sir Jeffrey, I accept your welcome most wholeheartedly and propose a toast in return. Ladies and gentlemen, our host!"

Eleven o'clock, by the chimes. The orchestra, small but energetic, took a brief rest and returned. Anne had danced at least once with everyone save Patrick, who, although invited at Anne's insistence, had been successfully relegated to a spot along the wall where he passed the time parrying Marie Lespenard's advances. Finally, when the rest of the guests were distracted by an argument between Sir Jeffrey and Artemus Powell, a local merchant, Anne managed to reach Patrick without being waylaid and steal him away from the widow. "Where have you been?" she asked innocently.

Patrick held his temper. "Waiting in the corner until madam might pry herself away from the rest of the men and find a moment to spare," he said icily.

"Oh, Patrick, don't be difficult. You see I have been kept busy. You might have joined me at least once or twice."

"Sir Jeffrey didn't want me to join you. Sir Jeffrey is my commanding officer. Sir Jeffrey's whim is my command and I am helpless," he said through gritted teeth. The music started, a ragged minuet. Patrick took

Anne's hand. "Will you dance with me, Anne, at last?"

Anne's eyes sparkled flirtatiously. "I should love to, Patrick."

For the first time during the evening, Patrick moved as graciously as he could. "I must confess, madam, you have missed one of the more intriguing confrontations of the evening. Mrs.—Widow, as she is here called— Lespenard has offered herself to me without reservation, suggested we scamper off into the night, and . . ."

"Fie, Patrick. 'Tis no more than I have done. Everyone knows six weeks at sea leaves a man famished. I think it most . . . generous of the widow to offer to attend to your great needs." She curtsied and circled Patrick, moving gracefully to the music.

"Famished indeed," Patrick noted over a raised shoulder. "But for one meal only, on which alone do I care to feast tonight. Beware, sweet Anne. There'll be no widows to call me from the table until I've filled you . . . and had my fill."

Anne blushed. "Sir, I pray keep your voice low."

Patrick bowed, chuckling softly as he introduced a light flourishing complement of steps, keeping in time with the woman at his side. "I warrant not a single ear captures the sound of my voice above the din."

"You are cruel, sir. They mean well."

"Mean. You have said it," he countered harshly. Across the room, Sir Jeffrey watched darkly, harkened to an interrupting word, scowled and turned to leave. "There he goes. Sir Jeffrey Amherst. He's raging with jealousy and hasn't taken his eyes off you all night. I'll wager he's unused to young, unknown officers who are bold enough to assert themselves."

"He did grumble something about young lieutenants," Anne noted sweetly. "His face got red when I asked if he had not been one himself."

The music paused and the guests broke for the tables and rum. Patrick pulled Anne to the side. "Once again they seek sustenance," he said in a voice urgent and husky with emotion. "Come, Anne. Let us be off before the General returns. Leave the common to dancing and feasting while we dance our own dance and feast on each other."

Not requiring a second invitation, Anne turned with his leading hand, slipped quickly into a shadowy corner of the room where the candles flickered dimly. Several merrymakers passed, their eyes dulled and heavy with excessive drink. Their departure went unnoticed. They hurried into the hallway and started up the stairs, Patrick rushing ahead, forgetting himself then halting to turn and hold out his hand. "My lady . . ."

Anne, a few steps behind, lifted her long flowing skirt from the floor and reached to accept his help. "You're very kind, good Lieutenant," she said lightly.

"Anne."

Anne's fingertips froze, barely inches from Patrick's. Her face went pale and her eyes widened in shock and disbelief, as if with that word one woman had vanished and another appeared to take her place. Yet both were Anne Gladwyn, who slowly pivoted away from a lover's importuning touch to behold the stranger who had called her name and spoiled the consummation of a romantic dream.

He was taller than she remembered, larger somehow. Had memory been faulty? "Henry?"

"The same, I should hope, madam," he answered formally, kissing her hand lightly and glancing at Patrick. "I don't believe I've had the honor."

"This . . . this is Lieutenant Patrick Campbell. Lieutenant, may I present my husband . . ."

Voices droned on in the ritual of introduction but the real conversation took place silently as the three gauged each other, assessed strengths and weaknesses. Why was Henry in New York? Had he heard of her affair?

"I felt a trifle out of sorts and asked Mr. Campbell to escort me to my room," Anne explained, the excuse plausible and delivered with no trace of guilt.

Henry and Patrick's eyes held a moment until the younger man conceded and lowered his gaze. "Lieutenant Campbell, eh? Major Lane spoke of you when I arrived. We shall be glad to have another lieutenant. It's been a long winter and my men will welcome relief. We'll start in the morning and get on with the business of teaching you something about the frontier. You've a lot to learn."

Patrick bristled at the implication of incompetence. A British officer, he was confident of his ability to function in any environment. More galling was the prospect of losing, once again, a chance to be alone with Anne. To have six weeks of frustration followed by this condescension! "Yes, sir," he responded formally. "If I may, sir, the men are woefully unprepared and I had hoped for a few days' grace, during which time they might learn how to handle such unwieldy boats."

"Nonsense. They'll learn soon enough. I did."

"Yes, sir, but the lady . . ."

Henry cut him off abruptly, dismissing Patrick with a negligent wave. "Thank you, Mr. Campbell, but I assure you the lady, since she will travel in my boat, will be perfectly safe. And now, I suggest you see to the men and arrange to have them assembled at the docks at dawn. Oh, yes. Send a wagon around to pick up my wife's trunks, if you will. We leave as soon after sunup as feasible. That will be all, Mr. Campbell."

Patrick suppressed his anger lest he do something rash. The Major was indeed a superior officer, and though it galled him no end, Anne's master as well. The fates had conspired to steal away the prize for which he had labored so diligently. No matter Gladwyn's rightful claim, Patrick fumed inwardly: Anne would be his and his alone. "Very well, sir," the Lieutenant managed, and stepping past the woman and her spouse, strode into the ballroom, barely avoiding a collision with Sir Jeffrey.

The broad, campaign-wigged General brushed past Patrick as if he didn't exist. "Major Gladwyn, eh?" he blustered. "Aye, I see him now." Henry bowed in greeting and shook his commanding officer's hand. "A surprise indeed, Major. You're just in time to join us for the shank of an evening dedicated to your lovely wife. Come tip the tankard with us."

Though the request of a commanding general carried the authority of a command, Henry was not to be dissuaded from a moment alone with Anne. "An honor, sir, but my lady pleads an excess of food and exhaustion after a long trip. If I might be allowed to accompany her to her room . . . ?"

"Of course, of course. The older man chuckled knowingly, trying to hide his envy. "But see you tarry no longer than is proper, or at least necessary, eh?" With an abrasive laugh, he turned and vanished through the entrance.

And so they were alone in uncomfortable silence. Henry marvelled at the beauty who was his wife. He had left behind little more than a girl. Now she was a woman, a powdered, rouged, coiffed and voluptuously sophisticated creature. A beauty mark adorned one high cheekbone and set off her pale, proud face like the rarest of cameos, albescent in candlelight. Swell of breasts rose and fell slowly. Could she be so calm, so unaffected? Could she care so little?

Anne's ice-pale eyes revealed . . . nothing, as she surveyed the man she had loved and wed, the man who, in the guise of love, had bargained for and bought her, bedded her violently and then compounding love's betrayal, consented to virtual exile by accepting the assignment contrived by Stephen and Charles. He was darker than she remembered, more incongruous than ever in the uniform of officer and gentleman. His boots were scuffed, his breeches patched with muddy stains. His massive shoulders strained the red wool coat which was water-marked and grayed about the wrists. A craggy, inexcusably unshaven and coarse jaw was the formidable base upon which was built a large-boned, handsome face dominated by deep brown eyes, too serious, too demanding. All in all, save for the remarkable eyes, Henry appeared more a vagabond than a man destined for high political office. She remembered the body underneath the clothes: the pale skin, the birthmark on his right side dark and the size of a penny. Great muscles broke his body into chunky slabs, deceptively soft on the surface. Flanks white and full, thighs thick and seeming too heavy for the calves which supported them. For an instant she recalled the morning after their wedding night when Henry had stood silhouetted against the window, his manhood sprouting from the thick hair at its base, already on the rise and ready again for her body. Blushing, she turned her head and, to Henry's puzzlement, looked away.

A soldier and his lady. Passing without words through trembling pools of candlelight, Anne led the way, pausing halfway down the shadowy corridor to reach for the door latch. Henry anticipated the movement, caught her hand, spun a too-long-absent bride into his hungry arms. Tongue forcing the kiss, bruising lips. A strong, deeply tanned hand clasped her throat. For a confusing moment Anne was back in Kensington Palace on the first night they met. Excitement welled. Responding hungrily now, she moved voraciously against him, her bosom pressed to his chest. Six weeks at sea and she hungered for a man. A heady, exciting man, strong with a strength beyond most . . . Forgotten the past, the disillusionment. Forgotten. . . .

And then she remembered—the hurt, the disillusionment. Remembered Patrick. Patrick was the man she wanted. Anne dug tiny fists into Henry's chest and forced him away in an attempt to stem the warmth springing to her loins. "Sir," she panted. "Would you take advantage of a lady in the passageway?"

"No. But when a wife seeks to escape her conjugal duties . . ." The words were awkward, overpompous. "You have grown more lovely than I remembered, Anne," he said, more softly. "I had not thought that possible. I journeyed here because I could no longer stand the loneliness, could no longer . . ." Again too overblown, too contrived. Why could he not speak simply? He bent to kiss her again but she turned away, face hidden. Henry stepped back, tilted her chin. "A barrier between us still, Anne?"

"One you constructed, sir, as I remember," she answered bitterly. "Don't tell me the stonemason has forgotten the product of his much-vaunted skills."

Henry bristled. "No. But I remember better a thousand poisoned reproofs and accusations, your intransigent insistence. You were bent on having your own way and mistaking mine. Will you never understand I love you, Anne?" His arms reached for her, but as he pressed close Anne tripped open the door and rushed from his embrace.

Henry straightened, embarrassed. The glow from a single candle betrayed the quick anger hardening his face. Anger changed to surprise and astonishment as a sleep-tousled Beth gave a stifled cry and sat upright in bed.

"Uncle Henry!" Clothed in nothing more than a light sleeping gown hardly long enough to cover a budding body, Beth jumped from under the covers and flung herself across the room.

"My God, is it Elizabeth?" he asked, wrapping powerful arms around the girl's slim frame. When he finally extricated himself enough to hold her off that he might have a better look, he found himself reddening. Here was no child, but a decidedly ripe young lady. "Get you to your clothes, niece, else I become enchanted by forbidden charms. I've trouble aplenty with one woman without another adding to my desire . . . *and* consternation."

Anne, finding herself strangely pricked with jealousy, glanced angrily at Henry as the girl bounded back to bed with an enticing display of bare limbs and crawled under sheet and quilt, smiling impishly at the man she loved as a father. Henry looked questioningly at Anne.

"She wouldn't take no for an answer," Anne began. Sighing, she found a chair, sat and recounted how it came to pass that Beth had undertaken the journey, being careful to emphasize the cancerous animosity between herself and Charles and the wicked way Charles had mistreated Beth. Henry scowled at his brother's misconduct, and to Beth's relief, agreed she should live with them until the times were more propitious for a return to London which, Beth secretly wished, might be never.

Explanations over, Henry yawned wearily. "It's late and I should go to bed," he said pointedly, the remark directed to Anne.

"I shall sleep elsewhere," Beth offered, rising.

"No!" Anne interjected, softening her tone immediately, not wishing to sound so urgent yet at a loss as how to continue.

Henry came to the rescue. "Your aunt is right. It's no hour to have you wandering the halls alone. Stay in bed. I'll go elsewhere. I must confer with the General anyway. Attend to your aunt, and tomorrow will be time enough for . . . uh . . . visiting." He rose, crossed to Beth and kissed her forehead. "I'm glad you're here, Beth."

Beth clasped both arms about his neck, pulling Henry off balance and forward to lean on the bed where his hand accidentally cupped one sweet breast, firm and virginal under the thin silk gown. Beth gasped, started to draw away but instead daringly pushed upward to increase the pressure.

Henry drew back as if scalded, berating himself for the less than paternal emotions this simple act aroused, then chuckling softly. The emotion could only be accepted honestly: whatever he felt at the moment was only a natural response to the girl's healthy sensuality. Beth would certainly find no dearth of eager young suitors at Detroit, he mused.

Anne waited at the door, returned Henry's intense stare with a wan smile and flinched when his thumb smudged the carefully applied powder and rouge. "Be ready early in the morning, wife, but wear none of this. It will only make the journey the more unpleasant."

Without waiting for an answer he swept her into a close embrace. More for Beth's benefit did Anne make a show of reciprocating, at least pretending to until taken by surprise by the rising emotion she had felt earlier. As their tongues met and played, calloused fingers insinuated themselves under the lace, found and gently caressed her breasts. Straining unconsciously, she found herself wishing the daring hand might completely rip free the bodice, the harsh lips and searing tongue might play about at will, that they might . . . She restrained a rising moan. "Henry, please. Beth . . . is . . . Not now, please . . ." Tears of frustration choked off the whispered plea.

Henry looked long at the woman in his arms, but failed to penetrate past those mid-winter eyes. "Very well, Anne." He started to say more, then shrugged, bowed slightly. "Tomorrow," he concluded, his voice tight and controlled.

A moment later he was gone into the darkness of the corridor. Anne watched the spot where her husband had stood, continued staring, confused by the desire she had experienced in place of the old bitterness. How had he affected her so? He was different. Stronger than before: a rock of confidence. Suppressing the disturbing emotions seething in her breast, wondering and frightened at her own ambivalence, Anne finally forced an unwilling hand to close the door and moved toward the bed she would share with Beth.

"Tomorrow," he said. "Tomorrow."

Sleep came slowly, and slowly did the great need for a man ebb, until finally Anne lay exhausted, eyes heavy and limbs numb. "Tomorrow," Henry's word, became a narcotic which twisted night and sleep into shifting images, erotic and confused. Henry . . . Patrick . . . Henry . . . with a confused and wavering dream-woman in the middle, torn between one and the other.

"Tomorrow. Tomorrow . . ."

CHAPTER 10

The conference with Sir Jeffrey during the early hours of the morning had been heated and, unwilling under the circumstances to presume on his own luck or the General's hospitality any longer than necessary, Henry was up and about at first light. The June morning was unusually chilly and he paused by the fire in the kitchen and summoned the night watch for orders before breaking fast on a pint of warmed hard cider. Instructions had been left for Anne and Beth and a private sent to rouse Lieutenant Campbell. But Lieutenant Campbell was nowhere to be found. Luckily, one of the house servants, bleary-eyed from the night's long revels, arrived before Henry left and offered the information that the Lieutenant had forsaken lodging under Sir Jeffrey's roof and was last seen departing in the company of Widow Lespenard. He more than likely escorted her ladyship home and continued on to pass the night where the men were billetted, the servant suggested with a knowing leer that died before Henry's scowl. The Major was not amused, and dispatched two men and an extra horse with directions to go to the widow's house, find the Lieutenant and take him to the river.

Borrowing a horse from Sir Jeffrey's stable and forgoing any more for breakfast, Henry spurred the ani-

mal south to Saint Thomas way, urged the mare
through the quiet avenues of the sleeping town, skirted
the heart of the community and veered to the west on
a little-used path leading to the Hudson. The morning
air was fresh and invigorating. Henry pushed the mare
to a dead run until he was in sight of the landing
place, marked by a pennant barely visible against the
trees.

The encampment was already awake and on the
move. Breakfast fires smoked as the cooks doused the
coals with water. A clean-up squad was busy swamp-
ing out the warehouse where the men had slept. Neat
rows of gear were laid out on a natural stone ridge
above the beach, ready for final stowing amid the piles
of supplies loaded the day before. Squads were formed
in ranks on the dock, waiting their turns to move in
groups to the *batteaux* tied up in a line downstream,
each craft pulled part way onto the sandy beach.

Jehu Hays had taken charge and was in the process
of sending one boat at a time into the water in order
to accustom the soldiers to the task of handling the
clumsy craft. Always prepared for the worst, the old
woodsman had talked Major Lane into lending him
two seasoned crews which stood careful watch in their
own boats a half-score of yards offshore, ready to assist or rescue the neophytes.

Henry dismounted unnoticed in the midst of chaos.
Jehu, crochety and gnome-like, was hurling abuse at
a crew of red-faced unfortunates trapped twenty
yards out, staring blankly at the shore, the water, their
oars and each other as the current slowly spun the unruly *batteau* past the point of embarkation, around a
bend in the river and out of sight. Their hapless progress was accompanied by laughter and jeers from a
gathering of local youngsters perched like so many

chattering magpies on the rail of a nearby fence. Laughing with them, Henry hurried across the sand and jumped onto the dock at Jehu's side. "Problems?"

The woodsman's face was beet-red. "Problems?" he mimicked, then raged, "Hell, no. Disaster's what we got!" His voice sank to a disgusted grumble. "Problems, he says!" and rose again to a roar. "Well, don't just sit there," he bellowed to the rescue craft furthest downstream. "Go get 'em before they try to float across to England!"

The soldiers on the dock were next to feel the lash of his tongue. "You!" He pointed to the crew next in line. "Get to your boat. And see you do better'n them sorry bean-eatin' bastards out there. Now git!" Eight men tumbled from the dock and ran toward the next boat.

Henry glanced around, quickly assessing the situation. "The first one, eh?"

"Hell, yes, it's the first one. You don't see no more out there, do you? I told 'em to put their backs into it an' pull together. Did they? Hell, no. Them oars looked like a bunch of dingle-bobbed cattails in a thunderstorm, slappin' water ever' which way. God only knows what they'll do when they see them sails."

"They'll learn, Jehu," Henry replied, clapping the wizened old trapper on the shoulder. "Keep them going. Just do the best you can."

The next group of soldiers had gathered about a boat, and on the word shoved it into the water. Several of the men slipped on the smooth rocks covering the bottom, and with yelps of surprise and pain, disappeared beneath the floundering feet of their companions. Others lost their grip and tarried too long before trying to jump into the boat. The craft slipped free, leaving most of the surprised redcoats chest deep in water, staring perplexedly as the *batteau* drifted out of reach. Of the eight men involved, only one hardy soul managed to clamber aboard. Water-soaked but proud, he perched on top of a bale of supplies. A moment later he realized he was alone and the look of success dissolved in dismay as he watched the shoreline and his bobbing cohorts slip further away. Jehu cursed in Iroquois and sent the second rescue boat into action.

"Need to talk, Jehu. Is there anyone who can take over?"

Jehu turned to the neat lines of men formed behind him. "Any of you musket fodder know *any*thing about boats?" he asked plaintively, obviously expecting a negative response.

"Where are the officers?"

Jehu spat into the water. "Officers? Having their mornin' tea, more'n likely. The hell with 'em, I say. Don't know about *batteaux* anyways. All they'll do is confuse matters worse, which we need 'bout as bad as an Injun needs another Englishman." He paused, glared at the ranks. "Well?"

A sallow-faced youth stepped forward timidly. "I'm from Portsmouth, sir."

"I didn't ask where you were from. Can you handle these damned boats?"

"Yes, sir."

"Good. Step over here on the quick." Jehu turned to Henry. "All right with you if we make him a corporal?"

Henry nodded, amused by his companion's practical and speedy way of solving a problem. "I suppose so."

"Good. What's your name, lad?"

"Jeremy Turner, sir."

"Well, Jeremy, you're a corporal now. Lay aside that Brown Bess an' see what you can do about gettin' these landlubbers into them boats an' workin' 'em like they should be worked."

Jeremy stared at the old man, at Major Gladwyn, then set down his musket as ordered. Never before had he been given so much responsibility or power. A corporal! Suddenly he realized he had no idea of how to act like a corporal, didn't know which way to turn or what to say or do.

"Don't stand there lookin' like a sick cow, lad. Get to work." Jehu turned to the ranks again. "Turner here's a corporal now. If you wasn't so damned ignorant you'd probably be one too. Listen to him an' do what he says or I'll be down on you like a catamount on a wee lamb." With a final glare, he strode off to join Henry, who had withdrawn lest the men see their major chuckling aloud at another officer's antics.

They found a quiet spot away from the commotion. Jehu lit his pipe. "Well, what happened?"

"I spent an hour and a half with Sir Jeffrey last night. Pontiac arrived a week ago. He left three days later."

Jehu sighed. "And?" He knew the answer but had to ask.

"Amherst refused to see him. In his own words, 'I've little enough time for the King's concerns without wasting it in the company of insatiable animals.'"

"Great Jesus!" Jehu swore, snatching off his fur cap and slapping it across his thigh. "Damn him to hell, Henry. Whose concern will it be if the Lakes Frontier goes up in flame?"

"I suggested no less. The General," he said, aping the man's pompous manner, "cannot conceive of any less than complete submission on the part of the tribes, and has so decreed."

"Decreed? What the consarned hell good is a decree?" the woodsman asked, thunderstruck. "What about guns, lead an' powder?"

Henry paused, reluctant to answer. "There's no change. Our policy remains the same. No guns, no lead, no powder, no knives—presents, he calls them—will be sold or given to any Indian. They are permitted to trade furs for blankets, beads, traps and tobacco. And rum."

"Didn't you tell him what's happenin'? We been lyin' through our teeth to 'em all winter long. They'll turn to the French for what they need an' there'll come a *re*-volt the likes . . ."

"Of course I did, Jehu. He blamed me for making promises I had no right to make and couldn't keep, exploded and threatened to have me out of there if I mentioned the matter again. Said I was on the edge of sedition and had better watch my step." The Major sighed, disappointment written on his face. "We have to convince him before the fall hunt begins, Jehu."

"Fall hunt? What fall hunt? Hell, they won't have to hunt. The rivers will flow red an' the trees'll be hung with dryin' scalps. They'll eat Englishmen." He sank into a silence prompted by anger too deep for words. "It ain't right, Major," he finally said. "Ain't right at all. He's drivin' 'em to the warpath." The woodsman looked up sharply at Henry, a worried look on his face. "You still want to bring your woman along? I hate to think . . ."

"That will be enough, Jehu," Henry interrupted sharply. Jehu jammed the pipe in his mouth, sucked noisily. "There may be disturbances, but I can't believe there'll be widespread warfare. Remember, Pontiac and I . . ."

"Beggin' your pardon, Major. Ain't nobody means as well as you. I know that. Pontiac knows it too, even if you are an Englishman. But that don't change the facts. His people damn near died last winter an' some for sure will this comin' one if'n Amherst won't let you at least sell 'em what they need, won't let you treat 'em the way they ought to be treated." The old trapper stood, ready to get back to the boats and the job at hand. He hesitated a second, knowing what he was about to say was direct insubordination, then plunged ahead. "Any man who wouldn't even show Pontiac the respect of sharin' a pipe is a damned fool, Major. Amherst, bein' top dog, is worse'n a damned fool. I'm tellin' you, Pontiac is gonna be forced to fight or lose face. He ain't about to lose face, for he's one proud Injun. The bad your so-called general is doin' with his *de*-cree outweighs any good you can do. Ever. You're stuck in the middle, Major." He started back to the strand, pausing only long enough to add dolefully, "Reckon we all are."

The British officer was left alone with only his disturbing thoughts for company. The morning had turned warm, humid and was already long beyond its hours. Damn Jehu's tongue for the ugly truth, Henry cursed silently, digging anxious fingers underneath the snug brown wig, attempting in vain to scratch plastered, tangled and sweaty hair, much too long for a wig. If the good general ever discovered an officer of the Crown wore regulation uniform and tight breeches only when around New York, there'd be hell to pay.

There'd be worse, though, if Amherst continued to ignore the Indians' plight. Jehu's predictions could very well come true. Should Anne and Beth be lodged in New York then? No. They might as well have stayed in England. It simply wasn't necessary. He and Pontiac were friends, had smoked many pipes together. Pontiac was a respected leader of his people, and while there might be disturbances, the war chief would keep the area around Detroit free of trouble. Besides, there was some sense to Amherst's reasoning. Without arms and powder, the tribes *were* basically helpless. Too many men in too many forts assured peace, even if the Indians were angry. He could safely take the women to Detroit.

A howl of laughter floated on the heavy morning air. Another party of soldiers heaved its *batteau* into the Hudson, this time completing a successful launch, only to find, once aboard, that they had left their oars ashore. It was going to be a long morning.

Patrick groaned, eased an eye open. Light. Morning. Something about the landing . . . The other eye snapped open. Good God, he was supposed to be— where the hell was he? *Pink* curtains? A sigh to his right reminded him with startling clarity. Widow Lespenard. His head turned slowly and he dared a closed-lid peek.

Her mouth half open, the widow—Marie—breathed softly. Under the sheet, mammoth breasts rose and fell gently, a not-so-subtle reminder of much more frantic . . . God! Daybreak . . . the waiting *batteaux* . . . If the Major was already there . . . ! Slowly, Patrick raised the coverlet a cautious inch and started to slide out of bed, stopped when the mattress moved and a heavy leg fell across his thighs. An unvoiced curse later, he turned to confront a lazy, sensual smile. "Madam . . ."

"My stripling. My dear stripling," she murmured, tongue darting out to lick her lips. Quickly, she shoved the covers down, revealing her breasts, sagging with great weight. "Good morning," she cooed, reaching out to catch and caress his manhood.

"Madam," Patrick groaned, "we cannot persist in this

enjoyment. I must depart. The Major is waiting and will be most upset. He left explicit instructions . . ."

"*Mais oui*, my little soldier stands to attention, no?" she crooned in the French accent she'd affected the moment they'd been alone. Her fingers played tantalizing tricks, pressing here and pulling there, leaving Patrick stiff and swollen, complaint forgotten. "Thrice *monsieur* pleasured Marie. Now I pleasure you, no?"

"Madam, I . . ."

Too late. Widow Lespenard, young in spite of more than forty years, rose and straddled her reluctant lover. The enticing, cajoling, clever fingers brooked no argument. "Shhh, *mon amour*. There is time," she whispered. "There is time."

Morning and majors ceased to be of any importance. The widow's hands roved over Patrick's chest and abdomen, traced intricate patterns ending at the swollen base where two bodies became one. An agile mistress, Marie rose, quickly descended and rose again, sliding sideways with the move. Never had anyone so aroused Patrick. He reached for her breasts but she stopped him. "No. I will do all. For you, *mon amour*. For you . . ." Heated hands became maddening instruments, branding and searing flesh already afire, with wilder and wilder movements, lifting, plunging, twisting until Patrick was no more than a helpless male toy in the widow's insatiable embrace. Suddenly, when he could certainly last no longer, she stopped, held him deep and motionless in the pulsing heat. Patrick caught his breath, gasping uncontrollably. Slowly, the ring of muscles tightened, and slowly rose, pulling him upward. The first convulsion caught him midbreath and he arched involuntarily, spilling, spilling as never before.

Marie sank back to the bed, caught one corner of the sheet and gently wiped the moisture from his limp flesh. "Now," she murmured, "you have spent the night with Widow Lespenard!"

"I didn't know . . ." Patrick paused, his voice weak.

"But of course not. Few young men do." She smiled lightly, kissed his chest. "You performed well, my little lion," she finished, and gently shoved him from the bed.

Nonplussed and weak-kneed, Patrick groped around, found breeches, boots, shirt and coat, and dressed as quickly as possible in the growing light. He turned, smiling stiffly. Marie lay naked on the bed, unperturbed and disconcertingly amused. Never before had a woman so completely dominated him, treated him like a child and left him bereft of dignity. "It's late. I must go," he stammered with the little force left at his command.

The widow pouted. "And will I see you no more, dear stripling?"

Patrick neared the side of the bed, took her hand and kissed it as gallantly as he could. "That is for restless fate to determine. But I can assure madam she will always be held tightly in the embrace of my memory."

"You are so poetic."

"Yes," he interjected rapidly. Damn it, what was the woman doing to him? Was she laughing? "And now, madam, I must bid you adieu," he hurried on, beating a hasty retreat before he became totally embarrassed.

"Patrick, don't for . . ." The door slammed, cutting her off. Marie Lespenard laughed aloud, rose from the bed and pulled on a light gown.

Halfway to the gate, Patrick was met by the two

messengers sent by Henry, bearing word the Lieutenant was to ride for the encampment immediately. Patrick's ire rose. He was already stung to the quick by the widow's belittling solicitude, and the Major's indiscretion struck him as intolerable. Now the whole company would know of its lieutenant's brief affair. The private handed over the reins, fighting at the same time to suppress a knowing smirk. Patrick whirled to discover the cause of such mirth and saw, to his utter despair, the good widow, her charms barely covered by a tousled night dress, waving a hat from the bedroom balcony. Mortified, he realized his head was bare. He mounted in one smooth motion and rode beneath the balcony.

"*Votre chapeau, monsieur,*" she whispered loudly, simultaneously dropping the tricorn and winking at the privates.

Patrick bowed, eyes tight with rage he dared not express. "Thank you, madam," he managed, donning the hat and wheeling the gelding away from the house.

The two privates waited, poker-faced, eyes front. But they'd seen, damn them. They'd seen. Patrick shot each a murderous stare, then slammed the spurs to the General's horse and pounded through the gate, leaving a cowed and choking escort to follow timidly to the rear.

Anne and Elizabeth were the last to arrive. Under the scrutiny of the soldiers, who were finally in position by beached and waiting craft, the women stepped down from Sir Jeffrey's coach. Anne groaned at the sight of the boats. Would there never be an end? The *batteaux,* though considered large vessels by those hardy souls who were forced, from time to time, to carry them on portages around rapids, falls or other obstacles, filled Anne with more than a little dread. They looked decidedly insecure.

Henry approached from the bank, and for the first time in over a year she saw her husband by light of day. Sunlight flattered him, emphasized the powerful physique and rugged features. She was pleased with what she saw, until a closer look took note of the rumpled military coat, frayed cuffs and threadbare breeches.

Henry kissed her hand and gestured to the boats. "Madam, we are loaded. The wind is upstream and we wait only your presence for our departure." Beth stood behind Anne, her emotions far more easily read than his wife's. "Excited, Beth?"

"Oh, yes. Terribly so," the girl beamed, avidly taking in the line of boats ringed by stalwart soldiers, the gulls screeching overhead, the sun-dappled watery sheet that went on and on to lose itself in the tree-shrouded distance.

"And who is this? Another surprise?" Henry asked, eyes raised. Sabrina, hoping to pass unnoticed until she was well out onto the river, timidly stepped forward. "Sabrina?"

"Aye, Master Gladwyn."

Henry glanced at Anne. "You made no mention of our extra passenger. Will there be others?"

"Sir Spencer gave his permission," Sabrina broke in hurriedly. "He said I could . . ."

"I'm sure Sir Spencer means well, but he has never been to America. Still, you're here and I don't see how we can send you back." His frown dissolved and he took the older woman's hands. "I'm glad to see you,

Sabrina. If I balked at first it was of concern for one of your . . . maturity . . . being put to such a rigorous test. Life here isn't easy, you know."

Sabrina smiled bravely. "I may be unused to forests and heathen savages, sir, but they'll be no less trying than rearing a young 'un, or keeping the wolves from the door."

"Perhaps you are tougher than you look. Like an old biddy hen, eh?"

"Say what you will, Master Gladwyn. An old biddy is as tough a creature as you'll find. I'll keep up, and do my share as well."

Henry hesitated. On second thought Sabrina would probably adapt more rapidly than either Anne or Beth, for she was already used to a harder life. Perhaps it wasn't a bad idea to have her along. Suddenly happy, he laughed outright. "Very well, Sabrina. Welcome, then, and let's be off." He took Anne's arm and led the women across the sand to the dock, avoiding the trampled and damp places in order to spare their cloaks and shoes.

"What is that?" Anne asked.

"What?"

"That . . . that funny little elf?" She pointed at Jehu, busy overseeing the redistribution of the cargo loaded on one of the *batteaux*.

"Elf! My God, don't let Jehu hear you call him that."

"Jehu?"

"Jehu Hays, a colonial. Part of a company of rangers. He and his men have proved invaluable. They know the land and the ways of the natives. I've learned a great deal from him."

Anne shuddered inwardly at what an uncouth gnome of a man such as this Jehu might have taught her husband. Henry reached over to brush back her calash with his fingertips. "I cautioned you against powder and rouge."

Anne squared her shoulders belligerently. "Sir, though I may be a continent away from family, court and England, I shall not forget nor abandon my position nor my heritage."

Henry shrugged noncommittally. By nightfall she'd regret the decision. But then, each new visitor had a multitude of lessons to learn. Most had to learn the hard way. At least the first few times.

They were lucky. All the first day the wind held and the sails stretched taut over the *batteaux*, driving the boats upriver. Henry, with Anne in his boat, took the lead. Beth was assigned to the following boat captained by the new corporal, Jeremy Turner. Jehu kept to the rear with an eye out for stragglers. With him was Sabrina, who, when she complained about being separated from her mistress, listened to the reasonable explanation that three women in one *batteau* would put undue demands on the few rowers. When presented the choice of an inexperienced crew—one she'd seen wallowing about like a great wounded duck—or the boat captained by a seasoned frontiersman, she quickly picked the latter.

Anne was at first determined to despise this new experience. Only weeks earlier she had been living happily in England. Now, through an improbable series of events impossible to unravel, she found herself on a strange river in the company of a hundred and fifty-odd men, heading into the wilderness and God only knew what frightful adventures.

But the brilliant sheen of diamond-hard sun on water, the calming effect of waves slapping gently against wood soon forced her to admit that this particular mode of travel was a good deal more agreeable than the ocean crossing. For one thing, there was more to see. At first, the eastern shore maintained a series of steep bluffs which soon fell off to a much more comfortable terrain of rounded wooded hills and shallow valleys dotted with so many gracefully cleared and tilled farms it appeared as if the entire land was one immense and carefully tended garden. The picturesque scenery was reminiscent of the English countryside. The western shore proved an entirely different story. There, broader, more heavily forested hills swelled to near-mountainous heights the farther north they travelled. Soon the hills ceased entirely and the shore became a miles-long perpendicular palisade blocking off all view to the west and dotted from time to time with massive rocky bastions, pale brick color contrasting with dark gray, jutting toward the heavens. The ridge above was topped with a ragged line of trees, and here and there the upflung rock wall held precariously perched clusters of oak. Anne marvelled at how any type of heavy growth could cling to and sustain life on such a barren, precipitous cliff. Now and then a lightning-blasted trunk gave mute testimony to the struggle.

"Anne, look!" Beth's voice rang out across the stretch of bright blue water between them.

Anne turned, shaded her eyes and searched in the direction Beth indicated. "What? There's nothing . . . oh!" A gray projectile exploded from the depths, rose and dove with a great splash when the fluked tail hit the water. Two more burst from the river in rapid succession.

Henry clambered aft from the bow. "Porpoises," he explained, repeating the information loudly enough for Beth to hear. "Friendliest creatures I've ever seen.

They'll be with us as far as the saltwater lasts." He noticed Anne dabbing at her cheeks where the water had played havoc with the carefully applied powder. Her troubles were just beginning, he thought, foregoing a biting comment when she pulled the calash forward to guard against further mishaps. Beyond, the porpoises leaped from the river again, in unison this time and blowing mightily through their airholes, either performing for or oblivious to the human audience. What remained of Anne's foul temper was powerless against the incredible grace of the display and the apparently smiling faces of the watery beasts. Henry grinned and relaxed for the first time since meeting her the night before. The porpoises were a godsend: his lady was smiling, at long last.

The day was nearly gone when the tiny flotilla struck sail and the soldiers bent to the oars and rowed to shore. Tasks were apportioned immediately. Jeremy was given the job of checking the *batteaux* and making sure each was tied securely for the night. Patrick, strangely quiet and restrained, set a perimeter guard, and with Sergeant Livingston, arranged for the watches. Jehu set to work preparing a crude enclosure for the women, stringing four long sections of canvas to a rough rectangle of growing trees and so affording them a modicum of privacy.

The long shadows raced across the river, enveloping the camp in purple. Soon the ring of axes stopped and the only noise left was the crackling of the cook-fires, the slow complaining of the men as they tried to ease cramped muscles and sunburned necks, and the soft whisper of the women's voices as they watched the sun set over the mountains to the west and compared notes of interest from the day's travel. In another thirty minutes it was near dark. The men were bedded down a hundred yards away after a hurried supper. Anne and Beth sat on a log inside their enclosure and watched the stars pop out, wild and lonely through the canopy of maple, oak and chestnut. They stilled when a cough announced the presence of a visitor.

"Can I come in?" the now-familiar voice of Jehu asked.

"Of course, Mr. Hays, by all means."

The woodsman carried a tin bucket strung on a rope handle, hung it over the fire to warm. "Brung you a little somethin' for yer first night. Make you sleep good." He paused as Sabrina rose from spreading blankets over beds of tender young pine boughs. "Injun tea, made from cherry bark and sassafras."

"I beg your pardon?" Anne asked, eyebrows raised.

"Well, you take a cherry tree, an' strip a piece of bark . . ."

"We have an extra cup, Mr. Hays, if you'll join us," Beth interrupted, her eyes twinkling at the idea of drinking 'Injun' tea.

"I hardly think . . ." Anne began.

"We opened a tin of sugared biscuits for supper, Mr. Hays," Sabrina added quickly, arranging the cups which had been drying near the fire.

"Uh . . . thank you kindly, ma'am . . ."

Sabrina drew herself up to her full five feet two inches. "I told you in the boat, Mr. Hays. You may call me Sabrina, like everyone else. I'm just a . . ."

"Is this . . . beverage . . . safe for civilized . . ."

"Oh, Anne! Of course it is."

"Please. Sabrina. For forty-three years . . ."

"It *does* smell nice. Maybe I'll have . . ."

"Is that *honey*?"

Jehu gave up trying to keep track. His stuttering increased and his face darkened beneath the heavy tan as Sabrina stepped closer, her gray eyes atwinkle. "Yes'm . . . uh . . . there be things . . . uh . . . needin' . . . to be looked after . . ." He turned and escaped from the enclosure and the questions, stumbling into Henry Gladwyn in his hasty departure from the women's camp.

Henry looked down at his buckskin-clad friend. "What's the matter with you?"

"Major . . . Major . . ."

"Well?"

"I'll be damned if they don't all talk to one time. I'll be hornswoggled if they don't!" he spluttered, hurrying off to the river bank and solitude, trailing a perplexed tone behind him. "Women! Durned if they don't bring consternation on a man."

Henry paused a few feet away from the canvas wall, softly lit from the inside by the fire. A shadow passed along the right side of the tent. Sabrina, by her posture. Another pair of shadows, seated, filled half the front flap. In pantomime, the shadows told a tale of a woman at toilette. The repetitious movement of brush through hair was a sensual dance, an intimate flowing sketch of disembodied flesh. Ought to walk right in, dismiss Sabrina and Beth and bed her here and now, he thought, at the same time having no hint of an idea as to where he'd dismiss them to. Of course, they could take a walk, disappear into the woods, find a quiet corner and there . . . Aye, and with soldiers on watch and a company of the King's First Regiment quickly in attendance to watch their major and his lady . . . Damn! How many trials must a man undergo before gaining his own wife's favors? He was a man, after all, and needed a woman. Needed this woman. Jehu was right. They did bring consternation.

A greeting called and answered, Henry shoved aside a loose flap of canvas, peered into the secluded campsite. Beth sat brushing Anne's luxuriant tresses, keeping slow time with a cricket hidden between two of the trunks. Henry walked to the fire and Anne turned to follow him, her face, washed of powder and rouge. Here was his wife as he had longed to see her: desirable and immediate, for in the same way the canvas had intervened and allowed only a shadowed misrepresentation, so too did the heavy makeup and powder keep Anne aloof, distant and unreal, a queenly fabrication of society, untouchable and unknowable. Here, Henry knew on the instant, was ample reason to summon Anne to America. Proud and spiteful she could be, but there was no denying her beauty. He had to believe her attitude and love for him would one day reflect that physical beauty. "Is all well with you, mistress and niece?"

"I'm afraid Grosvenor Square hardly prepared me for such an ordeal," Anne replied acidly. "You told me nothing of the bugs which . . ."

"I warned you about wearing paint. The 'bugs' are gnats and they are attracted by the odor of the rouge."

"I washed off the rouge. The gnats are still here, plaguing me."

"By the time you've gone without for three or four days, they will be gone completely and you'll no longer be troubled. Right now, with the wind right, a gnat—or an Indian—could smell you at a half mile."

Anne slapped aside Beth's hand. "Are you suggesting, sir," she began, rising angrily, "that . . ."

"Anne, hang one of your gowns outside the tent tonight. Let it air. Tomorrow, wear no cosmetics of any kind. You'll see what I'm talking about." He paused, his voice low. "This isn't London. It isn't even New

York. You don't need perfume out here. The whole countryside is perfumed with fresh air and water and trees and flowers. Tomorrow, you'll start to see . . . or smell the difference. It will take a few days, for your senses must get used to this new world. Before we arrive at Niagara, you'll know what I mean."

"Is it terribly far to Fort Niagara, Uncle Henry?" Beth asked.

"Depends on the wind and weather. With luck, less than three weeks, but we've green men with us. If the wind stops they'll have to row and our pace will slow considerably. If the weather is bad when we leave the Mohawk, the portage will be muddy and hold us up further. If the wind on Lake Ontario is bad we may have to camp for a few days."

Anne sat down, stunned. "I didn't realize . . ."

Henry took a cup of tea offered by Sabrina and sat across the fire from Anne and Beth. "I admit I withheld information from you," he began reluctantly. "But Anne . . ." His eyes looked beyond the night and his voice was intense with quiet excitement. "You too, Beth. And Sabrina. You won't believe what beauty you'll see. One hundred and eighty miles to Albany on the grandest river you've ever travelled. Every mile is different. Trees, birds, deer, bear . . . This place is so magnificent it will take your breath away. Smells, sights and sounds . . . And you still won't have seen the minutest fraction, still won't have seen the Great Lakes, which, if this land is beautiful, transcend beauty beyond description or compare. You will see, and your souls will be captured . . . As mine has been." He stopped, lost in the wandering words. For a moment, no one spoke, held by the mystery of Henry's vision, the inviolate sanctity of his dream. A light breeze billowed the canvas inward, stirred the flames and sent a shower of sparks into the living forest above.

"Best get to sleep," he said, breaking the spell. "We start early in the morning."

Anne, deeply moved by what she had heard, rose to accompany him to the perimeter of the protected camp. Henry bent to kiss her lightly on the cheek before raising the flap and staring toward the whispering river where the moon played upon the water. The mournful, reverberant call of a bird sounded, delicate, sad sweet notes ephemeral in the hidden night. "Whip-poor-will," Henry whispered.

"Nightjar, in England," Anne replied.

"Yes," he agreed, touching her cheek. "But we're not in England."

The canvas dropped and Anne stood alone. "I know," she said. And softly repeated, "I know."

CHAPTER 11

Catherine, her copper-colored flesh goose-bumped and glistening as she emerged from the chilly waters of Parent Creek, glanced up in startled recognition at the brave watching from the bank. She had made certain the grove was secluded before attempting to bathe and would have been offended to find a warrior intruding on her privacy were it not for the fact that this particular brave was her brother. Ten years separated them—Catherine was not quite eighteen—but such a difference hardly mattered so close were the two bound by ties of familial affection. With the death of their parents during an Iroquois raid eleven years before, Pontiac and Catherine had been left alone to make their way as best they could. There were, of course, aunts and uncles, grandparents and cousins, but it was Pontiac who kept watch over and all but raised her. That he had risen to such prominence among the Ottawas only further attested to the brave's exceptional force of character.

No trace of the deep love he felt for Catherine showed on his face as the slim, naked girl bounded shamelessly from the water and raced across the packed pine needles covering the forest floor. Her jet black hair clung to firm round breasts, masking the dusky flesh like a water-soaked cape. Diminutive, smaller than most Ottawa women, Catherine would have appeared to more literate eyes the very personification of a water nymph or one of Rousseau's noble savages. To Pontiac she was merely a sister, exasperating at times and maddeningly foolhardy. Catherine joyfully embraced the hard physique. Seeing Pontiac brought cheer to what had been a disturbing and glum procession of days.

"I am glad to welcome my brother," she whispered modestly, kissing his cheek in the Christian manner.

"And you, sister," he repeated formally, then laughed aloud, unable to control his mirth.

"Why do you laugh?" she asked, tossing back her head and showering him with drops of water.

Pontiac held her at arms length, hands gently gripping her shoulders. "Surely my little sister wishes to see our village go hungry this night."

"I do not understand."

Pontiac laughed again. "There is little game to be found in this part of the forest, yet the young hunters stalk imaginary trails leading to the fawn I have found." Catherine glared malevolently at the surrounding trees, now teeming with a hundred imagined prying eyes. "Of course, if my sister would take one of the People to her blanket, as is proper for the sister of a chief, she would enjoy her privacy as the rest of our women."

The girl shrugged away the weight of his hands, stalked across the tiny clearing to retrieve a buckskin shift from the branches of a currant shrub. "I have chosen a warrior already."

Pontiac's face clouded, the amusement gone. "You have chosen foolishly, little Flower."

"My name is Catherine."

"You are Ottawa."

"I have been baptized by Father Pothier. I am a Christian."

"Pah! Did the French Father erase the color of your skin? Or the kinship that unites us? Let the French and English dogs call you what they will. What is a Catherine? A meaningless word! To me, you will always be my sister, Flower-on-the-Water."

Catherine stepped close. Chastely, modestly, as befitted a woman of the tribe, she laid her head against his chest. "I would be none other, my brother."

Pontiac's anger receded, as always. Born out of love, it died for the same.

The days passed with the regularity of an undisturbed pendulum. Morning, and the smell of cooking fires sharp on the cool river air. Henry alert and authoritative, precisely thorough. Mountains and more beauty than Anne's eyes could take in, with each curve in the ancient river highway revealing a new vista to rival and overpower the one before.

Noon and heat, exacerbated by the sight of Newburgh, the tiny settlement nestled under cool trees. Rolling masses of fleece-white clouds, occasional high parasols. To the rear, Beth was chattering with someone—what was the boy's name? Jeremy? She turned and strained to see, but Patrick was missing, hidden somewhere back along the straggling line of sails. Henry was quiet, still intent, polite, solicitous. They passed Poughkeepsie, as inaccessible as Newburgh, for as long as the wind pushed, they would keep on and on.

Afternoon and dull fatigue. Eyes puffed and watering from too many hours of sun glare on water. Henry's touch, reassuring, imparting strength. His voice, weaving dream-like spell of the land, its beauty, grandeur, boundless generosity. His shoulder, the one sure haven of refuge, solid and real against the transient, drifting haze of undifferentiated blue and green and glare. To lean against him is to yield? No matter. There is comfort, as well.

Night at last, and the rush of cool air returning. Fire and food, solid ground. Henry's voice rising in occasional command, assurance of safety through the long night. Alone with Beth, still chattering, with all the comical, painful details of Patrick and the widow with the monumental breasts, as gleaned from the soldiers' gossip. A tear or two, shed quietly, wiped away quickly. Tired. So tired. Above, the unbelievable panoply of dancing stars and whispering planets. The rustle of leaves in the wind. Outside the tent, the sure presence of Henry and wistful calls of waking owls. Who? the owl asks of the night—of Henry watching over her. Who sleeps . . . ? Who dreams . . . ? Sleeps . . .

Ten days of fair wind and even climate found the *batteaux* beached on Dutch Island near the middle of the Mohawk River. Henry, eager to avoid delaying the journey for even a day, had bypassed Albany, the last village of any note north of New York. The decision earned surly grumbles from the men of the King's First, who with each passing day had become more eager for a respite from the rigorous demands of rowing and working the sails, the boredom of sitting in boats all day long and the inescapable and complicated task of setting up camp and mounting watches each night. Patrick, since he merely rode and did not have to work, had his own reasons for being disagreeably inclined toward Henry, the first of which was the Major's decision to place him in a craft far removed from Anne. Thwarted for the past weeks during the

ocean crossing, he found himself once again denied his
mistress' favors, this time by a superior officer whose
demeanor was unprofessional, whose attitude seemed
indifferent and whose dress was a shameful denigra-
tion of King and country. Henry's behavior fed the
stiffly proper Lieutenant's contempt of what he considered to be a renegade major. That Henry Gladwyn
was bound by rites of marriage to Anne mattered not
at all as far as Patrick was concerned, beyond the
obvious fact that in place of merely stepping in and
claiming her he would have to take her by force. In
the meantime he chafed bitterly, bided his time and
rubbed a sore back and sorer buttocks, taking small
comfort in the half-hearted belief Anne would surely
find a way to arrange a rendezvous before too many
more days had passed.

The first opportunity came at the island campsite.
They had stopped early for the supply of meat was
exhausted and the men had gone without for the last
three days. Leaving the others to set camp, Jehu had
taken the light canoe and ranged the shore downstream, beaching the craft and disappearing into the
forest. A half hour later the birchbark vessel returned,
low in the water with the weight of an elk. The ranger
hurried to the ladies' campfire where Henry, assisted
by Patrick, was involved in securing their privacy with
the canvas sheets, tying them in a random, multi-sided
configuration. Pulling the Major to one side, Jehu con-
fidentially reported the news of a burned-out cabin
and 'Injun' sign to the south. Henry left Patrick with
orders to finish the tent, then hurried off with the
trapper.

The final knot tied, Patrick waited inside, pleased
with his luck. Sabrina was at the center of camp
where, in a holiday spirit and to help lend an air of

celebration to their half day of leisure, she had decided to help with the cooking chores for the entire party. The cook grumbled, fussed and complained, but was happy enough for her company: for once in his military life he'd have someone with whom he might share the blame for the same old, generally tasteless provender. Beth too was gone, having conspired to meet with Corporal Turner—promoted, Patrick would never forget—without regard to rule or regulation—when he'd finished his duties. The two were exploring the narrow game trails that wound maze-like through the dense overgrowth covering the island. Patrick fidgeted nervously, adjusted his uniform and then feigned indifference when Anne entered with the soldiers who carried her trunks. Soon the privates were gone, leaving a tension hanging in the air between the bedraggled lady and her former lover. Anne and Patrick were alone for the first time since the trip had begun.

"Well," she finally said, the story of Widow Lespenard strong in her memory. "I suppose we're set for another night in the wild." The smile was too wide, the laugh too brittle. "Thank you so much, Patrick. You've been . . . very . . ." Her voice faltered. Silence.

Patrick held his ground, faced her across the tiny clearing. Anne, long since resigned to the impossibility of keeping up appearances during the voyage, had abandoned powder, rouge and perfume. Her hair, lighter from the sun's rays, was piled high and caught with a bow in a semblance of the day's fashion. Plain, she was, but strangely enough he found her even more alluring than she had been the night of Amherst's gala. Yet, why was she so reticent? "I don't think I understand, Anne."

. Anger, confusion, hurt pride tore at the false, inane

smile glued to her face. It wasn't fair. The endless, wearying travel without amenities and comforts was easier for a man who needed to be concerned with no more than the care of a wig and coat. In the face of such simple and studied elegance, Anne felt naked and unappealing, vulnerable and powerless. How to say what must be said when one looked like a peasant, a commoner? Another empty laugh, hollow and mirthless, filled the tent. "Understand? Really, I . . ." A slim hand touched her shoulder. Tapered, almost feminine fingers turned her with precise pressure. "You, sir, above all others, I should have thought would remain a gentleman."

Patrick, taken aback by the unexpectedly cool reception from one he reckoned as desperate as himself, struggled to regain with charm what had been lost through haste. "I would have thought my actions were a mirror to your wishes."

Anne stepped away. Words were a comfort. "Mirrors are deceptive, Patrick. Left becomes right, handwriting is reversed. Oft times men find it difficult to rightfully interpret what they see in mirrors."

The blouse of her travelling gown had come open at the top, revealing pale golden flesh and the slight hollow at the base of her throat where nestled a gold brooch Patrick longed to replace with kisses. "Anne, there are none to see us and we can hear if anyone approaches. We have a moment—however brief." She stood motionless, eyes downcast and unreadable. "My God, but I long for you, Anne. Must I wait until we reach our final destination in the heart of this damned wilderness?"

"If your hunger for a woman is so great, you could send for Widow Lespenard. Surely she would rush to your side."

Patrick blanched. Damn all wagging tongues, all prattling fools! A deprecatory chuckle turned into a weak giggle. "Really, Anne, you don't think . . ."

"I think you found one willing body to replace another. How fortunate the widow was so close at hand, and within the quarter hour at that!" Near tears with anger and frustration, she whirled and sat on a trunk, face hidden in hands.

Patrick stood as one stunned, groped for words. "My God, don't you understand, Anne? For six long weeks I'd hungered for you, six long weeks fasted in torment, only to have you snatched from me at the last moment. I was crushed and disconsolate. Wracked with visions of you . . . in the embrace of another man. I fell prey to . . . the first arms to beckon."

"What am I to do, Patrick?" Anne wailed, the words muffled. "Whatever am I to do?"

"Tell him," Patrick commanded, kneeling at her side.

"Tell him?"

"That you love me. Or I will."

"No!"

"Why? For God's sake, Anne, why?"

She closed her eyes against the tears that threatened, and saw images of sun-darkened, craggy face, firmly chiselled jaw and warm, thoughtful, laughter-filled eyes . . . Shoulders, arms and hands, strong and supportive, a bulwark against the wilderness. Had she changed that much? Fallen in love again with Henry? No. Impossible. And yet . . . "Because I'm not sure."

"Not sure!"

"Patrick, I . . . we . . ."

"I was sure. Sure enough to swallow my pride and beg and plead to be allowed to follow you. Sure enough to humiliate and humble myself before the . . ."

"Patrick, stop. Please, stop!" Sobbing, `Anne caught his hands, held them to her breasts. "I do love you, but don't you see how confused and frightened I am? Here we are in a strange land, surrounded on all sides by savages and wild animals. Henry is strong. He loves me. How can we . . . be together? He's my husband, Patrick."

Patrick rose, face colorless and hands trembling. "I came three thousand miles to be with you, Anne." Cold fury clipped his words one by one, laid them at Anne's feet in a precise line. "The choice is yours. Me . . . or Henry Gladwyn."

Wind crept through the trees. The sun dropped a little nearer the horizon, ticked off a second of eternity. "I don't know. I didn't want it to be this way," she whispered in agony. "Perhaps you'd better leave now, Patrick. I'm sorry . . ."

Patrick's countenance darkened, grew sinister. Then he bowed curtly, holding her in a fierce and piercing gaze. "No. Don't be sorry, Anne. Don't be sorry. Not yet."

Patrick stalked off into the forest without a backward glance, not even pausing to greet Beth as he passed her. Lost in jealousy and stunned outrage, he paid little heed to his direction. A bare three weeks earlier Anne Gladwyn had been panting with desire, willing to go to almost any length to be with him. Now she had cast him off, forsworn their love and mocked his sacrifice. Tears? Had she wept? Ha! Tears were an easy contrivance, as easily seen through. Damn! Just like the bitch Lespenard, using him and then casting him out.

Gladwyn. A major, indeed! And he had Anne as well. There was no justice. None. Then I shall conjure

justice myself, Patrick muttered, deliberately grinding
down a sapling in the middle of the path. I will have
Anne, I will have Gladwyn's ill-used authority. A
course will be shown me. The wary and the alert
always find a way. And if I am forced to wait too long,
this—he slapped the hilt of his rapier—will not fail.

Anne watched Patrick leave with longing, tear-filled
eyes. She wanted to call to him, but Beth's return—
and her speculative look—stopped her. So many complicated changes were taking place. Somehow Henry
and the wide country had insinuated themselves into
her mind and shaken her confidence. How had she
so blithely dismissed Patrick? She, who had always
loved the etiquette of love, delighted in the indulgence
of sensuality, celebrated beauty, poise and gracious
manners, had denied with sinking heart the one man
who best complemented her. And for what? For Henry
Gladwyn, the antithesis of the courtly admirer? But
why? For strength, had she said? There had to be
more, else she had taken leave of her senses.

"How fare you, ladies?"

Anne, startled by Henry's intrusion, looked away
lest moist eyes betray her consternation.

"Well, Uncle," Beth exclaimed happily. "I've been
exploring. The island is like a maze, and not too far
away there's a clearing where logs have been laid out
almost like in a church or meeting hall. It's so quiet,
so peaceful."

Henry chuckled. "The church. Twenty years ago
there was a small settlement a couple of miles from
here on the northern bank of the Mohawk. Dutch, they
were, and felt the same way about this island as you
evidently do. They felled the logs and laid them out

for a church. Every Sunday they'd come across the river in canoes and worship there in the glade.

"The story goes some Senecas had been traded a cask of rum for pelts. As it turned out, the rum was bad and one of the warriors died. The Senecas had warned the settlers about cheating and the brave's death was the final straw. One Sunday while the settlers were at their prayers, the Senecas moved in and killed the trader. In the blood lust that followed, they massacred the innocent worshippers as well. Only two got away. A boy of seven and an old woman."

"My God!" Beth whispered, shuddering as she remembered the quiet peace of the clearing and imagined the screams and horror of that terrible morning.

"Now," Henry finished, "the island is quiet. No one disturbs the 'church.' Not even the Indians. Jehu says they consider it an evil place and won't go near it."

The tale finished, a pall hung over the tiny camp and the women looked furtively about as if expecting a horde of screaming savages to descend on them. Henry's laugh jolted them back to reality. "Don't look so dismally grave. That was a long time ago." A call sounded from outside. "That will be Ensign Price, Niece, come to escort you to dinner, if you will."

Reluctantly, Beth rose and fabricated a smile. The ensign was doing his best to take over Mr. Simon's role, and though Beth would rather dine with Jeremy Turner and had done her best to avoid young Price, she could hardly escape this time.

Henry crossed to Anne. Dressed simply and without her rouges, powders and perfumes, she took his breath away. If only she could shed all her artifice so easily. Looking at her, desire overwhelmed him and it was an effort to keep a discreet distance. The wind soughed among the branches of the sassafras, murmured secrets of summers known and never to come again. The wind was wise and worried not. There would always be summers. And lovers. Who one day would learn to talk again. And touch again . . .

"Anne?" Hesitantly, he started toward her.

An echo of a distant shot sounded dully through the woods, a faint, lingering, hollow cough that stilled the hushed conversation of the soldiers and sent them scrambling to arms. Henry was gone as the sound faded. Anne stared out from the enclosure, amazed that such an ineffectual report should lead to so much activity. Officers moved men into a defensive perimeter around the camp. Bayonets gleamed in the sun's dying glare. Anxious soldiers of the King's First faced the forest, unnerved by the silence and convinced treachery lurked behind each tree and shrub.

Beth and Sabrina were quickly escorted to Anne's side in the tented quarters. The three women huddled near the fire, unable to see outside and imagining a multitude of horrors as elaborated by Beth, who was still affected by the tale of the massacred settlers. Sabrina finally rebuked the girl for a too-fertile imagination, then added in a worried tone: "Lieutenant Campbell was seen leavin' the camp. Master Henry and Mister Hays went out after him."

A stillness fell over them at her words, broken only by the whispered commands of officers, the sound of scurrying feet as men moved to new positions. Inside the tent, three women stared at the canvas walls and thought of the ghosts of Dutch Island.

They found Patrick on the other side of the narrow island, calmly reloading a discharged pistol. Henry and Jehu cautiously scouted and remained hidden, watching from the trees while Patrick swaggered to the water's edge and posed triumphantly over the limp, dark-skinned, half-naked form of a man spilled awkwardly across an overturned canoe. Jehu snorted in disgust at the Lieutenant's careless exposure of himself. "That's one soldier boy that ain't gonna live to see the geese leave, less'n I miss my guess," the trapper muttered, scouring the far shore before entering the clearing. "An' I don't usually."

Henry quickly crossed the distance to the Lieutenant. "What happened here?"

"One shot, through the head," Patrick boasted. "Came upon him as he was putting ashore."

"You fool!" Henry blurted angrily.

"Sir?"

"How do you know this man was an enemy?"

"He was an Indian," Patrick answered. He propped fists on hips and stood to his full height. "As I understand it, General Amherst's instructions regarding Indians are very clear."

"General Amherst has not been north of White Plains since he left Quebec. What he knows of Indians could be written on the point of a needle. The same could be said for you, Lieutenant."

"Sir, I take offense at your tone."

"Do you, Lieutenant? I will tell you . . ."

"Renegade Seneca, Major," Jehu interrupted, crouching over the dead man. "Looks to be a loner."

Henry's eyes narrowed dangerously with the information. "Do you agree, Mister Campbell?"

"Sir?"

"Do you agree with Captain Hays? Go on over and take a good look." Abruptly he turned and moved to the canoe, Patrick trailing after and wondering what came next. "What about it, Lieutenant? Seneca?

Huron? Ottawa? Iroquois? Cayuga? Oneida? Come on, man, speak up, since you know so damned much." He grabbed the dead Indian, held up the grisly head, half blown away by the shot. Blood stained Henry's hand, dripped into the boat. An uneasy silence reigned. "Come on, Mister Campbell, out with it!"

"I don't know."

"You don't know?" Henry asked, bitingly sarcastic. "Of course you don't know. What *do* you know? How nice this will look when the General finds out how the brave lieutenant shot an Indian from ambush. Damn!"

"Looks to have been scalp huntin', Major," Jehu reported, reaching under the corpse and retrieving a day-old patch of skin and blond hair.

"Aha!" Patrick exclaimed, recovering rapidly and beaming at what he considered an obvious vindication. "What do you say now, Major Gladwyn?"

"I say you've got a lot to learn, Lieutenant. The sooner you realize it the better for all of us. I say if that had been an Ottawa, Huron, Potawatomi or any one of another dozen tribes, you might well have begun a war and broken forever the tenuous bonds of friendship Jehu, I and a number of others have spent the last year laboring to construct. I say you've pulled a damned irresponsible stunt . . . and been lucky."

Patrick, incensed by the continuing harangue, drew himself rigid. His cheeks flushed with suppressed fury. "Must I remind the Major we are both servants of King George the Third? Soldiers of the mightiest army the world has ever known? It is our duty to make war on and subjugate these savages."

"No! Our duty, Lieutenant, is to make peace."

"Then we shall forever be at odds, Major Gladwyn. I had excused your less than proper attire and slipshod authority as being the result of the vigorous trials of frontier life, but I see now there are further and highly irregular insufficiencies of your character which extend beyond the excusable." The remark could only be answered with a challenge, a duel. Patrick waited for the response with growing excitement. He had his chance, more quickly than he had hoped. More propitiously, he had a witness who had heard Gladwyn's seditious speech. Recognition by Amherst, advancement and Anne Gladwyn's hand were closer than he had dared dream.

Henry stared long and hard at Patrick. Quick fury flared, then receded. The boy was an absolute ninny. To the Lieutenant's surprise, Henry merely shook his head in resignation. "Mr. Campbell, you are a damned fool," he finally said, letting the mutilated head drop with a thump into the canoe. Without another word, Henry Gladwyn headed for the brush.

"Sir!" Patrick shouted. To his dismay, the officer ignored the call and disappeared. Patrick swore bitterly, dug a scented silk kerchief from under his wrist cuff and held it to his nose.

Jehu, squatting by the corpse, suddenly stood, reached down and pulled the dead Indian's knife from his belt and held it out to Patrick. "There y'are."

Patrick gingerly took the knife and looked quizzically at Jehu. "Sir?"

"Well, you killed him. Scalp's yours."

"I beg your pardon?"

"Can't rightly boast on him less'n you got the scalp to prove it." Patrick's face whitened at the suggestion. Jehu laughed quietly. "That's the rules, Lieutenant. You kill an Injun, you got to scalp him."

"You're mad," Patrick whispered. "Both of you."

Jehu's laugh built as he started back to the camp.

After four paces he stopped, locked eyes again with the young lieutenant. The laugh was gone and the ranger's face was cold and humorless. "Son," the old trapper said softly, "if I was you, I'd be mighty glad the Major didn't turn around."

"We must talk."

Catherine glanced up from the buckskin moccasins, the object of her labors the past hour, as Pontiac entered the conical bark-and-hide-covered lodge, and let the door flap drop shut. "Yes, my brother?"

The war chieftain squatted with crossed legs beyond the fire and watched his sister without speaking. He was given to beginning important conversations in silence, a method that set him apart from most and conferred advantage when the pipe was passed and men spoke. Now, with the perceptive patience of a hunter, he sat silently, reading Catherine's innermost thoughts until sure of his approach. "Teata has returned to our camp." The words out, he ignored the wry, twisted expression that crossed his sister's face. "He is a brave warrior."

"He is a Huron," Catherine replied distastefully.

"All the more reason to accept him. The union of our tribes is to be desired. Ottawa and Huron would do well by such a bond."

"And I? Would I do well?"

"Teata is a great chief among his people. Men and women sing of his courage and deeds around the fires in their longhouses."

"He looks like a horse," Catherine parried, tugging on her chin to mimic the Huron's drawn, homely face.

Pontiac grunted in disapproval. "My sister has seen seventeen summers. She must choose soon—or end her days like old Yellow Eyes who never took a man and must beg from the others for food and skins. Teata is a mighty hunter who will bring meat to the fire, warm skins when the sun sleeps, and many fine sons. What more could a woman want?"

"Love. I do not love Teata."

"Love!" Pontiac scowled. "You have listened too long to the white man's words. You will learn to love Teata in our own manner, which will be sufficient. The love of the white man is as the ice of winter on which even the careful fall. The love of the white man is cold and comes from speaking great words but doing little. They love in word only, not in deed."

"I do not love Teata," Catherine persevered. "I cannot be his woman."

Pontiac sprang from the ground, fire flashing in his eyes. Though hardly more than average height, the massive breadth of shoulders and chest, outlined and glistening in the feeble light of the flames, made him seem a giant. "You will take Teata to your blanket," he ordered.

"No," Catherine replied, adamant in the face of his menacing countenance.

That anyone, especially a woman, should refuse Pontiac's command was unthinkable. But Catherine had done so. "Are you English that you disobey a chief?"

"The chief is my brother and I do not fear him as others do. I am a woman. One who loves her brother as life itself, but would keep her life. Already I have chosen a warrior. The Major Henri," she said, pronouncing the name in the French manner.

Pontiac leaned toward the light. "I said nothing when you went to Henri Gladwyn's blanket, for he is different from the others, a man of pride and respect. I knew he cared for you, and would not hurt you: he was a friend with the same loneliness as you. But the sun and the moon do not stay in one place. The seasons turn. I tell you, such a joining can never be."

"You are wrong, brother."

"Hear me, little sister. You know why Major Henri is gone these many days. He told us both he had sent the talking paper with words that would bring his squaw across the Great Water."

"The white squaw will not come."

"Would you come, if your man called?"

"*She* will not come."

Pontiac shook his head, and moved to a new argument. "You are Ottawa no matter what the white priest says. Henri Gladwyn is English and your blood cannot mix. You have seen the English dogs. They are greedy and do not respect the People or the land. Though Henri Gladwyn is as rare among Englishmen as is the Great White One among deer and elk, still, I would not have English blood in the veins of my sister's sons."

"Your blood is my blood." Catherine answered quietly but with great intensity so Pontiac would know she spoke from the heart. "I am a woman, but know my own mind. My strength and will are as great as yours. I tell you, brother-who-I-love, I will go to Henri Gladwyn. I will."

Pontiac did not answer, only shrugged and pulled aside the deerhide flap on the opening. "I will," she reiterated stubbornly, almost as if to convince herself.

Pontiac stood in the entranceway, his face dark against her will. "Do not see this Englishman again, Flower-on-the-Water. I have spoken."

"Why?"

Pausing, he turned and reentered the lodge. When

he spoke, the low guttural Ottawan passed no further than Catherine's ears. "This is not squaw's talk, but you are my sister and I will tell you because of your love for Major Henri.

"The redcoats' father in New York brings trouble to the People. When Teata, Nanais and I sought to council with him, he thrust us from the door like dogs, not deigning to smoke or talk. This was wrong. His men have been ordered to look down on the People, to laugh at their red brothers. There are many singing birds in New York, though, who came quietly and spoke what is in the redcoat father's heart. He does not like the People and would see our lodges empty, our women and children hungry and our braves weak and powerless. He has ordered the soldiers and traders to give us no more guns or powder or lead. Not even knives. Only rum, to corrupt the young braves, and bad blankets under which we will freeze."

Pontiac waited for the full import of the message to sink in before continuing. "I know the love you feel for Major Henri. I love him too. He is a man. I respect him. He tells me the redcoat father's words are not true, that the Great Father across the water will not let this great harm come to his children. He speaks with strength, but underneath his voice wavers and betrays doubt and weakness. He only hopes he speaks the truth.

"I am still Henri Gladwyn's friend. We will hunt together, smoke and council together. I will try to believe my friend as long as I can. But how long is that? Already, powder supplies grow short, shot rattles in the bottom of bags. The English continue to take land against our wishes and without paying. The trading post at Sandusky is now becoming a fort and our brothers the Wyandots are angry, speak harsh words and consider having their women weave the green belts of war. To the south, the agent Johnson speaks peace while the soldiers reinforce Fort Pitt. Many bad signs we see in the foul mist coming from the mouths of the Englishmen.

"I tell you, there will be trouble. Already the People meet to council alone where the English cannot hear. I go tomorrow to the north to speak with the Potawatomi chief Washee. Other chiefs will be there. Teata and Tatee of the Hurons, Great Turtle of the Shawnee, Mackinac of the Northern Ottawa. The runners left a week ago with belts to call more. Hudoc of the Senecas, to the Iroquois, the Mohawk, Delaware, Oneida . . . There will be a great council."

Catherine spoke for the first time. "There have been councils before, my brother. Why do you forbid me to go to Henri Gladwyn?"

Pontiac's eyes gleamed and his face hardened. "Today Henri Gladwyn is my brother, but he also must heed the words of the redcoats' father. I will trust Henri as long as I can and will speak for him at the council, but many others will speak against him. Tomorrow, Henri Gladwyn may be my enemy."

Fort Niagara lay a little over six miles behind them. There, Captain Portis had greeted the company cordially, treated everyone to a small feast and a night and day off duty, giving the men a much-needed rest. Anne luxuriated in the chance to sit down to a regular table and sleep in a real bed for the first time in more than two weeks. Two days later, with fifty of the men left behind to reinforce the Niagara garrison, they were under way again, upriver in *batteaux* to the base of the lower rapids and then aback sturdy packhorses going from the north end of the most demanding por-

tage in the northwest to the foot of the great escarp-
ment which rose over three hundred feet to the southern plateau.

Anne paled at the sight. Crawl-On-All-Fours, they
called this difficult passage where Seneca women and
children as well as the English soldiers loaded packs
on their backs and crawled up the face of the cliff.
Even Beth lost her usual buoyancy at the sight, swallowing her fear only after the climb had begun. The
women were helped from before and behind, Anne
half pulled up the incline by Henry, Beth by an apprehensive but brave Ensign Price and Sabrina by Jehu.
Foot by tortuous foot they clambered up and up, panting, sweating profusely in the July heat, suffering
scraped fingers and knees, torn shoes and mangled
dresses. Below, in a broad vista visible from a resting
place halfway up, the land stretched north, an un-
broken panorama of trees on either side of the Niagara
River to Lake Ontario.

A half hour for a little over three hundred feet.
Anne, Beth and Sabrina lay flat on a grassy slope,
gasping for breath, muscles quivering from the unusual effort. The men left them to their own devices
and set about forming the column which finally started
appearing over the crest of the cliff. A short hour later
and the provisions were again placed on packhorses
and the party set out due south along the edge of the
gorge. "Only a few miles and you'll be aboard the
Michigan and can rest. The rough part is over."

Sun. A cloud of gnats swarming to plague her.
Perspiration. Anne fell a little behind a once-again
ebullient niece who found strength to hurry ahead in
order to be one of the first to catch a glimpse of the
Falls. The trail bent and the trees thinned ahead. Anne
stopped dead in her tracks, straightened and marvelled

at the sight. Far ahead, an immense rainbow arched across the sky and a distant reverberation filled the air with a deep rumble more felt than heard. Here the path divided and the ragged file of men and beasts bore to the left, away from the gorge. A smaller trail went straight ahead and ran along the edge of the great chasm gouged from earth and rock. Hardly thinking, Anne struck to the right and found herself separated from the rest of the party, hidden by the dense foliage and walking no more than a half-dozen paces from the edge of nothing. With each step the rainbow seemed to arch higher into the sky and the tumultuous thunder increased. Below, waters rushed white-capped and furious, frothing like an endless charge of maddened beasts. Sound and wind lashed upward out of the depths, a tumult increasing to demonic levels, frightful and terrifying, yet insistently demanding she look into the maw. The air was damp and leaves dripped, loosing their droplets as she plunged through the narrowing trail.

No longer did she miss the others, no longer give them thought, drawn as she was to the rising cloud of mist ahead and the steadily increasing roar. How far had she walked? She no longer knew. A mile? Two miles? More? The trail twisted away from the gorge and tunneled through heavy timber; the rumble of the falls diminished and the air seemed drier. Deep shadows between the massive boles on both sides of the path hid frightful secrets. Where were the others? How far ahead, how far to the rear? There was nothing to do but push on. Ahead was the river and the Falls and so ahead also had to be the ship that would carry them further on the never-ending journey.

At last the trees thinned again. Rocks thrust upward, blocking the view. The air filled with water and an ear-punishing rumble so overpowering Anne could hardly hear her own thoughts. Doggedly she continued, scrambling over the line of grayish limestone projections jutting irregularly out of the ground, a haphazard battlement.

The Falls! Anne stopped, dazed. Never in her life had she seen anything to compare, anything to prepare her for the dread magnificence of the spectacle before her, the awesome creation of God and nature. Mindless, she stumbled down from the rocks to a grassy slope leading to the edge of the gorge. A wall of cascading water, mountainous in height, thundered over a cliff hundreds of feet across. Billows of mist rose, swirled, coalesced and faded, accompanied by a thousand and one shifting rainbows. A rush of air, moist and chilled, blew the hair from her face and plastered the torn dress to her body. Reason refuted any real danger, yet instinct cautioned she shrink back lest the promontory itself be sucked into the insistent stream, sucked into the raging maelstrom and swept away. Chaos! Tumbled water, tumbled rocks and tumbled air. A whirling, cavernous Hades into which helpless, hapless souls were plunged and swept to the earth's terrible depths.

"The Abode of the Gods."

Anne screamed, spun about and stared at the figure materializing through the mist. "Henry?"

Henry Gladwyn, a wry smile twisting his lips, bowed courteously, an incongruously courtly gesture for a man garbed in buckskin breeches. He was shirtless and gestured to a bundle of clothes, among them the scarlet coat and other military regalia, hanging from a tree limb at the edge of the glade. He no longer wore a wig and his hair hung shaggy and free like a great, flowing brown mane. Anne shook her head, bewildered.

Here was a Henry Gladwyn she had never seen, a husband whose body she did not remember. Gone was the white skin, the layer of softness. His whole torso matched the tan on his face. Never had she known an Englishman so brown. A jagged line of scar tissue marred his left side. Bulging muscles stood out in sharp definition, hard and taut, rippling beneath the lush carpet of thick brown curls covering his chest. Against the backdrop of rocks and trees, he appeared to be of them, a wilderness god of primitive sensuality, sprung from the earth itself. Her breath quickened. A satyr surprising a nymph, she thought, the male animal, strong, quiet, beautiful.

"Now that we're past Fort Niagara," he said, moving closer and shouting over the thunder of the Falls, "I can get rid of that infernal coat and those damned tight breeches. This is a good deal more comfortable— and offers less a target than scarlet and brass."

He laughed when she didn't answer, gestured to the Falls. "Beautiful, aren't they! Frightening but beautiful. Sacred to the Senecas and a dozen other tribes who follow this and other trails to listen to the gods speak. It's uncanny, but if you listen for awhile, you'd swear you can hear them."

A gray curtain enveloped them, obscured the rest of the world. Anne's cotton travelling gown, moistened by cool mist, clung to her body. A petulant, moist curl wrote an askew upside-down question mark on her cheek. Henry, now facing her, reached out to coil it at the corner of her lips, lingered to trace a line across dewy cheeks and down the slim neck. Pressed together by the mist, their bodies met, and their lips touched, gently at first, tremulous, hesitant, seeking . . . "No!"

Deny the pressure of his arm, stronger than any she had known before, circling her waist, forcing her closer. Deny the fingers firm against breasts and ribs as they loosened bodice strings. Deny the toughened flesh, scented by leather and smoke, the calloused hand searching, each caress a silent insistent demand. Deny the strong and unyielding thighs and the hard leather knot holding up the breeches, pressing through soft cotton to dimple softer skin.

The wind rising, swirls brown and auburn hair together, intertwining strands form a private tent inside which eyelids close and mouths open, lips move, kissing chin, cheek, nose. And now inside, tongues speaking the language of love, of need, of desire.

Her back struck the grassy carpet. His lips branded her throat and swollen breasts with one searing kiss after another.

Rearing, hungry flesh, thigh against naked thigh. Gown, underskirt pulled up, bunched at the waist. Scalding tongue raking belly, thighs, breasts. Fingers probing, pressing, stroking, holding. The richly furred chest harsh again her belly, a moment later crushing her throbbing breasts, bringing a flood of new sensation, driving her to the brink of a chasm as deep and wild as the greater one nearby . . . where the roaring song thundered.

Thighs spread, hips tip upward. On fire with the heat of passion, shining, swelling folds of hot flesh part to expose the inner bud, tumid and as hard as the engorged tool pressing to enter . . . His hips rise and a small hand grasps . . . and guides him.

"Yes! Yes! Yes!" she moaned aloud, unheard against the deafening Falls as he plunged, unable to withhold the wondrous length, hurting and healing with the growing momentum.

Nails rake sweat-streaked back. Male and female joined, heaving, bucking . . . Nature's carnal energy unleashed in mounting paroxysms to match the frenzy of the cataract. Straining, he stiffens. Deep inside he drives, pauses, surging wildly in eruption. Her scream is lost to the overwhelming voice of the gods in the mist and furious rapids, lost in the spinning, whirling maelstrom of love. . . .

They stood on the hill above Fort Schlosser, pausing a moment before descending to the outpost which controlled the eastern end of Lake Erie. Out on the pristine blue waters, the war sloop *Michigan* rocked against the prodding current, patiently awaiting the passengers to Fort Detroit. "They will have worried," Anne said.

"No. Not Jehu, at least. He'll know."

"Sir, you do not mean . . ."

Henry laughed and shook his head. "Jehu has a way, that's all. I suppose young Mister Campbell will be dismayed, though."

Color rose to Anne's cheeks. Did he suspect—or know—after all? "Mr. Campbell?" she stammered.

Henry gestured in a self-deprecating manner to himself. "My garments. I'm afraid the good Lieutenant expects commanding officers to be the epitome of English manners. I'm also afraid he is in for a great disappointment. That part of me is reserved for east of Niagara, General Amherst and all that. Out here . . . is home." The sweep of a hand emphasized the sense of his statement.

Anne sighed, relieved her secret was safe. A curious chemistry had taken place with their lovemaking, a strange, new longing resurrected from the ashes of the night in the garden so long ago. No longer afraid, she admitted Henry's ardor had fueled the miracle. The savage in him was exciting and she wanted to retain that part of him for herself. And when they returned to England? She smiled, confident the secret wildness could be captured, mastered and released on command.

But only on command, of course. The Langfords had been skillfully manipulating men for years, and Anne Gladwyn had learned well. She would mold Henry, shape him to the man she wished him to be—and *where* she wished him to be. "Home, husband?" She took his hand over a rough stretch and cautiously made her way down the last slope. "We shall see."

CHAPTER 12

They lay entwined, bodies warm together in the small bed. Niagara had been their tutor, unleashing passions to flood over precipitous cliffs and carry them gasping over exquisite rainbows and through giddy clouds of their own making. Against his better judgment, Henry had borrowed Captain Smalley's cabin, leaving Elizabeth and Sabrina to the mate's even tinier quarters. The *Michigan* was small—only eighty tons—and densely packed with men, but Henry was determined. Jehu could wink as often and as slyly as he pleased, and as for the men, what tales they might carry mattered not a whit.

A stir above-decks awakened him. Henry slipped from Anne's embrace, eased out of the bed and dressed rapidly, impelled by a slight shiver of anticipation. The *Michigan* was anchored below the mouth of the Detroit River for the night, and the next few hours would see home at last. Dressed and ready, Henry kissed Anne gently on the forehead, caressed her cheek with a finger. So aware of her presence, so tuned to her slightest movement, he could tell she had awakened and lay staring into the darkness. "It's morning," Henry whispered. "Sunrise in a few minutes. Would you like to come on deck?"

Anne's answering "yes" was a throaty purr. She burrowed into the covers and tried to sleep again but the bed was less appealing without a partner. Quickly, she slid from beneath the still-warm quilts, stood shivering and expectant in the cold morning air and groped for her gown.

On deck, Captain Smalley greeted Henry with a monosyllabic grunt. To the east across the vast expanse of Lake Erie, the horizon glowed dully, presaging dawn and a brisk morning wind. There was little need for words. The *Michigan's* crew was aloft, waiting for the signal to unfurl the sails. In another few minutes the wind would spring up from the southeast, the sails would be dropped and the sloop would pick up speed and run against the current, upriver to Detroit.

Anne arrived topside at the moment the first sail was sheeted home and filled with air. Picking her way through bales of supplies to the quarterdeck, she put an arm through Henry's and followed his silent gesture to a blaze of light shooting from under a cloud bank. The wind picked up, stiffening the canvas and pressing the gown to Anne's body. By the time the shifting pastels of morning dissolved to white and gray, the *Michigan* was on the starboard tack, a fine spray of white water hissing from her bows, heading into the estuary of the Detroit River.

And so the journey's end was near. The deck was crowded with men and officers. Henry pointed out each landmark, already described a dozen times by now. The narrow passage between Grosse Île and Île au Bois Blanc, Turkey Island, River Rouge. The river curved to the east. Sails were reset and the war sloop slowed as the wind fell off. No matter. Ahead lay Fort

Detroit, over which proudly waved the British flag, a bright and welcome patch of color against a background of gray clouds.

Bow and stern anchors hit the water simultaneously, almost unheard in the welcoming cheers and calls from the shoreline and from the men in a dozen *batteaux*, who were already paddling out to meet the *Michigan*. Anne watched the gate in the fort's wall open and a crowd surge toward the water. Could there be so many in this Godforsaken wilderness?

"Stay here. I'll see to getting the men off and then come back for you." He was gone again, leaving her alone at the rail to watch the babbling confusion. More *batteaux* were putting out from shore. A thousand greetings and questions mingled with nearly as many commands. Aloft, the sails were being furled. To Anne's left, men were clambering over the sides and spilling into waiting *batteaux*, overseen by a stern and white-faced Patrick Campbell. Across the stretch of water, the crowd milled in excitement. Men, women, even children—and Indians, she guessed, standing quietly on the fringes. Anne raised her eyes to the fort. Beyond the wall she could detect closely packed houses, and running from the opened gate facing the river to the blank north wall, a single street bisecting several side streets. The walls of the fort were of huge logs set upright in the ground. The land around was generally cleared for upward of a half mile, and was lightly populated with barns and houses of a French nature but adapted to the wilderness. Beyond these lay the ubiquitous forest, stretching to the horizon like a giant carpet covering the immense expanse of unsettled, unsettling land.

Excited and chattering, Beth and Sabrina appeared from below decks. Somehow, in all the bustle, Henry had returned and was escorting Anne over the port rail and into a *batteau* where eager hands vied for the honor of helping the commanding officer's wife take her seat.

Ahead on the shore, a ceremony took shape. Orders were bawled at the tops of sergeants' lungs, and within a short time the ranks of new soldiers had been drawn up to join the meager garrison of regulars and rangers in a semblance of parade ground order complete with wind-whipped banners and guidons at the head of each unit. Henry stepped ashore and gave Anne his hand. As he turned to face the crowd a hush fell over the assembled company.

"Atten-shun!"

"Present—harms!" The uncoordinated slap of wood and leather crackled in the clear air.

An officer detached himself from the parade and marched stiffly toward Henry, who, flanked by Patrick and Jehu, stepped to the front, leaving Anne alone again. A ragtag band—two trumpets, five fifes, a bagpipe and a brace of drums—struck up a ragged march as Captain Hilloe Davers, second-in-command, reported formally to the Major. When Henry finally returned the salute, the command "Ground arms!" ran down the line, followed by more slaps and a solid, resounding thud as well over a hundred musket butts hit the ground in near unison.

Perhaps Henry had been right after all, Anne was forced to admit. All was not irretrievably lost where pageantry—meager though it was—existed. Silently, and with some trepidation, she watched as orders were given and the ranks, the old hands at the lead and the new company following, marched into the fort.

The military formalities complete, officers and civilians crowded around. Henry stepped back to Anne and introduced her to Karen and Gus Schraner, a middle-aged couple from Holland, and Dr. Drummond, a tall, cadaverous man with arms too long for his captain's uniform and a face, it seemed, to match. Captain Davers watched over the proceedings with steely eyes, waiting for a chance to talk with his commanding officer.

Henry waited for a lull in the conversation. "Shall we, Ladies and Gentlemen? Anne, if you don't mind, I'd like to spend a moment with Captain Davers."

"Business. Always business with you men," Karen Schraner laughed. "Come, Anne. You walk with us, no?"

Henry smiled lamely and stood aside with Jehu and his second-in-command as Karen arranged escorts for Beth and Sabrina, then led the way into the fort. "We're glad to have you, dear," she said in a thick, melodious Dutch accent. "You're much prettier than we heard."

Anne laughed. "Henry never was a flatterer."

"On the contrary. Henry quite rightly informed us you were beautiful. The other reports were sketchier."

"Other reports? But how . . ."

"You'd be surprised. Already, two trappers who saw you in New York have been through, not to mention the courier, who I admit had his information second hand. And of course the Indians."

"Indians? We saw no Indians."

"Ach! Of course not. But they saw you."

The news was faintly disturbing, but quite soon forgotten, for they were entering the great gates. A hundred openly staring eyes inspected the new arrivals. The Indians weren't as fierce as Anne had pictured them; the women with black hair and eyes

looked positively harmless, even prosaic as they stood
about with blanketed, stone-faced husbands—who
didn't look nearly as dangerous as Henry would have
her believe they could be.

Karen chattered on about holidays, feast days,
dancing, parlor games and parties, but Anne hardly
listened, so intrigued was she with the new and strange
surroundings. The buildings were tightly packed but
neat and fairly well cared for. Few had glass in the
windows, but all within view were painted. Far from
sordid or squalid, the streets were clean and free of
waste or garbage, a pleasant contrast to any other
city she'd ever known. The architecture was basically
French—after all, Fort Detroit had once been known
as Fort Pontchartrain, and had been under English
control for less than two years.

Henry detached himself from Captain Davers and
resumed his place at Anne's side as they neared his
house. His grip tightened on her arm. "Well, here we
are," he announced enthusiastically, desperately wanting her to like what she saw, but afraid she wouldn't.
"It's not Grosvenor Square, but we've done nicely
enough, I think," he added with a self-conscious
chuckle.

The commanding officer's quarters—Anne's new
home, she reminded herself—certainly weren't that.
Two stories tall and freshly painted white, it sat by
itself at the end of the street and resembled a country
cottage transported to the wilderness from dear English soil. Henry expected an answer. "It's lovely,"
she said, surprised to find anything more than a hide-
covered hovel with mud-chinked walls. A white picket
fence and struggling patch of green lawn exceeded her
greatest hopes. She looked up at Henry and smiled.

"It really is, Henry," she assured him, determined to make the best of an awkward situation. "Can we go in?"

Henry grinned in obvious relief. "Come on. We've a surprise for you."

At a gesture, the front door flew open. Inside, an accordion struck up a bright tune and they entered to find a jovial, raucous welcome, as Henry's guests rushed to greet their commander and his wife.

A dozen and more names whirled in Anne's mind, and only gradually could she connect them with the right faces. Priscilla Hampton, widowed and one of the two teachers in Detroit's tiny school was plain of face and speech. Her husband had died at the hands of a renegade Huron, leaving her alone with a daughter to support. Beatrice Hampton, twelve years old, was a chunky girl almost Beth's size. A quiet child, she listened politely to Priscilla and Anne, moving off to meet and talk with Beth only after receiving permission.

Monsieur Louis Bouvier, tinker *par excellence*, according to himself, looked for all the world like one of Molière's more acidulous characters—black eye patch and all—and was the soul of wit. Good-natured and gleefully cutting, the Frenchman lost no time in infuriating Jess and Marian McBeecher, owners of the English trading post, who mimicked each other's dour faces with sour and gloomy tales about the depredations of the Indians, a race Bouvier stoutly defended.

The most surprising introduction followed the entrance of an elegantly dressed older gentleman whose deep-red velvet coat and breeches, black-and-gold *frac* and blazing white cravat and hose contrasted wildly with the starker earth colors worn by the rest of the assemblage. "Major!" the impressive newcomer exclaimed. *"Bonjour, bonjour! Comment allez-vous?"*

"Je suis très bien, Pierre," Henry replied in stilted and awkwardly accented French. "And Madame Charbonneau, is she well?" he continued, more at home in English.

"Oui, plus ou moins bien," Monsieur Charbonneau responded. "The fever has left a week past. She works already in the garden. Too much, I think." He turned to Anne. "And this one, by her great beauty, I take to be your wife, no?"

"Vous êtes très aimable, Monsieur Charbonneau. *Très heureuse de vous connaître."*

Monsieur Charbonneau positively beamed with delight, bowed, kissed Anne's hand and showered her with elegant Gallic compliments beyond Henry's meager understanding.

The rest of the morning passed quickly. The large living room which had easily held two dozen well-wishers slowly emptied as the supply of cider diminished and everyone remembered it was still Tuesday and business was waiting. Anne stole the chance to explore the remainder of the downstairs. The formal dining room with a massive dinner table practically begged for guests. A doorway opened onto a hall leading, on the left, to the upstairs, and on the right to a comfortable and spacious kitchen where pots and utensils hung in neat rows along the walls. Sabrina had already made herself at home in a small but comfortable room back of the kitchen.

Still exploring, Anne went back through the hall and up the stairs. She had barely examined the two bedrooms, a storeroom and library office that comprised the second story when Henry found her and brought her back down to say goodbye to the last of the welcoming party. Sighing with relief, they closed the front door and turned to survey the cluttered room. Sabrina stood by the kitchen door, her face drawn and white.

"Are you all right, Sabrina?" Anne asked.

"Aye, mum," the maid answered dolefully. "But I'm not sure . . ." A helpless gesture indicated the mounds of plates, mugs and leftover food.

Henry laughed. "Don't worry. I've arranged for help. Captain Davers is sending a couple of orderlies. They'll clean up. You look as if you'd better get some rest. Did anyone show you your room?"

"Yes, sir. Mrs. Schraner showed me." She glanced apprehensively at Anne. "Do you mind, mum? I feel a little under the weather."

Anne moved quickly to embrace the strangely subdued Sabrina. "It's all the excitement. Go lie down. We shan't need you for awhile."

"Thank ye, mum," Sabrina answered gratefully. "I'll be fine in a bit."

Outside, the weather threatened. Wind moaned around the eaves and distant lightning lit the room with soft brief flashes. Henry smiled, caught both Anne and Beth around the waist. "Summer storm on Lake Saint Clair. Probably won't get this far south. I'll have to inspect the fort, but you'll be all right. I'll be back before dark."

Rain. Anne wakened to the hiss of lightning and the crash of thunder, glanced around, ready to remind Henry he'd been wrong and then remembered he'd left over three hours earlier. The house lay quiet, a warm shield against the inclement weather. Sighing, she rose from the deeply cushioned chair in which she'd fallen asleep and crossed to the window. As if waiting only for an audience, the first drops splashed down, signalling that the sky had finally wearied of its burden, abruptly became a cascade that drenched the earth below, then courteously abated long enough to allow the few stragglers caught outside to scramble for shelter. In only a matter of minutes, the tempest began again in earnest.

The dormer windows of the bedroom provided a unique vantage point from which Anne could view the whole soggy spectacle. Rue St. Louis turned from packed dirt to a quagmire. The parade ground, barely visible, became a lake beyond which the white steeple of a chapel disappeared in the rain. A growing stream passed out of sight below, heading for the river wall and the marshy ground there. Detroit. How bleak it seemed in the rain, bleak and forbidding—like the faces of the unfortunate creatures who had lined the streets to gawk and stare at their arrival. New York had been a center of civilization compared to this tiny forted town.

The first glimpse of the frontier had been more instructive than Anne had wanted or needed: women in austere homespun garments with hands as calloused as men, women whose vitality seemed dulled by the horrible, endless procession of daily toil. Anne shuddered inwardly and stilled the rising panic with a stern resolution: "Not me!" The door squealed and she jumped in alarm.

"Anne? Oh, excuse me."

"I do wish you'd knock, Elizabeth," Anne said, tension straining her voice. "You startled me. What is it?"

"Sabrina. She's really ill. Remember Captain Drummond, the physician?"

"The tall, thin man? Yes."

"He walked with me from the gate and pointed out the surgeon's quarters on the way. I thought I might ask him to come see her."

"I'd rather you waited until your uncle returns."

"He'll be awhile, he said. Besides, Jeremy is here."

"Jeremy?"

Beth turned aside, cheeks hinting scarlet tones to match her hair. "Corporal Turner. He brought the last of the trunks. Uncle Henry has assigned him here as an orderly."

"You've spent a good deal of time in this corporal's company," Anne noted disapprovingly.

"He's . . . he's very nice."

"I'm certain he is, dear, but the lad is only a corporal. Now, Ensign Price . . ."

". . . is terribly stuffy. Besides, I like Jeremy."

"Dear Beth, there is little this world cares for our likes and dislikes."

"If that is so, then little care I," Beth responded heatedly.

"That's a very silly remark."

"Sabrina is ill, Aunt Anne," the girl broke in. "Ensign Price or Jeremy Turner notwithstanding."

Anne turned to the window, ashamed at having acted so peevishly. It must be the rain, she thought, the rain and the dismal bleakness. "You'd better hurry," she whispered. "Don't catch a chill."

"Thank you," Beth called, already moving. "I'll be back soon." Hurried footsteps on the stairway, a brief interchange, the bolt slid back and the door firmly slammed testified to Beth's departure.

Anne watched the couple slog down rue St. Louis. As an exercise to occupy a troubled mind, she struggled to recall what little she'd learned concerning the town. Four parallel streets running east to west. Rue

St. Jacques and rue St. Joseph followed, lined with a mixture of shops and residences, mostly of Frenchmen who wished to live within the safety of the walls. Since the French collapse and the surrender of all Canada, English traders and merchants had moved into the territory to join the disgruntled French and Indians, both of whom thirsted for a return to French rule. Under the circumstances, a tenuous peace prevailed on the Great Lakes Frontier, to which Fort Detroit, the English Army and Henry himself were crucial.

Was it possible to bring a modicum of civilization to an outpost surrounded by aboriginals and peopled with little more than soldiers and traders? The odds were against it, and yet . . . there had been some pleasant surprises. Monsieur Charbonneau was one. How amusing! Who would have thought this wilderness the home of an elegant, proper Frenchman who expounded at length in scintillating Parisian French on the realities of the redman *vis-à-vis* most of European society's philosophical and highly idealized portraiture of the noble savage? Seen in this light, the task of civilizing Detroit seemed not so great. If Monsieur Charbonneau was any indication, others of similar inclination would be found.

She turned away from the dormer and leaned against the sill. Against the far wall a massive, handsomely carved chest-on-chest reflected glowing highlights from the dancing flames. A fourposter bed dominated one corner, stout posts supporting a simple white tester stitched with a floral design along the border. The curtained sides added a feminine touch to what otherwise would have been a completely masculine decor. Closer to hand, a cushioned stool squatted before a rococo dressing table whose legs were intricately decorated with *singeries*, bizarre, intertwining monkey-like figures sporting human vestments. How such an unusual article of furniture had come to the northern wilderness defied imagination. The French were an enterprising lot, to say the least.

Dreaming of elegant at-homes, dinners and dances, Anne turned back to the window, fantasizing the hum of conversation, the clink of glassware and the sight of richly dressed men and women filling the rooms below. Perhaps, with luck, the enhanced social atmosphere would even help relieve the so-called "powder-keg" atmosphere around Detroit.

A movement below caught Anne's eye. A solitary woman draped in a blanket against the downpour stepped quickly along rue St. Louis and paused at the gate before hurrying toward the front door and out of sight.

Anne crossed the room, roused from thought to action. Late afternoon was deepening into evening and the stairs were gloomy. Anne shivered and realized it was not the damp chill but apprehension that had coursed through her. The orderlies had long since gone. With Beth away and Sabrina asleep, she was utterly alone.

The front door opened, and to Anne's astonishment the caller admitted herself without so much as a knock or announcement. Startled by such rudeness, and a little afraid, Anne stepped into the glow of the fireplace.

The figure whirled, blanket falling away to reveal a compact form clothed in a brushed and beaded buckskin smock. Long black hair hanging straight and dripping with water framed a face too angular to be called pretty, yet peculiarly attractive. She was hardly more than a girl, but her eyes flashed with animal ferocity. She stood absolutely still, a figure carved and molded by rain and wind, shaped by the artisan hands of nature. "What you do here?" the girl asked suddenly in a brusque and strangely accented voice.

"You speak English?" Anne asked in surprise. The girl was the first native woman she had seen at close range. She recalled Henry's description of the tribes around the fort. The Ottawa, the People-Who-Trade, he had assured her, were peaceful.

"I learn much from Eng-lesh. What you do here?"

"It seems *that* question would be more appropriately proposed by me. After all, this is my house."

"No!" came the angry response. "You go now!" With a strength her slim figure belied, the Indian girl grabbed one of Anne's trunks and dragged it across the floor with the obvious intention of removing it from the house.

"Stop it!" Anne commanded. "What are you doing? You have no right . . ."

The Indian ignored her and Anne, more out of reflex than new-found bravery, sprang at the girl and shoved her aside. "How dare you! You have proven yourself an unwelcome guest. As mistress of this house, I order you to leave at once."

The girl met Anne's impelling gaze with a murderous scowl. "Major Henri . . . You are his woman?"

Anne blushed at the Indian's bluntness. "I suppose . . . one could call me that. Yes."

The strange girl stumbled back as if struck, hissed catlike and whirled, slashing the empty air with a knife that gleamed evilly in the hearth's golden glow. The black hair whipped back and the girl's face contorted. Her knuckles whitened about the knife. "You not Henri's woman. You not!"

Anne stepped back, suddenly terrified by the unexpected threat. The child actually meant to use the weapon gripped in her mahogany fist. And there was no one to help. No one! Step by step, she retreated from the menacing steel pointed at her breast, backing toward the stairs.

The Indian girl narrowed the distance, cutting off her retreat. Outside, the rain pounded a thunderous cannonade; inside there was silence as Anne shrank from the blade, unable to speak. Her throat was constricted, every breath rasping and labored as she circled the intruder and moved cautiously to the door. This couldn't be happening to her. Savages didn't stab the Langfords of this world, didn't chase them from their houses at knife-point. Outside—only yards away from this strange room, close, confining and dark—was safety. She must get outside. . . .

She whirled for the door just as a fierce gust of rain and wind pushed it open then slammed it back against the wall. A brilliant bolt of searing lightning, vibrant blue-green-white and hissing viciously, split the evening and outlined an apparition in the doorway: stern, shadowed face under a shaved head adorned with no more than a tuft of hair. An animal, naked save for a loincloth and buckskin leggings, the torso disfigured by vivid tattoos. A figure of utter, unrelenting malevolence.

Thunder roared and Anne screamed in horror. The flashing knife behind, the hulking savage before! Then there was darkness, madly spinning, and she was plunged into its vertiginous depths, no longer aware nor caring.

Impressions of light came slowly back. She fought them, longing to return to darkness and her dream, in which she was fourteen again, a virginal beauty for whom each minuet, every galliard and gavotte produced a new courtier to bow, make gallant obeisances and request the honor of the next dance. There in the center of the room, lords and ladies in regal plumage strutted and dipped. From the corner of her eye she could see Sir Spencer proudly watching over his only daughter, while from a vantage point on the stairs, the old King, framed in a thousand pinpoints of candle-light, smiled beneficently upon his subjects. It was England. Home. An illusory, ethereal dream, the construction of a homesick, frightened mind, that faded as Anne returned to consciousness, and the dark face hovering above her.

"Henry . . . ?"

"Yes. You're in bed."

"Henry, savages. They tried to . . . to . . . Oh, my God . . ."

"It's all right. You're safe. See? Here's Beth. Everything's fine."

"But that savage man, that heathen . . . the girl! She tried . . ." The memory of the glittering blade clutched her in renewed fear. "Who was she? Is she still here?"

"No. That was Catherine. I'm afraid baptism failed to tame her unruly Indian temperament. She left before I arrived. Pontiac ordered her back to their lodge."

"Pontiac?"

Henry nodded. "When his sister disappeared, he suspected she might try something and decided to pay a visit."

"But I . . ." The realization dawned. The frightful savage in the doorway! "That was Pontiac?"

"You gave him quite a start," Henry laughed. "Sabrina too, but she's asleep again. Pontiac's not accustomed to ladies screaming at the mere sight of him. On the contrary, the maidens in the villages around here usually quarrel over who will be his squaw for the night."

"He's a monstrous brute."

Beth reached over and sympathetically patted her aunt's shoulder. "I should have swooned as well, were the same thing to happen to me. But Uncle Henry says he's very friendly, Anne."

Anne looked unconvinced. It was not easy to believe that Pontiac had saved her from that murderous woman.

"Shall I go back down and see to him, Uncle Henry?" Beth asked.

"Hmmm . . ." Henry reviewed the protocol required when dealing with a chief and decided, the hell with it. How many times had Henry Gladwyn cooled his heels while waiting for Pontiac? Anne needed support and comfort. "Yes. Apologize for me and say my wife needs me for a moment. I'll go to his lodge tomorrow."

Beth nodded and left the two alone in the bedroom.

Henry leaned forward and kissed Anne's shoulder, neck, lips. When she failed to respond, he pulled back, sat on the edge of the bed. "Are you still upset?"

She scrutinized his face, searching each line and angle. "That girl . . . tried to drive me from the house. When I admitted I was, as she so crudely put it, your woman, she flew into a rage."

Henry, sensing the conversation was leading to dangerous revelations, chose his words carefully, to avoid a lie without endangering the precarious new relationship with Anne. "Catherine has more or less attended to my quarters, prepared meals and the like. Indians can be pretty possessive sometimes, and I'm afraid she'd begun to think of the house as her own. Your arrival must have come as a shock, and childlike, she responded with violence, with the fury of the dispossessed."

Anne tried to listen to what he was saying. He was

trying to soothe her, she knew, but there was a discordant note in his voice, something that triggered an alarm in her mind. His words drifted away from her without making sense. Finally he stopped and there was a charged silence between them. There was something she wanted to ask but her lips would not form the words and before she could speak, he went on, bending over her, his lips brushing hers as he whispered, ". . . our bed, Anne. Ours to share." Deft fingers untied tiny bows and the gown fell open, freeing her breasts; he bound them with his hands that cupped and pressed.

"Henry." She fought against the warm arousal, fought the titillating roughness of his hand as it brushed aside her clothes and sought love's harbor.

Then he was naked, kneeling on the bed at her side, and the question was forgotten as her hand sought and drew his throbbing shaft between her breasts, pressed and held the warm flesh. She could feel his pulse heighten as she bowed to taste the tart sweetness of love.

His lips paused at her belly then continued down to feast on the moist well of passion, his tongue a probe of fire driving out all thought, his hands gently raising her—a willing victim, now. A long, low moan followed by a sharp intake of breath, and still he lingered throughout the first sweet convulsions.

Fingers entangled in long brown locks, she pulled him to her, felt the hardness enter her easily and drive deep inside. Her legs rose to wrap about his waist and pull him deeper and deeper, her one desire the exquisite, tearing fulfillment.

In the quiet aftermath, they lay still joined, warm and wonderfully weary.

*   *   *

Beth announced herself with a nervous cough and a clatter of footsteps on the stairway. The room was nearly dark, lit by a single candle on the center table. Pontiac stood by the fireplace, staring into the glowing embers. The fire had died for lack of fuel. There was no wood stacked by the hearth. Still, the dampness of the storm had been driven away and the room was warm enough.

Her father had kept similar private vigils. She had often entered a room to find him staring thoughtfully into ashen, fading embers. She wondered what Byron would think of his daughter now that she had travelled to a new land and was making a home among the savages in an untempered wilderness. Byron Gladwyn was a man who had ever challenged life, loved untamed freedom and fought and died for it. He would have approved.

Elizabeth matched the Indian's silence, as she gauged the savage chieftain, spawned of lightning-blasted forests, child of hill and tree and countless lakes. Here was a man her father would have liked to know, would have respected instantly. Briefly, she grieved for the first time in months. How Byron Gladwyn would have loved to stand where his daughter stood! How he would have drunk in all the sights and sounds and smells and tastes!

She stared at him, understanding Anne's reaction. He was an awesome figure, the red-bronze flesh covered with geometric tattoos—diagonals, loops, swirls, blocks and lines encircling legs and arms from wrist to elbow. On his back could be seen the head of an eagle, the eyes as bright and piercing as Pontiac's. Now, as he turned, she gaped at the blazing sun adorning his chest, the stylized rays intertwining with other less recognizable symbols. Rather than disfiguring, the tattoos seemed more to complement a sense of raw, primeval power. Short almost to the point of being squat, he must have matched her uncle's weight. Next to this chieftain, other men, with the possible exception of Henry, paled in comparison.

She wondered how she must seem to him but before the thought was fully formed, he had moved without warning and with the effortlessness of a cat, given her no time to quail or step back. A strong brown hand reached out and caught a length of scarlet hair. He gave a sharp tug, eliciting a yelp of pain.

"It is good," he said in halting English tinged with French and the harsher, guttural Ottawan tongue. "Many Eng-lesh men and women have two hairs . . . only one head. Fire hair is true. Good."

"My name is Beth," she said simply, concealing her surprise.

"Beth," he repeated, and made a wry face. "What does this 'Beth' mean?"

"Mean?" The question took her off guard. "I don't know. Does a name have to mean anything?"

"I do not like Eng-lesh names. They mean nothing." Beth colored defensively, but before she could think of an adequate reply, he spoke again. "Major Henri's woman will be well?"

"Yes. You frightened her."

Pontiac laughed, a ghostly rumble in his chest. "And I frighten you, no?"

The girl bristled beneath his stare. "Certainly not," she said emphatically, turning away and stepping into the next room. "You must forgive me. I am a poor hostess. Could I make you some . . . tea?" The girl colored, realizing how silly the offer must have sounded.

The Ottawa glanced at the stairway and the shadows above. "The Major does not come down."

"Well, he . . ."

Pontiac shook his head. "Henri is alone with his woman and will not be down." Again the disconcerting laugh, tinged with secret knowledge.

Beth blushed violently and hurried to light a lantern, as much to occupy hands and mind as to dispel the encompassing darkness. The yellow glare highlighted a thick necklace of beaten silver about the warrior's throat and the bands of metal above corded biceps. In the new light his body gleamed with a sheen of oil covering smooth, hairless skin. Beth smiled weakly. The buckskin leggings left his flanks naked and the loincloth concealed little more than manhood and buttocks. So much skin was certainly improper, yet he seemed totally at ease and unaware of the impression so much bare flesh created.

"I will go now. Tell Major Henri we must talk."

"He told me to tell you . . ." Beth gulped. Her throat was dry and the words felt harsh. ". . . he will come to your lodge tomorrow." She tried to disguise her discomfort with a smile, but failed.

Pontiac paid no attention. "Good," he grunted, stalking to the door before stopping and once more staring intently. "I give you Ottawa present . . . a new name. Your hair is as the leaves that sing of summer's end. The trees become as the flames of campfires when the time comes to dry meat, gather berries and prepare warm lodges for winter. So I call you Autumn Woman. It is a better name, no?" Without waiting for an answer, he was gone.

Beth felt the tightness slowly drain from her limbs. *I wasn't really frightened,* she insisted feebly, *just . . . nervous.* But what kept bothering her, nagging insistently in some heretofore protected corner of her mind? Something long ago, undiscussed and only referred to by the haunted look in her father's eyes. Some memory jarred loose by this Pontiac. Of course! Her mother, who had died when Beth was very young. Slowly an image took shape, an image of a woman of the northern lands, fierce and untamable, in many ways as primitive as the man who had stood before her.

She saw the magnificent Pontiac in a new light, saw the inscrutable face, the eyes of obsidian, impenetrable to the weak and timorous. Beth's eyes gleamed in the lantern light. She breathed deeply and her shoulders squared. She tossed her head and set the red hair swirling. "Autumn Woman," she whispered, savoring each syllable. "I am Autumn Woman."

CHAPTER 13

Pontiac sighted along the musket barrel, ignoring the beads of sweat forming above his eyes and threatening to spoil his aim. Fifty feet ahead, Henry Gladwyn crouched motionless in the brush, buckskin attire blending into the landscape. With painstaking slowness, Henry half-stooped and squatted to retrieve a flat chip of birch bark from the forest floor. Pontiac glanced at the powder level in the firing pan of his musket and wondered whether it was enough, then cursed the distraction and signalled he was ready. With a gentle flick of the wrist, Henry sent the piece of wood skimming into a particularly dense section of foliage. The chip careened from branch, vine and thistle, hardly completing its tumbled flight before a three-point buck leaped into the clearing and spun to the left even as Pontiac squeezed the trigger. The buck turned, swiftly transforming what should have been a kill to a painful crease across the rump.

Henry searched for a clear shot through the branches, but a second deer, this time a doe frightened from cover and running in the opposite direction, sent the Englishman sprawling, the musket discharging harmlessly into the air. Pontiac rammed another lead ball down the barrel while the doe scampered off into the underbrush and away from danger.

Pontiac strode up carelessly—no sense in quiet now —grinning as the fallen hunter struggled from the ground. "Grin while you may, Pontiac," Henry grumbled, pulling back the flint and checking the Brown Bess for damage. "It was not I who missed the first shot."

The Indian shrugged, stared down the trail their quarry had taken. "The blame is in him who accepts it, Henri."

Henry loaded and primed the flintlock. "Then I suppose it is the stag's fault."

"He is not here to deny it." Pontiac motioned for his friend to follow. Henry winced, kneaded an aching back muscle, and followed.

For two days they had been out, the first time this summer there had been an opportunity for such a venture. The shorter, broader muscled chieftain and the rawboned, lean and wiry commanding officer of Fort Detroit formed an unlikely-looking pair. That Pontiac should condescend to hunt with any Englishman was the talk of both settlement and tribal village alike Pontiac was known to have pledged brotherhood to Montcalm, and in fact still looked to the French and the day they would march up the Mississippi to retake Canada. Better known was his less than flattering opinion of the English.

Henry had not won Pontiac's friendship overnight. They had met dramatically enough, on the very day the Major had arrived at Fort Detroit. A violently drunk *voyageur* had decided to confront the new commander and test his mettle at the same time Pontiac, out of curiosity, had ventured to the shore to survey the new redcoat. The *voyageur* made some disparaging remarks and the Major, amazingly enough, had halted the soldiers rushing to arrest the lout, thrown off his coat and shirt and thrashed the hulking Frenchman then and there, receiving a vicious cut on the side in the process when the drunk pulled a knife.

Pontiac had never expected such bravery from an Englishman, especially from an officer—and resolved to know the man better. Over the following weeks, to his surprise, he found Henry to be one of the exceptional few who were both fair and willing to learn, were remarkably open-minded and detested the restrictive trade policies and attitude of calculated contempt promulgated by the Crown *vis-à-vis* the tribes. In truth, Henry's attitude forced Pontiac and other calmer heads to counsel against war, arguing to those who lusted for blood that in time this Henri might open the white father's eyes and the People would enjoy a relationship with the Eng-lesh like that which they shared with their French brothers. Had not the young Major Henri shown them this could happen?

Henry squatted by the chieftain and studied the surrounding forest, the path the buck and doe had taken. He swelled with quiet, unannounced pride. A year ago he would have been totally lost, totally confused. Jehu had been right: "Change you or bury you," the ranger had ominously intoned.

Henry had changed. London, George's Court, the rolling Chilterns; all seemed more remote than ever. Would they some day seem as distant to Anne? Each man and woman had to deal alone with the frontier. His conquest of her body above the splendid spectacle of Niagara Falls had been but a partial victory. Her mind and soul remained unconvinced.

Damn, just picturing her made a man's blood feverish—how, when in her passion, her aristocratic pretenses were stripped away to reveal the sensuous, carnal, tempestuous creature within. But could the

Henry Gladwyn who thawed those wintry eyes be the
same Henry Gladwyn who prided himself on spotting
the passage of a stag through the forest? The question
was deeply troubling. Anne Gladwyn was a woman
who would find it hard to love a man who preferred
savages to kings.

"Do you see the way?" Pontiac whispered, a tutor
addressing his pupil.

Henry soberly reflected on the double meaning of
the question and the emotional morass in which he felt
helplessly entrapped. He gestured toward a grove of
cedar. "Yes . . . and no."

The parade ground was a large flat square plot com-
pacted by the tread of uncounted soldiers engaged in
martial exercise. Anne paused and looked back. A tiny
cloud of dust, the only sign of her passing, hung in the
still air. Ahead lay the chapel—Ste. Anne's, she remembered with a wry smile—a combination of frontier and French architecture, and a reminder of Lakes
Frontier's former Roman Catholic governors. Unused
under English rule, the window glass had been removed for use in homes. A crucifix made of rawhide-
bound antlers adorned the peaked roof.

Anne pouted, not a little put out by Henry's eager-
ness to take to the woods in the company of a savage
only two weeks after their arrival. They had argued
the night before he left, but to no avail. He and Pontiac
had agreed to go, and go they would. Three days, he
had said, but of that there was no certainty.

She had visited Karen Schraner on her own the day
before, after Henry's early-morning departure. Last
night she had spent gossiping with Sabrina, an occupa-
tion never before even considered. Today she was determined to find something interesting to do, and had

ended up at the chapel. Who knows, she said silently. Perhaps I'll even take to the woods this afternoon.

The doors groaned open and she stepped into the eerie twilight. A field mouse scampered across the floor and disappeared beneath a broken bench. The wooden walls, devoid of any type of carving, showed only light shadows where the stations of the cross had hung. An altar dominated the opposite end of the sanctuary, but it too lacked ornamentation. Anne moved down the aisle and stood in the center of the room listening and enjoying the quiet that lingers even in the most abandoned of churches.

The sound of the door closing behind her broke the spell cast by the ghosts of former reverence. "Anne?"

"Oh!" she blushed, turning to see Patrick. "You frightened me."

"I watched you cross the parade ground." He removed his tricorn. His powdered wig seemed dulled by the dusty sunlight filtering through the cobweb-covered, broken shutters. "A fine, private place," he continued, running a finger across the dusty back of a pew. "The Jesuit who once tended his subjects and led them to Christ's peace within these walls now foments mischief among the Ottawas to the north."

Not one to accept enforced solitude, Anne could not hide the fact that she was happy to see him. Patrick did look dashing in scarlet. If only Henry would dress as well. Her brows knotted in confusion. Always Henry, she thought. Always Henry.

"We need a private place, Anne."

"Really?" she replied, the coy smile on her lips giving no hint of the turmoil in her breast.

"Come. You play the dutiful wife well. You reek with formal courtesy whenever your husband deigns to entertain his subordinates at supper. I commend your performance."

Anne laughed uncertainly. "So you think it a performance?"

"Of course. What? Have you succeeded in fooling yourself as well? Come, I will show you the truth." Patrick pulled her to him and covered her yielding lips with his.

Anne pressed against him, matching his ardor with her own. Her arms remembered the feel of him, crept around his shoulders. She couldn't recall how long since they had been together, could only remember the sweet bliss of their union. Moaning, she gave in to the passion of the moment as his tongue entered her mouth. She had missed him; missed the touch of his fingers, the weight of his slim body pressing against hers. Only Henry had kept the past at bay. Only with him had the empty nights been filled.

And there was the answer. At least in part. The past. Anne twisted away even as Patrick tried to guide her onto a bench. "No, Patrick!"

He caught her elbows. "Come, Anne," he entreated. "Be with me. We need each other. How long will you deny what has been, and will be again, between us?"

"Please, Patrick," she pleaded, biting her lip to keep from weeping. "Let me go, please."

"Is it the church? There are no relics here. It is naught but an empty, lonely room. Yet it can be sanctified anew, mistress. As we were once."

"No."

"Why?"

"You have said it, Patrick. Can you not hear yourself? 'What has been,' 'As we were once.' Dearest Patrick," she said, her voice gentle against the growing incomprehension in his eyes. "We are far from England. The past is long ago. I cannot explain. I don't think I completely understand myself."

She searched his face but failed to find a trace of understanding, only the beginnings of puzzlement and anguish. She started past him, pausing as if caught by an unseen hand or the tightening of the heartstrings that had bound them together in the cruel fashion of love. "I can't, Patrick. Not any more." She halted, barely able to whisper. "Please don't be angry. Please?"

Slowly, Patrick's hands relaxed and dropped to his sides. Anger and pain played across his face as he stared at her. He had come so far, paid so dearly. Now she was repudiating him, casting him off. A dull roar filled his ears. "Anne . . . Anne?"

"I'm sorry, Patrick," she whispered. "I'm sorry." Unable to linger, lest her tears betray her as she had almost betrayed Henry, Anne hurried from the chapel, leaving Patrick alone, surrounded by a complicated, impenetrable stillness.

Two days out and still the game avoided them, but both men were confident. Henry and Pontiac rested in the shade of a moss-covered granite ledge and ate pemmican, hearty little cakes made from dried meat, berries, nuts and wild honey, staple fare for braves on a hunt. The chieftain removed the worn flint from his weapon, replacing it with an unused stone chip. "My eyes will have to be as those of the hawk, my hands steady as a stalking fox, my aim nothing else but true."

"And if not, we'll track them down again, I warrant," Henry confidently replied.

"No."

"Why not?"

Pontiac turned over and shook an empty powder horn. "The Eng-lesh trader McBeecher refused me powder. He offered rum instead." Pontiac spat bitterly, indicating his opinion of the trader with one gesture. "I have never taken game with rum."

Henry sighed, sharing his companion's frustration. Yet orders were orders.

"My braves, our women, they come to Detroit. The soldiers treat them like dogs, follow us to the trading store that we might be watched and guarded against. This Lieutenant Cam-*bell* is worse than the others. When something is missing he is the first to accuse. He does not like us."

Henry chuckled aloud. "He doesn't like anyone, and he thinks less of me. I'm not what he expects a commanding officer and an English gentleman to be. It's a pity so many of the new arrivals look up to him. They've not passed two full weeks here and already the settlement is dividing into factions. Some of it is Lieutenant Campbell's doing, some of it the men's. They won't be happy until Detroit is just like London. Pontiac, I'll tell you, they're a bunch of damned fools."

"And the Americans? The rangers?"

Henry shook his head. "No. Jehu's boys were born here. They'd scream like wounded cougars if they had to be sent to England."

"Jehu will stay through the winter?"

Henry shrugged, pondering the question suspiciously. Although he respected Jehu, Pontiac had few dealings with the rangers. Why should he care whether the woodsman planned to remain at the fort or not? Of course, if Jehu left, so would the whole complement. The departure would halve the cadre of experienced men and dramatically weaken Detroit's defense.

Perhaps Jehu's warnings were correct, given the question. Henry cast a sidelong glance at Pontiac. The Indian gazed into the distance, seeming unconcerned, absolutely inscrutable. "I don't know," Henry finally said, answering on the safe side. "Possibly . . . possibly not."

Pontiac grunted, chewed on a twig and stared into the forest's dark shadows. "I do not think you trust me, Major Henri. Has some evil little bird whispered bad things of Pontiac, spoken lies of your brother's friendship that you no longer trust Pontiac?"

"What I have said is the truth. As for trust . . ." Henry unplugged his powder horn and emptied half the contents into Pontiac's. If the Ottawa war chief was surprised by the gift he did not show it, only nodded, stood and silently walked off into the forest. Henry watched, torn by doubt. Half a powder flask seemed a pitiful gesture compared to the unrest and conflagration that threatened to sweep the frontier with fire and blood if Jehu's dire predictions were right. And how well did Henry Gladwyn, Englishman, know Pontiac, Indian war chief, after all? "Well enough, dammit," Henry muttered to himself. "Well enough."

The sun crept diligently toward the western ridge of trees and lay like a fiery carpet over the undisturbed surface of Lake Saint Clair. Pontiac looked out on the glowing water and found himself thinking of autumn and the girl he had called Autumn Woman. He had seen her many times now, usually from afar, but once when she had come from the shallow water behind Île aux Pêches, he had glimped the outlines of a willowy, budding body beneath her light, wet clothes. Had she been naked, curiosity would have fled and he would have walked away. Did she not know that a man grew thick with curiosity and desire to see a woman so clothed?

Ha! You are a fool, Pontiac, he thought. He had three fine squaws, others when he wished. They were more than enough for any man, without looking upon white Eng-lesh flesh. Their bodies were firm; they fashioned leggings and jackets for him, brought food when he was hungry. Yet he had been unable to put the Autumn Woman from his mind.

The sun sank to touch the tree tops and the red shifted to gold, heavy with amber. The sound of Henry's gun speaking rang along the edge of the lake, rousing Pontiac from his thoughts. He moved before the last echo faded.

"My shot took her through the heart," Henry said, looking up as the Ottawa appeared from the shadows.

The Indian knelt, inspected the doe. The shot had been true and the doe lay warm in death. The size of the animal troubled him. She was so small. In the old days the People would not have taken such a small one, would have let her live to run free and bear many fine bucks. But now, with the English loose in the land, game was scarce and they must make do with what could be found. Gently, with hidden anger, he lifted the doe's head, gazed into the still-open eyes. How sad she looked, poor little doe. He whispered the ancient words in the silken ear, thanking her for the life given that others might live. Without any other word, he quickly eviscerated the tiny corpse, saved heart and liver for their supper and, as Henry buried the smoking entrails, lifted the cooling carcass and headed for the falling sun at the edge of the water.

"It is not the first heart you have wounded, my brother," Pontiac said, laying open for cooking the torn muscle, rent where the ball had passed through.

"I hope the other of which I speak is taken not so deeply as this one."

Henry colored visibly at the chieftain's none too subtle remark. Unable to frame the proper answer, he worked soundlessly for the next few minutes until a brace of steaks was severed from the haunch and lay on a clean flat stone taken from the water. Task done and hands washed, he squatted by the tiny fire where the heart already cooked. "I have come to your village four times since my return to talk with my brother and be with his sister, share her hurt and try to explain."

Pontiac held up his hand. "Our ways are different from yours, Henri, as Flower-on-the-Water knows. An Ottawa warrior may join with a woman yet not take her to his blanket. Like the thunder storm passing over the lake, the waters mingle with earth and sky yet both know the storm cannot stay. Lake and sky are grateful for the sharing, they give and enjoy . . . and let go. Thus should it have been with Flower-on-the-Water. I told her you would bring another woman but she would not believe.

"We are men, you and I. Warriors. As you have, so have I taken other squaws and thought little of the taking. You have no blame, my brother, for if I blame you, do I not blame myself? We must all be storms at one time or other. I am only sad my sister does not understand."

"You are wise, my brother, and your wisdom touches me," Henry replied. "Still, I have great affection for Flower-on-the-Water, and would not see her grieve overly much."

The chieftain had ceased to listen, instead stared out across the lake toward the mouth of the Saint

Clair River where the fierce currents sucked the water from the magnificent expanse of Lake Huron farther to the northwest. Henry followed his companion's line of sight without noting anything out of the ordinary. Suddenly Pontiac gestured violently, grabbed what little gear was in sight and fell to the ground, motionless. Henry, too experienced to question the Indian's action, crouched in the brush and peered through the reeds. Searching in the direction indicated by Pontiac, his attention was attracted by a rapidly approaching canoe in which three figures crouched. Indians, no doubt—yet why had Pontiac made such a hasty attempt to get out of sight?

The canoe was close now. Henry had been wrong. Not three Indians, but two—and a white man. A Frenchman. Henry's knuckles whitened as he clutched the musket barrel, relaxing only slightly when he realized they had not been spotted in spite of the fire. The canoe sped past, staying far enough away to miss the faint trail of smoke. Only when it rounded a densely wooded point of land did the two emerge from hiding.

"Dumas," the Englishman hissed. "And I with an empty musket. The disreputable blackguard. And the other two . . . Potawatomis!" He stared sharply at Pontiac. "What are they doing so far south and east, and with a troublesome scoundrel like Dumas? And why did you pull me from sight?"

Pontiac shrugged noncommittally. "I know of the bad feelings between you and Dumas. I would not have bad blood between two of my friends interrupt our hunt. Besides," he chuckled, "your musket was empty, the pan powderless."

"Yours wasn't."

"And you would have killed Dumas with Pontiac's gun? All the more reason to bring you to cover."

"Is not my enemy my brother's enemy?"

Pontiac paused, considering well before replying. "Dumas could as well ask the same question, as could I. You know many of the redcoats are Pontiac's enemies, yet you are their friend. Should Pontiac then kill Henri, his enemy's friend?"

Henry, properly chastised, was forced to accept the Indian's explanation, but pressed on another point. "Those with Dumas. One was Ningas, down from Michilimackinac. Why does a Potawatomi war chief come here?"

"To hunt," the chieftain grunted. "Why are we here? And you. Talk, talk, talk. Ask me questions without answers while fresh meat spoils on the ground and wet hide rots for want of care." With that, the brave turned back to the deerhide.

Henry stared toward the islands, uncertain what to believe. Why had Pontiac hidden? Hiding was not his way. The war chief undoubtedly knew more than he was telling, Henry thought. Dumas! Dammit to hell, something was up. One day he would find out what the Frenchman was doing in English territory and take suitable action. Until then, there was nothing to be done. But before he stooped to lend a hand with the doe, the Englishman loaded and primed his musket.

Ile aux Pêches. Peach Island. A perfect name, Beth thought drowsily as she finished the hard sweet fruit. Across the blanket, Jeremy sighed, sat up with a start and rubbed his eyes. "Oof! I slept."

"Like a babe."

"Why didn't you wake me?"

"You looked peaceful. I just lay back and watched the birds and the river and the sky."

"Still, you should have . . . Oh, my God!"

"What?"

"It's almost noon. We have to get back."

Elizabeth laughed. "You're such a worrier."

"It's almost five miles, Beth. Your aunt will be upset."

"It's downstream and you are strong. We've plenty of time."

"Little do you know, mistress." Jeremy leaped up, caught Beth's hand and pulled her to her feet. "Your hands are sticky."

"Peaches. Here." Beth picked one from the basket, playfully held it up to his mouth. "Come, good sir, eat."

"No."

"Eat or I shall force you to."

Jeremy ducked, ran away. Beth followed, laughing and tripping over skirts and downed limbs but finally trapping him behind an ancient peach tree. "Now. Will you eat?"

"Not if I have to make a sticky mess of myself, no."

Beth pouted, then brightened immediately. "I have it. Come here."

"Why?"

"I shall feed you." Jeremy cautiously emerged from behind the tree, watched as Beth tore the peach in half and extracted the seed. "Open your mouth."

"I . . ." Half a peach ended a sentence hardly begun. Jeremy was forced to chew. With no more words, the two young people stood face to face in the bright noon sun until the peach was gone.

"Good?"

"Mm-hmmm."

"I told you."

"Mm-hmmm."

Beth looked down, self-consciously. "I guess . . . we'd better get ready."

"I guess. Beth?"

"I'll . . . just wash my hands now," she interrupted quickly, blushing.

"All right."

Reluctantly, Beth took a slow step backward, turned and walked to the water's edge, kneeled on a flat piece of bark and dipped her hands in the swift current. Jeremy returned to the picnic site, caught up the basket and blanket and carried them to the canoe, his mind reeling with attempts to rationalize the just-missed opportunity. S'blood! She had *wanted* him to kiss her, and he'd been too shy. Well, the next time . . . !

Still, the morning had been pleasant. A good month, for that matter. Jeremy was proud of himself—a full-fledged corporal and personal orderly to Major Gladwyn to boot. The position required frequent excursions to the commanding officer's home and as many opportunities for chance meetings with Beth. Beth! Just the name set his heart thumping like a drum. Exhilarated beyond words, he loved her with the consuming totality of first love. That he would suffer any torment rather than invite rejection by speaking his feelings only heightened the emotion.

Beth rose as he approached, a round, flat, water-smoothed stone in her hand. "Bet you can't throw it halfway across."

Jeremy grinned, quickly looked serious. "Only one. Then we must go," he said in an authoritative tone worthy of an eighteen-year-old corporal.

"If there's to be but one throw, you must make it your best, then."

"Easy enough," the lad said with great assurance. Concentrating, he cocked his arm and sent the stone skipping across the steadily flowing river, striking and bouncing once, twice . . . six times before skimming like a leaf, finally losing impetus and succumbing to the water.

"Bravo sir!" Beth applauded. "That is twice you have impressed me. First, with the ease with which you handle Mr. Hays' canoe, and now . . . skipping stones."

Jeremy blushed at the compliment, and fumbled for words. "Would that I could impress you . . . in other more . . . meaningful ways, Beth," he said, trying to sound elegant but not succeeding.

"I think you have, Jeremy," she whispered in return, leaning forward slightly and hoping. "Jeremy?"

Her eyelids drooped and she leaned forward.

Jeremy steeled himself. Now, he commanded silently. Now. Heart beating violently, he forced leaden arms around Beth's waist and pulled gently until she came into his embrace, uncertain and then quickly bolder, arms about his neck, on tiptoes and pressing against him. A battle raged inside Jeremy's breast. *My God,* he thought, she's a major's niece and I'm just a corporal! The battle lost, Jeremy's arms dropped and he stepped away in alarm, stammering an apology. "Forgive me, Elizabeth, I . . ."

"No," she whispered, looking up with a slow and lazy smile, eyes bright and shining. "No. There is nothing to forgive, Jeremy."

"I took advantage. That was wrong."

"You took only as much as I gave willingly. And I will give more. Dear Jeremy, will you kiss me again?"

Suddenly he was jubilant, grinning wildly, almost laughing. Everything was all right. His heart was full and he was weak with joy and happiness. She loved him! The knowledge washed away the agonizing tension, left him free and lightheaded. "The last one. Then we must go," he said, imitating the old Jeremy Turner of five minutes earlier.

Beth's arms wound tightly around his neck, her eyes brimmed with newfound love. "The last one? I think not, sir. You'll not get away from Elizabeth Gladwyn so easily," she purred in a husky whisper, trembling as his hands freed her breasts.

Once more their lips met. This time, Jeremy neither hesitated nor held back. Nor apologized . . .

Anne stepped into the ugly wooden clogs that would keep the mud from her shoes, lifted the hem of her apricot gown clear of the freshly churned earth at the edges of the flower garden and stepped through the gate to accept Ensign Price's arm. Two privates struggled to a semblance of lazy attention and prepared to follow their commander's lady about, ready to carry purchases or run errands as ordered. A cooling breeze gusted off the river and dipped into the fort, forcing Anne to tighten the ribbon securing the broad-brimmed straw bonnet in place against the fierce summer sun. "I think we shall start with the Schraners', Ensign, if you don't mind."

Ensign Price, caught staring at the portion of creamy flesh visible above the apron bib, blushed, realized his interest was too obvious and started forward up the street. "I am . . . uh . . . sorry, madam, that Mistress Elizabeth is not able to accompany us. I took the liberty of inquiring, but Sabrina explained she was not about."

"I'm afraid Beth accompanied Corporal Turner on an errand today. With the Major gone, the boy had a free day, and . . ." At the mention of Jeremy Turner, the ensign's face suffered a dramatic change from pleasant inquiry to dejection. Anne noted the troubled look, realized how insensitive her remarks were. "She'll be back this evening, should you wish to call," she said a little too quickly, trying to repair the damage. "I'm sure she'd be more than happy to see you. Why, just the other day . . ."

Ensign Price listened without hearing, as he guided the lady down rue St. Louis onto Main Street, the thoroughfare running from the river gate to the gateless north wall opposite. At the intersection of rue St. Anne, they stopped to watch a company of regulars, Patrick Campbell at the lead, heading for the western gate to patrol, or scout, as Jehu called it, along the river. Two dozen men, red coats bright in the sun and muskets gleaming, marched in quick step behind the Lieutenant and stopped at a brusque command.

Ensign Price straightened and saluted respectfully as the Lieutenant neared. Patrick returned the salute, bowed stiffly, touching finger to tricorn. "Good morning, Mrs. Gladwyn."

"Good morning, Lieutenant," Anne answered brightly, her heart skipping a beat.

"And how are you faring?"

"Quite well, thank you. And yourself?"

"Very well, thank you. I trust you are becoming . . . acclimated to your surroundings?"

"When I can forget them, yes." She paused, searching for small talk. "Have you thought, Lieutenant, we are in the middle of a vast forest stretching for hundreds of miles in every direction?"

"I think of it every day, madam. But one must

adjust." Silence threatened. He was intensely aware of the waiting detail, of Ensign Price at Anne's side. "Well, I suppose we'd better be on our way," he began. "As you see, I've decided to lead a patrol myself, if for no other reason than boredom. If you will allow me?"

"By all means, Lieutenant. You were kind to stop."

"Yes, of course. Ensign." The two soldiers traded salutes and once again Patrick bowed curtly to Anne. A short command later, the patrol was marching briskly away.

They started up the main street again, but Anne, preoccupied with the memory of their meeting two days before, paid little attention to the scene. Her inner vision had focused on Patrick—had penetrated his icily courteous demeanor. Behind it lay frustration and plodding bitterness. She could hardly blame him, in a sense, for in England she had been free to indulge herself. But here there was Henry, a stronger, fiercer Henry than the man who had once left her. Here was the man-stallion who sheathed his magnificent scepter deep inside her, whose heated kisses and caresses cared little for art, but carried her to the heights, not just at the last, but again and again, howling and weeping with the joyous liberation of total consummation. How different he and Patrick were. Poor Patrick. He had come all the way to Detroit for nothing.

"Brutes!"

The exclamation shattered the dream. "Sir?"

Ensign Price pointed at a knot of buckskin-clad rangers who had burst into a chorus of coarse, raucous laughter. Across the street, an unlucky pair of the King's First scurried into their barracks, out of sight of the rangers. "They laugh at us and the men and have the gall to call themselves Americans. They keep to themselves and flaunt their so-called wilderness knowledge as if the King's First were a bunch of idiot lackeys."

"Jehu's men *are* seasoned veterans," Anne pointed out gently.

"Brutes, I say. Worse than vagabonds," the ensign continued. "Subjects of the King yet lacking all but the narrowest loyalty to His Majesty. Mark my words, give them another few years and disregard shall grow to treason. As for Mr. Hays, he is downright contemptuous of us."

"Disreputable they may be," Anne countered, "but effective. Surely you exaggerate their mischief-making powers, Mr. Price."

"I think not. It would do my heart good to be allowed to hand them a severe thrashing. I'm not alone, you know. There's many a man of the King's First just waiting for the excuse. I swear, madam, they make my blood boil. If the occasion arises, I vow I'll step out of my officer's uniform and join in the fray. Look at them! Scruffy faces, vulgar manners, rag-tag clothing . . . An army? Hah! More like heathens instead of good Christians. Why the Major allows . . ." The ensign caught himself, suddenly very aware of the lady's privilege and position in the garrison as the commandant's wife. "I beg your pardon, madam. I spoke out of turn and had no wish to be insubordinate nor to o'erstep my bounds."

"The apology is accepted. I hope in the same manner in which it was given, that is with the best of grace. But perhaps another subject would be more appropriate, and our discourse might pursue some other more temperate direction."

"By all means, Mrs. Gladwyn," the ensign answered, relieved that he had not been called to task more strongly.

Anne smiled graciously, willing to let the lad think her generous, rather than admit his remarks had touched on the one lingering point of her own disaffection—Henry's reluctance to oversee Detroit's affairs in a more formal, more English way.

Rue St. Jacques throbbed with activity despite what Anne considered to be the earliness of the hour. There weren't that many people about, but the narrow street and small, crowded shops gave the impression of a great gathering. Still, what they might have lacked in numbers, the crowd more than made up for in diversity.

Indians wandered about the streets closely watched by wary English soldiers. Anne had learned the names of some of the tribes, marvelled at how many there were. Ojibwas, Menominees, Miamis, Ottawas, Hurons, Kaskaskias, all mingled in half-naked, tattooed, beaded and feathered splendor. She still couldn't tell them apart. Trappers and *voyageurs*, roughly clad in leather and canvas clothes were distinguishable to her only by the knit wool caps the *voyageurs* wore. No group of men had a reputation to match these restless French rivermen whose arms and backs supplied the brute power necessary to drive supply-laden *batteaux* through the fierce currents and manhandle supplies and boats over the impossible portages that joined the northern rivers. They were little more than savages themselves, and the tales of incredible feats and unendurable hardships they lived through never failed to impress her.

The rest of the throng was of more gentle stock. Most were farmers from the outlying areas, and most of them were French although more and more English had arrived with each spring since the fall of the French empire in Canada. Docile women disciplined squealing children wide-eyed with excitement at a visit to the fort. Bound to their holdings for most of the year by their rigorous chores, they might journey to town no more than once or twice during the summer. What winters must be like for them, in their ice-bound isolation, the newly arrived Englishwoman couldn't imagine.

Since Anne's appearance in Detroit, word had spread of a lady whose influence and family heritage were closely allied with royalty. To most of the simple farmers of the area, so bereft of recreation or activity other than work, Anne Gladwyn was someone to look at, to show their children, some of whom even now stood in the streets and gawked at the veritable queen.

Anne entered Karen Schraner's shop, sighing with relief to be free of the pressing crowd. "Good morning," she called, surprised to see the shop empty. Karen was considered the best tailoress in the settlement, and the day was rare when she could not be found at work.

"Why, Mrs. Gladwyn! A good morning to you." A heavyset, jovial-looking man of middle age emerged from a side door, ran a roughened calloused hand through close-cropped snow-white hair and wiped the beaded sweat from his brow.

"Good morning, Gus," Anne answered, always happy to see this chunky man who looked as if he'd been hewn from the same wood with which he worked. "Where's Karen?"

"Ach! She has gone to McBeecher's to pick up some silk—real silk, too, brought in yesterday. She will be right back. Come. Sit and have some tea."

"No, thank you. I should hate to interrupt your work. How are my chairs?"

"Two of them are nearly done. Come see."

She followed the Dutchman into the adjoining shop where the smell of freshly cut and planed wood and the heavy pungency of resin hung redolent in the air. Woodworking tools were arranged neatly about the walls and a number of projects in planning, in progress or completed, took up most of the corners. The center of the room was dominated by two handsomely carved wainscot chairs, high backed with broad comfortable arms, lacking only a final polishing to bring out the cherry grain and the delightful and intricate pattern carved into the backs. A confusing welter of parts for the next four of the set lay in piles on the floor. "They're beautiful, Gus."

The cabinetmaker beamed with pleasure. "I'll have the others finished in a fortnight, I think."

"That would be wonderful." The door of the dress shop opened and closed. Anne looked toward the noise.

"Karen!" Gus called.

"Ya."

"A surprise," he shouted, leading Anne next door and into Karen's shop. "Mrs. Gladwyn is here to visit."

Anne had taken a liking to the Dutch tailoress from their first meeting when they had, by mutual though unspoken agreement, become fast friends. The two women were a study in contrast—Anne lightly built and pale-skinned, Karen a buxom, sanguine woman of nearly forty, almost twice Anne's age. Anne couldn't remember knowing anyone so totally happy in all her life. The Schraners had been landed gentry in their native Holland but had fled to the New World in

1747 when William IV of Orange became Stadtholder and decided he'd be better off without a few of his more vociferous opponents around. Strangely enough, to Anne's way of thinking, there had been no weeping on either Karen or Gustav's part. What amazed her was that the couple did not mind at all the events that had so completely altered their lives; rather, they seemed to revel in the changes and treat each new turn of fate as a great adventure.

"Shame on you, Gustav Schraner! You've not brought our Anne a cup of tea. Nor a single one of those cakes I baked just last night. It is poor hospitality you have shown." The carpenter held out calloused palms in a gesture of despair, but Anne came to the rescue, explaining she had refused his earlier offer of refreshment.

"And so! How is my *liebchen* today?" Karen asked, plopping her parcels down on the counter and shooing her husband back to his woodworking shop.

"Very well," Anne responded. She picked up a corner of the luxuriant white silk, spied a roll of pink ribbon. An idea crystallized, full blown on the instant. "Elizabeth will be sixteen on the second of September. Would you have time to construct a summer gown of this material?"

Karen's strong Dutch features contorted in a frown. "I have other work promised. Ah, but I have one of her dresses to alter for Widow Hampton's daughter. I could take my measurements from that, and . . ." She paused, beaming. "Something I have to show you. Wait." Karen bustled off to the back of the shop, reappeared moments later with a fashion doll.

"Why, it's just like a gown I saw last summer in London." The doll was dressed in a light gown, complete with panier, made of *camelot* and lined with *cartek*. Off white, more of an ivory really, it mirrored exactly the fashion of the year before. "This is exquisite. Do you have more?"

Karen could only admit she hadn't. "A new one arrives every month in New York. This is the first for me." Her face brightened. "But I have made arrangements. Each time the traders come, they will bring at least one. Soon Detroit will be as fine as New York, no?"

The two women giggled at the thought and set about planning Beth's gown. The *camelot* was unavailable, of course, but silk would hang nearly as well. The *cartek* lining was unimportant: cotton would do. Gus would fashion the panier himself, keeping it large enough to be fashionable, but small enough to pass through narrow frontier doors. "Five weeks," Karen finally estimated. Which will give me a week to spare. Elizabeth will be surprised, no?"

"Yes." Anne felt positively warm. She herself would help with the lace trim. Not only would she be kept busy, but the project would be exciting.

"The dress will be splendid," Karen continued, "and we'll have a party to match." Bubbling with enthusiasm, the older woman flew into a flurry of description, hushing Anne when she tried to intercede. "No, dear. I shall see to everything—the party will be your treat, too. You'll see what a party we shall have."

Overwhelmed, Anne could only nod in reluctant approval, eyes dimming with memories long put aside. "I remember balls and parties where every room was bathed in light and alive with fine music," she began aloud. "And the clothes! How they glittered! Fine young men, beautiful girls dancing and dancing with elegance, bowing and curtsying . . ." Unable to continue, she breathed deeply through fingers tented prayerlike below eyes bright with wistful tears. "I am silly, no?"

"No!" Karen replied, her throat husky with sympathy. "Not at all." Impulsively, she embraced Anne, kissed her cheek. "Dancing, glittering gowns, gracious young men . . . These are things I have seen, too. You shall see what we can do."

"You must miss home very much," Anne said, suddenly aware Karen came from a similar background.

Karen Schraner drew back slightly, her expression serious. "But dear, this is home," she said. "Our *new* home . . . as it is yours."

Jess McBeecher, the grouchy merchant of rue St. Jacques, jabbed a thumb toward the cluster of Ottawa women streaming into the store. Thick features wrinkled in disdain around a nervously twitching nose. "It'll be an hour, by m'oath, ma'am. I dare not take me eyes off'n the likes o' these heathen. Given half the chance they'll steal the place empty as new," he said hurrying off to rescue a remnant of cloth from soiled hands.

Anne glanced around apprehensively as voices rose in anger, and cringed against the counter when a soldier roughly grabbed a woman and unceremoniously shoved her out of the shop. The other women, eyes glittering with hate, crowded around, falling back only when presented with the raised muskets of two more soldiers. The atmosphere was brittle with tension. Anne summoned Ensign Price with a gesture. "Sir, would you please be so kind as to bide here until the order for the Major's household is filled? I'll be visiting Monsieur Bouvier."

"Aye," the ensign answered noncommittally, touching his hat and bowing slightly.

McBeecher watched out of the corner of one eye, waited until she cleared the door and was well into the street. "What would a fine lady like the Major's wife be wanting with that old reprobate?" he asked, when the Indians were once again reduced to surly quiet.

Ensign Price shrugged. "What the lady does is none of my business and should be none of yours, storekeeper," he said coldly. "I believe you have an order to fill, if you would be so kind."

Louis Bouvier slammed a manicured hand down on the table and roared with unabashed vehemence. "Cheat, sir? Do you say I cheat?" He was on the shadowy side of fifty; he had never been so insulted in his life.

Dr. Amideus Drummond, his pointed chin and long nose a harsh, puritanical antithesis to Bouvier's plum-pudding face, remained unimpressed. Neither noted Anne's entrance. "I merely said my pawn was at Queen's Bishop six, where by virtue of attacking your Queen's Knight three square, enabled me to mate with Queen to my King's Bishop four."

Bouvier studied the board patiently, knowing how silence drove the doctor to the verge of madness. "Well!" he finally admitted, sucking in the word. "Indeed you are correct." Drummond smiled, opened his mouth to speak but didn't get the chance. "*Were* it placed precisely where you say," he went on. "But from where I sit, the pawn appears to be at Queen's Knight six and therefore in no position to attack the square mentioned, which means of course your Queen's move does not constitute mate. Of course, if you moved your Queen . . ."

"Touch it not, you French cutpurse, or I'll . . . Oh, good morning, Mrs. Gladwyn," Drummond exclaimed, standing quickly, the argument forgotten for the moment.

Bouvier rose, brightened also. "Ah, madame, you do me a great honor!"

"I knocked, then heard your voices. Good morning, Captain Drummond. Please don't let me interrupt. Mr. McBeecher is filling an order and I thought I'd pass the time with your books, monsieur."

"But of course. I will join you as soon as I vanquish my neophyte friend, the sawbones here. Another five minutes should suffice to . . ."

"Vanquish! Neophyte? Ha! You'll not live to see the day!"

Anne had been fooled the first time she had heard them quarrel, mistaking them for mortal foes when for all their bluster just the opposite was true. "Since you two are obviously deep in philosophical considerations," she interrupted sweetly, "perhaps neither of you would mind if I adjourned to your library, monsieur?"

"Not at all, madame. Voltaire, Rousseau, Swift, Pope —even the Bible."

"Bible! Hah! The one I gave you," the physician expostulated.

"True, sir!" Louis Bouvier bowed sarcastically, turned once more to Anne. "I admit I have had to read the Bible. Our honored friend here hasn't read anything else, so in order to discourse on even a moderate level of intelligence, I've been forced to read down to his level."

Drummond looked about to explode. "Voltaire! Swift! What would the world come to if everyone read such nonsense? They are men dedicated to the dislocation of society. Totally mad."

The Frenchman's round cheeks flushed and his wig seemed to settle awry to one side. "Mad they may be, but with the madness of genius."

"Genius, pah! Rather malcontentment. Civilization is a complicated structure, the work of ages! Your iconoclastic heroes are revolutionary asses and fools who do not understand it is good to have a place, to belong, to know what one must do to live. But enough. Not another word. I came to play chess, not to be forced to listen to infernal garble, and play chess I will."

"Not with your pawn at Queen's Bishop six."

Dr. Drummond went livid. Anne stifled a giggle. It seemed Louis had finally gotten the poor physician's goat, toppling philosophy and all with no more than a Queen's Bishop's pawn. The good doctor managed an unintelligible curse and brutalized his hat in jamming it on his head. "Good day, madam," he managed to gasp to Anne, and bolted from the room.

It took a moment to control the laughter. A giggle broke into an outright laugh, the first Anne had enjoyed, it seemed, for months. "Monsieur," she finally choked, "he is the only physician for hundreds of miles about. You should not vex him so. I fear he'll not be back. You've seen the last of your friend."

"Friend? Humph! After what he said about my books? Ten books I have in there. Ten of the best books in the world. Certainly more than anyone else for as many miles around as there are no physicians. He'll come back. They infuriate him, but he reads them. One day my wordy friends will convert him." He paused, a wry frown puckering his mouth. He pulled at the patch over his eye. "And how dull things shall be then! In any case, he'll be back. Meanwhile, would you have some sherry?"

"If I'm not keeping you from anything."

"Never, my dear," he said, leading the way to the sherry, set on a table below the lovingly cared for shelf of books. "You call tinkering with clocks and gambling, playing chess, mending pots or philosophizing or any of the thousand other little tasks which I manage to involve myself, 'work'? Consider, madame. I play. Had I to work, I should die of boredom."

He gestured to the shelf of books, his prized possession. "There are my treasures, and here below a pair of finely wrought cups won from Monsieur Charbonneau at faro." He poured from a bottle, handed one of the cups to Anne. "Enjoy, my beautiful friend. The finest nectar from Monsieur Charbonneau's larder, also won at faro." He raised his cup. "To Monsieur Charbonneau! May he continue to play. Have a seat, my dear. I hope that somber fellow McBeecher takes his time. What shall we discuss? Voltaire? He's a fine fellow for a fine morning, eh? Has a new book I haven't yet read. *Candide,* I'm told, though what it's about, my informant had not a wisp of an idea. More the mystery then, eh? And more the delight when I finally get a copy. What's the matter, madame?"

Anne shook her head, sipped at the wine. "I have read some Voltaire. Those who dislike him, do so violently. Are you sure Dr. Drummond will be back?"

Bouvier laughed, crossed to the chessboard. "Madame, I am sure. I am the only one in Detroit our poor doctor can beat at chess." With a sly wink, he returned the pawn to Queen's Bishop six, where it had been before he had managed to displace it without the doctor's knowing.

The privates set the last boxes of provisions down on the dining-room table, retreated with salutes. Ensign Price placed a tiny bundle with the larger ones, bid Anne good day and likewise retired. Sabrina bustled in, the aroma of flour and fresh peaches wafting through the kitchen door.

"Hrumph. In such a hurry they couldn't carry these into the pantry and save an old woman's strength."

"I'll help," Anne said, her mouth dry from Louis Bouvier's sherry.

"No . . . no, child. I'll take them piecemeal. I don't know where to put them all anyway. Any word of Master Henry?"

Anne pouted. "Not a single one. He's still in the company of that odoriferous savage, and little anyone can say to dissuade him. Still, he might return tonight. Three days, he said, and this is the third."

Sabrina clucked with satisfaction at locating a crock of honey among the supplies and, totally absorbed in the fabrication of a pair of pies, hurried off into the kitchen. Anne considered following, then thought better. She would just be in the way, as Sabrina had implied.

How still the room, she thought. Well, there was much to be done. But what? A strange loneliness settled over her. How useless she felt, and more than a little bit lost, unable to find a niche in the bustling life filling Detroit.

But I do not want a niche here, she thought. This life where one revels in the meagerest of comforts,

embraces the merest of amenities. No . . . If only
Henry were here . . .

And then what? The duties of command would more
than likely keep him from her side, and she would be
left lonely still. What was it Dr. Drummond had said?
It is good to know what one must do to live, to belong. It is good to have a place.

To belong . . . in a place.

And where, indeed, was Anne Gladwyn's?

CHAPTER 14

Moving soundlessly, moccasins treading lightly over bark and bough, Catherine gathered tinder for a campfire, ranging the tiny clearing to probe beneath tumbled roots and under windfalls in search of dried bark and pine needles. When the fuel was gathered, she paused to partake of the forest's abundant harvest, robbing berry vines and fruit trees and returning to the lodge with a bulging sack of blackberries in one hand and an armful of firewood bound by thin vines thrown over her shoulder. She and Henry had built the wigwam less than a year before, nestling it securely in a shadowy clearing. Whatever disturbing memories the hidden sanctuary held she had brushed from her mind, for given the choice of staying in the wild or going to the Ottawa village where she might suffer the indignity of encounter with the English Major, Catherine chose the wilderness. The bark and deerskin structure offered adequate protection against the elements and the surrounding thick forest assured privacy. The wigwam was a good place to be alone. Except she wasn't.

Stooping to feed the hungry embers of the small cooking fire, she sensed intrusion and whirled about as Teata walked into the clearing. Only Henry and Pontiac knew of this secret lodge and the very idea that

Teata should have discovered her lair was infuriating. The Huron crossed the clearing confidently, placed hands on hips and waited across the fire, expecting a warm greeting and daring to hope for much more.

"What are you doing here?" the girl blurted out in angry Ottawan before the brave could speak.

Teata, a chieftain in his own right, glowered at the aggressive tone. "A squaw does not speak this way to a chief. Not among the Hurons."

"You are not among Hurons."

Teata started to retort in kind, refrained in the name of dignity. Instead, he scowled and looked away, shedding the words like water. "Where my people live, by the great lake our French brothers call the Lake of the Hurons, many times the sky darkens swiftly and, without warning, hurls fire arrows at our Mother Earth. This the Hurons have learned to live with and accept. You are much like that country—the sky and water— all of it. Storms rise in you without warning, lash out at any who stand before you. Thus it is with the best land. Always."

"Why have you come here?"

Teata squatted, revealing a waist that had thickened since the last time Catherine had seen him. He had come to the village the previous winter to ask Pontiac's permission to take Flower-on-the-Water to the Hurons. He smiled, teeth yellow and canine-like, and Catherine glared at him. He was a powerful warrior who had assumed control over his people through sheer force. As far as Catherine could see, he had little of the intelligence that made her brother a natural leader. "I come because Pontiac is still away from his village and I thought my Ottawa brother's sister might be in need of a warrior's service."

"My brother is gone?"

Teata nodded, spat into the fire. "Four days now. With the Eng-lesh dog Gladwyn."

Catherine started at the name of the white man with whom she had shared her blanket, much to the delight of gossiping squaws and the discomfort of disgruntled warriors. "Where?" she asked.

Teata shrugged. "To hunt. Upriver. Maybe Pontiac will have good hunting—bring back Eng-lesh scalp."

"No," Catherine responded a little too quickly, then turned from Teata's stare. "How did you find my lodge?"

The Huron chuckled softly. "I followed you when last you came to the village. Your brother wishes our tribes be joined, that I take you to the lodges of my people."

"But that is not my wish."

Teata frowned with displeasure. "Your brother speaks plainly. The white French priest taught you evil ways which your tongue mirrors as lake water mirrors the insolence of clouds. Pontiac is your chief, woman. I am here to take you."

Catherine tensed in alarm, backing away from the warrior. "My . . . my brother . . . told you . . . to do this?"

"You will go with me," he said again, rising and stepping over the fire to grab her arm.

"No!" Flower-on-the-Water struggled in vain to free herself from the Huron's grasp. In response, Teata gripped her hair, forced her head back and half-carried, half-dragged her into the lodge and threw her on the pile of blankets in the corner. Catherine lay quietly, not struggling, not crying, eyes betraying such furious hate for the Huron warrior that Teata was forced to look away.

"Listen well, Huron. To satisfy yourself you will have to kill me. If you do not, the tale I will tell my brother will so outrage him, that were you a hundred warriors and as many days' travel from this place, he would find and kill you and cast your heart and liver to the dogs to fight over in the dust. Hear my words, mighty warrior, for they are true."

There was no way to tell if the warning would stop him, but that it would have some effect was certain. Teata had proven himself a resourceful warrior, but he was no match for Pontiac. The Ottawan's exploits in battle were legendary. "Well, O mighty conqueror of women? You have invaded my lodge against my will. Now what will you do?"

Silence.

"Do I not please you?" Catherine mocked. The silence continued, broken only once by the sudden rush of wind through the briefly opened, quickly closed entrance flap as Teata stalked away.

When she was sure he had gone, Catherine rose, dusted jade slivers of grass from her smock. Tomorrow she would go to the village and wait for her brother's return. That she might catch a glimpse of Henri Gladwyn mattered not in the least—or so she repeated over and over again, unconvinced.

The anguished groan of a wheel disturbed the morning's quiet and brought Anne from bed to stare through the narrow window down on an ox-drawn vehicle whose sorrowful squeal had vanquished the last vestige of a dream. The sky, dotted helter-skelter with glimmering, fleecy clouds, brightened over the jagged edge of tree tops delineating the distant hills. She yawned, wondered if recapturing the dream was worth the effort and decided not: the empty bed

looked unappealing. Five days—this was the fifth—and
still he was gone. Could there have been an accident?
Did Henry lie hurt and in need of aid? Or did he simply prefer the company of a savage?

Moving from the window she shrugged off her sleeping gown, bathed with a spongy clump of fragilely
scented moss given her by Karen Schraner and dressed
in a simple cotton gown decorated only with circlets
of plain lace around wrists and throat. Restless and
without direction in mind, she drank a cup of tea in
the kitchen and quietly left the house, cutting over to
rue Ste. Anne and heading for the east gate. The
sleepy youth on duty at the entranceway fumbled to
alertness as the commanding officer's wife approached.
"Good morning, Mrs. Gladwyn."

"Good morning, Private. Would you be so kind as to
open the gate, please."

"Ma'am?"

"Please open the gate."

"Well, ma'am, I ain't supposed to . . ."

"What's your name, Private?"

"Uh, Rexrode, ma'am. Doody Rexrode, American
Rangers."

"Very well, Mr. Rexrode. As a favor, would you open
the gate, please?"

"You mean so you can go out by yerself?"

"Yes."

"But the mist ain't even off'n the river yet."

"Is there anything particular about which I should
be alarmed, Mr. Rexrode?"

The youth caved in before her probing smile. He'd
never been this close to a real lady, not one come all
the way from England, and especially not one so
pretty that just being near made him feel bumbling
and awkward—not to mention the fact that she was the

Major's wife. "No ma'am. Nothin' I s'pect to be troubled over. Seems like you oughta have an escort, is all."

"I assure you I'll be perfectly safe, Mr. Rexrode. Now if you don't mind . . ."

The ranger lifted the bar and opened the access door, allowing Anne just enough room to pass. "Ma'am, you're supposed to tell me where you're bound. Major's orders for anyone leavin' the fort, an' I cain't disobey."

Anne paused, stared blankly at the forested shore. Where . . . ? "If anyone asks, I will be visiting the Charbonneau farm."

"Yes'm," the youth answered, swinging the gate shut.

The bar slid into place behind her with an ominous, final sound. Still, Anne had resolved not to pass another hopelessly aimless day within the walls waiting for Henry's return. She started down the path that wound across the cleared ground leading to the farmlands and comfortable cottages of the French farmers, stopping to watch when a great white bird, long and graceful, flopped through the air from the river and landed on one of the pines bordering the forest to the north. Intrigued, Anne veered away from the path, sighing in disappointment when the ungainly bird rose into the air and disappeared. Alone, she stood at the edge of the treeline, then took a tentative step into the shadows. The air was fresh, tingling cool, inviting further exploration. She hesitated, deciding her fears were foolish. Nothing would happen. Besides, it was much too early to go calling. Bolstering her courage she entered the dark mystery of virgin timberland.

Slatted beams of sunlight slanted through the leafy canopy above. The ground was freckled with broken light, leaves, pine cones, bits of bark and acorns, the scattered treasure of squirrels. A dozen species of birds, sweet-throated and multi-colored, sang from the cool jade shadows. Wild roses nodded fragrant pink cups. A puddle of silvered water caught in a leaf sprayed a shower of molten light on the wings of a butterfly. Her footsteps were muffled on a carpet of matted brown pine needles. Soon the settlement, the river, were lost from sight. Anne subdued a shiver of apprehension and, scolding herself as she might a child, set off deeper into the forest. The air was pungent with the smell of rotting leaves and the fragrance of wildflower and pine pitch. Massive granite outcroppings rose from the soil, formed ledges, overhangs and crevices. Austere gray surfaces splashed with startling bursts of red, orange, green and gold where moss and lichen strove against reluctant stone, cracked open the ancient rocks, forcing crumbled footholds where seeds of birch or aspen might germinate, take hold and further reave the granite shelf with probing roots. It was like some wondrous garden, she thought, then corrected herself. No garden was ever like this. This was beauty untouched, almost contemptuous of human efforts to shape and mold and impose symmetry or form. So close to the fort, Anne felt as if this primeval world had swallowed her, borne her away from the world of men. Her dress caught on a bramble bush, and stooping to extricate herself, she spied a cluster of dark purple berries. Curious, she plucked one, tentatively nibbled, then plopped the many-globed fruit into her mouth and yanked several more from among the brambles, her face registering delight with the discovery of the rich, sweet-tart taste. Finally satiated, she pressed to explore further.

As if sensing intrusion and wishing to protect itself, the foliage and brush thickened and, against her will, forced her onto a narrow trail which led to a clearing dominated by a stick and mud-dammed creek. Felled birches and aspens littered the ground around the water and Anne searched for the beavers Jehu had told her of, the fat, flat-tailed creatures who dammed creeks and built their homes in the middle of the ponds. Sure enough, a pile of twigs and branches rose from the flat blue sheet of water. As she watched, a dark triangular patch of shadow bobbed to the surface, rising further out of the water as it reached the pile of sticks and clambered on to the top of the domed lair. "Busy as a beaver," the settlers said. The beast adjusted a few branches, turned at the snap of a twig and dove instantly into the water, signalling alarm with a resounding slap of its tail. Another beaver, larger than the first, scurried rapidly from behind one of the fallen aspens and forsaking dinner, beat a hasty retreat to the water. As suddenly as she had entered the tiny glade, the animals had disappeared.

Anne lay back on the cushiony ground, closed her eyes and listened to the gurgling stream song, the bright melodies of lark, thrush, robin and dove caught in harmony with the soft drone of the wind among the boughs. Here, where snow and beavers had cleared the trees, the sun sloped into the circular glade, dappled with diamonds the pristine pond, turned to God's golden nectar the dew that sparkled from leaf and branch. Suddenly, a rustle of brush to her left turned rapture to unsettling concern. Edging over slightly, Anne peered above the irregular tree trunks. A fawn nervously neared the water's edge, frail hooves poking the mud and brown-spotted coat trembling as the babe muzzled the water and drank its fill, punctuating every few swallows with a cautious uplifting of its tiny head. Anne sighed with relief, happily returned to her own examination of the fairy-land glade.

The songs of water and forest, the gently bobbing motion of lily pads boasting tremulous butter-gold blossoms, the whirring crescendo of darting bees conspired to lull her, still the hurried passage of time and aggregation of worries, until she lay perfectly still, as placid as the pond, and drifted into sleep.

The heat on her face woke her. The sun had passed above the pointed crests of birch and red pine to illuminate the glade with radiant fire. How long had she slept? Remembering Henry's painstaking lesson, she gauged its position and guessed it to be late morning, then looked around her wondering if the fawn had kept her company. She peeked above the fallen tree and caught her breath.

The fawn was nowhere to be seen. Catherine stood where the deer had trembled and drunk. Had the fawn been a mystical illusion, or was it the girl who was the phantom conjured out of the land's eternal mystery? No, the Ottawa girl was real, and was watching Anne, watching and waiting. With no other alternative, Anne rose, keeping her face as composed as she could and flattening the wrinkles from her skirts as she stepped to the water and moistened a silk kerchief to freshen her neck and face. This time no one was there to intercede, to step between knife and soft flesh.

Anne trembled inwardly, marvelling at the ill-considered audacity which had led her to wander from the safety of Detroit's palisades as if the forest were nothing more than the King's garden. Where a few hours ago had been Eden, now lurked a furtive stillness. The gentle breeze had become a menacing whisper, the noble grandeur of towering pines a leering barrier impeding flight. She dabbed at her face with the cool cloth, considering which way to run.

Catherine advanced slowly, savoring the English-woman's rising panic. Anne backed away and slipped in the mud, soiling her slippers and the hem of the dainty dress that had been designed for parlors and not forests. The Indian laughed outright.

Laughing at me, Anne thought. Laughing at . . . me! Her anger overwhelmed the panic and she struck a rigid pose, eyes matching the Indian's elemental fire —fear and apprehension at bay.

Catherine, curious at the sudden change, sat on a fallen tree trunk. "You are not afraid, Eng-lesh woman?"

"Certainly not." Anne ventured a step nearer to demonstrate her confidence.

"Before, you frightened plenty."

"That was before."

"And now?"

"If you wished me harm, you would have struck while I slept and was at your mercy."

Intrigued, Catherine paused to consider the answer and the woman who had given it. Somehow, the white woman had changed. Instead of fleeing, she displayed the demeanor and bearing befitting the daughter of a great chief. "I think maybe you go. You do not like it here, I can tell. Why you do not go?"

"Perhaps I will before too much longer. Major Glad-wyn and I together."

Catherine shot to her feet. "No! Henri will not go with you. Never."

Her concern for Henry aroused Anne's own suspicions anew. "And why will he not?"

"You do not belong here." Catherine spun about,

long black hair flicking whiplike in the sun. The girl stared across the pond, then back at the English-woman. "You do not understand our ways."

"I am not Ottawa, but I hardly see what that has to do with anything."

Catherine laughed harshly. "I do not speak of Ottawa." Her arm swept the surrounding woods, alive with echoes, unseen movement and unquenchable, teeming life. The gesture was of one who knows every crevice and corner of an old habitation. "You do not understand the land. Henri does. His place is here in the land he loves."

"With you?" Anne asked calmly, not knowing why she should, yet unable to resist in spite of a sinking feeling that the answer was obvious.

"Yes," Catherine replied firmly. "I have shared my blanket with the Major Henri. We built a lodge to-gether. Henri understands, listens and has heard the Great Spirit. I too have listened. The Great Spirit's breath has moved the trees and called our name with the east wind. I am Major Henri's woman. It is so. Now you will leave."

Anne reeled. How foolishly blind not to have seen the obvious. But Henry with . . . with . . . Was it so inconceivable after all? Other white men had lain with savages. Why not Henry? But still . . . ! How could he? The answer was ridiculously simple, stood no more than five paces in front of her. That hair, trim figure, small but firm breasts pushing against the soft deer-skin smock, those tanned and strong legs. My God, she thought, stunned and confused.

"You will leave now!"

The words reverberated through the pristine setting as if Catherine had shouted at the top of her lungs, when in fact she had merely whispered.

Expecting Anne to crumble and flee, the Ottawa maid was surprised when the Englishwoman whirled and answered with a certainty belying doubt or fear. "Not yet," she declared emphatically. "Not yet."

Pontiac left him a mile upstream when he stepped over the side of the canoe and vanished into the forest. Henry paddled downstream and skillfully guided the canoe across the tricky current to pull ashore at the river gate landing. He had stayed away longer than planned, he thought guiltily. Anne would no doubt be furious. Davers would be anxious.

The gate sentry snapped to attention and saluted sharply. Henry returned the salute and cast a practiced eye over the interior of the fort. Everything looked in order. Nothing seemed to be amiss. Perhaps a short stop at the house wouldn't be a bad idea. He frowned. Anne would want an explanation of why he'd been gone so long, and would get upset all over again when he had to leave for the office to get Davers' report. No. Everything considered, it would be better to get checked in and business out of the way. Duty first. He'd surprise Anne at supper. And then pleasure: he'd have a full night to make amends for the five-day absence.

The sleepy office came to life with the commanding officer's entrance. Davers had everything under control. The Indians had been quiet. There'd been a brief fight between one of the rangers and a pair of the regulars, but other than that, nothing of note had happened.

Henry Gladwyn rubbed weary eyes and listened to the remainder of the report, then Davers' request to depart for Niagara as speedily as possible. Henry's quill poised over the Captain's orders. "You must be in a hurry, Captain. I had thought you might reconsider during my absence."

"No, Major. I'll be pleased to see the last of the wilderness. I'm glad I was sent here but I'll be happier to return. I try not to think of my family in Coventry, for they are an ocean away and many a day's journey ere I see even the welcome chimneys of New York. Yes, I am impatient, sir."

Henry sighed, dashed pen across paper. "I am sorry to lose a capable officer, Captain."

"You have Lieutenant Campbell, sir. He seems to be coming along well. Better than many I've seen."

"Yes. I suppose so."

"He's in the outer office waiting to speak with you. Shall I tell him to come in?"

Henry nodded, reluctant to face the abrupt and trying personage of Patrick Campbell before a bath and a night's sleep, yet knowing as well there was no sense in delaying. He acknowledged the Captain's salute. "Yes. Please do. Oh, by the way. There's a party of eight heading for Niagara before long. There'll be room for one more unless you want to wait for the *Michigan.*"

"That's not necessary, Major. Captain Smalley says he'll need another three weeks before she's shipshape, and I can be in New York by then."

"Very well. You'll be in good hands. A man named Menelaus Buell will be leading the party. Bunch of traders from Michilimackinac. Should be tying up now, and they'll be ready to leave in the morning."

The Captain relaxed. "Thank you, sir."

"Captain?"

"Yes, Major."

"I neglected to express how sorry I was to hear of

your father's untimely death. I expect you'll be assuming the welfare of the entire family?"

"Yes, sir. But it's a task I'll enjoy. There's the chance of a seat in Parliament, which is something to look forward to, too. Thank you for your sympathy, Major. I'll stop by before I leave, if you have letters."

"Thank you." The door closed and Henry returned to the dispatch at hand, the latest in a long series of letters to Amherst attempting to explain his opinion of English policy toward the Indians and French. Damn, he thought. There must be some way to open the General's eyes. The five days with Pontiac had been a long lesson in just how far the situation had deteriorated and how perilous their position was. Policy *had* to change or Pontiac would be forced to send out the red-and-black belts of war.

The door opened again and Patrick Campbell entered, saluting crisply. Henry sighed and put aside the dispatch, braced for the worst. "Yes, Lieutenant?"

"Major Gladwyn. Is it not true I was supposed to be second-in-command here in Detroit?" Patrick asked without greeting or preamble.

"Originally, yes."

"Then I request to know why I was not placed in charge during your absence."

"I can appreciate enthusiasm and desire to exercise ability and rank, Lieutenant, but that does not excuse your peremptory manner or your tone of voice."

"I have a right to know, sir. The men laugh behind my back because I wasn't even told you had left, much less that Captain Davers was to remain here and in command."

"It just so happens Captain Davers . . ."

". . . was scheduled to leave this Godforsaken wilderness prior to your hunting excursion with that savage."

"Lieutenant, you interrupted me."

"You requested Davers to stay in lieu of relinquishing command to me!"

"Damn, but you vex me, Mr. Campbell!" Henry shouted, slamming his fist down on the desk.

Patrick, somewhat taken aback, replied half-heartedly. "I have the right to command, sir."

"You have no rights whatsoever except those dictated by the duty your uniform requires."

"I wish I could say the same for the Major," Patrick countered, casting a brazen glance at Gladwyn's attire. Henry's face colored beneath his bronzed complexion.

"Do not try me too far, Lieutenant. Very well. I will tell you why I asked the Captain to stay until I returned. You, Mister Campbell, are green as new-cut wood. A tenderfoot, a pilgrim, as Jehu and the other old-timers would say. You need seasoning, Lieutenant. You're not ready for command. When I feel you're experienced enough, I shall be all too glad to place you in command of the most important link of His Majesty's defense and foothold on the Lakes Frontier. Until that time, I suggest you hold your peace and learn as much as possible from those who do know."

"I'm sorry to disagree, sir, but I feel I am ready for command."

Henry stared closely at the young Lieutenant who stood at rigid attention. Slowly, he leaned back in the camp chair, tossed quill to desk and considered a single idea that might solve a multitude of problems. "Very well, Lieutenant," he said suddenly, the decision made. "Perhaps you are ready for command, so command you shall. Today is the twenty-third of July.

After outfitting yourself properly and acquainting Ensign Price of your duties here, you will take five men of the King's First—I'll make sure you've a scout to help you find the way—and relieve Ensign Mallory at Michilimackinac."

"Michilimackinac!" Patrick exclaimed, paling. With a total garrison of thirty-five men, the fort was little more than an outpost; a duty there tantamount to being buried alive.

"You heard me."

"But . . . but I was posted to Fort Detroit."

"And under my authority. You yearn for command so I place you in command. Where I think you'll do the most good—or the least harm. The sergeant there is a man named Fulton. I suggest you watch closely and listen carefully to what he has to say. He's a good man and knows his business better than most officers. I'll have orders written out by tomorrow and you will depart the day after, weather permitting."

The door flew open and Jehu barged into the room, cutting off Patrick's protest. The ranger cast a sideways glance at the Lieutenant and doffed his cap in deference to Henry. "Sorry, Major. Didn't give the corporal a chance to tell me you was busy. Heard somethin' I figure you ought to know."

"That's all right, Jehu. We were done here."

"Seems Mrs. Gladwyn took it in her head to take a stroll," Jehu hurried on. "She's been gone since nine or ten this mornin'."

Henry rose from his seat. "Alone?"

"Appears so. The young'un who let her pass says she went out alone."

"My God," blurted Patrick. "I'll form a detachment. We'll . . ."

"You'll do nothing of the sort," Henry interrupted.

He turned to Jehu. "Which way did she go?" he asked, masking his apprehension.

"West."

"Anything going on out of the ordinary?"

"Not that anyone knows."

Henry paced the room, considering the best course of action. West. A few farms. Not much else. The main Indian encampment was to the east. The best thing to do was to remain calm. If Anne was lost, she was probably wandering around in circles and was closer than she thought. "Very well, Mr. Hays. Find her and see she's safe. Tell Corporal Hanks you'll send up some smoke if you need help. Make sure he assigns a man to watch for it."

"Yes sir," the ranger said, hurrying from the room without wasting any more time.

"Major. One man! You should have every available man out looking for her."

"And they'd be cluttering up the trail, getting in each other's way. No. Believe me, Mr. Campbell, this way is best."

"I protest, sir. Anne's . . . that is, Mrs. Gladwyn's life is at stake! Sending one man to find her is criminal negligence of the . . ."

"That will be all, Mister Campbell." "Anne," he had said, quickly amending it to "Mrs. Gladwyn." Henry refused to give credence to a growing suspicion. After all, Anne and Campbell had been shipmates, knew each other well enough. But there were more important things to worry about. "You are dismissed, Lieutenant."

The two men stared at each other for a long moment. Patrick stood poised on the balls of his feet, wanting but not daring to continue the argument. Suddenly he remembered his last two meetings with Anne. The sour realization that he had lost her before she had wandered into the forest cut through his anger and he relaxed. If anything had happened to her, the loss was her husband's, now. There was nothing more he could do. "Sir. About Michilimackinac."

"You have your orders, Lieutenant. I suggest you obey them. Immediately."

Patrick's mouth opened, then clamped shut. "Yes, sir!" he said, sarcastically accenting the final word. With a stiff salute, he whirled and stalked from the room, slamming the door behind him.

Henry stared at the closed door for a moment, sighed and picked up the quill and got back to work. "And maybe you will learn, lad. Just maybe . . . in time." Five minutes later, work forgotten, he was standing at the west gate, anxiously waiting for word that Anne was safe.

"A marvelous roast, Sabrina."

"Thank you, Mister Gladwyn." Sabrina placed a shallow clay dish on the table and Henry sniffed the brown crusty covering, inhaling the sweet aroma of fresh peaches.

"I picked them myself," Beth offered. "Well, Jeremy and I." She searched her uncle's face for some adverse reaction to the news. His expression failed to alter. "Sabrina showed me how to bake it."

"A peach cobbler, then, is it? You shall spoil me. Had I known this waited, I would have paddled all night and chanced the snags and rapids."

"It's nice to know something would have parted you from that heathen's company," Anne snapped. "Or from your office."

"Anne," Henry tried to explain for what seemed the tenth time since Jehu had brought her back that afternoon. "If I had gone looking for you instead of Jehu, we might both be still out there lumbering around in the woods."

She did not see the humor in that. Henry looked to Sabrina and Beth for support, but both women were occupied with their plates.

"To be found by that vulgar person you call a friend! He frightened me nearly out of my wits. And then had the nerve to lecture me about venturing out alone because there were probably a hundred young Ottawan bucks who would give their eye teeth to . . . well . . ." She looked at Beth and rephrased the thought. ". . . to force their favors on me."

Henry's mask of sympathy crumbled. "Force their favors? I've never heard it put quite like that out here. In any case, not on *my* wife. They wouldn't dare."

Sabrina turned away. Beth stifled a snicker.

"Oh!" exclaimed Anne in disgust and anger. Slapping down her wineglass, she quit the table and stormed up the stairs without so much as a fare-thee-well.

Henry stoically bore the uncomfortable silence following Anne's departure, finally shattering it with a rueful chuckle. "Elizabeth, your uncle is not the most tactful of men."

"Neither was Father, but I loved him anyway."

Henry smiled appreciatively and ladled some of the cobbler on his plate. "I trust you'll forgive me if I don't eat the whole thing. The rest will keep, won't it?"

"Anne was terribly worried, Uncle Henry. I think we all were when you failed to return on time."

Henry paused, seemed about to say something by way of explanation, then thought the better of it and turned back to the pie, blowing away the steam before tasting it, lest he burn his tongue.

* * *

Anne snuggled into the warm, soapy depths of the bath, and scolded herself for her brief outburst. Still ... "Peach cobbler, by my oath!" she muttered, allowing herself an unyielding pout that refused to be erased by Henry's entrance.

The fire lit earlier to heat the water made the room almost intolerably close in spite of the open window. Henry unlaced his shirt as he approached, knelt by the metallic tub. Anne's hair was piled high atop her head, one curl defying all restraint and coiling on her forehead. His hand turned her face to him. "The forest is seldom a punctual place, Anne. I'm sorry if you were upset. I was worried when I learned you had left hours earlier, and alone."

"Not enough to come looking for me."

"Jehu is ten times the tracker I am. I knew he'd find you. And bring you safe back to me."

Anne gasped as sunburned arms dipped into the tub and hoisted her from the water. "Sir!" Her arms were already circling his neck, when she realized honor demanded a protest and frantically began to pummel his soaked shoulders and chest.

Henry laughed, dropped her, naked and dripping, onto the bed. Anne made to roll away but fell into a cunningly contrived trap of cupped hands and an encircling arm, the enticement of lips tormenting neck and breasts.

She was struggling still, when the battle turned. Suddenly she was at his soaked shirt, running tapered fingers over his chest. She waited breathless as Henry kicked free of moccasins and breeches. The frustrations of the past week and the revelations of Henry's affair with Catherine were forgotten as flesh met burning flesh and entwined on the drenched covers. The smoldering troubles with Indians and French were forgotten with the touch of thigh and breasts. Only the bed existed now, only male and female, only the man above and the woman below, both demanding, both capitulating to love's demands with passion-driven thrusts carrying them to the shuddering climax where body and soul melded and became one.

A faint line of crimson indicated where Anne's teeth had pinched flesh at the height of release. She touched the wounded shoulder with her fingertips, wondering if he had felt pain. A muscular arm draped across her waist, imprisoning her. But she did not want to move. The candle on the table sputtered, sent shadows flickering. The room flared, then fell into darkness, which in turn retreated before pale moonlight suffused by the curtains. Twice he had emptied the feverish wine of passion, each time carrying her to muscle-wracking consummation, leaving her lax and languid, delightfully exhausted yet strangely refreshed.

Henry had drifted into sleep, but Anne remained awake, drowsy, comfortable, in a half-dreaming state into which the nagging memory of the confrontation with Catherine intruded. She read the lines of his face —jaw, lips, nose, eyes and noble brow at rest, composed —and tried to imagine Henry with the Indian girl, cursed herself for doing so. The Indian child could never give him what I can, she thought, drowsily recalling the contortions of their passion. A man like this needs a woman. He was alone a year. Certainly, I can't blame him for being a man.

Henry stirred, rolled over, exposing the stark outline of shoulder, waist and hip. On his side the jagged scar furrowing the smooth flesh was a reminder of the harsh existence to which he had subjected himself. To forget the horrible months in London when she'd been

such a shrew? Possibly. The scar hadn't been there
then. But what other unseen scars did he bear? How
else had he changed? In many ways he was more a
stranger to her now than on the day she had married
him. Could she ever truly win him from this primitive
world and the elemental passions that governed it?
Instead, an unsettling premonition that she would
never see London again, never return to the grace and
comfort of that life, swelled to fill the darkly shadowed
corners of the room with a blackness that seemed to
close in on her. She moved closer to Henry, taking
comfort in his warmth, his slow, even breathing. But it
was almost dawn before she fell asleep.

Morning. Sabrina had left an hour earlier, with Beth
disappearing moments later. The house was empty and
silent for the first time since Henry's return the day
before. Anne sat in the front room sipping a cup of
tea and enjoying the quiet when a knock came at
the door. Sighing at the interruption, she rose and put
aside the tea, headed for the door to find Patrick waiting outside, hat in hand. "Patrick! Whatever . . ."

"May I come in?" Anne paused indecisively. "There
is no one watching, if that's what you're worried
about."

The smile on Anne's face froze in a hard line. "Sir,
your rudeness could best be displayed elsewhere."

Patrick slapped the door, preventing its closing.
"Come, Anne, have you not even a fond farewell for
me?"

"Farewell?" she asked, not understanding but stepping away from the door. Patrick entered, took in the
empty room at a glance. Before she could speak again
he caught her in an embrace, forcing a kiss on unwilling lips.

Anne did not resist, rather remained passionless, tasting with curious dispassion the faint familiar urgings, memories of a lost love she now knew they would never recapture. Sensing her mood, Patrick faltered and stepped away, angry at what appeared to be disdain. "Aye, farewell—as well you know." Anne raised hand to mouth in a gesture of bewilderment. "What? Confused? How so, madam? Your plan worked. Tell me how you put the scheme afoot. A wayward suggestion over tea? A cooing favor asked of a cuckold as you lay in bed?"

"Kindly refrain from raising your voice, Patrick, until you've told me what you're talking about."

"Why? The withered maid holds forth among those louts who call themselves rangers. The errant niece keeps company with an upstart corporal and the equally scandalous Bouvier. Your husband, as usual, is hard at work dictating the fate of the garrison. We are alone. Are you afraid to be alone with me, Anne? Why? Now that you've seen to my banishment . . ."

"Stop it! I don't know what you're talking about."

"Yesterday Major Gladwyn saw fit to appoint me commander of Fort Michilimackinac."

"And where is that, pray tell?"

"Ah! Just my point. North and west—far from here, where you'll have little to fear from me. I must admit the idea was brilliant, Anne. After all those hours wondering when I'd let slip an impertinent remark or otherwise embarrass you . . . But to go to such an extreme!"

"Patrick, whether you believe me or not, I had nothing to do with this. I swear to you, I didn't know."

"Ha! How the truth is transformed when shaped by such beautiful, treacherous lips. I wish I could believe you, mistress." Mocking graciousness, he bowed deeply, a tight-lipped smile lined below virulent eyes. "Know one thing, Anne. I loved you sincerely, and though you have spurned me openly and arranged for my exile, I love you still." Pausing to regain control, he continued in an ominous whisper. "I shall persist despite you or your husband's efforts. I will not abide this . . . this . . . burial, but like Lazarus shall rise from the dead and return—and on that day have Henry Gladwyn at sword's point. And how will you plead then . . . mistress?"

The door slammed and Anne was left alone. Patrick Campbell was gone—for a while.

CHAPTER 15

England had never seemed so far away. Captain Hilloe
Davers had tried to make the best of a bad time by
reminding himself that he was leaving the wilderness
for good. Four days out of Fort Detroit and becalmed
for a day and a half, the disgruntled conglomeration of
traders, trappers and a single English soldier leaned
into the task of rowing the nearly two hundred miles
across Lake Erie to Niagara. Forsaken by wind, they
prayed, cursed or bore their troubles in grudging silence. Half-ruined hands, strained muscles and backs
soured the disposition of the entire party. They had
expected to extend a meager larder by adding a deer
or two to the supply of salt pork and biscuits, on
which they'd made an unpalatable morning meal, but
the hunting had been poor, the men returning empty-
handed. For some time a trio of fishing lines had
trailed the *batteau,* but neither bass nor trout would
have anything to do with the strips of bacon bobbing
through the water, too slow for a living animal, too
fast for a dead one. After a full day of rowing, they
could look forward to little more than finding a likely
spot along the shore, making a fire, gulping down more
salt pork and bread and wearily bedding down to
spend a restless night hoping morning would bring a
breeze.

Usually good-natured, the Captain found himself grumbling and short-tempered. "Will there never be a wind?" he complained. "Shall I be forced to row my way home, to the very mouth of the Thames?"

"The ocean will be a bit of a go, Gen'ral," a trader named Rubin Crane interjected.

"I am not a general, Mr. Crane. Captain Davers will do just fine."

"Your pardon, Captain. Anyway, best you set your sights on winterin' in New York."

"God! Why?" Davers asked, falling for the bait like a tenderfoot.

"Well, can't never tell what ship'll be in the harbor and when it'll be leavin', with them new regulations they got."

"Aw, hell, Rubin," Menelaus Buell retorted. "Quit joshin' the Gen'ral. Don't be listenin' to Rubin Crane none. He ain't never been to New York. As for regulations, he ain't got no idea of what they are."

Davers scowled at the banter. If only the wind would come up! He gritted his teeth and pulled harder on the oar. The brilliant afternoon sun, unchecked by roof or leaves, glared down and sapped the strength from a man's muscles. The lake surface, nearly flat, reflected the blinding rays like a sorcerer's mirror until the Captain's eyes ached with the effort of staying open.

By late afternoon, when they were more than ready to make camp, they sighted a thin tendril of smoke along the shore ahead. Buell could be heard in the stern, cocking his musket. Crane ceased all banter and stabbed a heavy knife into the gunwale where he could get it quickly, all the time keeping one hand on the oar. Davers peered across the distance, alert and questioning. "Who be they?" someone asked.

No one answered, instead they kept pulling at the oars, the pace slowing as Buell steered further out into the lake until they could identify the campsite onshore. Ten minutes later the man in the bow turned and faced the rowers. "It's young André Charbonneau, the old man's son."

"A Frenchie," Buell grumbled.

"Do you know him, Gen'ral?" asked Crane.

"Aye. Passing but not well. Know his father better. Still, we've always been cordial."

"Who's the other one?"

"I don't know," Davers answered. "But I'm sure they won't mind us joining their camp. See, André's waving us over."

"I don't like it," Buell grumbled. "Never trusted a Frenchie yet."

"Damn, but I smell venison!" another of the party exclaimed.

"I warrant they'll trade or sell, or even give us some if we ask," suggested Crane. "I'm for pullin' in."

"And I," Davers answered. The others, with the exception of Buell, joined in famished agreement.

"Ho! André Charbonneau!" Davers called across the water. "Captain Davers and party making for Niagara. May we join you?"

"But of course, monsieur. You are welcome here!" he hailed in return. "There's fresh meat, cooking and ready to be eaten."

André Charbonneau cut a trim and dashing figure despite the trappings of a *voyageur*. He boasted his father's aristocratic good looks. Only dark flashing eyes hinted of a volatile nature. The young Frenchman stepped into the water to lend a hand. "It is good to see you, Captain Davers," André said, catching a thrown line from the *batteau* and helping pull the keel onto the bank as the travellers leaped out of the boat and slogged ashore.

Rubin Crane followed his companions onto the sandy bank. "Come along, Menelaus," Crane called. "The war's been over a long time."

"In a moment, Rubin," the older man answered gruffly. The second man by the fire was now recognizable as Thomas St. Aubin, a weaselly sort, to Buell's way of thinking. Gangly, with a sallow complexion and scraggly tufts of graying hair protruding from a knit cap pulled close over his head in spite of the late July heat, St. Aubin was not the sort to inspire confidence. But if André Charbonneau vouched for the man, perhaps . . . No, Buell decided. There was something wrong about the camp. "You go ahead," he said, "I'll be along in a minute."

The savory aroma of venison steaks sizzling on a spit, the juices dripping into the flame, drew the party to the campfire. "There's plenty for all of you," André said, indicating the meat. "Now, Captain, what brings you so far east?"

"Home," Davers sighed. "I'm bound for England and home. That is, if this damnable calm ever ends."

"A pity you do not travel by canoe. Thomas and I have made good time."

"It's good of you to share your food. I've had my fill of pork and the bass have made a point of refusing our bait."

"It is an honor, monsieur." Grinning, he removed his cap and wiped the sweat from his forehead.

Buell watched from the *batteau*. Perhaps he was being foolish. Nothing seemed amiss. The young'un showed no pistol and the musket laid to one side posed no threat. The sickly one was armed, but what could one man do? One man? He could count more than a dozen chunks of meat spitted over the flames. Enough to feed . . . Damn!! He bolted erect. "Rubin! Gen'ral! Look to your . . ."

The shot from St. Aubin's musket ripped open Buell's throat, cut short his outcry and knocked him from the boat into the muddy shallows where torn arteries sprayed the water red. The shot served as a signal for a volley. Smoke gouted from the forest's edge and a hail of balls swept through the men about the fire, sent them tumbling and reeling to the ground, frantic hands clawing at desperate wounds. Davers alone remained unscathed as a cluster of Huron warriors sprang from the trees and fell upon the wounded survivors, dispatching them in rapid and grisly fashion with knives and tomahawks. The Captain took to his heels, forsaking the cumbersome *batteau* and lurching, panic-stricken, into the water. Too late he fumbled for the pistol at his belt, only to have the weapon knocked aside as two braves reached and subdued him, bringing their prey back to shore to be greeted with shouts of laughter and hoots of derision. He turned his pink fleshy face toward André Charbonneau who had watched the massacre, unmoved by the terrible spectacle. Davers recognized the Indian striding through the carnage to the Frenchman's side. "Teata!" he shouted. "André, for the love of God, help me!"

The youth, eyes blazing, strode to the unfortunate Captain and spat in his face. *"Imbécile Anglais. Cochon!"*

The braves howled and dragged the Captain into the trees. Teata remained a moment to inspect the mutilated corpses. "Pontiac will be angry," he grinned. "Eh? Eh?"

"And move at last," St. Aubin sneered, heading for the boat to find what booty he might.

André looked over the water. To kill men—even English—in cold blood, went beyond honor. He was not proud, yet what else could he have done? Orders were orders. At least the massacre would serve a purpose. Pontiac would be forced to take precautions against reprisals, and would so find himself drawn closer to open warfare against the English.

The moon rose to the anguished screams of Captain Davers reverberating through the forest. Bright-eyed with rum and the lust of torture, bellies full of the hearts and livers of the other dead men, the Hurons returned over and over again to the unfortunate victim. Still he lived. Empty eye sockets streamed blood. The muscles of his left arm stood out in stark detail where the skin had been stripped from it to make, when cured, a tobacco pouch. Innumerable knife wounds had been cauterized with live coals. With the first streak of light in the east, the last hoarse croak and wheeze of pain stopped suddenly when the Captain's chest was torn open and his still-beating heart ripped out. Mercifully, the sagging, pitiful corpse could not see the dancing Indians toss his flesh about the clearing before devouring it raw.

As the sun rose, the *batteau* was emptied and burned, the beach smoothed over. Not a trace remained of the tragic occurrence. Even the severed, mutilated and partially missing remains of Captain Davers were consigned to the ground, buried with the rest of his unfortunate companions and the faded dreams of wife and children and home. The Frenchmen departed by canoe. Teata and his Huron warriors disappeared into the woods. The peaceful site was as it had been. By mid-morning, a strong north wind ruffled the empty water.

CHAPTER 16

"It's . . . it's beautiful!" Elizabeth marvelled. "But you can't mean . . . ? Is it really for . . . me?" Giggling nervously, she put down the parcel, part of the ruse Sabrina had concocted to lure the girl from the house. Cheeks flushed, Elizabeth examined the beaming faces of the three conspirators, then returned to the royal creation that dominated the room and spawned visions of palaces and glittering balls: a gown of white silk tucked at the waist, circled by a flurry of ruffles about the hips and hem. The sleeves were of elaborately stitched lace from mid-arm to wrist. The silk was so richly ruffled that the depth of the fabric created an illusion of varying hues, a billowing cloud of ever-changing depth. The bodice was fashioned of fairy pink silk, low cut and slim to accentuate not yet full breasts. A single tear, homage and testimony to Karen Schraner's craft, glistened on Beth's cheek.

"Happy birthday, Elizabeth," Henry said, crossing to take her hands and kiss her on the cheek. "Sixteen! God, but your father would have been proud."

Beth looked helplessly at Anne and Sabrina, then haltingly approached the dress and brushed tentative fingers through the shimmering silk. "It's too wonderful. Why, wherever shall I wear it?"

"At your party of course," Anne said.

Beth gasped in amazement. "A birthday party? For me?"

"Of course. Who else?"

"I . . . I mean . . . I've never had a birthday party before."

"Then there is no time like the present," Anne announced firmly. "And best you hurry, too. Your escort will be here before long."

"Come, child. Karen and I will assist you," Sabrina said, helping Karen with the gown and leading the way.

Beth followed dutifully, pausing once to look back at the smiling faces below. "Just think, a party for me! But what shall I do?"

"Feast and laugh," Anne began, "and dance with all the handsome young officers. Stroll beneath the boughs with your evening's favorite . . ."

". . . and let him steal a kiss and seal his fate, for he will be famished for another for all his days," Henry concluded with a hearty laugh.

Elizabeth blushed again, managed an "Oh, Uncle Henry!" and darted up the stairs.

His arm around her waist, Henry pulled Anne close. "It is nice to see her so happy," he said softly, lifting her face to gaze into misty eyes touched by Elizabeth's innocence and glee.

"Yes. So beautiful, and . . . Sometimes I wish I were sixteen again."

"No. If you were sixteen again, I shouldn't have met you. The world would be a bleak and lonely place." Gently, his lips brushed hers, once, twice, a third time.

Anne hesitated, then melted into his arms. Still she hungered for him. "We had best repair to the upstairs as well, sir . . ."

Henry nodded, took her hand and was part way up

the stairs when a knock sounded and a voice called
from outside. Henry saw to the door. Anne glimpsed
a buckskin-garbed figure and felt misgivings at the
subdued conversation. Henry's face was troubled when
he turned back to the room. "Anne . . . I'm afraid I'll
have to be a bit tardy. Jehu asked me to meet him at
McBeecher's. Something he wants to show me . . ."

"But the party!"

"The party will be splendid, I'm certain." The spell
broken, he moved about the room, finding and strap-
ping sheath and knife to belt, grabbing a pistol from
the case. "If you'll please inform the Charbonneaus of
my delay and apologize . . . ?"

Anne didn't know whether to be angry or cry.
"Henry, please. I beg of you, this is Elizabeth's . . ."

"Jehu wouldn't summon me unless it was important,
Anne. From what little he said, it's very important. I
promise not to be long."

A second later the door closed, the hollow slam a
hammerblow to the evening's festivities. Anne ascended alone to the quiet of the bedroom. Henry's
dress uniform lay across the bed. She patted the scarlet
coat, admired the golden buttons, polished and gleaming in the candlelight. Why did the interminable duties
of command always have to interfere? Thoughtfully,
she turned away and began her toilette.

Evangeline Charbonneau had offered her home for
the party, noting that the spaciousness and touches of
European gentility would enhance the social affair.
Anne and Karen had gratefully accepted and worked
throughout August to make sure all would be ready.

Now, recorder and viola joined the plucked and
trembling harmony of a harpsicord in the delicate,
difficult passage of a work composed for the occasion

by none other than Monsieur Bouvier. Louis himself was at the harpsicord, frowning whenever an inappropriate pause or discord broke the elegant rhythm. Evangeline, a slight, genteel wisp of a woman still recovering from the illness that had kept her bedridden much of the spring and into summer, rushed away to hurry the preparation of the food, leaving Pierre, Anne and Elizabeth the task of greeting the guests.

Anne assumed the role of hostess with aplomb. Half of Detroit had been invited, it seemed, along with a host of French families whose names jumbled together within the first few minutes. It was no small relief when the flood of arriving neighbors and friends slowed to a trickle. Bouvier had begun to play again and couples joined in the dance as they waited for the feasting to begin.

Beth, resplendent in the new gown, found herself the object of not only Ensign Price's and Jeremy's vying attention, but of André Charbonneau's as well. Jeremy, swelling with pride, left his scowling rivals behind and led Beth onto the earthen dancing floor. The air was filled with polite chatter and eager laughter, the gentle smell of pine carried by a fresh breeze from the river. Overhead, a thousand stars danced in time to the music and a single, small and curious cloud gazed down before being driven from its perch by a radiant moon. As the evening wore on, Anne searched the river path for Henry, but he was nowhere to be seen.

Evangeline Charbonneau and Karen Schraner had outdone themselves in preparing the handsomely kept grounds. Candles and storm lanterns perched on gaily decorated pedestals enclosed the festive throng in a glittering halo of warm light. Long wooden tables draped with cotton sheeting and decorated with flow-

ers formed ample barricades at both northern and
southern boundaries of the lawn, and though they'd
borne the groaning weight of countless dishes at the
beginning of the festivities, the half dozen soldiers
pressed into service as waiters were sent scrambling
to keep them full. More than a hundred hungry guests
crowded about platters of ham, wild turkey and venison. Mince meat, apple, peach and blackberry pies
vanished during lulls in the music and dancing. Karen
Schraner had prepared earthen bowls full of rich
custard baked to a golden brown, a delight to every
palate. There were fresh garden vegetables, many of
which had been used to stuff the turkeys, and veritable
battlements of freshly baked bread. Cider, beer and
wine kegs were tapped and hearty thirsts slaked.

Anne looked about at the homespun garments and
laboriously preserved, hopelessly dated fashions and
was grateful she had chosen a silk gown of simple
French cut and the color of a cloudless afternoon sky.
Her finest would have been appallingly out of place.
For once she was content to take second place: Beth's
dress was the talk of the partying throng, though it
was to Anne's sensuous figure that the attention of
many a masculine eye wandered.

The music ended and the musicians disbanded to
claim a share of the rapidly dwindling mountain of
food. Louis Bouvier moved heavily about the tables,
loading a great earthenware platter with thick slices of
venison, at the same time snaring a leg of turkey and
brandishing it like a club. The musician's face literally
glowed with cherubic enthusiasm and excitement as
he tore away great chunks of the dark meat.

"You play well, Louis," Anne said as he approached.
"And an original composition . . . Bravo!"

"I thought it a bit pagan," Amideus Drummond replied, intruding into the conversation. He produced an exquisite box of intricately worked silver, inhaled a pinch of snuff, turned aside and sneezed. "If you are finished with your musical pretensions, perhaps you would like to watch Pierre and me at a game of chess. I have already conquered him twice this evening."

"Today must be your birthday, too, Doctor. Surely Monsieur Charbonneau let you win as a present, no?"

"And this? How do you explain my winnings?" Drummond crowed, producing a £10 note and waving it under Louis' nose.

"Chess!" Bouvier snorted. It was an admission of defeat. "And how would the young men and ladies dance without music?"

"Dancing, pah! Let them wander into the brush and go a-romping. That's what they'd truly like to do."

Bouvier glanced piteously at Drummond and set down his plate. "You are a doctor. An *English* doctor. What can you know of love, eh?" Having regained both offensive and self-esteem, he quickly stalked back to the harpsichord. Drummond scowled and would have followed to continue the argument, but Pierre called from the house. Anne acknowledged his farewell, stifling a giggle until the physician was well out of hearing.

The party was going well. Anne moved aside from the more vocal revellers whose laughter swelled as the wine casks emptied. French and English had put aside whatever rivalry and discord tinged their everyday lives. A concession had been made, mostly because of Beth's feelings for Jeremy, and even a few enlisted men were present, a development the younger officers —Ensign Price especially—had at first discouraged. To one side, Beatrice Hampton spun by on the arm of Private Rexrode, the lad Anne had spoken to briefly at the gate.

"But you do not dance, Anne?" Evangeline Charbonneau exclaimed, approaching on the arm of a dapper gentleman dressed in a coat of royal blue and spotless white breeches, a generously powdered wig framing a face whose aquiline features lost their serious set on seeing Anne. "May I present an old and dear friend, Jean Dumas." The gentleman bowed gracefully. "Jean, this is our commanding officer's wife, Mrs. Anne Gladwyn."

The Frenchman's eyebrows raised in reaction to the name. "Jean was a major in the war, Anne. He . . . oh, *mon Dieu,* where is Pierre? You must get acquainted, no? The wine . . . the wine . . ." she fussed, hurrying off.

Dumas remained silent for a moment, watching their hostess depart. Anne took the opportunity to study him. He seemed a gentleman of breeding and position. Yet there was something disturbing in his sharp features and the sardonic glint in his dark-blue eyes. Anne sensed he knew the effect he made, and enjoyed it. A thin moustache, waxed and perfumed, curled down at the corners of his mouth, hinting of boredom denied by full and sensuous lips. Anne blushed, realizing those deceptive eyes had turned to study her with no small amount of appreciation.

"Gladwyn," Dumas began, rolling the name off his tongue, relishing the word. "Gladwyn. But I know this name, madame. Some few years ago . . ." An eyebrow raised in surprise. "But surely it is not the same man. This Gladwyn and I met . . . at Quebec. For a brief moment, one might say, for in truth there was little talk at the time." Dumas smiled graciously. "Forgive me. I reminisce of strangers and a matter that little concerns you, eh, madame?"

"Perhaps not," Anne replied. "I have heard my husband speak of Quebec, though not of you. At least not by name."

"Wed to Lieutenant Henri Gladwyn then . . . ?"

"Major Henry Gladwyn, Monsieur Dumas."

"Major, *mais oui*. Commander of Fort Detroit and a beautiful bride as well. The Major is a fortunate man."

"You are too kind, monsieur. And you say my husband is a friend?"

"No no no," he chuckled. "Perhaps an acquaintance. As soldiers—how shall I say?—allied to different causes, we tried to kill each other once. But my good friend Bouvier has begun to play and the dancing begins. I am far from Louis' Court and would be grateful for the arm of a beautiful lady. I do not see Monsieur Gladwyn and must assume you are alone, as am I, else surely the Major would be at your side. He is ill, perhaps?"

"No," Anne stammered, a little taken aback by the casual reference to killing. "There was some matter that needed tending. He will be here soon."

Dumas shook his head in dismay. "Such is the trouble with Englishmen. Duty must always be the most demanding of mistresses. I should let less important matters wait their turn were you *mon amoureuse*."

"But I am not, monsieur."

"Then I will, as a child, pretend for but the moment of a dance, if madame will not refuse."

Anne's quick, flirtatious smile was answer enough. If Henry preferred duty to wife, then so be it. Perhaps when he arrived and saw her arm in arm with Jean Dumas, Major Gladwyn would think otherwise. Be-

sides, she mused, taking the Frenchman's arm and
letting him escort her to the dance, Monsieur Dumas
is terribly handsome.

The new partners moved with assured grace and
timing across the dancing floor. A glorious chandelier
of stars flickered and spun overhead in a startling clear
sky. Bow and curtsy complemented each other in a
sensual statement of amorous intrigue. They neared the
trees at the edge of the well-kept grounds and as the
music ended, Dumas' arm lingered about Anne's waist.

"Sir, the music has ceased."

"There will be more."

"But . . ."

"Walk with me among the trees."

"Monsieur, you presume . . ."

"Nothing. But I would be away from this crowd."
Anne allowed herself to be eased into the shadows,
then had second thoughts. Turning, she brushed
against the Frenchman, who murmured a soft compliment in French and pressed his lips to hers.

A kiss, then another. He was too used to conquest,
too confident, too sure, Anne thought, but two can play
that game. Deliberately she moved closer into his embrace, returning his kiss with an ardor that surprised
Dumas.

They parted. Dumas caught his breath, then noticed
the slight mockingly contemptuous half-smile that vanished as soon as glimpsed. The Frenchman was not
accustomed to being vanquished at his own game.
"Madame is most . . . adept."

Anne arranged the daring cut of her bodice, smiled
at Dumas from beneath demurely lowered eyelids.
"And monsieur provides a most interesting and lovely
divertissement."

Dumas grinned wolfishly. "Madame, I confess I like you. Perhaps we shall be friends, no?"

"Perhaps, monsieur. Only perhaps." She took his arm and led him into the glow of candles made jubilant by a light breeze that freshened the air and wafted the aroma of honey-glazed hams and hens roasted coppery gold over the clearing.

"Do we dance or feast?" Dumas asked.

"That is no true question for a chevalier."

"So be it. We dance. But madame must be warned."

"Of what, monsieur?"

"Of shadows," the Frenchman replied, laughing meaningfully.

They moved into the galliard. Bowing low, Dumas softly loosed a jest fraught with innuendoes. Anne expertly, cleverly riposted. Now was a time to enjoy; Dumas made a captivating partner, as gallant as the London gentlemen she had left so far away. Anne surrendered to the lively rippling cadence of the music, until suddenly the music ceased.

Dumas muttered an oath. Anne, surprised in midstride, caught her balance. Jehu Hays had stepped into the light, musket in hand. Henry stood by the musicians. Heads turned to stare in amazement as he ignored Evangeline Charbonneau's greeting. Anne's anger at seeing Henry still in rustic attire of coarse blousy shirt and buckskin breeches gave way to alarm as he stalked across the clearing. There was not one moment in Anne's upbringing to prepare her for what followed.

Dumas began an elegant bow. "Ah . . . Major Gladwyn, it has been indeed a long . . ."

"What are you doing here, Dumas?" Henry interrupted coldly.

Anne stepped in before he could answer.

"He was dancing with me as I am unescorted. Jean has been kind enough to . . ."

"Kind? You *have* changed, Major Dumas."

"I am a major no longer. I am a civilian here on business for my king."

"This is English territory, monsieur."

Dumas' eyes narrowed. "I have friends among the Ottawa and thought to visit them. Surely . . ."

"You may visit elsewhere. In French territory."

"Sir," Pierre Charbonneau stepped up. "Monsieur Dumas is my guest, and will pass the night in my home. I invited him."

"Then you showed poor taste, Monsieur Charbonneau."

Both men bristled at the insult, but before either could speak, Anne intervened.

"Henry, this is a poor way to show our gratitude. Pierre and Evangeline have arranged this party in Beth's honor. The least you might do is put aside past differences. Monsieur Dumas has."

"Has he indeed? I wonder as to the real reason for his presence in the Lakes Frontier."

"Henry!"

"Keep out of this, Anne."

"You wrong me, sir," Dumas said.

"Do not talk to me of wrongs lest I lose all control."

"Elizabeth's party is no place for such base conduct," Pierre began, his voice trembling with anger. "We are here to celebrate."

"I have not come to celebrate," Henry said in a voice tinged with remorse, "but to jeopardize our friendship, Monsieur Charbonneau, though I do wish otherwise." He took an unusual pear-shaped watch from his belt. On seeing it, André sidled toward the shadows. Thomas St. Aubin cast a quick accusatory glance at the youth.

"What is this?" Pierre remarked, obviously confused.

"A watch that belonged to Captain Hilloe Davers."

"Belonged?"

"A Huron brave attempted to trade it to Jess Mc-Beecher for a keg of rum. Jehu was in the trading post at the time and recognized it as Captain Davers'. I cannot conceive of him parting with it willingly."

"I have yet to understand," Pierre Charbonneau protested.

The brave, under questioning, revealed he obtained the watch from your son, André Charbonneau."

The youth bolted for the shadows at the mention of his name, but found himself at bayonet point as a group of English soldiers entered the grounds.

"Sir, surely you do not think for one moment . . ."

"I am sorry, monsieur, but it is my unfortunate duty to remove your son to the fort. He shall have comfortable quarters."

Pierre Charbonneau staggered as if struck. "My son a prisoner? Impossible!" he stammered weakly.

"A guest—until we can ascertain what happened to Davers."

"He gave it to me, Papa," André blurted out, frightened and casting about for support. "The *anglais* Captain gave it to me for some venison."

The old man stared at Henry waiting for a response.

"Monsieur, the *Michigan* sails for Niagara in the morning and carries a dispatch requesting information on the well-being of Captain Davers. We should receive an answer within three weeks at the latest. I am required to force my hospitality on your son until then. I am sorry, but with Monsieur Dumas in the area, I must take this precaution."

"Again I am made the object of your derogation, sir," Dumas angrily interjected. "You have inconsiderately interrupted our host's party and most uncourteously impugned my honor. As before, *Lieutenant*," he sneered, "your tongue is bolder than your actions. I grow tired of your insults."

Henry turned slowly to Dumas, stared coldly into his eyes. When he spoke, the words were plainly enunciated for all to hear. "And I grow tired of your honor, sir, which is that of a viper."

The crowd sighed in anticipation. The challenge meant a fight—one of the few diversions offered on the frontier. Dumas' eyes flashed with the fires of hatred and his hand clutched for the silk kerchief at his sleeve, snapping it up to slap Henry's cheek.

"Please, I beg you!" Anne cried, but Henry was not to be denied. He lunged for the Frenchman, who, caught off guard, fell prey to a startling fist to the jaw and another to the neck as he dropped to the ground.

Jehu let out a blood-curdling whoop of joy at the prospect of a fight. Anne backed away in horror. The color drained from Beth's face. The crowd formed a large circle.

Dumas rolled to his feet and charged, ignoring a savage kick to the shins. The two bodies collided and separated part way, linked now by Dumas' hands clasped about the Englishman's throat.

A roar erupted from the crowd and the handful of English soldiers stared apprehensively at the many French faces. Still, three of the more seasoned veterans kept a determined eye on André.

The corded muscles in Henry's neck strained against the stranglehold while he sent hard rights and lefts into Dumas' stomach. When the Frenchman could take no more, Henry broke free, grasped an outstretched arm and fell backward, simultaneously driving booted heels into Dumas' belly and tossing him over onto the ground.

The circle around the fighters shifted, reformed. Dumas clambered to his feet, taking a smashing right on the mouth. Toe to toe, the opponents hammered one another, not even trying to block the brutal blows.

Anne ran across the clearing to Jehu's side. "Mr. Hays, you must stop them!" she screamed.

"Ma'am, I couldn't even if I had a mind to. Fella'd have to be plumb crazy to step between them two."

Another roar from the crowd and Anne spun about as Henry staggered and sank to his knees, stunned by a looping right to the temple. Breath ragged and forced through a flattened nose that would forever mar his aristocratic features, Dumas backed away then rushed to the attack, aiming a vicious, killing kick to the Englishman's head.

Henry rolled, took the kick on his forearm and drove a desperate fist into his opponent's groin. Dumas gasped and lurched away. Henry shakily regained his feet then waded in, delivering blow after blow, fists slamming like a machine, forcing Dumas toward the fringe of the crowd that hastily parted as the combatants neared.

The spectators formed a new circle, mercifully hiding the view from a weeping Anne. The sound of fists connecting with flesh and bone was too horrible. And then there was silence. Henry, battered, bleeding about a swollen mouth, cut eye and bruised cheekbone, but with a look of wild victory, stumbled from the onlookers, and stood before Pierre Charbonneau.

"Pierre, I wish there were some other way, but I will do what I must . . . what my authority demands. I am sorry. Truly."

"Major!" the voice lashed out, barely more than a whisper yet cutting and clearly audible. "From this moment on, our friendship is ended."

Henry sighed, drew himself erect. The answer was soft but firm. "So be it, monsieur. Take him away, Captain Hays."

For a moment, Anne thought the old man would not be able to restrain his fury, but at the last second he stepped aside as André was led past. The murmuring crowd, divided in their loyalties, gazed at one another suspiciously and drew apart as the English guests began to leave. Anne gasped as Dumas' unconscious form was carried into the house. The flickering light revealed eyes swollen shut and a nose that was a twisted glob of flesh against a mask of dripping red.

Soon the tables were emptied and removed. Most who made their homes along the river started for the long row of tied canoes. Others chose to walk the distance despite the late hour, for the dirt path was clearly delineated against the ripening crops and fallow meadows from which the forest had been driven back. Soon only Anne, Henry and Pierre remained. Anne was still shocked by the party's sudden and dramatic conclusion. She could feel the tension between the two men, but when the Frenchman spoke it was to her.

"Madame, I do not hold you responsible. My house is open to you and your niece. And now, if you forgive an old man, good night."

Together but alone, Anne and Henry walked away. In the dark depths of the far forest an owl sounded one long, ominous, mournful note.

"My God, Henry! How could you?" Henry glanced at her, cupped more water and bathed his cut face.

Anne, all the more angry for his silence, continued to rail. "And your conduct toward Jean—Monsieur Dumas —was contemptible. You bullied, and when he sought redress had not even the courtesy . . ."

"Courtesy!" Henry shouted with such vehemence that Anne sat upright in amazement. "One doesn't show 'courtesy' to the Jean Dumases of this world."

"He seemed a perfect gentleman."

"Seemed?" Henry glared, water mixed with blood dripping unheeded to chest and floor. "Your ignorance . . ." He stopped, more angry than Anne had ever seen him, his eyes slitted with fury. "Enough. I'll not speak more of the man lest I lose the sweet release these bloody fists have gained." He grinned at the memory of Dumas' prostrate form and the satisfaction of seeing the man crumple and fall. It had been a long time in coming, and if there were to be no other revenge against the Frenchman in this life, at least there'd been that one moment. He wiped the moistened cloth over his naked torso, a growing desire for Anne driving away the events of the past hour. Reaching out, he tugged askew one curl from Anne's coiffure.

Anne suddenly grew quite aware of her husband's arousal. She started to rise from the bed only to fall back, overpowered by bruised hands with still-bleeding knuckles. "Sir!" An outcry cut short by a kiss. "No . . . !" And another. "No . . ." And once again. His lips were salt-sweet with the taste of blood and he smelled of sweat and animal exertion. "No!"

Henry paused, lips still close. "I will, proud dove." He caught her wrists as she struggled anew, laughed aloud. "The sweet dove has talons. Shall I bind them again?" he said, trying to thrust her arms behind her back.

Anne tore free, and rolled from his grasp. Her

tousled appearance excited him further. "You will not, sir!"

"I would have you by my side, sweet Anne. Or know the reason why."

As if the phrase were a fuse burned short, the months of frustration and slow-burning anger exploded. All the words, all the pent-up reasons, gushed out at last, unrestrained. "Reason? A thousand! Look at you! Cut, bleeding, a barbarian clothed in skins . . . I had hoped this exile had not altered the English officer and gentleman I once knew, the man to whom I joined ambition and energy, in whom I had faith and with whom I was determined to win place, honor and fortune. But I was wrong. What gentleman would disgrace his wife and niece, brawl like a common lout and betray a trusted friend? You're a stranger, a stranger I don't know and don't care to know!"

"Hold your tongue, mistress."

"I cannot hold your lust at bay, but there will be no pleasure for you unless you find abject, flaccid surrender to animal rape exciting!"

"I said be still!"

Surrendering totally to rage, Anne ripped at her bodice, baring her breasts. "Take me then, sir. Reave me as is your pleasure."

"Damn it, Anne, will you stop it!"

"Well? Go on. What's stopping you? You took me against my will once. Surely you've learned enough from your savage friends to rape a helpless wife again, eh? Smear a little fresh blood around, show what a strong, domineering stallion you are!"

Furious beyond reason, Henry grasped her. His fingers dug into the soft flesh of her arms. An awesome, white-lipped rage contorted his face and he raised a hand to strike.

"Come, sir," Anne taunted, voice cracking with contempt and fear. "Do you need help? Shall I lie down or wait for you to knock me down? Shall I pretend I'm Catherine and match your savagery?"

Henry gripped her hair, jerked back her head, cutting off the insults. Anne yelped in agony as he bent her back onto the bed. With a vicious swipe, the soldier rent the gown completely asunder. Smouldering eyes raked the wondrous, supple treasure, naked now and helpless. Anne closed her eyes and held her breath as Henry trembled above her.

Suddenly the pressure was gone. She was free and sat up in time to see him bolt from the room, shirt in hand. The door slammed and his steps sounded on the stairs. Drained, exhausted of all emotion, she did not move. "I should feel victorious now," Anne whispered to the empty room.

But she didn't. Searing, bitter tears coursed down her cheeks and, sobbing, she sank into the pillows and wept alone.

Henry ignored the sentry at the gate, brushed past the youth who at the last minute recognized his commanding officer and managed an uncoordinated salute. The moon hung low in the west, bathing the earth below and turning the air to vibrant silver. He followed his shadow into the trees and paused to get his bearings before realizing he didn't give a damn about bearings or anything else. Heedless of danger, he plunged through the forest, his vision slowly adapting to the night and carrying him past barely seen dangers on the trail until the dull glow of a campfire beckoned.

The clearing was overgrown where the forest strove to reclaim its own but the lodge he'd helped build was little changed. A tiny cooking fire guarded the door.

She was there. Better leave, his mind raced. Turn and go back to the fort.

Weary from the confrontation with Anne and troubled still by what he considered her abuse, his heart bade him stay, demanded the first forbidden step. Empty of thought, he crossed the clearing, cautiously ran his palm over the rough bark, knelt and dropped a handful of twigs into the fire.

"I knew you would come." Sleek and naked, glistening reddish-brown in the bright new flames, she stood by the narrow entrance.

"How did you know?" He faced her and did not move as deft fingers opened his shirt.

"Because I waited," Catherine said.

They lay side by side on the cool earth, the blanket kicked away. His arm encircled her shoulders and he lay quietly, not yet asleep.

"You must send her away," Catherine whispered.

"No."

The girl stiffened, then relaxed as the soothing hand played along her spine, lowered to caress the trim curve of her buttocks. She yawned and pressed close.

"If she is to leave it must be of her own choosing. Not mine."

"I will make you send her away." Even, white teeth nibbled animal-like at the thick muscle reaching from neck to shoulder. Lower then, her lips enticing further. "I will make you forget."

Boiling tides of love engulfing him, Henry groaned as Catherine rose, straddled him and suffered sweet impalement. Slow rolling waves, the surging, ancient rhythms, the sea swell of lust unharnessed, swept through her very being as the fierce storm of passion erupted, leaving Henry breathless and Catherine moaning his name, falling forward to bury sobs against his neck.

Slowly, the sobs diminished and Catherine slept, her breath even and strong. Henry watched through the entrance as the final ember of the fire flickered out. It would soon be morning.

CHAPTER 17

Pierre Charbonneau, an old and weary man, sipped at the cup, made a wry face and tossed the tepid liquid into the fireplace. It wasn't a time for tea anyway, he reflected, opening the spirits cabinet. Uncorking a fine old bottle of cognac, he returned to the table and poured a healthy two fingers. Thomas St. Aubin snared the bottle as soon as it left his host's hand, but replaced it immediately when he saw the look in the old man's eye. The rum would have to do.

Charbonneau frowned in displeasure. He did not like rude men, and especially this rude man who had gotten André into so much trouble. It was the twentieth of September and almost three weeks had passed since the party and André's arrest. The courier had returned that afternoon to Detroit with the unsettling report that Captain Davers' party had yet to pass through Fort Niagara. The Captain and seven other men had disappeared without a trace other than the damning evidence of the watch. Pierre tried to console himself with the belief that the missing men might have fallen victim to one of the many violent summer storms that sprang up over Lake Erie, but such daydreams held little reassurance: André remained confined to a cabin in the stockade, under heavy guard.

The dream fled once and for all with the visit from

Jean Dumas, who even now leaned against the window and stared at the fort in the near distance. Bearing the marks from Henry's beating, he peered at the high, imposing palisade as if the wood had become transparent and he could focus on the man within, whom he despised not so much for the thrashing but because Henry Gladwyn knew the hidden truth and therefore would always be a threat. "Continue, St. Aubin," Dumas firmly ordered.

"There is no more. We buried the bodies, erased any sign of a struggle and sunk the *batteau* in deep water. I ordered Teata to refrain from taking any booty. Everything went into the ground."

"Not everything, monsieur," Pierre curtly corrected, taking bare delight in the way St. Aubin's sallow tones paled in embarrassment.

"But you know these savages," Dumas interrupted smoothly. "It is impossible to keep them under total control. They follow orders only when the whim strikes."

"I do not care about savages, whims or warfare!" Pierre exclaimed, emphasizing the point by slamming his palm down on the table top. "I care only about my son. What is to become of André? When Major Gladwyn learns . . ."

"He will learn nothing more than he already knows, and if he does, it will not matter," St. Aubin offered boldly.

"What does that mean?"

"He means," said Dumas, "that Major Gladwyn may soon be occupied with other more pressing matters. Teata and Mackinac and a half-score of other chiefs have demanded a council with Pontiac. They will convince him to make war upon Detroit—upon all the English forts along the lakes and across the wilderness

road down to Fort Pitt. Our chances of victory are
very high, if not certain. The English foothold is insecure, and with luck, we shall drive them from the continent."

Pierre slumped in his chair, stunned by the enormity
of the endeavor. "That's . . . impossible," he muttered
weakly.

"No, not with French assistance—and that of General
Amherst, who could not cooperate more were he in our
employ. If Pontiac can show sufficient success in this
region, most important in the destruction of Fort Detroit, I feel confident our sovereign will renew France's
commitment to the Americas. A French army will be
formed and landed. With a concerted Indian effort,
we cannot fail."

"Illusion, Monsieur Dumas. Mad illusion. Conjure
what you will, but not at my son's expense. Must I
continue to remind you that André is in jeopardy?"

"André will be free by morning."

Charbonneau started violently. "But . . . but how?"

"Never mind how," Dumas said with a controlled
smile. "You will see him this night. André is a most
valuable companion, Monsieur Charbonneau. He has
kept his hatred. It is a pity you have not."

Jehu, back from Niagara and sitting down to his
first decent meal since the ill-fated party, slathered a
second thick slice of steaming bread with freshly
churned butter and groaned with pleasure when Sabrina filled his bowl a third time with a hearty stew
full of carrots and fresh, succulent onions, knobby po-
tatoes and haphazardly cubed chunks of venison in a
rich brown bubbling broth. "Beats trail food, for a
fact. Was you a little younger and not so tough, I'd
consider . . ."

"Younger? I'm ten years younger than you."

"An' just how do you know that?"

"From the looks of your scrawny neck, is how."

"Woman, you . . ." Jehu suddenly shut up, aware the conversation had taken a disturbing turn. What the hell I been sayin'? he asked himself. "You sure you got enough o' this ta go around?"

"You're much too late in worrying of that. Everyone here has gone off their heads. Like mice, they are, coming to nibble, and separately, too."

" 'Tis a sad way to go about the world. I only seen him for a minute, but the Major looked like he was in a dark mood."

"No worse than the mistress," the servant retorted. "I've all but raised that child—as my own, I have— and never seen a tantrum take so long in the easing."

"A terrible row, was it?"

Sabrina raised her eyes to heaven and shook her head. "Not that it's the business of such as yourself . . ." She glanced about the empty room and finished seriously. "It's terrible, Jehu. Just heartbreaking." She poured a mug of tea and sat down at the table. "Go on. Eat your fill. There's none to dispute you. Each night I cook and must watch the food cool, untouched, or abide alone with young Elizabeth, who can't wait to be off and away from this unhappy house. Now and again Anne joins me, silently picking at her food. And the Major? You'll find him sleepin' downstairs, or more often as not gone Lord knows where. Passing the night at his office, I'm told, preferring the uncomfortable solitude of a cot to his . . . uh . . ."

"Marriage bed?" Jehu offered, eyes a-twinkle. "You'd not find me sleepin' on a cot had I a woman to lie with."

Sabrina suddenly found her teacup of utmost interest and fell to studying the leaves intently. The ranger kicked himself for letting his tongue lead him astray again. Quickly polishing off the stew, he pushed back the bowl. "Well," he sighed, "I suppose there's no sense in not tellin' you, in case it comes up. First thing I heard when I got back. It's been but few nights the Major has endured the loneliness of a cot, old lady."

Sabrina jerked forward. "What are you saying?" she whispered hoarsely, knowing his meaning full well.

"Only this," Jehu began, eyes narrow and voice lowered. "When one is willing and one ain't . . . another willing will be found."

Sabrina grimaced. " 'Tis a pity such a talent for clarity has been wasted on a slanderous tongue."

"Slanderous? Aye. The truth is now slander, eh? Very well, if you'll have it so," he said, rising and pulling on his cap.

The servant rounded the table and grasped his arm. "I'm sorry, Jehu. But such talk makes my heart heavy."

Jehu softened, patted her hand. "And mine too. But I tell you this for what it's worth. Your mistress would do better keeping a less contentious tongue in her head and staying home to bear babes instead of sending her husband off to get others with child. Henry Gladwyn is a man who knows his business and duty. He's a good officer and a better commander, rare as a redcoat can be. What he did at that party, he did with good reason. If he gets naught but anger and silliness at home . . . ?" The rising inflection at the end left unsaid the obvious.

Troubled, Sabrina withdrew to the fire. "I'll not say

you're wrong, but can't agree aloud you're right." She looked up at him, her face pained. "I can't say those things to her, Jehu. 'Tis not my place."

"I know," came the soft reply. "I know." Quickly, Jehu crossed the room, laid his hands on Sabrina's shoulders. "We'll talk of it no more. Will you dance with me this Saturday?"

Sabrina looked up, a smile erasing the lines of concern. "Aye. I will. And gladly, too."

"Good. I'll be on my way, then."

"Be careful."

Jehu grinned. "Old lady, I been bein' careful so long I don't know how to be anything but." Turning, he strode from the kitchen and closed the door against the chill in the hall.

"Sir!"

Jehu stopped, whirling toward the sound and half drawing his knife until he saw Anne. Bundled in a shawl, her face white as a sheet, she stepped from the shadows and faced him in the gloom. Not a word did she speak, only stared with burning eyes.

"Ma'am?"

"Come with me, please," she ordered without looking back. Jehu cursed his luck and followed like a puppy about to be whipped. Inside the living room, she dropped the shawl and stood in front of the fireplace. Jehu waited, shuffled his feet. She'd heard every word he'd said, dammit. What a fool . . .

"Well?"

There was nothing but to admit the sin and apologize. Maybe she needed to hear it straight out, anyways. Clear the air. Still, those eyes . . . "I reckon I been talking outside my business, ma'am, but . . ."

"Why, Mister Hays, I hardly should imagine that bothers you in the least."

"Ma'am, you've a sharp tongue. Nothin' I can hope to match. An' seein' as I deserve it, I'll hold mine and offer an apology. I don't apologize to many."

Anne was not to be dissuaded from rubbing salt into the wound. "Oh, my! I'm flattered, Mister Hays."

The trapper let the insult sink in, felt the rising tide of anger. The lass had gone too far, as was the trouble of too many of the high-born. Never knew when to quit when they were ahead, always had to keep barging on. The time came when a man had to speak plain truth. "Ma'am, you don't think much of us rough sorts, I can tell. Never have. Maybe it's our clothes, maybe 'cause we lack learnin' of the proper way to this an' that. We're different from your London-born-and-bred ways an' I'm sure you could teach us a good deal. But there's a couple of things we practice that wouldn't hurt you to take to, an' if you're any example of English folks, well, I reckon it'd do for the whole blame country."

"And that is?" she asked icily.

"When someone offers you an apology to fit the crime, well, then you accept it an' go on from there. An' when that someone is old enough to be your father—an' I reckon I got forty years on you—then he deserves the same respect no matter what he wears or where his mother dropped him. Especially if he's got the common sense you ain't. Good evenin' to you, ma'am."

Her voice stopped him before he reached the front door. "Jehu!"

"Yes'm?"

The words were strained and came with great difficulty, but she went on. "Does that first hold true for women, too?"

"Yes'm, it does."

"Then, I'm sorry, Mister Hays."

Jehu looked over his shoulder. The apology had cost a great deal. Anne stood stiffly by the fireplace, near tears. "Don't go, Jehu. Please?" The dam broken, tears streamed down her cheeks and she sank into a chair, weeping violently.

Jehu watched uncomfortably, finally went to her and laid a rough, comforting hand on the trembling shoulder. "Now, now . . ." he intoned awkwardly, at a loss for more.

"So many things pile up so quickly," came the muffled cry. Anguished tears overcame words again, leaving Jehu to pat her shoulder and, feeling vastly incompetent, wonder what else he could say or do.

Gradually the tears slowed and she sat up, wiping her eyes. The very picture of dejection, she swallowed a hiccup and started talking, the words spilling out. "You were right. I listened to you talking to Sabrina and knew it was the truth even though I hated every word. But where do I begin, Jehu? I wanted so much for everything to be beautiful and nice. I tried so hard . . . to . . . accept all the newness. Well, maybe I didn't, but I tried to try. And then, just when I thought everything was going well . . ." She paused, picturing the night of the party. "That fight was so terrible! Poor Monsieur Dumas and the Charbonneaus. But it reaches beyond that. I . . . I know where he's been going, and I know I drove him there, but still . . ." She took a deep breath. "It was my fault he went in the first place, but he . . . he's still going, and I'm afraid, Jehu. I'm so afraid. I carried on like a shrew and nagged him and tried to change him when I should have known better. Wouldn't listen, put on airs . . . How do I apologize for that?"

Jehu coughed nervously. "Some things there just

ain't no fit apology for. They got to be lived down,
is all."

"But how? It's too late."

"Beggin' your pardon, ma'am, but it ain't never too
late. All you got to do is make a start an' then keep at
it. That's more'n enough apology for any man."

"But . . ."

"An' there ain't no buts about it," he went on, not
allowing her to continue. "You start an' then keep
goin' an' time an' nature'll be on your side. The Major
ain't a complete damned fool, after all. He'll be back.
You're too much of a woman for any man to forget,
an' Henry Gladwyn's too much of a man to let you go."
He paused, looked around uncomfortably, unused to
talking so much at once. "Well, I reckon I better go.
Goodnight, ma'am." Once again he turned and headed
for the door.

"Jehu?"

"Yes'm?"

"Thank you."

The old trail blazer looked back. Anne was sitting
up. The tears were gone and a look of determination
had taken their place. He grinned. "I guess I lied when
I said apologizin' comes natural to folks here, ma'am. I
reckon it don't come natural anywhere. You'll do all
right, Missus Gladwyn. I reckon you'll do just fine."

Too embarrassed to enter with the musket, Doody
Rexrode leaned the Brown Bess against the wall and
opened the door to André's quarters, a crudely fur-
nished one-room cabin fronting on rue Ste. Anne.
"Need anything before you turn in, André?"

"Yes. My freedom," the French youth grumbled from
the dark. "How can you do this to me, my friend?
Have we not hunted together? Trapped beavers? Now

you stand watch over me as you would a common thief."

"I'm sorry, André. I volunteered for the job figurin' you'd rather have a friend nearby, rather'n one of them redcoats. It don't please me to see you like this. I'm sure the matter'll be cleared up in a few days' time. You'll see."

"Leave me alone."

The young American shrugged. "As you say, André. Good night." Doody stepped outside, locking the door behind him and thrusting the iron key into a belt pouch. A soft footfall in the shadows alerted him. The private reached for the musket, stood quietly, listening. Must have been my imagination after all, he thought. Well, time to turn in. The noise again. He spun around, glimpsed the familiar face. "Oh, it's you . . ."

He did not see the blade, only felt the sharp bite as the steel slashed through his throat, then as quickly withdrew. Doody spat a mouthful of blood, shook his head with surprise and pain, unable to believe the spewing blood that covered his hands. When he recovered enough to attempt a cry of alarm, the blade slid through his ribs and found the final target. The dying private's knees buckled and he slumped silently to the earth.

The assailant went to work quickly, slit the key pouch and opened the lock. André looked up as the door swung open and his benefactor entered. "What are you doing here?"

The figure only thrust the dead ranger's musket into his hands. "Where's Rexrode?" André asked suspiciously.

"We are nearest the west gate," came the answer. "There is one sentry. I could do nothing about him, nor dare I risk being seen by others. I would hurry if I were you."

The figure vanished. André leaped from the cot, slipped into chilled boots, anxiously peered outside and gasped at the sight. But if he felt remorse at all, it did not show. Bolstering his courage, the youth darted through the door and slipped in a puddle of mud. Realizing with horror it had not rained, he furiously wiped his hands on his breeches, then started toward the gate at a slow, measured pace, as naturally as possible to avoid detection.

The rampart was empty. Only one man was on duty. A soldier stepped out of the sentry box. "You're early. But never mind, I can use the extra . . ."

André bludgeoned him with the heavy musket, slammed the stock thrice more onto the shattered skull until the body ceased to twitch. In the quiet, with his ragged breath the only sound other than the cry of a bittern in the far marshes, he slid back the bolt, swung open the gate and walked into the night.

He was free.

Henry shifted about on the cot, trying to find a comfortable position. If he could only fall asleep, perhaps he could find relief from the raging emotions that filled his night with agony. Nothing helped. Finally he gave up, rose and lit a candle. Davers' watch lay on the desk top. The hour was late. Orion the hunter would be well into the west. Catherine, perhaps, would have finally fallen asleep, alone and wondering.

Catherine. She was a fine copper-skinned wench who knew how to move beneath a man, knew how to pleasure him. But she wasn't Anne. Anne was . . . He sighed aloud, facing the truth at last, the truth that had kept him from his usual nocturnal sojourn in the forest and imprisoned him in the austere office.

Henry cursed the room's closeness and slipped into soft and well-worn buckskin breeches. A turn around the fort—maybe even a check on the house to make sure everything was all right—wouldn't hurt. Mind made up, he stepped outside and collided with a young soldier whose name he couldn't recall. "Major! He's gone. Never seen the like. Christ in heaven, blood everywhere . . ."

"Calm down, man. Who's gone?" he asked sternly, but late. The youth had taken off like a shot. Running, Henry followed, catching phrases and words. Deducing the rest, the officer forged ahead and hurried toward the prisoner's cabin.

The alarm bell sounded as he rounded the corner. Trouble at the west gate! Doors slammed open. Soldiers and civilians poured out of barracks and houses. Lanterns were turned up and the street came alive with light.

"They killed him!" someone shouted. His further cries were drowned out by a confused babble.

"Close that gate!" Henry recognized Lieutenant Busby's voice. A dull thud of wood striking wood indicated the fort was secure once again.

Rexrode's corpse was visible in the moonlight, the ghastly smile on his lifeless face repeated in a wide crescent on his neck. Henry cursed violently as another private burst through the gathering ring of curious onlookers with news of the murdered sentry at the gate. "Keep back!" Henry shouted. "Private, get everyone away from here. And tell them to leave that damn bell be!"

There was no point in searching the cabin. André

Charbonneau was certainly gone. Henry kneeled by the dead boy, noticed the thin slit left by the blade that had pierced Rexrode's heart. This was not done by André. At least not alone. Someone from inside the fort had helped him escape. Across the gruesome expanse of bloody ground, a series of footprints pointed toward the heart of the settlement before disappearing in the jumble of tracks left by the seething crowd that had come running at the first sound of the alarm.

Jehu, followed by Lieutenant Busby, forced his way through to Henry. "One dead, Major. The gate's closed. Far as we know, whoever come in is gone." He paused and kneeled at the dead boy's side. "Damn. Rexrode was a good man."

"Shall I put everyone on full alert, Major?" Lieutenant Busby asked.

"No. The last thing we need is panic. Get the bodies out of sight and your men back to their posts. Those that aren't on duty will be inside their barracks within the next five minutes. Check with me when you're done. I'll be in headquarters."

Busby saluted quickly and started issuing orders as Henry and Jehu made their way to the west gate. A second later they were outside and the diminishing clamor was left behind. The ranger squatted and studied the earth with a practiced eye. "Hard to tell," he finally said.

"I guess it's too late to catch him," Henry muttered.

The woodsman nodded and stood. Both men stared out at the distant border of trees. "I could try," Jehu offered. "Mighty difficult to follow sign over this ground, much less at night. I got a feelin' he took to the trees and then cut over to the river. Wouldn't surprise me none if a canoe was waitin' for him, neither." Jehu spat into the dust, thought of Rexrode and the promise the lad had shown. "I reckon maybe I'll be waitin' for him too. Find him, one of these days."

"What worries me more is those tracks leading away from the gate," Henry replied.

The night hid Jehu's rueful grin. "You noticed them too," he said matter-of-factly. "Too bad that herd trampled 'em up."

"Whoever it was, he didn't leave. Are you thinking what I'm thinking, Jehu?"

"Yup. He lives inside the fort." It didn't need to be said, but Jehu said it anyway. "Looks like we got us a problem, Major. Yessir, a first-class problem."

CHAPTER 18

October lingered among the oak trees, had yet to drape the rough bows with russet and sienna. Tiny moccasin flowers were never thicker than at the moment. Fleurs-de-lis with delicate yellow-gold hearts protected by rapier-like emerald leaves nodded in a nippy breeze that hinted of winter. Beyond a gleaming border of marsh marigolds, lady ferns in more profusion lifted leafy fingers in secretive, humble supplication to the distant, partially concealed sky.

Although the forest might refuse to admit summer's end, the woodland creatures knew well the signs. Even the most primitive beast sensed the subtle cyclic motion of earth and sky, heard the silent warning of dogwood and the protestation of stone and grumbling roots. A furious burst of activity enveloped the forest then as bramble thickets were invaded, seeds and nuts gathered. The bear felt the quiet sluggish churning of his blood and knew the time was near, fought with lessening resistance the urge to return to his lair for a long, wintry sleep.

Inside the fort, preparations for the coming winter were nearly finished. Cracks opened by the summer sun were chinked with new mud. Wood by the cord had been stacked. Slabs of cured meat hung in the smokehouses. Grain had been ground and lay in sacks, waiting to be made into warm loaves to be eaten with melted butter. The heavy work had been done. Soon the Indians would leave for their winter hunting grounds. The inhabitants relaxed in preparation for the lazy months.

Anne lay abed, half asleep, half awake. The dainty chimes from the clock downstairs floated through her dreams. "Hark to the chimes, come bow your head," she sang drowsily in time to the melody. "We thank thee, Lord, for this day's bread."

One . . . two . . . Anne counted each stroke. Three . . . four . . . five . . . Too early to rise. Six . . . seven . . . eight? Impossible. Eight o'clock? The sun should be streaming through the window.

She opened her eyes to stifling darkness. An all-pervading stillness hung over the room. Anne touched the empty half of the bed, fashioned Henry's shape from memory, the rise and fall of his easy breathing in slumber: pictured him turning to her. Was he with Catherine, wrapped in feverish coupling, enjoying his Indian mistress?

The anguished thought swelled in the darkness like a great ugly beast and filled the morning. "No," she whispered, holding back the tears. "I don't want to think this. I don't want these thoughts. I do not want him back. Why should I care?"

The truth lay forming in her womb, growing steadily. She'd known for a certainty only a week before, when her time had passed for the second month in a row. If only Henry were near, she thought, dispelling the lurking evil. If only he were here to lay his hand on my stomach and touch the child growing here. But how to tell him? Run through the streets to headquarters? Run and plead? The idea was tempting but Anne Langford would never run to any man. Never.

The price was too great. If Henry Gladwyn didn't come back for her, Anne Gladwyn wouldn't abide his returning for the child's sake.

Anne rose from the bed and hurried to the shutters, casting them open and reeling from the somber, lowering panoply of unhealthy blackish-green storm clouds stretching into the distance. The air seemed thick and made movement sluggish. The flag on the headquarters staff hung limp and unmoving. Nary a bird sang; not a sound emanated from the packed settlement. Nothing stirred. She stood watching. A creak of shutter and another head popped out of another window. Anne looked closely. Four—no, five—others stared into the ominous sky.

Waiting . . .

Pontiac stood, cast the blanket from his shoulders and faced the east, waiting for the sun. Three days ago he had strode into the hills, keeping to the north where the land rolled into massive monuments to an earlier earth's tortured upheaval, bound for the hilltop sacred to his people, the Back-of-the-Turtle. By the time the sun sent its first rays to the Mother Earth, Pontiac was well up the forested hillside, strong limbs bearing him up the steepening incline with no more effort than had the ground been flat.

He had been weary even then, for the previous night's council had been an exhausting ordeal. Hudoc of the Senecas; Ningas of the Potawatomis; Mackinac, a rival Ottawan chief eager to assume Pontiac's position among the seven tribes. And Teata. Pontiac scowled. Teata was troublesome and rash but a brave warrior. That night, in stirring detail, he had revealed to the council the successful attack on Davers' party, proudly displaying the eight scalps taken and boasting

of the meal he had made of their flesh. The rest of
the warriors were duly impressed, but Pontiac barely
managed to conceal his fury at the Huron's deed.

Teata had set the tribes on a collision course with
the English, for the deaths would surely be discovered. All night Pontiac argued the folly of war, but
the hope that Henry Gladwyn and the scant few who
supported him could sway the redcoats' father in New
York did little to offset the innumerable grievances
the other chiefs brought to bear.

"Without guns and powder we have been unable to
prepare for the winter. Where are the racks of meat
that should be stored to fill our bellies during the time
the Earth Mother sleeps?"

"The Eng-lesh trader's rum and whiskey corrupts
the young men of our tribe, leaves them surly and
hopeless, weak against those who would harm us."

"The white man's disease that spots the flesh has
taken the lives of half our village. Our women weep
and we bury our children."

"They take our land, treat us like dogs to be kicked
out of the lodges."

All were arguments for which Pontiac could find
no reasonable rebuttal. Worse, Henry Gladwyn had
come to Pontiac and spoken of André Charbonneau's
escape and Pontiac had had to lie, protesting he knew
nothing of the matter. The situation was deteriorating.
Winter was approaching fast and the following months
would be difficult, but Teata called for immediate
war, as did Mackinac. After all, Dumas had promised
the French army would come to aid them once the
first blow was struck. But how, Pontiac questioned,
would they fight a war during the winter? How could
the French march across the frozen land to help them?
The others grudgingly decided Pontiac was right, but

he was forced to make a concession: in return, he would reassess his position.

He had left immediately, in the middle of the night, to search for the answer, to be one with the Great Spirit and pray for a sign, reaching the barren summit of the Back-of-the-Turtle before the slight layer of frost had melted from the rocks. There, eyes closed, he offered a chant to the wind and sky. Hands outward and legs wide apart, Pontiac faced the primitive splendor of earth and heaven. For three days, he had waited for the sign that comes only when the Great Spirit dictates. On this, the fourth day, the sun failed to appear. One man stood alone under the awesome bleak array, the turbulent domain of ghosts and gods, knowing the Great Spirit had at last deigned to notice his son.

Catherine drew away from Henry's unresponsive lips. "What is it, Henri?"

Without answering, he strode from the lodge and stared up to the terrible configuration of deepening gloom—clouds to mirror the deepest, innermost feelings. Catherine sensed with quickening heart that something was amiss. "Henri?" She followed, slim, naked and worried. "For three weeks you have not come to me."

Had three weeks passed already? Henry wondered. Twenty-one lonely nights spent on the office cot? And how many days, out of stupid, overweening pride, since he'd been alone with Anne? The settlement was rife with gossip. He had sent orderlies to gather clothing from his house. He and Anne had seen little of one another, and when their paths did cross, shared only uncomfortable cordialities which served to fuel new and even more malicious stories. His relationship with Catherine had come to an abrupt halt, not for lack of passion, but because, suddenly, he had come to a painful realization, one that had brought him to Catherine for a final visit.

"Henri, my brave warrior." Tawny arms encircled his waist.

"No, Catherine, you must not," he began, extricating himself from the embrace. Catherine stepped back, eyes downcast as Henry continued. "I do not mean to hurt you, but . . . Oh, damn it to hell, I will hurt you and there's no way out."

"I do not like you this way, Henri," Catherine pouted. "Perhaps you return tomorrow."

Henry reached out and caught her shoulders, preventing her from leaving. "What must be said must be said now."

"An evil spirit darkens the sky. I have moved my fire inside. Come with me."

"I can't. It is a lie. All of it. We have been together yet we have not. What you took for love was no more than anger at another. This I know now. I used you, Catherine, while in my heart I loved and needed Anne. To continue would be to hurt you more."

Catherine's face contorted into a mask of hatred. Retreating, she fled into the lodge, emerging moments later dressed in the buckskin shift.

"Catherine . . . ?"

"Do not touch me, Eng-lesh man," she spat, then whirled and scurried to the safety of the forest, pausing once at the edge of the clearing to look back. But there was nothing to be said. Neither tried. She was gone.

The crackle of flames distracted Henry. Catherine had scattered the fire inside the structure the two had built together in what seemed another age. The flames licked through the top, paused as if hampered by the oppressive air, then sprang to new life. Slowly, the bark was consumed and the lodge caved in. What little remained uncharred soon succumbed to the voracious fiery tongues. Henry slumped dejectedly on a nearby log and waited for the one remaining vestige of his relationship with Flower-on-the-Water to burn away to ashes.

Forest, farms and fort hung suspended between earth and the single, nearly black cloud mass. Twilight, false and out of time, darkened men's spirits and promised an angry God's wrath. Not a sound issued from the expectant silhouettes of trees or houses.

Animals looked about, trembling, wild-eyed and testing the still air with flared nostrils. Some scurried fearfully for holes or dens, there to cower until the unknown passed. Others, too large to hide in the earth, sought refuge in the depths of the forest where the thick foliage offered the hope of safety.

Men held their breaths and turned their faces to the sky, looked up to the ponderous cloud or glowering gods. It made no difference. Redman or white, all were afraid of the spirit storm waiting inside the heavy, oppressive mattress that hung motionless over them.

Finally, when man and animal could no longer bear the tension, a single sinister drop fell. Another, huge and black, followed. Then, as if slashed by the knives of a thousand evil spirits, the cloud ripped apart.

Black rain. Who had seen or could comprehend black rain? Jet-black drops stained leaves and roofs. Soot-black drops sizzled on abandoned fires. Evil-smelling, the noxious liquid gathered into foul rivulets which puddled in horrid sulphurous pools under the rapidly wilting flowers. With the rain, a forceful wind ripped the branches into frenzied motion. The first winter wind from the north tore the stagnant atmosphere and slanted the rain in morbid cascades.

Anne stared in frightened disbelief at the black rain. "Mum? Mum, do you see it?" Sabrina called, bursting into the room and joining Anne at the window. "What is it? It smells of brimstone!"

Beth hurried into the room, her hand stained by the jet-black substance. "Look!" she cried.

"Oh, my God!" Sabrina screamed, and fell to towelling the girl's fingers.

"It doesn't hurt," Beth protested. "I have set out an ink well to be filled."

"Which we shall throw away immediately, shan't we, mistress?" Sabrina declared emphatically.

But Anne was lost to her own thoughts as the palisades blackened beneath the somber curtain and the road turned to black mud. The outer walls of the houses, white only moments ago, darkened, streaked with black streams. "It's as if all Detroit were draped for a requiem, as if the whole world was in mourning."

The first drops jolted Henry out of his torpor. The ink-rain matched his mood as it doused the smouldering coals of the remains of the destroyed lodge. A fitting end, he thought, as he slowly turned and headed back toward the fort. A fitting end. But not an end to everything. The fort waited. So did Anne. Suddenly alarmed, he began to run.

Fifteen minutes later he bolted through the gate. Hair and buckskins stained black, he sloshed through the empty streets to headquarters. Lieutenant Melton, the duty officer, rose to attention. Everyone was frightened, he reported, but other than that nothing had gone amiss. Henry ordered him to carry on and ducked inside his office, there to doff the soaked garments and down a mug of hot buttered rum brought in by Jeremy.

"I've never seen the like, Major," the youth said, obviously unsettled. "No one else has, either. Private Moore says it's the end of the world."

Henry laughed to hide his own disquiet. "Nonsense. It's black rain. Nothing more."

"Still an' all, Major . . ."

"Look. I was outside. Soaking wet. Now I'm here, still alive and in perfect shape. There's always a dozen Private Moores around to announce the end of the world, and they're always wrong."

Jeremy looked and sounded doubtful. "Well, if you say so, Major. Still, I wouldn't be so sure it don't mean somethin'."

Henry stared out the window, unable to dispel the oppressive feeling that Jeremy might be right. Perhaps the rain did mean something. The Indians would be sure it did—and Indians were seldom wrong in such matters. Not that they'd tell him, of course. Turning back to Jeremy, he forced himself to shrug off the growing dread of what was probably a perfectly natural phenomenon. He was, after all, a rational man. Superstition and the belief in omens was for the unenlightened. "Corporal. Cover yourself as best you can and see to Mrs. Gladwyn and Beth. They may need some reassurance."

"Yes, sir," Jeremy answered glumly, starting to leave. He stopped in the doorway. "What do you want me to tell them, sir?"

Henry looked up, caught by surprise. The corporal was waiting and he had to be told something. "Tell them everything is all right," he finally said. "Tell them they're safe."

Jeremy disappeared. Henry pulled on a dry shirt and went back to the window. Safe, had he said? Was anyone safe? Outside, the black rain streamed down, staining the world.

The chiefs gathered in the council lodge in the center of the Ottawa village. From time to time, one would rise and peer through the opening, mutter an incantation aloud and return to his place. This most certainly was a sign. Pontiac's magic was powerful, his affinity with the Great Spirit close. Now they waited for him to return, to hear his words and, from his decision, formulate their own plans.

The time of morning was a secret, for night had lasted under the macabre rain storm. There was a tribal recollection of a similar storm in the old days, but it was remembered only in an old story. No one, not even the oldest of the medicine men, could remember what had happened or when. There was nothing to do but wait, to huddle about the fire and try to ignore the chill gloom, the hushed patter of the diminishing spirit-rain.

Suddenly, the flap was shoved aside and Pontiac entered. His flesh glistened, streaked by the spirit-storm. His eyes glowed with feverish light. The braves made ample room by the fire but Pontiac ignored the gesture and answered their questioning glances with a single shrill outcry that made the blood hesitate in their veins and the flesh prickle. Finally he approached the fire and crumpled wearily in the warmth, panting from the long run from the Back-of-the-Turtle.

Teata, eyes wide with wonder, spoke first. "The Great Spirit has spoken?"

Pontiac nodded, exhausted.

"What will you have us do?" asked Hudoc of the Senecas.

Pontiac searched each chief's face before speaking. "Winter comes. Return to your tribes and lodges. Prepare for the hard times as best you can, and see that your warriors have food and keep their strength. We will meet in the spring. This time, bring all the people. I will send belts of wampum to tell you exactly when and where."

Teata, ever anxious, scowled in disapproval. "And what will happen in the spring, Pontiac, chief of the Ottawa?"

Pontiac sensed the younger warrior's derision but chose to ignore the question. Instead, he rose and strode out into the dwindling rain. Warriors and chiefs followed nervously. Pontiac stood before an intricately carved post a foot in diameter and jutting five feet into the air. The tribal totem told any stranger who entered the village that the Ottawas were at peace. Without a word, Pontiac knelt, dug in the mud a moment and straightened, holding a steel-bladed tomahawk that had been buried at the base of the peace pole. His powerful arm swung over and down and a resounding, splintering crash followed as the tomahawk split the totem and lodged a foot above the ground.

Teata's question had been dramatically answered. There would be war. The last drop fell, ending the black rain. The Great Spirit had spoken. His children would obey.

* * *

The bitter north wind that had carried the black rain the day before whipped the shores of the Detroit River and filled the sails of the *Huron,* pushing the sturdy little sloop down the current. Henry watched the craft from the ramparts. There was nothing he could do of course, but the sense of urgency felt by everyone in Detroit had caught him, brought him into the deteriorating weather. Winter was coming early and the *Huron* had to make at least one more trip before the weather closed in.

"Sorry to see her go, sir."

Henry looked at his companion, the young corporal Jeremy Turner. He had taken a liking to this youth who had so adapted to the frontier. Given half a chance, he'd be one to last. "Why?"

Jeremy bundled down into the thin coat, shoved his hands under arms. "I guess I took a comfort, just seeing her out there, sir."

Henry smiled. "I felt the same way. We'll get snow, soon. Maybe it will mean an early spring." Jeremy seemed lost in thought. "Corporal?"

"Excuse me, sir. Watching them leave, an' all, got me thinkin' of Captain Davers. I mean, what did happen to him? Where is he?"

"I doubt we'll ever really know, Corporal. The wilderness has a way of swallowing up people. They disappear, maybe caught in a sudden storm, injured miles from any help. Killed by Indians, maybe. Young braves eager for scalps. Many things there are in the howling wilderness, which is the danger and yet the great joy of living here."

"And if it was Indians, sir, then might we not be in danger?"

"No. At least not until spring. Let's go." Commander

and corporal scrambled down the treacherous steps, gained the more easily traversable ground and hurried toward the Major's quarters.

Inside, a heavy oaken desk squatted in front of the north wall. An iron stove glowed in the near corner. The floor space was further diminished by three extra chairs, and in one of these was sprawled Jehu Hays. "How do, Major. You'll pardon my not standin', but my feet are near froze." The ranger shifted closer to the stove. "I must be gettin' old. Not winter yet an' here I sit, bones achin' an' feet chilled numb. What'd you think of that rain? I never seen the like."

Henry doffed his coat and pulled off his boots. Still cold, he took a seat behind the desk, poured himself a healthy portion of rum and tossed the bottle to Jehu. "I'm more interested in André Charbonneau," he answered shortly.

"Probably holed up for the winter. I scouted half the damned northwest, seems like, and nary a sign of the scoundrel. 'Course, the folks hereabouts ain't about to talk, seein' they're French. What worries me ain't so much that young'un is the one who freed him."

"We'll find him in good time, Jehu. There's any number of Frenchmen within these walls. And who knows, it could have been an Englishman more interested in gold than country. But we will find him . . . or her," he added thoughtfully.

Jehu nodded, wearily rose from the chair and muttered something about getting some sleep before somebody sent him out again. He opened the door to find Beth waiting.

"I hope I'm not interrupting," the girl announced as she entered. "Hello, Mr. Hays."

"Hello, miss. See you tomorrow, Henry."

"All right, Jehu." The door closed and Henry turned

to Beth. "And to what do I owe this honor, niece?"

"Your absence," she answered bluntly.

Henry stiffened. "I don't feel particularly welcome in that house, Elizabeth." The girl shook her head in disbelief. Henry caught her meaning and continued. "We have been through this before. You are still a child and I do not expect you to understand."

"But I do. I have thought and thought, and Sabrina —you needn't frown, Uncle—Sabrina and I have talked it out thoroughly. Oh, I understand very well."

"If you've come to belabor what isn't any concern of yours . . ."

"I have come to speak my piece, and shall. I am sixteen, a child no longer. It is you and Anne who behave as children. You love her, know well you love her. And Anne loves you. I am not so gullible as not to be able to see the obvious." Tears spilled down her cheeks. "Uncle, you must return. Can you not see? Are you blind even to your own self?" She stopped, arguments failing before his stone-faced silence. "Oh, never mind! I shouldn't have come here. It isn't any of my business." Suddenly she ran, threw wide the door, bolted out the front and disappeared into the whirling snow.

"Corporal Turner!"

"Yes, sir," Jeremy responded, quickly alert to the Major's tone of voice. He didn't know what had happened but was taking great care not to make things any worse.

"I'm not seeing anybody for the rest of the day. Do you understand? Allow no one in."

"Yes, sir!"

Elizabeth's outburst—the very words with which, in his heart of hearts, he had struggled for so many weeks—stung to the core. Henry slumped into the chair recently vacated by Jehu. His hand fell to the side and settled on the stubby-necked bottle of rum. He lifted it from the floor and took three hearty, fiery swallows. The bottle was almost half full.

He stared at the cot placed in the corner. Damned lonely cot. Slept on them before plenty of times. Never had worries like this before though, he thought. Never let a woman, even Anne, drive him to quivering indecision.

Anne. God, she was beautiful. But too damned proud. Well, nothing wrong with that. He was proud. No reason why his woman shouldn't be proud, too. It was one of the reasons he loved her. He paused, the bottle halfway to his lips. Hell yes, he loved her. Had, ever since that first night.

He stared at the cot again. "Then what the hell am I doing here?" he said aloud, standing and tossing the bottle onto the rumpled blankets. "Damned fool silliness," he swore, stomping into a pair of dry boots and stalking to the back door. Henry had forgotten his coat, but it didn't matter. It was time to go home.

Anne helped Elizabeth throw another log on the fire and returned to her guests. Guests! Spies, was more like it, come to ferret out the latest on what the reclusive Mrs. Gladwyn was up to with her husband away from home and hearth. Anne was in no mood for niceties. Imagine, she reflected indignantly, Priscilla Hampton and Marian McBeecher paying a visit. Impugned by a teacher and a shopkeeper! The very idea was galling. As for Karen Schraner, what had prompted her arrival on this windiest of days? Was she in league with the others? No. Not Karen. Suspicion slowly ebbing, Anne asked Beth to go to the kitchen to help Sabrina with tea and cakes.

"Two fires and it still feels chilly in here," she commented nervously, more for the sake of sound than anything else. A log slipped and she hurried back to the fireplace to poke it back into position. A shower of fiery diamonds exploded in the air, winked out as quickly as they had appeared. Anne jerked back in surprise, stumbled against the sideboard, jarring Henry's sabre loose from its place on the wall. With shaking hands, she replaced it and turned to face her guests.

"The Major's sword? I thought he was . . ." Priscilla's voice faded and she avoided Anne's frown and Karen's virulent stare.

"So that's why you've come after all!" Anne snapped, rubbing her side and holding her stomach where the still-unseen child lay.

"Now, Anne," Karen tried to intercede.

"No. My husband is not here, as you surely know. Nor do I expect him. I leave it to your fertile imagination where he is."

"Attending to duty, no doubt," Marian McBeecher interjected, a sweetly condescending smile on her lips. The *double-entendre* did not go unnoticed, but what could have been an unpleasant scene was averted when the kitchen door opened and Sabrina entered.

"Tea and cakes," Karen exclaimed brightly. "Sabrina puts us all to shame with her abilities."

The servant blushed and placed the tray of delicacies on the table. Beth followed, carrying teapot and cups. Priscilla glanced with distaste as Marian's fleshy fingers gathered three of the cakes and, oohing with delight, plopped the first, followed quickly by numbers two and three, into her mouth.

Anne poured. Karen reached out, her eyes meeting Anne's and flashing a brief signal of courage and wry humor. The Englishwoman chided herself for ever doubting Karen's intentions. Somehow the seamstress had learned of the visit and come to lend support.

The wind gusted against the door, which strained against the bolt. The chimney sang a mournful note. "A strange year," Karen said. "A short summer, then that horrid sulphurous storm."

"Aye," Marian agreed nervously. "Jess said it's ill times we'll see, too."

"If you ask me, we've seen them already," Priscilla added.

Marian McBeecher nodded in agreement and swallowed her fourth cake. "It's the truth you've spoken, Mrs. Hampton. Why, Jess does nothing but complain these days, and I can't blame him. It's been a rare thing, indeed, the past month, when we've had a customer from the surrounding farms. The French keep away from the settlement, and those as do come in admit as they already have most of what they need."

Anne bridled at the useless chatter. "To what do I owe this visit, ladies?" she asked, beginning innocently enough, the anger rising with each word. "We have discussed the weather, your businesses and that which is not your business."

Beth, who had remained silent, stifled a chuckle. Karen discreetly looked away.

"Really!" Priscilla Hampton exclaimed, shocked by her hostess' bluntness.

Anne rose, near tears. "I'll tell you what. Because you're bored and can find nothing better to do than nose about for gossip. Well, I have some information you might . . ."

A forceful pounding at the door interrupted Anne's remarks. Priscilla glanced about, eyes wide and frightened. Beth rushed to the door as the knock sounded again, freed the latch and let the door burst open. The girl leaped away, squealing in surprise.

Henry Gladwyn strode into the room, his wild un-kempt mane windblown and a reckless smile splitting his face. "A party, is it?" he roared. The wind whipping about his shoulders ruffled the white blouse open to the waist, revealing the forested musculature of his chest.

Priscilla blushed and averted her eyes. Marian choked on her fifth cake. Anne was plainly amazed, more so than the others.

"Then 'tis a party that has just ended. Good day, ladies." His arms yawned open as if to gather them up bodily. None moved, could only stare. "I said, I wish to be alone with my wife. And so good day!"

Priscilla screeched and headed for the door. Marian, better sustained by all she had eaten, managed a more determined defense. "Sir . . ."

There was no chance for more. The trader's wife yelped in terror as Henry scooped her into his arms and carried the struggling woman to the door, caught her wrap from the stand and deposited her outside, desperately trying to keep warm. Karen Schraner, ges-turing in mock surrender, for in truth she thought Henry's intrusion great fun, ran past. "Nay, sir, I tarry not. Goodbye, Anne . . . Beth . . ."

Sabrina, hurrying from the kitchen to determine the source of all the commotion, caught sight of Henry and with a shy giggle just as quickly retraced her steps.

"To the kitchen, niece!"

Beth jumped away as the towering figure shooed her after Sabrina. "But . . . but . . ."

"Away! Sabrina's calling you."

"I hear nothing," she protested.

"By God, then you must be deaf, for I hear her

plain as day. Now off," he roared, advancing and laughing as she fled.

Henry whirled on the one remaining figure. Anne backed away, anger giving way to alarm. She had never seen him quite like this—wild, raw, an untamed titan spawned by the north wind. "Sir, you've lost your reason."

"Nay. I've found it at last." She tried to elude his grasp but the man was too powerful and agile. Anne felt herself lifted in his arms. "A welcome weight you are, Anne. Blessed relief compared to Jess McBeecher's portly wife."

"Henry, for decency's sake . . ."

"To hell with decency. For my sake. And yours." He mounted the steps.

"Enough, sir!" Her fists pummelled his shoulders, chest and neck. "The humiliation! My friends chased in disarray . . ."

"Friends? Now there's a laugh. Your friends will understand, and those who don't will tell tales in any case." Laughing, he kicked open the bedroom door.

"You can't mean to . . . I mean, after what you've . . . done . . ." Words gave way to a struggle to keep her gown laced, a struggle quickly ended when their lips met.

Breath rising thickly, his teeth and tongue enticed neck and shoulders, breasts—bare now, nipples taut and swelling—warm flesh against warm. How long without that touch? How long had passion been reined, lying pent up and waiting? "Sir, you are cruel," Anne finally gasped, eyes moist and voice trembling.

"Not I, my dear. Love is cruel—and kind. Matching only to break apart, breaking apart to make reunion all the more sweet. I love you, Anne. I was angry and tried to deny my love, and failed. I am a cripple without you. I love you with all my heart and soul, as you love me."

"No . . ." she struggled.

"Yes. Say it."

"No. I . . ."

He entered then and Anne knew the sudden fullness, the sweet piercing ecstasy. She arched her hips to gather him in and called his name. Her fingers remembered the familiar shoulders, roved down the bunched and corded muscles, down to stroke his hips and blend with their motion . . .

Time lost, then found again . . . The peak reached, and again the flooding of passion's nectar. Impossible to get close enough . . . to touch fully enough . . . to taste enough, to smell, to see, to hear . . .

Breaking apart and reuniting . . . Accepting, weeping, repeating, unashamed of lust or love.

"Yes, Henry. I love you. Yes . . ."

Later, while the wilderness world slept and the early hours slipped into dawn, the two lovers lay awake and drowsy, a wondrous, lazing entanglement of dreamy warm flesh, intimate and alone. When the eastern sky spread a band of light across the horizon, Anne remembered and placed his hand on her belly where the life quickened. For a long moment, Henry did not understand.

"Why did you not tell me?" he finally asked.

"I wanted you to come back to me for me. Not just because I was going to bear your child. Are you happy?"

"Yes, I am. Very." Gently, he leaned down, kissed her stomach and laid his head just below her breasts as if to listen for the faint, as yet unheard whisper of life.

Outside the open window, a fragile, flaming beacon from the east bounded from the clouds and lit the earth. A new day, Anne thought, no longer resisting the downward tug to sleep. Surely, a new and wonderful day.

CHAPTER 19

The first snow came later in October, two days after the Indians left for their southern hunting grounds. The next storm hit on the tenth of November. With increasing fury, the wind howled through the streets and battered the walls of the houses. The first patches of ice could be seen forming along the edge of the river. Activity quickly dwindled throughout the settlement as the inhabitants contemplated the mending of harness and tools, the repair of furniture and weapons, the thousand chores that would have to be done before the seasons turned again.

Winter. Bright morning of ice. Afternoons of blowing snow. Nights of bone-cracking cold. Silent months of cold fleecy drifts piled up against the stockade walls. One day spun like a strand of spider's web into the next.

There was time for everything: time to linger over tea, to sleep, to sit and talk. Time for hushed plans; Beth and Sabrina plotted to welcome the sleeping yet-to-be-born child, nestled in the quiet of the womb. Time to lie abed and dream, to be carried by the unhurried passage of time, to sit before the fire and imagine other days and a life to come after the child's birth. He would know England, know the English heritage from which he sprang and to which he owed

allegiance. This was Anne's singular resolution, formed
in quiet contemplation while reading one of Bouvier's
precious books.

Winter, despite solitude, was a time of renewed
confidence for Anne. Her gentling, and the winter
quiet had combined to subdue some of the wildness
in Henry, who even now entered from the chill, dusted
snowflakes from his scarlet coat and accepted Sabrina's
offered cup of spiced tea. Only the night before he had
shrugged off his military regalia and stood in bronze,
naked glory, basking in the warmth of the fireplace.
Warmed, he had dived into the bed, and to Anne's
squeals of mock protest, made playful, lusty love to
her.

She had won, in part, a victory over Jehu's howling
wilderness. Henry's appearance approached that suitable to an English officer. She had steered his conversations away from the petty and immediate problems
of the fort to the more interesting world of politics
and society back home, and his thoughts focused even
more on that distant world.

January, February . . . The hours slipped past in
lengthy amorous encounters—lovemaking before the
hearth in their room, with Henry worrying he might
cause her harm and Anne teasing, coaxing, guiding,
wanting. Harm? Not in the slightest, dear, she assured
him. Not in the slightest.

The snow still heavy on the ground, Pontiac stood
on the crest of a granite ledge and looked down at the
silent encampment where his people struggled to keep
warm and hold on to life. Restless children, he
thought, running roughened fingers over the belt of
wampum and reading the story of harsh times among

Huron and Potawatami. The Ottawas had fared better, though many of the old and very young would never see the summer. How much better off they would have been had the Indians never learned to depend on the white man's equipment. Guns, powder, knives, blankets, pots and pans—life was hard before the first strangers from across the great water came, but at least they had been prepared for the worst. Well over a hundred years with the white man had made the red man soft and easily broken, hanging onto the unnatural tools of a different civilization like a captive wolf cub who forgets how to hunt. Now that the Eng-lesh had seen fit to deprive their red brothers, even a child could see how necessity had dulled the instincts and driven the once-proud nations to weak-kneed beggary.

His thoughts were broken by the popping of a twig. Flower-on-the-Water stepped from the trees and warily approached. How long since they had spoken? He had hardly seen her since the move south.

"Are you angry with me still, brother?"

"I cannot tell."

"I am sad that a chief as wise as Pontiac does not understand his sister well enough to know the pain that fills her heart and leads her to defy his will."

Pontiac waited until the words were clear in his mind. "I see you alone and silent before the campfire. I hear the women rattle their tongues, talking of Flower-on-the-Water and how the Eng-lesh Major brought a curse upon her, how she will not lie with a proper man of the People and bring forth strong sons and beautiful daughters."

"I am sorry, brother."

Pontiac scowled. "You are sorry? White man's talk.

Tell me why you refuse little Flower, when you know it would give me pleasure to see Ottawa and Huron united through the joining of my sister and Teata. It is out of love for you I wish this."

"I do not love the Huron. I would rather be alone than with Teata. He is a dog."

"Hold your tongue, sister! He is a warrior."

"I have not seen him in battle."

"You will," Pontiac said, his face darkening as he turned away.

Catherine drew her blanket close against the cold. She, as well as anyone, knew what spring would bring, and feared it. Never before had she dared broach the subject with Pontiac. When they left for the winter camping grounds he had approached the war reluctantly, but the cruelty of the season had altered him. As the old and weak perished, and the babies grew silent and eventually died for lack of sufficient food and warmth, his heart had hardened. As each body was carried out and the pitiful blanket given to the one who most needed to survive, Pontiac's hate for the British grew until it was a flame that warmed him, kept him alive and yearning for spring and revenge. No longer was he a friend of Henry Gladwyn.

"Brother, must it be?"

For a long time, Pontiac did not move. Finally he spoke without turning. "Go back to our camp. Count the empty lodges and do not ask again. I will not hear Henry Gladwyn's name again, from you or any man."

Demurely, Catherine stepped away, stopping only when he called. "Yes, my brother?"

Pontiac's voice was strong, allowing no room for argument. "Do not tempt me to wrath, Flower-on-the-Water. You will take Teata. Go now."

Silently, as befitted a woman of the tribe, Catherine

descended to the village. Her heart was heavy, but she did not weep.

Finally spring began to thaw the frozen arctic winds. February gave way to March. The ice on the lakes began to break up. Perhaps the slumbering bear stirred in his lair, grumbled and complained with the quickening of sluggish blood. Deep tubers remembered the light and marshalled strength to re-explore the world above. White tendrils broke from brown skins and sent knobby fuses burrowing upward.

Inside the fort, Detroit stirred and wakened. The window in Henry's headquarters office stood open and a soft spring breeze promised peach and apple blossoms. A time of rebirth, or so the poets said, Henry mused, returning to the dispatch brought only hours ago by Captain Smalley. The letter recounted his brother's death. Sir Charles Gladwyn had suffered a choking spasm while dining at Stephen Berkely's apartments and died that night with a chicken bone lodged firmly in his throat. The Gladwyn estate and fortunes had at last passed on to Henry. Destiny had contrived to strengthen his bonds to England, and he could not dismiss the feeling that it was tempting fate to remain in the Americas.

For the tenth time in as many minutes he reviewed the arguments leading to his decision. Perhaps his fall from grace wasn't irrevocable. After all, half the conspiracy that forced his posting was gone. He was a wealthy man again, and could afford the necessary expenditures which led to political advancement. As important were Anne's feelings. She had wanted to return all along, and would be delighted. With a final deep breath, he dipped quill in ink and scrawled his signature across the bottom of the page.

April 20, 1763
General Sir Jeffrey Amherst
Headquarters at New York

Sir:

With the death of my brother, Sir Charles Gladwyn, and the subsequent succession of myself to
the Gladwyn estates, titles and emoluments, my return to England for the settlement of the estate
has become imperative. I hereby solicit your
interest in this matter in the form of posting to
England.

I trust this request does not come at an inop-
portune moment, and would be most grateful if
it were to receive your immediate attention. My
wife is with child, and should deliver within a
month, after which we shall be able to travel.

I remain

  Yr. most obedient, yr. most humble servant

     Henry Gladwyn

There. It was done. No need to add that Pontiac
and the Ottawas had returned, that Jehu had brought
word of how poorly the tribes had fared. Little use to
repeat that the strict trading regulations had led to
death and deep-seated bitterness among all the north-
western tribes. No need to mention that Pontiac would
no longer council with Henry, nor to depict the drawn
faces of the old, the sullen hatred burning in the eyes
of the young. Massive unrest, especially among the
proud, volatile young bucks, promised an explosive
spring. Henry could only hope that the weakened condition of the Indians and the strength of the garrison,

would help contain the uprising that was almost sure to come.

But Amherst's response would have been predictable. Well, it didn't matter any more. Since Pontiac was no longer his friend, the current commandant of Fort Detroit had nothing special to offer. Henry reread the contents of the sparse note and marvelled how so few words could indicate such sweeping changes.

The door to the study opened and Anne entered from the hall. "Am I intruding?"

Henry shook his head, held out the letter for her perusal and was rewarded with a startled outcry of happiness as she flung her arms about his neck. "Henry . . . Oh, my darling!"

"I did not think you hated it so here."

Anne blushed. "No, I don't. Not truly. At least any more. But England, Henry. England! How soon do you think General Amherst will act?"

"In his own good time, knowing the General. Still, there isn't that much of a hurry. After all, there's still a child to be born."

"A son, sir, I've decided. Will that please you?"

Henry's strong hand clasped about the back of her neck, drew her down to his lips. Anne prolonged the exchange, loving the rugged pressure. Then suddenly she broke away, was up and pacing excitedly across the office. "There's so much to do. Wait until I tell Sabrina. We'll have to pack, of course. Oh, dear. What shall we do about Beth? You know she's quite smitten with Jeremy—Corporal Turner. I don't know where to begin. First I . . ."

Laughing, Henry reached out and caught her, pulled her onto his lap and silenced her with a kiss. "There's time enough for everything, sweet mistress. Have you learned nothing this winter?"

Tears of happiness filling her eyes, Anne beamed at him. They were going back to England, to civilization. "I'm so happy," she whispered, resting her head against his shoulder. "I'm so very, very happy, my darling."

Jehu Hays sighed and shoved himself away from the table, glanced longingly at a remaining morsel of turkey. "Go ahead, Jehu," Henry laughed. "Unless Captain Smalley has been eyeing it."

"No, not I," the sailor protested, patting a well-filled stomach and loosening his belt. "After a winter of Fort Niagara's drab fare, this will do 'til the real heaven comes around. Pity Mr. Gilbraith had to stay aboard."

Anne rose from the table, managing to stifle a yawn. "With your leave, gentlemen? I tire early these nights."

"Aye. You must sleep for two, Mrs. Gladwyn," the Captain said with the authority of one whose wife had borne eight. "With a beauty like yourself so near, it's a wonder the river ever managed to freeze at all, and must surely be the reason spring has come so early this April."

"You are too kind, Captain."

"I'll come with you, Anne," Beth said. The two women bade their good nights and left for the upper bedrooms. With their departure, the dining room fell silent. Henry brought pipes and tobacco for each man, then filled three pewter-lined hard leather tankards of rum from a special cask Smalley had brought from the ship. Mugs raised, the three toasted each other silently. Henry resumed his place at the head of the table, filled a pipe, lit it from a nearby candle and exhaled a thick bluish cloud of smoke.

"Now, gentlemen," he said purposefully, "let's talk about Indians."

Not far from the fort, a family reunion was taking place around the kitchen table of Pierre Charbonneau. What should have been a festive occasion, the home-coming of André after a winter in hiding, was marred by the portentous news he bore. The onset of spring would see a determined effort to end British rule on the Lakes Frontier. Huron, Potawatami, Seneca and a dozen other tribes had united in secret confederation with the Ottawas under Pontiac's leadership. Unnamed French agitators had fired the Indians' hate and were promising, if not open aid, at least moral support and eventual assistance in the form of a French army marching up the Mississippi.

Furtive steps outside the house brought André to attention, gun drawn. Pierre motioned and his wife, Evangeline, hurried from the room. The precaution proved unnecessary, for when André nudged the rear door ajar, two familiar buckskin-clad figures, Thomas St. Aubin and Jean Dumas, entered.

"Well, messieurs," André said, closing the door quickly. "We are all here, then."

Dumas nodded to André, turned to the elder Charbonneau. "But are we together, monsieur? That is the question."

Pierre paused only momentarily, then raised his head. A hint of sadness tinged his words, but passed unremarked. *"Oui, monsieur. Nous sommes unis. D'accord?"*

"D'accord!" Dumas said, taking a seat without invitation. "Then we may begin. *Messieurs,* let us talk of Englishmen . . ."

* * *

Pontiac sent the girl away, for she did not please him. Not this night, with his mind racing toward the next few days and filled with a thousand plans and contingencies. The wampum belt handed him just that afternoon confirmed his plans had been acceptable to both Teata and Ningas, who to show their enthusiasm were already on the journey to Detroit. They planned to arrive with their warriors just before the Calumet Dance.

For the past three years, the Ottawas had welcomed the return of spring by dancing the Calumet ritual within the walls of Fort Detroit. This year would be no different, though Pontiac had arranged a far more startling conclusion to the celebration. They would welcome more than spring. They would welcome freedom from the English once and for all. A wolfish grin of determination split his face. Great deeds of valor were in the offing, and when they were done, at Detroit and at every other fort in the northeast, Pontiac would stand on a peak no other chief had ever occupied. And all was ready. Pontiac relaxed at last and fell into a deep, untroubled sleep.

Night. Henry fought his way through the last tabulations, sorting on paper which supplies should be sent to which of the lesser outlying forts under his jurisdiction. He was grateful Captain Smalley had delayed his departure: Amherst would be pleased at the early report and might look more favorably on the personal note he'd receive at the same time. The top sheet itemized the supplies sent to Fort Michilimackinac. Lieutenant Campbell's terse, infrequent reports were stacked underneath. Henry could read the young officer's angry frustrations between the shortly clipped phrases and grinned at Patrick's complaint of Sergeant

Fulton's insubordinate attitude. For a second a seed of guilt sprouted. Hell of a thing to do to Fulton, saddling him with a greenhorn that way, even if there'd been little choice. In the long run, Campbell would thank them both.

Somewhat fondly, Henry remembered the times he'd spent with Fulton. A damned good sergeant, the type of man who kept the army running, by God. How ironic they should both end up in America. And Fulton had said marriage would be the end of the Lieutenant that night in the pub in South London. How far away that was. Almost like a dream. Yesterday seemed more elusive than ever on this silent spring evening. Pity there would be no chance to bid farewell to the sergeant before leaving with Anne. A note would have to do.

It was cold in the office. Henry thought of Anne and the warm comfort of their bed. Maybe he had grown soft after all. Resolution fled and he put pen and paper away. Well, a man traded one thing for another. A wife he loved. A son—surely, a son—to raise in the brisk air of the Chiltern Hills . . .

A sound in the outer office roused him. The creak of a door as someone entered. No soldier had business there at that time of night. "Who is it?" Henry called out.

A groaning floor board betrayed padded footsteps approaching, and the image of Private Rexrode's corpse, throat slashed and blood-drenched in the night dew, sprang to Henry's mind. Silently, he primed a pistol and positioned himself to one side of the door that even now eased open on its leather hinges. Henry caught the hand that curled around the wooden edge and spun the intruder into the room.

"Catherine!"

The Indian girl stared at the floor in shame-faced surrender, then spied Henry's weapon. "Will you kill me now, Henri?"

The soldier scowled and placed the pistol on the table. "Don't be ridiculous." Unable for the moment to think of anything further to say, he sat on the edge of the desk and waited for Catherine to begin. The girl remained silent, head lowered and long black hair sweeping forward to curtain her sorrow. "What is it, Catherine?" he finally asked, more harshly than he should have. "Why have you come here? I should imagine I'd be the last person you'd want to see."

Catherine slowly circled the soldier, paused for a moment to linger near the pistol. She glanced up to see how this affected Henry, who remained outwardly indifferent. Satisfied that despite the uniform he had not changed all that much, she took the candle and stared into the dancing flame.

"I hate you, Eng-leshman. I hate you for what you have done. I tell myself this many times. Two days ago I returned to the forest where our lodge stood. The ashes were scattered by the winter wind. Only one small knot from the center beam remains. I mourned, for what I wanted was lost." She looked up from the candle and met Henry's gaze. "Do you know there are flowers there, Henri? Tiny green buds sprung from ash and burned earth? My brother tells me I am a silly girl, that these thoughts will bring destruction. He tells me I must hate the Eng-lesh Major, but the hatred has died. It could not stand against the flowers of spring." She paused, continuing wistfully, "Flower-on-the-Water is no longer Flower-on-the-Water. Catherine is no longer Catherine. Not Indian, not white woman. What am I, Henri?"

Henry tried to find an answer but could not. "I

don't know, Catherine. I'm sorry, but I don't know."

Inexplicably, Catherine smiled. "Then I tell you, Henri. I am the woman who loves you. That is why I have come. Not to beg for what you cannot give, but to betray."

Henry stood abruptly. "What does that mean?"

"The warriors of our tribe will come to council and dance the Calumet tomorrow. It is then that my brother will slay you."

"I cannot believe," Henry began, stopping as he realized how foolish that sounded.

"It is the truth. I have heard from one who knows." She smiled ruefully.

"But I allow only sixty braves to enter the fort for the dance and council. What can so few accomplish? And unarmed at that?"

"The women will enter, too. Beneath their blankets they hide muskets, filed short to be easily concealed. My brother Pontiac will give you a belt of wampum, one side of white beads, the other of green. At the end of the council and before the dancing, he is to hand you this gift. He will turn the green side up. This will be the signal for the warriors to attack. Within a minute, most of the officers will be dead and the fort will be his. By this way he hopes to avoid a terrible battle and many deaths. The Eng-lesh will be sent naked from our land. My brother does not wish to kill all, but I do not think he will be able to control his warriors. Not this time."

Henry listened, stunned. "But why?"

"A bad little bird has come among my people and whispered that you and all the other Eng-lesh must be destroyed. I fear they have listened too long and too well." She drew near him, touched her lips to his hand and brought it to her face. "I am a Christian and would not see this terrible thing happen. And I do not wish to see my Henri hurt, though I will never know his warmth within me again. No. Say nothing. For it would only be words speaking of dreams."

Catherine whirled, started out and paused at the door, her face thoughtful and sad. "Am I not true to my name, Henri? A flower on the water blossoms only once. Only once . . ."

Jeremy shielded his eyes from the sun's fierce blaze and stared off in the direction of the Ottawa village, obscured in the distance by a curtain of trees. Already that morning they had seen canoes crossing from the east bank of the river, and from the amount of smoke rising from the camp, it was evident many Indians had gathered. Soon a party of braves would start for the settlement. When that happened, Jeremy had orders to alert Major Gladwyn. Until then, his duty was to watch and wait.

The gate was open, letting anyone who wished enter or leave, with the exception of the English-women, who had been ordered to keep inside the fort. All morning long, Indian women had been drifting in one by one, innocently going to shop and trade. A larger than usual number of French settlers had likewise drifted out, suspicious to Jeremy only because he knew why they were leaving: someone had passed the word to the trusted.

Suddenly a familiar figure passed through the gate. "Beth, wait!" he called, jumping down from his post. "You know your uncle's orders. No one's to leave the fort this morning."

"Jeremy Turner!"

"Orders are orders, Beth. You know that."

"Oh, be still," she flared. "Mrs. Charbonneau is ill

again and Monsieur Bouvier had some of the elixir she's been taking. He thought it might be nice if Anne and I delivered it, but Anne doesn't feel like the walk."

"That doesn't change the fact . . ."

"I asked Uncle Henry," she lied, "and he said since it's only a mile I could go alone."

Jeremy looked around, disturbed. "He didn't tell me."

"Do you want me to go get Uncle Henry and have him tell you himself?"

"That's not what I said. I just don't think it's a good idea, is all."

"Whether you do or don't is none of my concern. Good morning, sir!" With an arrogant flip of scarlet curls, Beth strode down the path, scolding herself for making up such an outrageous tale and being so abrupt when it wasn't really Jeremy's fault at all. Besides, it didn't matter. It was a nice day and Mrs. Charbonneau *was* ill. Besides, she'd be back in half an hour. Uncle Henry would never know.

Major Henry Gladwyn shifted uncomfortably in the highbacked wainscot chair brought to the council house from his quarters for the occasion. He loosened the stiff braided collar which made each breath an effort, and went over the plan for the hundredth time. It had to work. Too much was at stake. It was already past noon. "Ensign Price?"

"Yes, sir."

"Anything new from Sergeant Livingston?"

"No, sir. Just that they're ready and waiting, out of sight and quiet."

"Good. Carry on." Damn! What was keeping them? It seemed as though hours had passed since Corporal Turner's anxious report that the braves could be seen on their way to the fort. All morning the squaws had been coming in. Without advantage of foreknowledge, none would have suspected they carried weapons beneath their blankets. Quickly he added the numbers. Sixty braves inside the fort, more outside. More than a hundred squaws inside. It could be touch and go unless . . .

The first signal! A steady tap-tap-tap of a single drum, announced the arrival of the braves. Through the door he could see the escort of rangers round the last of the barracks and enter the parade ground before splitting into two groups. Behind them came the Indians, sixty strong, garishly painted and led by their chief. Pontiac cut a powerful, noble figure, dressed in beaded buckskin leggings and loincloth. His body was painted a dusty blue and the tattoos on his chest and back were outlined in vermillion and ochre. A single eagle feather was tied into the knot of hair at the top of his head. The chief, followed closely by the subchiefs, Nontenee, Winnemac and Natee, led the dancers into the council room.

Henry rose to greet them, showing no trace of the tension that sent rivulets of sweat pouring down his sides.

"We have come, Henri, to council and dance in welcome of the Earth Mother's wakening, that she will increase the bounty of the forest and lakes so her children the Ottawa will have plenty to eat and may rejoice with her. We would have our Eng-lesh brother watch our dance, that all may know there is naught in each other's hearts but peace."

Henry extended his hand and shook Pontiac's, gestured to an orderly, who passed out tobacco and bread, as was the custom. Outside, the drum kept up the steady, ominous beat. For an hour, no one spoke.

The Indians sat placidly, politely finishing off the bread, filling the pipes and passing them back and forth until the tobacco had been smoked. The heat in the council room rose despite the open windows and doors, and with it the tension, keyed to nerve-breaking brittleness by that single, continuous tapping.

As the hour passed, Pontiac's face darkened and he strove to burn away every vestige of friendship for the red-coated Englishman sitting in the great chair. Success was elusive. He and his brother Henri had shared many good moments. They had shared hunts and campfires, respect and trust. But the Great Spirit had decreed they should be enemies: perhaps kill one another. Images of the winter-dead and the spring-grieving kindled his anger anew. The Great Spirit, the Father of All Thunders, had spoken. Pontiac would obey, in the name of the People.

Henry sat calmly, smoking when the pipe was passed, saying nothing. The longer Pontiac waited, the more the drum and the ranger escort waiting inside the council house bothered him. Outside, he could see the squaws in position along the street. Barely under control, he finally rose. "We have come," he began abruptly, "to show the face of peace to our Eng-lesh brothers. Why, then, do we hear the roll of war-like drums and see lines of men with guns. I would like to know the reason for this. Surely, some naughty bird has not been telling the Eng-lesh bad things of his red brothers?"

Henry rose, betraying no emotion. "Well does Pontiac know the drum beats many times in an English fort. Well he knows that the rangers drill to be prepared against those who would harm us. There are many tribes about whom I do not know and therefore do not trust. Not wanting to hurt their feelings, I have let the drum sound and the rangers stand guard to show them that we are always ready to receive Pontiac, our brother and friend, but are prepared to meet with musket and bayonet any who would come to do us harm. I beg Pontiac not to take offense at an action that surely does not concern him."

They were both lying. Each knew the other lied. The tension climbed another notch. Pontiac hesitated, his face dark with anger. Henry forced himself to remain calm. The moment of truth was upon him and he dared not quail.

Pontiac grunted and reached behind him. A brave handed him the wampum belt. It was white on the top; Henry could see the green underneath. To his left, he could hear Ensign Price suck in his breath. Outside the drum beat sounded like a giant heart, filling the parade ground. The Indians' faces were impassive. Henry steeled himself . . . His hand crept toward the pistol at his waist.

Pontiac rose, held out the belt. He was a mere three paces away. "We have brought a gift of peace for you, Major Henri," the chief said, giving no indication the braves were tensing for the signal to kill all in the room. "This belt of wampum will signify the bond between your people and the Ottawa nation."

They dared wait no longer. As Pontiac took the first step, Henry nodded. The sergeant at the door repeated the signal. Another step. Pontiac was only a pace away.

Suddenly the crash of drums, rolling now like thunder. Pontiac stopped, looked around. Outside, wood crashed against wood as every shutter along the street was flung open. A glance showed armed redcoats, bayonets fixed, at each window along the street. Another glance showed that the soldiers and rangers lining the walls within the council house had cocked and primed their weapons. Furious, Pontiac glared at Henry, wondering who could have told him. As he watched, the Major nodded his head briefly. Outside, the thundering roll of drums diminished abruptly to the steady tap-tap-tap of moments ago.

Silently, his face frozen into a distorted caricature of rage, Pontiac handed the belt, white side up, to Major Gladwyn, commanding at Detroit, then, wheeling, stalked from the council room, followed by the rest of the braves. Within fifteen minutes every Indian in the fort had left. As the gates closed behind the last, Henry sank down in the chair. "Ensign Price?"

"Sir?" The ensign's voice was weak and thin.

"A 'well done' to all. God knows what happens next, so keep the men on watch."

"Yes, sir."

"Oh, yes, Mr. Price. Tap a cask of rum for the men."

Jehu strode up from where his rangers had gathered. "Well, Major, I doubt we'll see the Calumet Dance this day," he grinned.

"Quite so, Mr. Hays, quite so." Henry examined the wampum belt; the sun glinted with ironic brilliance off the white beads. White, for peace.

"What would you have me do?" Pontiac roared to the glowering braves surrounding him. "Give the signal and see sixty of my bravest warriors slaughtered by the Eng-lesh soldiers? Watch while our women were murdered? That is what would have happened. And the weeping in our lodges would have sounded for many moons and all the while the Eng-lesh would have listened safe within their walls. No, my brothers. We were betrayed. One among us has turned upon those of his own blood." The war chief raised a pistol overhead. "My heart cries out for vengeance . . . vengeance on this traitor! Show him to me and I will kill him myself."

"Not *he!* She!" Teata shrieked, bursting through the circle of redmen and hurling Catherine to the ground in front of Pontiac.

Pontiac's face contorted into a horrid mask of malevolent rage at Teata's accusation. "What does this mean, Huron dog?"

Teata ignored the insult, only glared at Pontiac in triumph. "Ask her. There are those who saw her leave the fort last night, then run and hide in the shadows. Why? Does she go to lie with the Eng-lesh Major or . . ." Silence rung in the huge common lodge. ". . . to betray her people? Ask her, Pontiac, chief of the Ottawas!"

Pontiac stared at Catherine, his face unreadable against the rising hum of voices. "Silence!" None dared defy him. When he continued, his voice was flat and deadly calm. "Sister. Tell me this dog lies and I will cut out his tongue and feed it to the fish. Tell me he lies and the bonds between Huron and Ottawa are broken and there will be war between us until this insult is avenged!"

Catherine looked up at Pontiac, the brother she loved. Her eyes were bright with tears which would never flow, no matter what torment ripped her breast. The silence was a cage. Finally her eyes dropped.

"I cannot," she whispered.

A sigh from the crowd as all breathed at once. Pontiac closed his eyes and held his body rigid to contain the awesome inner struggle. "You . . . told Major Henri . . . of our . . . plans?"

"Yes."

"Are you a man of your word, noble Ottawa chief?" Teata asked smugly.

Pontiac stared at the faces around him, demanding the penalty for a traitor. "Flower-on-the-Water. Stand," he said.

The girl shakily struggled to her feet. For the first time in his life, Pontiac knew indecision. She was his sister. Sister . . . the word wailed silently inside him. Catherine, what have you done? I must kill you. It is the way, my Flower. It is the way of our People!

His finger tightened on the trigger. Catherine seemed calm. She read the torment in his eyes, was aware of his agony and knew with a surety he could not shoot, that he would rather be an outcast.

Love and hatred warred in Pontiac's breast. Love for a sister, hate for the English. Love and hate set to the drum beat of blood pounding through his heart and head. Her eyes were clear, as clear and direct as they had been when she was a child and he had first sworn to watch over and care for her. Flower-on-the-Water. How many times had they run through the woods together? How many times had he guarded her as she slept? How many times . . .

A brittle explosion shook the lodge and echoed dully throughout the encampment, followed by stillness. No one spoke.

An urgent fist hammered the door. Anne motioned for Henry to remain seated. The day had been difficult; he needed to relax. Would they never let the two of them dine alone? Besides, it was probably nothing more than Sabrina, who had left a half hour earlier to see if Elizabeth was with Jeremy. If that failed to turn her up, the girl was more than likely helping Karen Schraner with a dress or tarrying over a game of chess with Monsieur Bouvier. Anne opened the door and uttered a small cry of surprise when Jehu rudely bolted past without even the courtesy of a greeting. "Mr. Hays . . ."

"Major. You better come with me."

Henry looked up, tired and not wanting to go. With Jehu's evident concern, he snapped alert. "What is it?"

"You gotta come to the river gate."

"Really, Mr. Hays, this is hardly . . ." Anne began.

"Pontiac's there an' wants to see you, Major," Jehu interrupted. At the mention of the Ottawa's name, Henry rose, and bolted for the door, right on the heels of the ranger.

The river gurgled softly, its unceasing song disturbing the night with pleasant memories of youth and far more innocent times. Henry stepped through the gate. Upon his orders, the complement of rangers Jehu insisted on bringing remained beyond the gate with their trailwise leader while the Major continued on a few paces alone.

"Pontiac?" Henry called softly.

The war chief stepped out of the shadows. He was carrying something in his arms.

The moon slipped from behind a cloud. Only then did Henry realize what the Indian's burden was. "God in heaven, Pontiac! What have you done?" He pressed his hand to her heart. It came away sticky with cold and drying blood.

"Not I alone, Henri, though it was by my hand," Pontiac replied in a voice laboring beneath crushing grief. "I wanted you to see, for it is by your hand as well as mine that my sister is dead."

"Why, Pontiac? Why?"

"It is too late to ask why, Eng-lesh man, for we

both know the reasons. It is the way of my People."
Pontiac looked down at her face, frozen in sleeplike
repose. "She understood this . . . and forgave me at
the end."

"But Catherine . . . your sister," Henry struggled
for the words, lost them as he tried.

"I wanted you to know this sorrow and carry it with
you as I will all the days of my life, Henri." No more
to say, he turned and strode down to the bank of the
river, lowered Catherine's body into a canoe and
climbed in.

"Pontiac . . . !" Henry managed, his voice shaking.
But the cry went unanswered.

Suddenly Jehu was at his side. "Major. One of my
boys just come a-runnin'. They're all there. Potawatomis, Hurons, Senecas—warriors from Lord only
knows how many other tribes. We better get back in,
'cause we got us a regular first-class uprisin' on our
hands."

Henry needed a second to understand. Even then
he had to ask. "Are you sure, Jehu?"

"Sure as can be, Major. We're at war."

Henry did not notice that Sabrina had returned, nor
that Jeremy Turner was with her. He scarcely felt
Anne's lips brush his cheek in greeting. The paleness
of his usually ruddy bronze complexion told her
something was amiss.

"Darling? What's happened?"

Henry stared at the half-empty goblet of wine and
felt no wish to drink more.

"Well, it can't be all that terrible," Anne said, trying to alleviate his concern. "We've finally located
Beth. She went to the Charbonneaus' to deliver a
package and evidently plans to spend the night."

Henry erupted from the chair, caught Anne in a bruising grip. The grim expression he had worn on his return was nothing compared to the look of horror that now crossed his face. "What are you saying? Beth outside? By the blood of Christ!" he shouted, slamming his fist onto the table and spilling the wine. White-faced, he slumped wearily into the chair. His head throbbed. He welcomed the pain, wished it might increase to blot out every vestige of consciousness, that he might not have to face the monstrous trick fate and circumstances had played.

"We are at war," he finally said, his voice hollow, sepulchral. Anne gasped, Sabrina sat heavily, hand to her heart. Jeremy looked about like a trapped animal, panic for Beth rising. "We are surrounded by God knows how many savages bent on visiting fire and destruction on this fort and its inhabitants. And Beth is outside."

BOOK III

CHAPTER 20

"Good luck, Jehu. Be careful." The English Major and the American ranger shook hands briefly. Henry nodded and a private pulled open the secret gate in the south wall. Jehu and a dozen rangers, and Jeremy Turner, who had insisted on coming, slipped into the darkness. Each was armed with no less than a musket and a brace of pistols. Most carried an extra knife or two thrust in belt sheath or boot top.

Jehu grinned and slipped into the old pattern of night fighting. Too bad the Major couldn't come along, he thought, but there was no question the commander's place was in the fort. Still, it didn't matter all that much. If anyone could free Beth, he was the man. Now their only hope was speed and surprise. The ranger calculated quickly. No more than an hour had passed since they had learned the Major's niece had left for the Charbonneaus'. Not even Pontiac would suspect the white men would mount a raid so quickly. With luck, the girl would still be at the Frenchman's farm. With luck.

The night was a wall between him and the forest on his left, the fort to the rear and the river running softly off to the right. Sensing the presence of someone ahead, Jehu stopped, motioned the others to a halt and pressed his ear to the earth. Jeremy stirred, earning a peremptory wave from Jehu for his impatience. Night-sensitive eyes watched the woodsman gesture for them to stay put. With no more sound than a falling leaf makes, Jehu drew his special thin-bladed knife, the one honed to razor sharpness on both edges. If they were to get to the Charbonneaus', this was the only way. He crawled forward.

Kioqua rubbed drowsy eyes, stared at the log-strewn shoreline and wondered if his woman was truly with child. Perhaps she had only said that to keep from being beaten for letting the cooking fire go out. It was a thought. He vowed to keep close watch on her. If she did not swell before long, he would beat her for lying as well.

Bored with guarding the empty river and tired of cradling the heavy musket, he lay the weapon close at hand on the ground. There was no danger. The Eng-lesh cowered behind the walls of the stockade. It made Kioqua feel good when he thought of their fright. It made him feel powerful. There was magic in the white man's fear. More magic and power to be gained in killing them. Kioqua hoped they would fight bravely when the time came. He hoped . . .

The knife slid into the side of the warrior's neck and cut completely through the arteries and trachea. There would be no cry to warn the other watchers. Twisting the blade expertly, Jehu ignored the jetting blood that covered his hands and arms and spurted against his chest while he kept the dying man from thrashing against the underbrush. A moment later he let go and the brave slumped over next to the musket he had so foolishly placed to one side. The blood-stained knife lifted in a quick signal. The log shadows on the shore stirred and took on life, and the rangers crept forward to gather around Jehu and Kioqua's corpse. Quickly, Jehu led them into the trees.

Proud of how silently he moved, Jeremy worked his way forward. When he finally stopped and looked around, he realized he had blundered by not paying close enough attention. Preoccupied with only one thought—to find Beth—he had missed Jehu's signal to take cover. Now he was alone. Suddenly, voices sounded ahead. Forcing himself to stay calm, he stopped and crouched just as a cluster of vague silhouettes came into view and silently moved toward him like so many ghosts.

"Kioqua." A whisper, barely heard.

Jeremy clutched the musket tightly as he glimpsed the knit cap of a *voyageur*. The others were Indians, he was sure, but the Frenchman was in the lead. Jeremy remained motionless. If he moved, they would surely spot him. But they were walking directly toward him! He would have to move—have to do something.

Not receiving an answer, the party halted and the *voyageur* called once again. Then silence. The warriors and the Frenchman advanced cautiously. Jeremy's lungs began to burn and he realized he'd been holding his breath. Sweat streaked his forehead and his hands, clammy and cold, trembled on the musket. He thought of Beth. Sweet Beth, who had been captured, possibly abused—or killed!

An anger more somber than the night rose in him to quell fear, replacing it with a fierce will to vengeance. The *voyageur* was almost on him, and called once again in a hushed whisper to the lifeless brave. "Kioqua!"

"*Oui*," Jeremy answered, shoving his musket forward until it almost touched the *voyageur*'s face and jerking on the trigger. The Brown Bess roared and the Frenchman was blown backward into his Indian companions. Jeremy whooped, dropped to one side and fired his first pistol. He drew his second as a volley of musket fire erupted around him, and shot a knife-brandishing warrior in the stomach.

Another brave leaped astride the youth, lowered his musket and then suddenly spun away, crimson gouting from his chest. Jehu grabbed Jeremy and pulled him behind a tree. The firing had miraculously ceased. Jeremy realized the rangers had drawn abreast of him and opened fire when his first shot killed the *voyageur*. One of the rangers held up two fingers. "Damn," Jehu said. "Let's get out of here."

"But Beth," Jeremy protested.

"There's probably a hunnerd redsticks for each one of us headin' for this spot right now, boy. I got a lot of faith in me, but not that much. We're leavin'." Jehu turned to the ranger who had signalled him. "Who?"

"Charley and Otho," the almost invisible figure replied.

Jehu shook his head in disgust. "Bring 'em along. Now let's run."

If sneaking from the fort seemed to take an eternity, running back took even longer. Jeremy trailing behind, they broke from the trees, forsaking cover for a clear field of flight. Muskets exploded from behind, their number increasing as a huge war party swarmed out of the woods and across the cleared ground. Jehu and three others slowed, loading and firing on the run to harass the Indians.

Finally, they were in range of the fort. Jeremy realized the flashes of light from the walls were musket fire. Behind him, the howling pursuers relinquished

the chase rather than incur further losses. The gate
ahead swung open and men poured out to help bring
in the dead and escort the living. Jeremy slumped
against a friendly shoulder. Somehow, they had made
it back. Major Gladwyn was waiting as they filed into
the gate. The look of hopeful expectation died in his
eyes as he watched the last man enter. No one needed
tell him. They had failed.

Two mornings after the ineffective raid, on the
third day of the siege, Henry stood atop the east
wall, looking at the distant stretch of trees beyond
which the Charbonneau farm nestled in its clearing
surrounded by neatly plowed farmland. So close. He
could walk the distance in fifteen minutes. But fifteen
minutes might as well have been an eternity for all
the good it did him. Why the hell had the attackers
made no attempt to communicate with him? What
was Pontiac up to? For that matter, was Beth still
alive? The thought froze the marrow in his bones.
She had to be! Surely Pontiac wouldn't harm an innocent young girl. But this was not the same warrior
with whom he had hunted and shared a campfire.
Had Pontiac so grown in hate, had he so changed that
he would hurt Beth? Did I not harm Catherine,
Henry thought. No, that was different . . . or was it?

He turned as Jeremy reported that the officers were
assembled for the morning staff meeting. Henry
cast one last baleful look to the east, then descended
to the street.

In his quarters were gathered the fort's officers.
Jehu, Captain of Rangers, shuffled to his feet while
the others bolted to attention. Another officer might
have interpreted his casual response as a personal
slight, but Henry knew the frontiersman had led a

party of rangers outside the walls during the night and had had little rest since returning. "Good morning, gentlemen," he said, taking a position directly behind the desk. "Please make yourselves comfortable."

Henry glanced at the other faces in the room. Captain Smalley and Lieutenant Gilbraith, old hands both, looked relaxed. Dr. Drummond looked ill at ease. Lieutenant Melton, the supply officer, checked the totals on his inventory sheets for the hundredth time. Lieutenant Busby, the duty officer, was absent, probably on the wall. Of the noncommissioned officers, only Sergeant Livingston, the oldest Indian fighter with the exception of Jehu and some of his men, and Corporal Turner, there because he was Henry's orderly, were present. Four of the fort's five ensigns fidgeted anxiously, trying to hide their nervousness. Only the one who was absent, Mallory, who had come down from Michilimackinac and was confined to quarters with a fever, had any experience of note. Damn, but he could have used a few more officers. Another captain, certainly a pair of experienced lieutenants . . . But now was not the time for wishes. Now was the time for work.

"Very well, gentlemen, let's have our reports. Jehu? You weren't able to fire La Grange's farmhouse?"

"No sir, Major. Lost another good man and two wounded. Them redsticks was as thick as hens at a seed trough. I'd like to try again a few nights from now when they figure we've given up."

"We can't delay too long. They can pester us at will with fire arrows, and three men have already incurred gunshot wounds. As long as those marksmen can see into the fort from that damned roof, the west wall is untenable. We'll discuss a few plans after this meeting. I'd like you here, too, please, Captain Smalley. Ensign Johnson?"

"Sir!"

"I want a close eye kept on that fire detail, especially at night."

"Yes, sir. Only four arrows yesterday. All extinguished before they did any harm."

"Good. Mr. Melton?"

Melton, prematurely balding, stood with a sheaf of notes. "Everything under control, sir. Lucky for us the ships came in ahead of time. We have plenty of shot and powder and enough corn, wheat, molasses, tea, dried beef and pork to last at least four months, if we're careful. I've instituted strict rationing, with a close guard on all stores. We'll have nothing fresh at all, but I've assigned a few men to set trotlines in the river at night. They'll use the secret entry port to minimize the danger. We should have fish once in a while, at least for the women and children. That'll help."

"Well done, Lieutenant. Ensign Price?"

The reports went on, covering every aspect of life in a besieged fort. By the time an hour had passed everyone had a good idea of the status of Detroit and orders had been issued to cover the next twenty-four hours. Henry finally sat. "Very well, gentlemen. I think we're in good shape. Only two things more. Relax." He turned to Dr. Drummond. "Captain, I've decided that in case anything should happen to me, you will assume command," he began.

"I must remind you my rank is more honorary than practical, Major," Drummond interrupted hastily. "I have no desire to . . ."

"That will be all, Captain. Next to myself, you hold the highest rank here."

"What about Jehu?"

The woodsman chuckled softly and Ensign Price stiffened noticeably. "I'm afraid Mister Hays would have little success in attempting to exercise control over the King's First. We'll let Jehu attend to the rangers and a King's officer to the regulars."

The physician grumbled a final complaint but managed to assure the Major he would do his best should the need arise.

"Very well. Starting after this meeting, you will familiarize yourself with the workings of the fort and its defenses. Sergeant Livingston, you stick with him, give him a hand."

The sergeant acknowledged the order without change of expression. He disapproved of appointing a doctor as a commanding officer, but he would never have questioned the Major's decision. Drummond sat back, reflecting. Commandant! Lord keep Major Gladwyn, he thought. And yet . . . He had to suppress a chuckle. The notion of letting the conditional appointment slip out during a chess game would put Louis Bouvier in his place. Responsibility had its good points.

"Captain Smalley?"

"Aye, sir."

"How soon can the *Huron* sail?"

Smalley glanced at Lieutenant Gilbraith, who shrugged in response. "Within the hour if you wish."

"Not that soon. This evening?"

"Begging your pardon, Major," Melton interrupted, "but I've counted on the *Huron*'s cannon for protection at the river gate."

"Can we get them off and bring them inside, Mr. Gilbraith?"

"Yes, sir. If we have to."

"Very well. Do it after dark. As far as the Indians know, they'll still be aboard. Once they're off, head downriver. We have to get word of this to Fort Niagara. That is, if it's still there."

Henry stilled the flurry of questions and protests with an upraised hand. "Gentlemen, we must face facts. This is no ordinary insurrection. There are more than a half dozen tribes outside these walls."

"Why don't they attack and get it over with?" Ensign Price asked, a little too shrilly.

"For the same reason they didn't carry out the attack at the Calumet Dance. The Indian mentality won't permit the sacrifice of that many warriors, no matter what the goal. The result is not worth the loss.

"Second, it is Jehu's and my belief there's more afoot here than we suspect. We are under siege. Indians, by nature, do not mount sieges, and yet Pontiac somehow has united the tribes and done precisely that. He wouldn't commit himself to such an elaborate, uncharacteristic undertaking if he weren't certain of victory, and he wouldn't be certain of victory if he didn't have something up his sleeve. In short, we must assume the other forts have been reduced." A small buzz of excited comment rose and quickly subsided as Henry continued.

"It wouldn't be hard. Michilimackinac has thirty-five men. Presque Isle only twenty-one. Le Boeuf, Sandusky and Venango, fifteen each. With control of the Lakes Frontier, all he has to do is wait us out. If I am right . . . Well, I only hope I'm not."

Everyone sat quietly, turning over the possibilities. Henry turned his attention to Jeremy. "Corporal Turner, I'm placing ten men under your command.

You will accompany Lieutenant Gilbraith on the *Huron* to Fort Niagara, and thence, if necessary, to New York to report to General Amherst."

"But sir . . ."

"A sizable force will have to be assembled to our relief. Unfortunately, the *Huron* has a crew of only six, woefully inadequate under the circumstances. Ten won't be enough, but it's all we can spare. Captain, you may sail at your discretion after the cannon are put ashore. Corporal, I will have dispatches prepared for you. Will there be anything else?" No one answered. "Very well, gentlemen. Remember, we're on hard times and the morale of your men is of overriding importance. I want every soldier here looking sharp and acting sharper. See to your duties and we'll have another staff meeting tomorrow morning at the same time. Dismissed."

The meeting broke up quickly, officers filtering out in clumps of two and three, discussing duties and problems. Jehu, Smalley and Henry stayed behind to plan attacks on the nearby houses and barns that offered cover for the attacking redskins. The morning was half gone when the door opened and one of the orderlies assigned to the Gladwyn household entered. "Pardon me, Major, but Mrs. Gladwyn asked me to fetch you."

Henry felt his heart quicken a notch. "What is it, Private?"

"You've a visitor. Mrs. Gladwyn is entertaining him until you arrive."

"A visitor? Who?"

"A Frenchman, sir. Name of Dumas."

Anne refilled Jean Dumas' goblet. "You are too gracious, madame. And in such ungracious times."

"Horrible times is more appropriate. Why, you were fortunate to gain entry to the fort alive and whole, what with those dreadful savages all around."

Dumas allowed a thin smile of faint amusement. "But madame, I am *with* those dreadful savages."

Anne's eyes widened, but before she could answer, Henry burst into the house. Dumas bowed eloquently. "Ah, Major Gladwyn. Your wife is a charming hostess."

"What are you doing here?"

Dumas grinned wolfishly, touched a finger to his battered nose. Anne rose to leave, still shocked by her guest's revelation. "You should stay, madame," Dumas said curtly. "After all, this concerns you also."

"Monsieur Dumas," Henry began, keeping rein on a rising temper, "before I summon the guard and have you taken away, have you any . . ."

"Threats? How callous, Major. But no. You will not have me removed. In fact, I think it will be the other way around." With a contemptuous laugh, he helped himself to a third glass of wine.

"I am appalled by your conduct, monsieur," Anne said, suddenly nervous.

Dumas allowed his eyes to sadden expressively. "*C'est regrettable,* madame. Another day, perhaps, another place, we might have been . . . Ah, but small matter now. Our own fortunes are set and who is to say whether they lead us to ill or good?"

"I might have known you would be at the heart of this matter," Henry interjected angrily.

"You give me too much credit, Major. The fire was there, set by the fool Amherst and the Crown's own stupidity. I only added fuel." Deliberately, he drank and set down the empty goblet. "And now, Englishman, Pontiac's terms."

"Pontiac's?"

Dumas smiled. "You will abandon this post within the day, leaving behind all provisions and supplies save those necessary for the journey to Niagara. Of course, all weapons and powder will be left behind."

"I've heard that before, Dumas. What happens if we refuse?"

"Major, we have been men of the wilderness long enough to know what becomes of the poor soul who falls captive to these savages. I have seen prisoners kept alive for days and scream for the mercy of death until their throats bled raw and they strangled on their own blood. It would be a pity if young Eliz—"

Henry's fist slammed against the side of Dumas' jaw, sending him reeling across the room, stumbling against a chair and falling to the floor. Anne stifled a scream and backed away. Beth! She fought for control.

"Get up," Henry ordered, fists clenched as he advanced on Dumas.

"You always lacked civility, Major," Dumas said through puffed and bleeding lips.

"And you lack honor," Henry retorted. "You follow a senseless, ill-conceived dream, Dumas. France is beaten in North America, as every fool knows. Here are *my* terms, which you may carry to Pontiac. Disband. Desist this unwarranted violence and I will instigate no retribution. Return my niece to me at once."

"Really, Major Gladwyn, you . . ."

"Listen well, Dumas. I'll tell you this once. If any harm comes to her, I shall not rest until I have brought you and Pontiac to account for the crime. I leave it to your imagination what your punishment shall be. Now get out before I decide to keep you as a hostage. Guard!"

Dumas scoffed. "The English Major is grave with

the life of a woman. He threatens when the warriors of six nations besiege his fort. You are helpless, Gladwyn. Detroit will fall, if not today, then tomorrow. Do not be so foolish as to think you might receive assistance from any other outpost, for even as we talk they have fallen, their paltry complements overwhelmed. Detroit stands alone, Major. I offer you the one opportunity to save your niece and the lives of everyone in this settlement."

"You heard my terms, Dumas. Now get out."

Jean Dumas smoothed his coat, bowed to Anne and departed under armed escort.

For a long moment, the house was silent. Henry finally moved, set the overturned chair upright and dejectedly sat down. Another long minute of weary silence passed. "I cannot believe it," Anne began. "I hate to lose the things I brought with me, but to have Beth back and be rid of this place for good makes it seem almost worthwhile."

"We aren't going," the slumped figure of her husband replied.

"What?"

"I said we aren't going. I have surrendered only once in my life. No, maybe twice . . ."—he looked at Anne— ". . . but not again. Turn Fort Detroit over to Pontiac? Never."

"But Beth . . ."

"There is nothing I can do."

"But there is. Monsieur Dumas just told us . . ."

"I cannot do that."

"He was right then. You would endanger Beth's life. Your bravery does not become you, sir, when another's welfare is at stake."

"Damn it, Anne, all our lives are at stake. More so than you know. What do you think would happen if

I opened the gates and surrendered to Pontiac and your good monsieur?"

"Just what he said."

"The hell it would," Henry said bitterly. He folded his hands, stared down at his entwined fingers. "I will tell you a tale of the noble Jean Dumas," he softly began. "We first met at Fort Munro. Yes, Munro, not Quebec. Major Dumas had brought siege to us. There was little we could do save try to withstand assault after assault. His troops were aided by a large war party of Huron braves. Eventually sickness and dwindling supplies took their toll and our commanding officer ordered me to sue for terms. I was a lieutenant then. The Major was more than gracious—his terms were identical to those he proposed only minutes ago. Our commanding officer agreed and soon the entire settlement—weapons and goods left behind—filed from the fort. One hundred and fifty-nine soldiers and civilians.

"Dumas waited until we were well outside the walls before unleashing the Hurons, and then stood and smiled and watched, without raising a finger to help. Men, women and children were slaughtered, mutilated and dismembered. Some were thrown into cooking pots still alive and screaming."

He paused, the memory twisting his features. "I was charged with protecting them . . . I ran. Like a frightened deer. The others of my detachment stayed, fought with fists, rocks . . . They died . . . everyone . . . dead. Except me. Somehow I escaped. The brave, gallant Henry Gladwyn. Only Jehu knows. And now you."

Anne stared in disbelief. "But you were young. What good would it have done you to die, too?" she asked sympathetically.

"I ran, damn it to hell, Anne. I ran! I left them to die! All of them!"

Such treachery was unbelievable. Nausea tearing her stomach, Anne gasped for breath. The tale was too awful. Not the gallant Jean Dumas, with whom she had flirted, even kissed! "I cannot . . . believe . . . any man . . . Pontiac is your friend, Henry."

Henry laughed ruefully.

"She is to be left at the mercy of those savages, then?" Anne asked, the past horror fading under the pressure of the present crisis. His silence was answer enough. Anne paced the room angrily. "I wonder if it is the welfare of Detroit you are striving so hard to protect. Tell me. If you had never met Monsieur Dumas until this very moment, and you believed as I do that every condition pertaining to our safety and Beth's would be met, would you relinquish your precious command and accept a just and honorable surrender that we might return, safe and sound, to England?"

She stopped in front of him, waiting. Finally Henry looked up. "It won't work, Anne. I forgot my duty once. I'll not run again."

CHAPTER 21

By the afternoon of the fourth day, word of Dumas' proposal had reached everyone in Detroit. The civilians, unaware of Dumas' previous treachery, listened with regret to Henry's refusal; to withdraw until an army could be sent to clear the frontier once and for all seemed the easier and wiser course. Why endanger lives needlessly? they asked. What could be gained by the Major's actions but the destruction of everyone under his protection? Protection, indeed. If the way he protected his niece was any indication of what was in store for the fort, then all were doomed. As for the soldiers, their lot was to carry on as ordered and not think of such matters. They stood watch, cleaned their weapons, manned the walls and looked with no small amount of trepidation at the tendrils of sooty gray smoke drifting above the tops of the trees and signalling the campfires that waited, taunting and numerous, beyond the woods.

Their concern was not without merit. Only that morning, Ensign Mallory, still weak from the fever but determined to enjoy a breath of fresh air, paused too long to examine the field of action. The cracking pop of a musket from almost directly below his position on the wall disturbed the quiet and poor Mallory tumbled back into the street, his jaw shattered and

the top of his head taken off by a musket ball. His
assailant, with a roar of triumph, scampered across the
hundred yards of cleared land to the safety of the
woods, as if impervious to the shots searching his zig-
zagged path. Once among the trees, Pontiac held up
his musket and empty shot pouch to show he had
carried only that one load, thus adding another exploit
to his growing legend. In the fort, morale slipped and,
for the first time, men grumbled, looking over their
shoulders lest an officer was listening.

That night, after Mallory's funeral, Anne stopped at
Karen's shop, looking for a moment of respite from
tension and jangled nerves. She marvelled at the
Dutch woman's seeming unconcern for the fort's plight
and sat, basking in the quiet, while Karen moved
about cleaning up after supper. "Where's Gus?" she
asked, suddenly aware the house was inordinately
quiet.

Karen shrugged, stacked the dishes and carried
them to the kitchen where a cauldron of water bubbled
on the fire. "On the wall, I suppose," she said, dump-
ing a mismatched array of plates and mugs into the
kettle.

"But is that safe?"

Karen shook her head in resignation. "In times like
these, nothing is safe." She looked at Anne, noticed
the worried lines etching the young woman's clear,
smooth skin. Beth gone, a captive, and a child on the
way. No wonder Anne looked so distraught. Karen
had seen the wilderness test the mettle of countless
numbers, and though many had survived much worse,
she realized that for each, the moment of testing was
a unique experience, a challenge and sorrow to be
borne alone. The seamstress left the dishes to soak
and reached down to take hold of Anne's clasped

hands. "I will tell you this, *liebchen*. I do not think any harm will come to Beth."

Anne's eyes glimmered with new-found hope at the words. Karen continued. "Once, when first you came to Detroit, Beth was helping me in the shop. We had only just become friends, and she told me about meeting Pontiac. He had given her a name. Autumn Woman. He called her Autumn Woman. An Ottawa, and especially Pontiac, does not bestow a name lightly."

"I remember. She told me the same thing," Anne replied. "You're right. I'd forgotten. And Henry said how important such a name could be—like a trust." Tears came, unbidden, and she stifled a sob. "I laughed at her then, Karen, and now . . . Do you really think a name will matter all that much?"

Karen frowned at the tears, caught the hem of her apron and brusquely dabbed at Anne's face. "What is this?" she asked huskily. "Tears? And to what purpose, eh? You must set a better example. At least we have reason for hope."

Ashamed, Anne shook her head, forcing a tight-lipped smile. "Yes," she said bravely, placing her hand to her stomach, "we *do* have reason for hope."

Night wrapped the settlement in gloom. Anne had not meant to stay so long, to leave so late. Rue St. Joseph was foreboding in the eerie silence. The back of the barracks was to her right and a row of abandoned houses to her left. Perhaps she should have summoned an escort, Anne thought belatedly, for though the way was no more than three or four hundred feet, the walk alone through the empty street held all the terror of a childhood nightmare. She wished for a fleeting moment she hadn't felt the necessity to prove her courage or independence. But no matter. No more than forty feet ahead, the open parade ground, partially lit with the lanterns hanging in front of the church, offered security.

Suddenly she stopped, aware of a shadow crossing the faint light at the intersection. Shuffling footsteps aproached. "Who is it, please?" she called in a small voice that was swallowed by the squat, dark, empty rows of houses to either side.

The steps were nearer now. Panic welled, made each breath an effort. The urge to flee rose to screaming proportions, but she could not. Transfixed, she backed away slowly.

"Please. Who is it?" she implored. The shuffling steps came closer. Something ghostlike moved in the shadows, moaned. Moonlight, diffused by heavy clouds, glimmered faintly to outline . . . to identify at last the lurching shape.

"Oh, Dr. Drummond!" Anne giggled, caught on the edge of hysteria. "What a naughty trick. You frightened me."

He did not speak. Again the pleading moan. He advanced on her, his feet dragging with each deliberate, heavy step. "Dr. Drummond?"

Closer still! Anne backed onto a porch. The railing prevented further retreat, trapping her between unyielding wood and the splayed fingers of the dreadful apparition. Bile burned her throat. Her lungs raged for air and she tried to scream. The leering face came closer and closer until she could see the eyes burning with utter horror. His left hand reached out for her. With his right he clutched his slashed throat, from which sprang a horrid, spurting fountain. He stumbled, falling against her, striving to talk, to form words, to name his murderer. All that issued was a bubbled froth that spilled down his chin and masked a distorted whisper. At last, he crumpled, slid down her length and left an obscene red trail soaking her gown.

A long, terrible scream split the night. Anne stared down at the lifeless body lying at her feet. The scream rose, and she became aware it came from her own throat. Unable to stop, she clamped her hands over her mouth to stifle the sound. In the silence, she knew something else was wrong. Her hands were slippery on her face: slippery or sticky.

Footsteps pounded through the night. Lanterns bobbed down the street. The men who carried them lacked legs. Anne stared at the sight, only gradually became aware that the legs were missing only because the lanterns lit the men from the waist up.

"What's wrong, ma'am? You all right?" He was staring at her, aghast. "My God!"

"What's happening here?"

"It's Miz Gladwyn."

"You all right, ma'am?"

"Jesus God, an' the doctor!"

The voices went on, a confusing babble. Anne was circled by concerned men. Someone finally took her by the elbow and led her off the porch, away from the blood-soaked corpse and toward her house. More men met them as they reached the corner.

"It's your missus, Major."

"An' Captain Drummond. Someone killed him. Slit his throat."

Henry moved quickly. "What happened, Anne? For the love of God, what happened?"

If they'd only stop asking her what had happened! Anne realized she still had her hands over her mouth. She pulled them away.

"Oh my God!" someone gasped.

She looked down. Her hands were covered with blood! Sticky. A curious salt taste . . . The moan started low in her throat. "Henry . . . Henry!" Suddenly a searing pain tore through her abdomen. The faces in front of her were frozen as the moan stopped. Barely able to draw breath, air hissed through her clenched teeth as the pain struck again and again in wrenching waves that split the dizzily spinning world into which she plummeted. She was falling . . . falling . . .

Someone caught her. "Light the way," she heard someone say. "Get Karen Schraner to my house. Quickly, man!" The voice was Henry's, but it sounded as if he was far, far away.

Henry's feet had all but worn a path in the living room floor. From time to time he stopped and stared upward, as if trying to pierce the beams and planks that separated him from Anne. The clock on the mantel chimed for the fourth time since he had carried his wife in and handed her over to the ministrations of Sabrina and an out-of-breath Karen Schraner. "Two o'clock! What the hell is going on up there?"

Gus stirred in the great chair by the fire. "There is nothing to do but wait, my friend," he sighed for the tenth time, with all the wisdom of a man who had been through the waiting ordeal before.

"Wait? It's been four hours!"

"It's her first, Major. They take longer."

Henry stopped in front of the chair. His fists clenched and he stared at the Dutchman as if he were to blame for the delay. "Longer!" he exploded. "What the hell do you mean by longer?"

A piercing cry from Anne interrupted him. Henry started as if the pain had torn through him, threw up his hands in despair and started pacing again. The sound of a door opening stopped him. With a single step he was at the bottom of the stairs in time to see Sabrina poke her head over the railing. "More water. Quickly," she ordered, and ducked out of sight again.

Henry raced for the kitchen, but Gus stopped him at the hall door. "I'll carry it, Major."

"I'll do it."

"No!" the Dutchman ordered. "You stay." Without waiting, he disappeared down the hall and reappeared a moment later carrying a large, steaming iron pot.

Henry watched helplessly as Gus hurried upstairs. Before he could start pacing again, the door opened and Jehu entered. "Well? Did you find anything?"

"Nothin'. I been over the whole place like I was lookin' for a lost needle. His throat was slit, just like Rexrode's. Stabbed, too, but I reckon he missed the heart this time. I followed the blood, but it don't lead nowhere that tells me anything." He shrugged, looked up. "How is she?"

Henry slumped in the chair vacated by Gus. "The same. Hell, I don't know. Nobody tells me anything." He sighed, dragged a hand across his face. "Dammit. Drummond. Did you see her? Face all covered with blood. What the hell kind of thing is that to do to . . ."

"You're blamin' the wrong man, Major."

"I suppose so," Henry agreed reluctantly. "Still . . ."

A long scream from above cut him off in mid-sentence. "The hell!" Henry bolted from the chair and bounded up the stairs. Gus was in front of the door, barring the way. "Get out of my way!" Henry roared.

"You'll be under foot. Let the women work."

"Curse it, man, that's my wife in there!"

"And she doesn't need her husband. Not right now. Please, Major."

The cry faded. Henry sagged against the door. "Nobody tells me anything," he complained again. "Not a thing."

Anne strained against the rags binding her wrists to the headboard. "Oh, God! Please God."

"Press down, Anne. Press down with the pain. Help it." Karen hovered over her and wiped her forehead. Sabrina brought a new cloth, traded with Karen. "We'd better feather her," the Dutch woman said, a worried frown replacing the confident look she reserved for her patient.

"Feather? What's feather?" Anne asked weakly.

"Hush, child. It won't hurt. Now relax. Relax while you can. It will be over soon." Karen left the head of the bed to check under the covers. She was worried. Anne's water had broken two hours before and the girl was having trouble. The soiled bed clothes had been changed. Now a new, darker stain sullied them. Coolly, Karen pulled up the covers again, patted Anne's knee and smiled comfortingly.

Sabrina returned to the bedside, handed Karen a chicken feather and moved quickly to Anne's head.

"I'm cold, Sabrina."

"There, there, sweetheart." The girl's face was wan and pale, haggard with pain. Her forehead was clammy and beaded with tiny drops of sweat. Suddenly her eyes closed and her teeth clenched as another wave of pain hit. Her lips pulled back and her back arched.

"Press down!" Karen ordered sharply. "Press *down*, child."

Anne tried. Through the white haze of pain, she

looked down at the tent formed by her bent legs and concentrated on pushing her back into the mattress. She could feel the covers pulled off her and steady hands kneading her abdomen. Just as the peak of the pain passed, something light began to tickle her nose. She turned her head but the sensation followed, maddeningly persistent. She couldn't help it. Sucking in a great gulp of air, she sneezed violently, and then again. The pain below grew to monstrous proportions until it filled the world. She was being torn to pieces. Unable to stop herself, her head bent back and her lips pulled into a protracted scream of agony.

"Easily, child! Easy. It's coming. The worst is over. The worst is over." Sabrina's hands were warm and calming, her face only inches from Anne's.

"Relax, now, *liebchen*. Just steady pressure, not too fast. We don't want it to come too fast. Just steady . . . Steady . . ."

The pain diminished slightly and Anne could open her eyes. With Sabrina's help, she lifted her head and looked down. And suddenly the pain didn't matter any more, for there between her legs, springing from her body, was the miracle of new life.

"Press, *liebchen*. Gently. Help us out."

And she could! Face twisted with concentration, Anne pressed. For a moment, the tiny shining head cradled in Karen's competent hands didn't move. Anne pressed again. The pain rose, but she could bear it now, for a shoulder had appeared. And then another . . . and a tiny arm and torso . . .

Her child! Exultation swept away the pain. Karen was lifting the babe, holding it up, free in the air, the sweet air. Anne sagged back, spent. Her child. Flesh of her flesh. As in a dream, she heard the first, faint wail.

* * *

Nothing. The clock chimed the half hour. Nothing except hurried footsteps since that last protracted scream. Face white under his rugged tan, Henry stood rooted to one spot, staring into the flame. Gus sat in the big chair. Jehu squatted Indian fashion, back against the wall. Neither so much as moved.

Jehu heard it first. He looked up, waited until a second, heartier cry filtered through the heavy plank door. "Major," he said softly.

Henry's head came up. Eyes wide, he held his breath. A third cry. A thin protest. Like a shot, he was up the stairs, Jehu and Gus following.

The door was locked. A quick look of anger flashed across his face and he raised a fist to knock on the door. "Easy, Major," Gus advised. "They'll be busy. Give them time." Another wail interrupted him.

Jehu grinned. "Sounds healthy enough. Sassy, too. It's a girl."

Gus snorted. "Boy. Girls only cry once."

"How the hell would you know?"

"I've helped. Been there. How would *you* know?"

Henry stared at them, dumbfounded. His child had just been born and they were arguing . . .

The door opened and Sabrina poked out her head. "Major? Shhh."

Numb, Henry slipped in, leaving Jehu and Gus outside. He tiptoed across the room, eyes glued to the bed. And then he was there, staring wildly down at her. She was so pale! Her eyes were closed! "Anne?" His heart beat violently. My God, he couldn't help thinking, my God she's . . .

Anne's eyes opened and she looked up at him. A slow, weary smile covered her face. "Henry?"

"I'm here, my darling." A slow tear formed in her

eye. She looked so proud, so exquisitely happy, so utterly beautiful. Her left arm was crooked beneath a tiny bundle of soft covers, and with a nod of her head, she indicated he should look. Slowly, hesitant fingers trembling, Henry pulled back the top blanket.

A tiny, pink, wrinkled face appeared. The hair was still damp.

"Your daughter, sir," Anne whispered faintly. "Are you pleased?"

Speechless, Henry could only nod as a silly grin covered his face and a wild, buoyant sensation of joy filled his heart. "She's beautiful," he answered simply. "She's beautiful, Anne."

Her eyes were closed. She was asleep. Gently, Henry pulled the cover from the tiny face. A daughter, by God. A daughter. Sabrina was smiling at him. Karen was chuckling softly. "You let them sleep now, *ja?*" she asked.

Still stunned, Henry shook his head and backed silently out of the room. Damned if he wasn't a father. Damned if he wasn't.

Jehu and Gus were waiting for the news.

CHAPTER 22

They had tacked back and forth for four days against strong headwinds. On the fifth, the wind eased off and swung to the south. Lieutenant Gilbraith ordered full sail and the *Huron* forged ahead, racing for Niagara to bring news of the uprising. The storm that hit on the sixth morning was on them with no warning, churning the placid surface of Lake Erie into a veritable sea of Hades. Plumes of spray jetted upward over the bow and gunwales like the misty breath of sea beasts. Gilbraith, trying to make the quickest possible time, had too much canvas spread. Before the men could get aloft, the churning cauldron of punishing waves washed two overboard, snapping the mainmast and holing the hull beyond hope of repair.

The following morning, the storm was gone, having diminished during the night as quickly as it had arisen and leaving no evidence of the furor save the pitiful wreck of the *Huron*. Lieutenant Gilbraith, nursing a broken leg, ordered the wreck blown up to keep what little could be salvaged from falling into enemy hands. The sad task done, the remaining soldiers and sailors camped on the beach, drying out and nursing their bruises, preparing for the long overland trek to Fort Schlosser, beyond which lay the Niagara River and Fort Niagara.

Unfortunately, a war party of Wyandot Hurons had other plans. That afternoon, the Indians fell on the valiant and unsuspecting little band and slaughtered them. Gilbraith, seeing the hopelessness of the situation and fearing the torture stake, put pistol to forehead and pulled the trigger. He did not live to see the last of his crew overpowered, nor to hear the long, drawn-out tremulous screams of those not fortunate enough to have dry powder and a ready sidearm.

One survivor cowered in the woods, holed up under a deadfall. Jeremy Turner, out to find game to sustain them on the march, had just headed back toward shore when the first shots sounded. Throughout the night he lay shivering under the logs and piled leaves, trying not to weep aloud at the terrible shrieks of the victims and victorious ululations of the Wyandots. Somehow, with dawn and the last cry, fatigue and shock overtook him and he slept through the day until sunset. Hungry and thirsty, he waited the night before daring to move.

With dawn, Jeremy crept from his hiding place and sneaked back to the camp. The war party was long gone, and finding the scalped, mutilated and partially cannibalized remains of his companions, he wept again, for them, and for himself. Only he remained to reach Fort Niagara with word of Detroit's plight. He didn't think he was brave enough even to try.

At last the moment passed and Jeremy forced weakness aside. Time was wasting. Cold-bloodedly, he picked through the camp and gathered what he could find that would be of use, made up a pack, shed scarlet coat and breeches, washed out a blood-soaked set of seaman's clothes, donned them and headed into the emerald heart of the forest, avoiding the more frequently used lake-shore trail. Jehu spoke of the howling wilderness, Jeremy remembered, which changed all men, some for the better, some for the worse.

His way was east, away from the setting sun.

Juliet Elizabeth Gladwyn snuggled against her mother's milk-laden breast. Six days old, Anne thought. Six days already. She lay back against the pillow and yawned, enjoyed the tugging pull of tiny lips and gums. Rested at last from a night haunted by dreams of poor Amideus Drummond's pawing corpse, she lay drowsily in the sunlight streaming through the window.

Juliet gurgled and Anne hitched herself up on the pillow to stare down at the child. "I wish I could give you better than this, sweet one," she whispered. "I wish I could give you a world of culture and civilization, not this outpost in the wilderness; not the threat of death." As if to emphasize her thoughts, the muffled report of musket fire from the forest drifted in through the window. A second later the Indians' fire was answered by the soldiers stationed along the east wall.

A knock sounded at the door and Sabrina came in balancing a teapot, cups and biscuits on a tray. Anne straightened the covers. The tea smelled wonderful. "Thank you, Sabrina."

"It's little enough, mum," the servant sighed. "We've plenty of flour and staples, but there won't be any fresh meat, vegetables or fruit for long with those heathen savages all about the walls."

Anne patted Sabrina's hand and realized how very much like finely textured parchment the older woman's skin had become, how time and hardship had tracked her face. "We'll make do, Sabrina. We'll make do."

The door opened again and Henry entered, a smile replacing the frown so firmly affixed to his face these days. "You look well," he said, bending down to kiss her. Juliet's eyes rolled back to see who was interrupting her dinner. "Aha! Looking at me, eh?" Henry asked with a pleased laugh. "Recognize me? Know who I am?"

This single addition to Detroit's population had increased Henry's concern a hundred-fold, but now, close to her, worry disappeared. "Come here, daughter. Come see your father," he said, awkwardly taking the child into his arms. Juliet protested immediately. Her tiny arms flailed helplessly until she caught his finger. "Surprise," Henry chuckled as she tried to nurse his finger. "You'll not get much there, child."

Juliet wailed. Henry laughed aloud, which only upset her the more. "Very well. Back to mama. But beware I don't snatch you away when you've finished." Sitting down on the edge of the bed, he handed his daughter back to Anne. Juliet hungrily went back to her supper.

"Your daughter is voracious, sir."

"And stubborn. I did not think one so small could make so much fuss," he said, caressing Anne's cheek. "She gets it from her mother."

"Henry Gladwyn . . ." Playfully, she nipped at his finger.

Henry pulled away in mock alarm. "A perfect example. Detroit is under siege and you go around biting the commanding officer."

The smile disappeared from Anne's face at the mention of the momentarily forgotten outside world. "Henry? What is happening? Is there any word of Elizabeth? Have you seen Jean Dumas again?"

Henry's face darkened. "We won't talk of him now."

"But . . ."

"You have a visitor," he said, not letting her finish. The subject was closed. "Monsieur Bouvier. Will you see him?"

"Louis?" Anne experienced a moment of panic as a dozen scenes of the acidic Frenchman and choleric English doctor at their beloved arguments filled her mind. "Do I have to, Henry?"

"He hasn't let on, but the last few days have been painful. It would do him good to see a mother and child. Sometimes a man needs reassurance, needs to be shown the loss isn't absolute."

Anne blushed, ashamed she had thought only of herself.

"Of course." She patted her hair, pulled the cover over the nursing child. "But Henry, we must talk, you know."

"Later." He patted her arm and walked from the room. Anne could hear voices downstairs. Seeing Louis Bouvier would awaken painful memories, but she couldn't bear the thought of sending the Frenchman away. Life would be empty and sad for him with the untimely passing of his friend and rival.

She heard the muttered words, "a vicious killer," and Henry's reply: "No one has yet come under suspicion." Anne shivered and hugged Juliet close for protection. It wasn't bad enough they were under siege, but a murderer was at large within the walls of the fort and might strike again at any time. Had he seen Anne? Watched while Drummond gasped his last in her arms? Did he perhaps suspect she knew his name? Of course not. How silly! No one was looking for him so he had to be safe. Didn't he? She shuddered.

Bouvier paused in the door. "Pardon, my friend. I did not mean to frighten you. The Major said I could come up."

"Yes, of course, Louis. I was just . . . just lost to an unpleasant thought and you startled me."

"These days . . ." He sighed eloquently. "I know what you mean, madame. The times are conducive to unpleasant thought. But enough of sadness. You show me the little one, eh?"

Anne carefully turned back the cover. Bouvier gazed down at Juliet. Quickly, he glanced back and forth from mother to child. "Six days old and already a beauty! Just like her mother, eh? See? The nose, no? And the eyes. Such tiny little fists."

Juliet stirred at the sound of a strange voice, opened her eyes. "Aha! She knows me." Bouvier laughed, beaming with delight. "I can tell. Here, little Juliet, I bring you a present. A very special present, though you may not realize it now." He placed a leather-bound book at the baby's side.

"Louis, not the Shakespeare! Why, that is . . . You shouldn't!"

"But why not? I want to. She is English, so I give her a book by the only Englishman who knew how to write. What I want to do, I will do. When she is older, perhaps you will speak to her of Louis Bouvier, that she will remember, if not the gift, then the man, eh?" He spoke with forced gaiety, the tone harsh and false. Anne found herself near tears in response to the touching gesture, smiled brittlely in return.

Bouvier sat, leaned forward and stared at Juliet. "We are born, we die. What more is there? What more? Nothing else really matters, does it? What we choose to do—or don't do—all our deeds are as nothing compared to those two simple truths. Still, we go on. Why? Because we must. She is beautiful."

"You are too philosophical, sir. Shall we have a game of chess?"

"Chess? I have not played . . . recently, madame." He sat straight, unmoving for a moment. *"Mais oui. Let us play!* We have enough time for sadness without making more. I see you have a table nearby, and a pot of tea . . . So, we have all we need, yes?" He laughed, the exuberance forced and hollow. Anne did not like the sound.

Colors shifted from dark to light. Time slowed to a crawl in the shimmer of an unreal sun ripe with orange and purple and magenta. As usual, she had started somewhere along the path on the way to the Charbonneaus', floating, it seemed, toward the silent, waiting house. Utter silence enveloped her until her feet suddenly struck the front steps with resounding thuds out of proportion to all reality. The front door was closed. Rare, for a fine spring day, but not rare enough to cause alarm. She knocked. The sound reverberated through the house. Strange, how the knocking continued, echoing into the distance. An inner sense told her to flee, but her feet were now rooted to the planking.

Suddenly the door opened. André Charbonneau stood there, a smile on his face. Beth pretended not to notice, although she knew Uncle Henry was searching for him. "I've brought the medicine for your mother."

His white teeth gleaming, André laughed. *"Entrez,* mademoiselle."

She took one hesitant step. Someone hidden inside the doorway grabbed her and spun her into the room where another man waited. Instinctively, she clawed at him as he reached for her. The man howled and jumped back. An ugly reddening groove crossed his cheek.

The door slammed. Four men faced her. "What are you doing?" she asked in a high-pitched voice that sounded off key. "What have you done to Mrs. Charbonneau?"

None of the faces changed. One of the men walked toward her, kicked a chair away from the table. "Sit."

"I most certainly won't sit. I demand to know . . ."

His hand lashed out faster than she could duck. "Sit."

If she could have run! Instead, some dreadful force made her feet move toward the chair. She turned, and someone shoved her into the seat. Footsteps from behind . . . "No!" Rough hands caught her wrists and jerked them around the back of the chair. Before she could protest, a leather thong looped around her wrists, another around her ankles. The men stepped back and disappeared from the room. She was alone, helpless, a prisoner.

"If you are very, very lucky, my dear, nothing worse will happen to you."

Beth struggled, stopped immediately when a hand fell on her neck and started to squeeze. "I could break your neck, you know. Quite easily." Jean Dumas appeared in front of her, stood gazing down at her.

"What are you doing?" Beth asked nervously. "Why have you . . ."

"Shhh." He put a finger to his lips, wagged his head. Beth stared at the strange display. "You are a hostage, my dear."

"But . . ."

His left hand slapped her, rocked her head back violently. "Do not make the mistake of questioning me. You are a hostage. For now, you will stay here. Later, you will learn what you need to know." He smiled, stepped back and bowed with exaggerated politeness. "Do not try to leave, mademoiselle. There are those who watch." He was gone.

She waited alone, tied to the chair. Time passed slowly. Once she heard a muffled drumbeat from the fort, but nothing else save the sounds of birds or insects broke the quiet. Desperately, she tried to figure out what was happening and why. Had the uprising against which Henry had warned come at last? Once, an ashen-faced man she'd seen before came and untied her to let her go outside for a minute. There was no danger she would run away. She could barely walk. A quarter hour and a single dipper of water later, she was tied in the chair again.

It was dark. Terrified of why she was being held, she fabricated tales to keep herself from screaming against the pitch black. Far away, someone fired a gun, which was followed by more of the maddening silence.

The screams started later. They seemed to come from the direction of the fort, but of that she could not be certain. For the first time in her life, she prayed, but uncertainly, for she did not know how. Her whole body grew numb. Once she dozed, waking to the pain where the leather thong bit into her wrists. She doubted her sanity. Nothing was sure. Perhaps she was sleeping. Perhaps the meat pie the night before had been bad. If so, her dreams were worse.

Suddenly there was light outside. And people! The door burst open and a veritable demon bounded into the room. Nearly naked and covered with war paint and blood, the Indian walked directly to Beth. A knife was in his hands. André stepped forward quickly to speak in rapid French. The only word she could make out was "Teata." At the sound, her heart went to ice. Teata! His name more than any other was to be dreaded.

The Indian answered briefly, scornfully. Before anyone could interfere, he cut her bonds and pulled her to her feet. "White woman come," he said in broken English. "Come now." Without another word, he was dragging her across the room. Beth screamed, but he hit her across the face. André watched, white-faced and powerless.

She had no idea of where they went or how long it took to get there. Her legs were lifeless appendages. A branch tore her skirt. Another slapped across her face. Stones dug into her bare feet, but there was no time to cry out. Ahead, a blaze of light shone through the trees. Beth tried to hold back, but was pushed violently into a large clearing on the edge of the forest, where she stumbled and fell to the ground.

Ear-splitting screams filled the night. Terrified, Beth looked around. No less than three large fires and perhaps a hundred Indians surrounded her. A large black cooking pot hung over one of the fires and something pink and white poked above the rim. Beth stared, unable to believe her eyes. A leg! A human leg! Something warm and acid burned her throat, and she retched over and over again.

The next hours passed in a daze. Finally, a dull line of light glowed in the east. She was tied to a tree, her arms stretched cruelly around the trunk. The night had been filled with one horrid episode after another. At least half a dozen Englishmen had been caught outside the fort when the siege began, and the Indians had tortured and killed them, one by agonizing one, in a blood lust that never seemed to abate.

Mindlessly, she had been forced to watch their ingenuity. A redheaded farmer was the last. Naked, he was driven to the center of the clearing where a thick stake had been implanted in the ground. While four savages held him down, a fifth cut open his abdomen, and to a roar of approval from his companions, slit the victim's intestine, pulled out the loose end and attached it to the stake with his knife. The others pulled him to his feet, and the howling mob forced him to walk around and around the pole. Strangely, the white man made no sound, which drove the torturers to even greater frenzy. Finally, he fell. Beth knew he was still alive because he looked at her then, and smiled. She fainted when they poured the hot coals into the emptied cavity.

Daylight. She regained consciousness, looked around dully. The fort was visible through the trees. In the foreground, the grisly remains of the night's tortured souls hung on display in clear view of the defenders. She tried to get up, but her arms and legs were still tied.

Someone was approaching. Beth closed her eyes and feigned sleep. Between slitted lids, she saw a dozen Indians, led by Teata, enter the clearing. Two of them carried a long plank-like affair which they threw down beside her. She couldn't help it. She opened her eyes and tried to squirm away from them. One caught her ankles, another her wrists. The rawhide thongs were cut and she was thrown onto the planks and retied.

Teata waited until they were finished and she lay propped against a tree. An evil leer crossed his face and he walked slowly toward her, stopping less than a pace away. "What . . . are . . . you . . . doing?" she croaked weakly, barely able to talk.

Teata pulled his knife, reached out and caught the front of her dress. Beth closed her eyes. "It's my turn now," she thought, too stunned and sick at heart to even cry out. "It's my turn now."

The fabric tore and Teata pawed at her. The morning breeze bathed her breasts and naked torso. She opened her eyes again. "What . . . will you do?" she whispered.

Teata grinned. "Red hair show Eng-lesh how die," he said slowly. With a grunt of approval, he reached out and touched her breasts. "Send to Major. Red hair die slow."

At his signal, two of the braves moved to the board and lifted it. Beth tried to scream, but no sound would come. She thrashed about, but her arms and legs were leaden, would not move. The fort was out of musket range, but they could surely see her. The Indians set down the board again and propped it upright on a pair of poles another had carried. Beth was sobbing. Huge spasms wracked her body.

A cry, and then another. Teata howled and the fort listened. She could see figures moving along the wall. "Uncle Henry! Uncle Henry! Help me!"

When he was sure they were watching, Teata walked up to her and drew his knife. The tip touched her breast, started to cut . . .

"No!! No!!" she screamed, thrashing on the floor, waking up at last and thrusting away the chilled muzzle of the musket Thomas St. Aubin held. Still half asleep, she sprang to her feet, ready to flee. She was in the garret at the Charbonneaus'.

Groggily, she struggled to separate fact from fantasy. The dream had been true, up until the time the braves had started to carry her out of the clearing. For then Pontiac had intervened. Naked save for garish war paint, he had appeared from nowhere. Only Beth and the braves lifting the board had seen him. Eyes narrowing, they put her down again. Teata's warriors faded into the trees before Pontiac's wrath. A moment later two Ottawa braves had helped her back to the farmhouse.

Seeing St. Aubin before her now, Beth could not help but think the dream's horrible ending might well come to pass.

Fully awake now, she cast about for some sign that escape might be possible from this attic prison. None was. St. Aubin barred the path, his musket to one side and his left arm, hand flat against the wall, to the other.

"Your face is healing well, monsieur," she managed to say calmly, inwardly cringing at the thought of his touch.

St. Aubin scowled and touched the ten-day-old scab on his cheek, a legacy of the fight to subdue her on the day of Beth's ill-fated visit to the Charbonneaus'. "The wounds of love, *ma putain*," he smirked, leaning forward to kiss her.

Beth's fingers swept up to rake his eyes. St. Aubin jerked back and threw up his hands, in the process letting the musket drop while Beth lunged for the door and stairway beyond. Off balance, Thomas could only curse and stumble from the attic in pursuit, taking the stairs two at a time.

A flash of skirt at the end of the hall . . . St. Aubin raced to the kitchen to find Beth struggling in Dumas'

powerful grip. With a disdainful motion, the Frenchman shoved her into a chair. A slap across the face
stilled her protest.

Thomas St. Aubin dutifully stood to one side,
assiduously ignoring the girl's torn bodice, not out of
a sense of decency but because he wished to avoid any
undue association with a prisoner he had almost allowed to escape. He could sense Dumas staring at him,
and shrank inwardly. Dumas slid the ringed fingers of
his right hand underneath St. Aubin's chin, raising the
younger man's head until their eyes met. Dumas had
slapped Beth with his left hand. Had he used the be-
ringed right, her face would have been torn open from
chin to ear. Thomas closed his eyes and shuddered,
aware only of the coldly glittering jewels that delicately stroked his jaw. "I am sorry, Monsieur Dumas."

"You are an imbecile, are you not?" Dumas purred.

"*Oui*, monsieur."

"But even an imbecile can learn?"

"*Oui*, monsieur."

"How?"

Thomas straightened, stared blankly into Dumas'
face, acutely aware of the musket at his side. But he
made no move. Thomas St. Aubin had proven himself a formidable opponent in many a brawl. What he
lacked in strength, he made up for with treachery.
There was only one man in the whole world he feared,
and to whom he gave total allegiance. That was Jean
Dumas. "I . . . I don't know, monsieur."

"Imbeciles learn through punishment. Like children,
n'est-ce pas?" The smaller man gulped, nodded, dread-
ing what was to come. Dumas only smiled. "Do not
let this happen again."

"No. It will not," came the weak reply.

Dumas turned to Beth, who had remained silent

and not a little frightened throughout the eerily quiet but threatening interchange. "You will cook for us now. I am hungry."

"I will do nothing of the sort," Beth answered clearly in spite of the choking fear in her throat.

The Frenchman struck again. Beth's bodice ripped further, revealing one white rounded breast. This time St. Aubin watched. Beth's cheek reddened from the blow, yet she continued to stare at her captor through watering eyes. "*Monsieur chien* . . ."

Dumas' right hand twitched and she stopped in mid-sentence. As if addressing a child, Dumas bent and spoke softly, gently, the poison in his words hidden by a beatific smile. "Did I not save your honor just now, *ma petite chérie?* Ah, how you English forget your benefactors. But no matter. You will cook, no? If not for us, then for Teata."

Beth shivered uncontrollably. The idea of being sent to Teata was horrifying. "I will cook for you."

"*Bien!*" Dumas said, rising and starting for the door. "Thomas, you will be more careful with our guest. I will return after talking with Teata. There must be some way to convince Pontiac an attack should be made. Then we will not need the girl, eh? And you may do with her what you will." He laughed aloud, bowing with exaggeration as André entered with a load of wood. "You *and* André," he chuckled, "if Teata doesn't get her first." He was gone.

"What happened?" André asked after the door slammed. "What has gone on here, Thomas?"

St. Aubin adjusted his knit cap and frowned. "Nothing," he growled, angry at Beth and everything in general. "Watch her. She will cook." Mumbling an oath, he grabbed a tankard from a shelf, poured the remaining contents of a nearly empty wine bottle into it and left the kitchen for a more comfortable chair on the front porch.

André crossed the room, reached out and tugged on the ripped cloth, tearing it until Beth's left breast was totally exposed. She shrank from his touch. "Please, monsieur . . ."

"Please what?" André asked. "Keep you from Teata? You would rather have me, no?" Beth closed her eyes, trying hard not to cry out as he reached to toy with her breast. "No?" he reiterated harshly.

She dared not speak lest she dissolve in tears. Hurting and humiliated, she could only shake her head "no."

André shoved her away. "You disgust me." He jiggled an empty teapot. "There is no tea. Make some, now!" Trembling, Beth started for the back door. "Where are you going?"

"For water. I must heat water if you are to have tea," she whispered meekly, continuing outside, aware that André watched from the doorway as she went to the well. Briefly, she considered making a break for the trees. But even if she were able to elude André, what then? To traverse the Ottawa camp unseen was impossible. Desperate, she searched for an alternate route to the fort. What about the river? The shore appeared deserted. Downstream, the *Michigan's* masts were barely visible. Of course—the ship's cannon. The Indians would keep well out of their range. If she could make it to the water, there was a chance.

"What does Autumn Woman see in the river?"

Beth jumped, cried out. Pontiac had appeared from the trees, moving as silently as the wind to materialize at her side. His upper torso was naked, the natural copperish brown skin streaked with vermillion and ochre, over the burning sun and intricate geometric scars. "You were watching the river." He glanced toward the house, fixing André with a formidable stare until the hotheaded youth quit his vigil and went inside.

Beth pulled the torn fabric across her breast. "I . . . I don't know. There are clouds, on the surface, in the sky. But which is the real sky, the true river?"

Pontiac nodded, a trace of a pleased smile softening his face. "You are well named, Autumn Woman."

"My name is Elizabeth," Beth replied curtly, recovering some of her confidence. With a toss of flame-colored tresses, she walked toward the empty barn.

Pontiac followed, troubled by the unpleasant memory of a similar interchange with Flower-on-the-Water. The wound on his soul was still raw. "Why do you say this?"

"Because," Beth said, temper flaring, "Elizabeth is my name. My English name. And as you surely intend to hurt me, it would be far easier to think of me as one of the English, whom you hate."

"Autumn Woman forgets too fast."

Beth whirled, caution forgotten. "Elizabeth! And I have not forgotten. I know you've only saved me for the right time. André Charbonneau told me of Dumas' terms."

"They are *my* terms."

"Well, whoever's. My uncle did not accept them, nor will he, I hope. That leaves a brave warrior no other choice, does it? Is that why you are here? To take me away?"

"Fear makes Autumn Woman speak ugly thoughts," Pontiac answered calmly. "I came to see you. To talk. To forget about that which must be."

"Why forget? Why *must* be? It's what you wanted, isn't it?"

"No. This was begun many moons before you or I were born. The trees knew it would happen. The rocks knew. My people only waited until we could stand no more, until the time had come and they could wait no longer." Pontiac's words were sad, tinged with the desire to be somewhere else, some free place. Why did she stand so, half in shadow? Why did she meet his stare with such bravery? "You will not be harmed," he said, starting to go.

"I have heard the terms. I have heard Pontiac is a man of his word. The Frenchmen have told me. Not even for his sister's life will Pontiac break his word."

Hands lashed out to grip her arms. The muscles of his shoulders and arms bulged in a stark display of tremendous strength, bound only by will. The slash of ochre paint across each cheekbone made him seem almost demonic as his lips drew back in a brief, tortured smile. Beth stared in terror as Pontiac's face tautened in a terrible transformation of rage. In that fleeting rictus, Beth glimpsed her own demise and the heinous destruction of her loved ones. Then the powerful arms loosened their grip.

"Go . . ." Pontiac managed, his voice almost a croak.

"I'm . . . I'm sorry," Beth said. She had trod very dangerous ground.

"Go back to the house," the chieftain repeated, betraying unmeasurable sorrow. "Pontiac has said you will not be harmed."

Beth nodded dutifully, turned away and hurried from the barn, impelled by the intense stare that burned into her back as she ran.

CHAPTER 23

Pontiac had evidently told the truth. Two weeks passed, during which the Frenchman made no new advances. Early on the morning of the sixth of June, Beth woke from a curiously vivid dream. A red-haired woman had stood alone in a forest, surrounded by an audience of animals and men. The red-haired woman stood straight and tall, proud and fiery-eyed, waiting for her lover who would soon join her on the densely packed carpet of leaves and pine needles, soft and springy under her feet. From afar, through the dark boles of massive trees, she could see him striding toward her. He was short and muscular, covered with vivid tattoos and streaked with vibrant paint. His face was stern and serious and his gaze threatened to melt her to supplication. Footsteps drummed on the path, announced his coming. The dream was so real, that even now she could see him advancing . . .

The attic door flew open, outlined by a faint orange glow. Two shadowy, bedraggled figures stumbled into the room. "Company, *ma petite putain*," Thomas St. Aubin grumbled. The door groaned shut.

Beth cringed in the corner, listening with alarm to the labored breathing of two men. She tugged the blanket close against the chill. "Are . . . are you English?" she asked, afraid to speak, afraid not to.

A vague shape stirred in the darkness. "Aye. And you?" a man replied.

"Yes."

"What is your name?"

Beth could see nothing. She was speaking to and answered by a spirit. Trembling, she answered. "Elizabeth Gladwyn, sir." A macabre chuckle spread through the darkness. "And . . . yours?" she asked.

"Patrick Campbell."

Patrick, Beth and Private Will Jolline languished for three days. Each was let out for a few moments in the morning and again at night, allowed to use the privy and then returned to the attic. Their meals were passed in by an unspeaking André Charbonneau. For the first day, Patrick and Jolline slept, exhausted by long journeys, physical maltreatment and lack of adequate food, water and rest. On the second day, they talked.

Jolline had been captured at Fort Presque Isle, some three-quarters of the way to Niagara. Rumors of Indian trouble had been rife all winter, and with spring at hand, Ensign Christie, the fort's commander, had ordered all hands to keep a tight watch. On the fifteenth of May, they had sent out a *batteau* to intercept the *Huron* and so learned Detroit was besieged. A day later a runner brought word of the siege of Fort Pitt and the fall of Forts Venango and Le Boeuf, all to the south. The whole frontier was aflame. A week later they were holed up in the blockhouse, as well prepared as possible when the Indians attacked.

Fort Presque Isle—twenty-seven men and one woman—held out for two days against burning pitch, fire arrows and the muskets of more than two hundred Shawnees, Senecas, Ottawas and Chippewas. When at last they surrendered, the prisoners were divided among the Indians, some to be ritualistically tortured and killed on the spot, others to be kept as slaves. Jolline's ordeal had been long and harrowing. Marched first to the remains of Fort Sandusky and there held for three days while the Indians dickered over his fate, he was finally sent to Detroit. He preferred not to speculate on what was in store for him.

Patrick listened to the story with growing fury. Obviously, Amherst's policies hadn't been restrictive enough. As for the French . . . But there was no time for useless conjecture. Their duty was to compile as much information as possible and then inform the fort. To that end, he interrogated Elizabeth at great length, extracting as much as she knew about the rebellion, and recounted the fall of Michilimackinac to his fellow prisoners in case one of them should make it safely back.

For Michilimackinac controlled the straits between Lake Huron and Lake Michigan. Thirty-five officers and men made up the cadre and kept a benign eye on the more than three hundred trappers and traders, most of them French, who lived in and around the fort and plied the far northern waters of His Majesty's American territory. As with Detroit, the Indians were still largely inclined toward France and French rule.

Sergeant Fulton had been warning of trouble for two weeks. A half dozen traders had told highly suspicious and inflammatory tales of Indian preparations. Patrick refused to listen to them and dismissed the warnings as defeatist thinking. It was springtime, after all. The Indians were known to gather around the fort for their spring games. Eyes blazing and voice trembling, he told of the attack that had come in spite of his disbelief.

The Sacs from across Lake Michigan were visiting the Chippewas, who were in league with the Ottawas and Pontiac. For a week, the large temporary camp throbbed with life and the beat of drums as the two tribes renewed old friendships, traded slaves and other goods, and played baggataway, or lacrosse. On the morning of June second, there was to be a huge meet between the two tribes.

The day dawned bright and clear. Squaws and non-players filtered into the fort to trade and visit. By nine, the game had started on the field in front of the fort. Officers and men lined the walls and stood by the open gate to watch the play. Over twenty men to a side rampaged up and down the field in a fierce contest more noted for cracked skulls and broken bones than finesse. Armed with a four-foot pole equipped with a webbed basket at one end, the players flung a carved wooden ball the size and shape of a turkey egg back and forth. The object was to score by touching a post at either end of the field.

Patrick stopped in the middle of his account, chuckling uncontrollably. Beth handed him a cup of water and he drank deeply, spilling some down his chin before continuing. "We never had a hint. One minute the game was progressing normally. Suddenly, someone threw wildly and the ball shot through the gates. In a second, forty savages were after it. Like a boiling pack of dogs, they thundered into the fort. And then . . ." Patrick stared in her direction, his eyes focused somewhere far away.

"Go on," Beth prompted.

"And then they struck," he whispered, visualizing

the scene. "Squaws opened their blankets and tossed hidden weapons to their men. The soldiers at the gate were killed before anyone even knew anything was wrong. I . . . watched . . . suddenly found myself running madly for safety. A tomahawk passed over my shoulder and struck the man in front of me . . ." He grimaced horribly. "His brains . . . his brains . . . his brains . . ."

"There's nothing too cruel for the likes of them heathens," Jolline muttered.

"I know," Beth said softly, remembering Teata's crazed triumph.

The rest of the story came out in agonized bits and pieces. By the time Patrick was captured, eighteen of the thirty-five lay in dark splotches of their own blood in gruesome attitudes of death. Within the hour he was taken from Michilimackinac and marched south for Detroit. To make matters even more discouraging, another captive, brought part of the way with Patrick and killed before reaching Detroit, had carried news of the burning of Fort Sault Sainte Marie, the abandonment of Fort Edward Augustus and the downfall of Fort St. Joseph. All the far north forts were gone. At Detroit his captors had handed Patrick over to the Hurons and the officer had experienced firsthand Teata's personal brand of humor. The clothes ripped from his back, he'd been mocked, beaten and spat upon before being given a dead soldier's ill-fitting breeches and thrown into the attic.

Their situation was desperate, indeed. Captive and expecting death, there was nowhere the three could look for succor. It appeared as if the Indians had wiped out the whole of the English force in the Lakes Frontier, save for Detroit, which was in dire jeopardy. That night, they all slept uneasily, tossing and turning on the bare boards, wracked by their individual nightmares.

Patrick lay awake, as he had all night long, listening to the drawn-out shrieks of agony. One or two prisoners had been brought in from most of the reduced forts, and Detroit was being treated to their slow, humiliating death. Patrick was no different from those inside the walls: he didn't need to see the atrocities. The screams were enough.

The last cry faded with the night. Satiated for awhile, the Indians would sleep until midday. The defenders on the walls would not. Bleary-eyed from fatigue and fear, their tempers would grow short.

Patrick considered. It would soon be his turn. He would have to escape that morning, before the Indians finally woke up after their night-long orgiastic spree. Determined, he roused Beth and Jolline and explained the necessity for escape. Groggy after only an hour's sleep, the private and the girl helped in the feverish search of the attic for any implement that could be used to slip the latch or serve as a weapon, stopping only when André showed up a half hour later to lead them out one by one and then leave what would pass for breakfast and a fresh bucket of water. He would be back at noon, he told them, with a surprise for the two soldiers. As soon as he left, driving the bolt home and dropping the bar into place, they fell to frenzied activity, working desperately in the weak light that peeped in through cracks of the wall. Beth stood guard, watching through a chink in the wall, as André and Thomas disappeared into the forest.

It was Jolline, rummaging in a dusty corner, who found a suitable tool—a broken section of an old hickory ramrod. Patrick grabbed the stick and set to work, shaping it to his needs on the brass corner of a trunk.

A half hour later he had worked the slim stick between the door and sill and eased out the bolt. The bar was their sole remaining restraint, a problem Beth solved. Using thread from the hem of her skirt, she braided a long string which, with the aid of the ramrod, was shoved through a crack, worked around the bar, pulled back through the same crack and tied in a knot. Seconds later, the bar was pulled up and the door eased open.

Alone, Patrick reconnoitered. The house was empty of all guards. Five minutes later and he was back in the attic, carrying shirts for himself and Jolline and a loaf of bread and a huge chunk of cheese which he handed to Beth. "Hide these," he said, taking a final drink of water. "You may need it."

"What about me, sir?" Jolline asked, afraid to stay and even more apprehensive about leaving.

Patrick paused in the doorway. "We'll make a break for it right through the middle of the camp." He grimaced, gestured to their bare feet. "The path is open through there, clean and well worn. Without shoes we'd never make it through the fields."

Elizabeth faltered, "I'm going too."

Patrick stared at her, decided quickly. "No. That will be impossible."

"I won't be left behind," she said, beginning to panic. "You can't leave me here. When they see you're gone, I'll be blamed and they'll . . . Oh, my God! Don't you see? They . . . they'll . . ."

Patrick caught her by the arm, violently shook her. "Calm down, Elizabeth. Calm down, now!" She stared at him, eyes wide and pleading. "Now listen carefully. We're the ones they'll kill. Pontiac won't let you die, but he'll gladly watch Teata torture us. You'll not be harmed!"

"You can't leave me," Beth sobbed. "You can't, Lieutenant."

"We must. It's our only chance," he insisted impatiently. "Two men, with these clothes, might be mistaken for *voyageurs* just long enough to let us through. But a white woman? Never. You'll stay."

"I'm coming whether you want me to or not."

Patrick dropped her arms. His eyes were cold and calculating. "Very well," he said at last. "Wait here while I find something for you to wear."

He was back sooner than she had dared hope, but instead of clothes, carried a piece of rope. Elizabeth paled. "What are you doing?"

"Escaping," Patrick answered shortly. "And wasting no more time on words. Now, will you let me tie you, or do I have to do it the hard way?"

Beth looked to Jolline for help, but could see the youth was too frightened to disobey a direct order from his superior. She sagged, defeated, and listlessly allowed Patrick to wind the rope about her wrists and ankles, then tie it tightly. "If I ever get out of here and tell my uncle," Beth began.

"You won't have to. I'll tell him myself. And I think he'll understand. Now, if you'll wish us luck? We have no more time." Patrick considered, turned to Jolline, "Speed and surprise will be our hope. A weapon will only be extra weight. Are you ready?"

Jolline couldn't keep his eyes off the tomahawks, quickly grabbed one and returned to the door. "Just in case. I'm ready if you are."

"Very well, Private," Patrick smiled, calm now. He opened the door, stepped onto the porch and stretched nonchalantly, as if he were a host, wishing a visitor Godspeed. "Good luck, Private."

Jolline tucked the tomahawk in his belt, hitched up his pants. "Same to you, Lieutenant. Nice morning for a stroll."

Patrick shuddered, strangely exhilarated. Never before had he felt so alive. The path ahead lay beckoning, promising escape . . . or doom. He stifled the urge to laugh as they stepped from the porch and walked across the clearing, heading for the woods. The morning was still. No one appeared to be moving or watching, but each felt as if a thousand eyes followed his every step. Patrick strode along briskly, looking neither to left nor right. Jolline kept up, making his head stay forward, but casting about with his eyes. A rivulet of sweat poured from each armpit and down the small of his back.

Fifty yards, and still no cry. "So far so good, Private. We start running at the edge of the trees."

"Yes, sir," Jolline answered, his throat dry.

Another twenty-five yards. Patrick's heart was beating violently, the blood pounding in his head. Less than a mile to go. Each step was a calculated risk, each added pace increased the chances of detection. Objects stood out clearly. Each rock, each stone, each tree . . . "Now!" he whispered hoarsely, breaking into a silent run.

The path was clear before them. Patrick was swifter, broke into the first camp a half dozen strides before Jolline and kept on going. As he had hoped, the Indians were still asleep and they traversed the camp without rousing the slumbering braves. Only on the perimeter was one Indian awake, leaning against a tree to relieve himself. Patrick plunged into the woods before the startled brave could react, and Jolline caught him with a tomahawk just as he raised a shout.

The dying Indian sank to the ground, thrashing in the underbrush. Somewhere, a dog barked and the camp behind them awoke in time to see Jolline disappear.

On they ran, bleeding feet pounding on the packed path. A cry from behind, and Patrick pushed faster. Jolline, winded already, felt his lungs catch on fire, burn through his ribs with knife-sharp pains. How far? What about the other camp? Thought was muddied, nearly impossible. Behind them, the cries of alarm swelled and running feet pounded closer.

Suddenly they were in the next camp, the edge of the woods visible ahead. Patrick had his second wind, spurted around one campfire and leaped another. Jolline, his breath coming in labored rasps, struggled to keep up, blundered through the first fire without seeing it, lurched around the second. The braves here were awake, and though taken as much by surprise as those in the first camp, reacted more swiftly.

Patrick slammed into one, sent him sprawling into a temporary lodge, knocking the structure to the ground. A brave ran toward Jolline, screaming a war cry and raising his tomahawk. The sight and the sudden, looming thought of the torture stake drove the pain from the private's feet and aching lungs and spurred him on. Ducking under the whistling blade, he knotted both fists into a ball and sent the brave spinning into a campfire. On all sides, startled, infuriated Indians rose from the ground in time to impede the progress of those from the first camp, now pouring from the path.

Ahead, a cry from Patrick. The forest was thinning, Jolline saw. They were through! He could see the fort! Only another quarter of a mile. They'd done it after all! He cut through the remaining fringe of trees. The pursuers had no clear field of fire. The Lieutenant was well ahead, passing the burnt-out remains of a barn and rapidly covering the open ground.

Something thumped Jolline in the back, with the sound of a fist hitting a ripe melon. He felt nothing at first. Then, suddenly the whole world went off balance and the ground rushed to meet him. Jolline slammed into the dirt, scrambled frantically, trying to rise. Can't stop now, he thought, spitting soil and struggling to his knees. He coughed and something spewed from his mouth, covered his forearms and hands with red froth. Tiny puffs of gray-black smoke rippled along the walls of the fort and the Indians turned and ran back.

Good. They were covering him. In a moment he'd reach the walls and be welcomed into the arms of friends. All he had to do was run a little faster . . . Something struck his head and he fell once more and was pulled upright by the hair. He felt a searing pain along his scalp and a curtain of red descended, to cut off the light.

Gasping for breath and barely able to stand, Patrick was rushed to the dispensary. Henry arrived while Private McManaway, acting medic since Drummond's death, cleaned and bound the cuts on the Lieutenant's feet. When Jehu showed up five minutes later, McManaway was hustled out. Henry passed Patrick a tankard of spirits and sat back, waiting for him to regain enough strength to speak.

Patrick began slowly after downing a gulp of rum. "They hit us on the second, sir. We didn't have a chance . . ." For an hour he talked, covering the events at Michilimackinac and adding the intelligence garnered from Private Jolline and Elizabeth. Neither senior officer interrupted. Instead they sat impassively, listening and correlating the news he brought with what they already knew.

"Damn!" Henry beat on the arm of the chair. "Why in hell didn't you at least try to get her out?" Patrick pulled the blanket closer about him. "Just to tie her up, leave her alone in there. What the hell kind of man are you?"

"I did well to bring myself out, Major, and you know it," Patrick countered.

"You did well," Henry repeated sarcastically. "You did well to lose Michilimackinac, too, I suppose." Patrick's faced reddened. "Some of the best men on the frontier are dead, and you did well? Damn it, man, some of them went through the continent with me. Fulton taught me half of what I know, and you did well?" He leaned forward, barely under control. "Do you know what, Campbell?"

"Sir?"

"It's a damned shame, I think, that they don't eat the lieutenants and save the sergeants."

Patrick stiffened. "I don't think Pontiac will let her be hurt, sir, if that's what . . ."

"You don't *think!*" Henry roared, coming to his feet. "That's my niece, Lieutenant."

"She never would have made it," Patrick responded flatly. "I did what I thought best, at the time and under the circumstances."

Henry stared at the blanket-wrapped figure, then dropped into the chair, drained of emotion. "Very well, Lieutenant. I'm sure you did. I wasn't there."

Patrick roused himself to take the initiative. "As a matter of fact, sir," he began forcefully, "sitting here in safety inside the fort, I submit you have no idea of how hopeless the situation is. We are at war with a monstrous enemy, and they are winning."

"No one knows that better than I, Mr. Campbell."

Patrick laughed derisively. "Prove it. We have a hundred and eighty men of the King's First."

Henry cast a glance at Jehu, who leaned back and studied Patrick knowingly. The lad's stay with the Indians had affected him badly. "Not quite so many," Henry answered softly. "Not any more."

"Enough, then. Give me my men. I'll march through those savages to the tune of volley and bayonet and bring you Pontiac's carcass."

"I think you'd best see to yourself, first, Mr. Campbell."

"You must! All right. A hundred. They're the King's own, Major. No half-naked heathen can stand before them. At the first show of strength they'll break."

"I'm sorry, Mr. Campbell, but Pontiac would like nothing better than for me to attack his position. He'd have us at his mercy. All of us."

"Preposterous!"

"I hate to disillusion you, Lieutenant, but Detroit is the last bastion of resistance in a widespread and extremely effective rebellion. With Pontiac, nothing is preposterous."

"Pontiac!" Patrick spat venomously. His eyes blazed as he stared at each of the two men in turn. "Tell me, Major. Is your concern for this settlement or for the welfare of that savage butcher you call a friend?"

Jehu raised his eyebrows, glanced at Henry, who rose, and fixed the insolent officer with a stern and unwavering stare. "Mr. Campbell, you have had a rough time. You're tired, hungry and hurt and just escaped, so I will overlook your insubordinate remarks. However, should you ever speak to me with such insolence again, I will thrash you within an inch of your life, and then clap you in irons. Is that clear?"

Patrick blanched, tried to rise and fell back in his seat. Tears of rage blurred his vision and his throat burned.

"Is that clear, Lieutenant?"

"Yes, sir," Patrick whispered, slumping in defeat, looking terribly small and worn in the ragged blanket.

"Very well. That will be all. Jehu?"

The grizzled ranger followed Henry out of the room and into the street. Neither spoke until they were almost to Henry's office. Finally, Jehu grinned. "March right through 'em, will he? You oughta give some thought to lettin' him try, Major. All by hisself."

Henry stopped on the top step to his office. "I do not need advice on how to handle my officers, Mr. Hays," he snapped.

"No, *sir!*" came the caustic reply. "I 'spect you don't. Anything else, Major?"

Henry stopped and collected his temper. "Sorry, Jehu. Three more of him and I think I'd let Pontiac have the place, lock, stock and barrel."

"Agreed," the ranger grinned. "Still, he means well."

"Jehu, my friend, meaning well isn't worth an empty powder horn. Come on. We're late for a staff meeting. There's still a fort to run."

Late afternoon and Juliet. The tiny bundled infant lay bound in a beribboned coverlet, deep in the generous sleep of innocence. "As tough and hardy as the wilderness," Anne thought proudly, brushing her lips across the downy blond hair before stepping quietly from the room. "Twenty-one days," she said softly, mentally adding the number. "Three weeks old."

She started down the hall. The part-way open door to Beth's room caught her attention. Sabrina had no doubt left the door ajar while cleaning. Anne paused, staring at the unslept-in bed, the unlived-in room, empty for nearly five weeks. Joy turned to bitterest bile and a worried frown creased her face. "Oh, Beth," she whispered. "Please, God, keep her safe and bring her back to us unharmed." A sound downstairs. It was time for Henry to be back. "Henry?"

"No, Anne," a familiar voice replied.

Anne drew back into the shadows at the top of the stairs. Patrick's escape—and the news that Beth was alive—had been the sole topic of conversation since his return that morning. Each time his name was mentioned, Anne had pretended easy nonchalance, though she dreaded facing him again. Now panic welled anew. What would they talk about? What was there to be said? "Patrick?" she called nervously. "Is that you?"

Moccasined, bandaged feet appeared, followed by a rumpled uniform that hung loosely on a frame made spare by ordeal. Patrick stood at the foot of the stairs, gazing up with darkened eyes that seared through the gloomy hallway. "Hello, Anne. Surprised to see me?" There was a forced lightness to his tone that made her wary.

Anne descended the stairs. "Henry said you'd escaped and were back. I . . . wondered when you'd come." But not now, she thought, not with Henry due home at any moment. She had reached the last step. He waited, gaunt and a little stooped. "My God!" she gasped. "What did they do to you?"

"Less than they did to Jolline." He giggled briefly. "I'm sorry, you don't know him. Anyway, I'm here at last." His eyes raked her body with a strange intensity, magnified by the months of separation. Anne could not help but be affected. Without realizing, she swayed slightly. Patrick reached out without warning and swept her into a hungry embrace. "Here at last, Anne. Here at last." Before she could answer, his lips covered her mouth.

Giddy and half-dazed, Anne momentarily succumbed, melted into his arms, overcome by his miraculous return and aroused by such feverish need so passionately expressed. And yet . . . "No, Patrick!" She squirmed free, pushed him away. "No. We can't!"

Patrick peered closely at her, refusing to understand. "You didn't feel that way once. Anne, once can be again. Now. Don't you understand? I still love you, in spite of everything." He hobbled forward, wincing with pain. "I have forgotten and forgiven those machinations that sent me north and from your side. Your wrongs were purged by the long wintry nights, exorcised by loneliness and solitude. Each night, each day, I saw, walked, ate, slept, worked with your image before me. With each passing hour I realized anew I must return. Each empty day assured me we would be together again. The wilderness left me with one thought branded on my mind. Anne Campbell by my side, forever."

Anne backed away slowly, frightened by the sudden madness in his eyes. "You've misconstrued, sir. I . . . I . . ."

"My vision did not lie, Anne. I will remain here no longer than necessary. Together, we will return to England. I know you still love me, Anne. Admit it."

"Why, Patrick, I . . ." Whirling, Anne eluded the importuning arms and adroitly stepped into the living room. Memories of the past collided with the emotions of the present. Patrick was still handsome, pride and bearing still evident despite the ravages of captivity. For a fleeting second she mourned the passing of their affair and regretted the unhappiness it was fated to bring him.

Undaunted, Patrick followed. He caught her by an arm, spun her toward him and saw in those ice-gray eyes not love but fear and reticence. "Anne . . . ?"

"We cannot, Patrick. I do not love you."

"No," he said flatly, shaking his head in disbelief. "No."

"There is too much at stake, too much you don't and can't understand. Here and now is the real world. We were fools living in a fairyland existence."

"A world to which you long to return," Patrick interrupted, his voice a desperate whisper. "That's where your place is."

"Is it?"

"Certainly not here in this dreadful country. Hordes of vicious primitives lie in wait outside the walls. The frontier lacks in every single aspect of civilization. Your beauty alone makes the wilderness bearable. How long will even those perfect features last before deprivation turns you haggard and sour?"

"Stop it," Anne ordered harshly. "I'll hear no more of such talk."

"You will. If I have to scream."

"Lower your voice immediately."

"I won't."

A cry issued from the upper floor. Patrick's face went blank. "A child?"

Anne nodded. "Yes."

"It's true then. I refused to believe them." A manic smile covered his face and he looked around the room. Suddenly the smile disappeared and he grabbed her arms, pulled her close. "Whose?"

"You're hurting me, Patrick."

"Whose, dammit? Whose? Whose?"

"Mine. Mine and Henry's. Her name is Juliet. Juliet Elizabeth Gladwyn."

Patrick shoved her away and lurched to the table, pressing his knuckles into the wood. His head was bent, and Anne thought she heard a sob. "Then you are lost to me," he said in a pitifully small voice. "Perhaps we are all lost. I followed you to this wilderness out of love, sacrificed everything, and am left with nothing." He turned, his face mercurially changing, twisted now with fury as the tortured words issued in a near shriek. "You have broken me, madam. You have renounced our love and destroyed me!"

"No. Do not blame me for your brittleness, Patrick. I will not accept the burden."

Patrick laughed mechanically, the sound strident and unnerving. "Brittle?" he asked, gasping for breath. "Burden? Madam is amusing, and must pardon my laughter . . ."

Anne forced herself to remain calm. "Lieutenant Campbell, my husband is due home. My child is crying and needs me. I'm afraid I must beg your indulgence and ask to be excused."

"Of course." The barking laughter died away. "Thank you, madam. I will take my leave." He bowed and stiffly walked to the door, opened it to see Henry standing outside.

Anne saw Patrick jerk as if slapped, then turn. A secretive smile played across his face. "It is a pleasure to see you so . . . content, Anne. Pray you stay that way. Perhaps I might regale you with my adventures among the savages, some day. After all, you might be experiencing them for yourself before long." He nodded to the unseen child, who was complaining more vociferously now. "Juliet Elizabeth. A delightful name. Good day."

He was mad, she realized. Quite, quite mad, capable of anything. Wearily, she stumbled toward the door, stopping with a gasp of alarm at the sight of Henry. Jaws knotted, he stared, a statue depicting shocked comprehension. "Oh, you're home," she said inanely. How much had he heard?

"Yes."

"I . . . I must see to Juliet."

"Yes."

He knew. Blinded by tears, she started up the stairs, away from the pain in Henry's eyes.

"With him?" Henry asked, his voice strangely hollow. Anne hesitated. "With him!?" he bellowed.

"Yes!" she said, spinning to face him. "In England. Not here. I was alone. Can you understand that? I resented you, your leaving. I took a lover. It's not unheard of."

"The virtuous Anne Langford! I should have known from the first . . ."

"You could not know because you were not there." Anne blazed. Now it was in the open and she could not stop. "You were here in this interminable wilderness, playing the primitive with your sweet, murderous savage. So don't talk to me about Patrick!"

Henry stepped forward. For a second, Anne feared he would strike her. Instead, he stopped. "Very well, madam," he said icily. "I shan't. Good day."

"Henry!" His back was ramrod straight. "Don't leave. You are my husband. I love you. I cannot say any more. I do not mean any less." Not waiting for his reply, she hurried on up the stairs, shut the door behind her and gathered Juliet in her arms. "There,

there, baby. Mama's here," she said, trying desperately
to hold back the tears. "Mama's here. Mama's here."

She expected to hear the front door slam. Instead,
the bedroom door opened and Henry walked in. For
a long, long moment, he stood motionless, studying
her, then walked to the bed and stared down at Juliet,
quiet now at her mother's breast. His mind made up at
last, Henry sat by Anne on the bed. He put an arm
around her. Together, they sat in close silence, watching the child.

Priscilla Hampton sipped, found the tea still too hot
to be swallowed and replaced the nearly full cup without so much as spilling a drop. Her lips did not even
appear moist. Jess McBeecher entered the schoolroom
and closed the door behind him, clearing his throat
as he walked to the front of the room. The small gathering quieted gradually, Gus Schraner sighing loudly
and Marian McBeecher whispering a final indignant
comment to Priscilla in order to be the last heard.

"What I got to say," Jess began, "can be said pretty
quick. Then I reckon we'll all have to sit back an'
listen to Gus tell us why I'm wrong." The schoolroom
was crowded with the English settlers living in the
fort, many of whom were fairly recent arrivals, having
taken refuge within the walls since the outbreak of
hostilities. Most were English farmers who had sought
to work the land with their French neighbors. Now
their homes lay in charred ruins, grim repositories
housing the remains of a parent or child lost to the
marauding tribes. All settlers of French extraction
were excluded from the gathering.

"Go on, Mr. McBeecher. What you got to say makes
a lot of sense to me, an' the rest o' these folks ought
to hear it straight out."

The storekeeper nodded and continued. "Thank you, Mr. Barr." He coughed, pleased with the importance of his position. "The problem's mighty clear. We got that damn redstick Pontiac outside the walls, an' he wants Detroit bad enough to keep us penned up 'til we rot. When he gets in—well, you all seen what they did to them they caught."

He paused, considering, taking time for the words to sink in. " 'Course, Pontiac has offered us, our wives an' children, safe passage to Fort Niagara. Same as anyone else, I hate to see what's mine fall into the hands of the savages, but I got to ask myself: What's a few goods worth when my scalp is hanging from some heathen's belt?"

The crowd mumbled in answer to the rhetorical question, each visualizing Indian atrocities being visited on themselves and their families. McBeecher raised a hand and the room fell silent again. "You all know Major Gladwyn has seen fit to refuse Pontiac's generous offer. It's all well an' good with me if the Major wants to risk his family's life, but it's my feeling he shoulda consulted with us before he saw fit to jeopardize *our* lives."

"Detroit is my home. I do not like to be driven from my home," Gus Schraner interrupted, his deep bass voice and slow speech lending authority to the pronouncement. "Once is enough for me."

Jess sighed as if to say, "I told you so." "We wouldn' be leavin' for good, Gus. The idea is to go to a safe place until an army can be raised to punish Pontiac an' the rest of 'em. What good does it do us to stay if we're all to be slaughtered?"

"But we do not know this," the Dutchman protested. "The *Huron* has been gone for almost six weeks. Help is on the way."

"Not true." The voice came from the back of the room. All heads turned to see Patrick Campbell step out of the shadows. McBeecher smiled in satisfaction. The Lieutenant's arrival had generated the appropriate response.

One of the farmers shot to his feet. "Mr. McBeecher," he exclaimed belligerently. "We were told none of the fort's officers knew of this meeting. Have we been betrayed?"

"Mr. Decker, please. Quiet . . . all of you. Let me explain."

"I can adequately defend my presence, thank you," Patrick said, taking a position in front of the suddenly nervous, volatile assembly. "Mr. McBeecher was kind enough to invite me because I feel the same as you. And I am not alone. A great many, possibly a majority, of the military share your concern and sentiments. However, as long as Major Gladwyn is in command there is little we can do short of outright insurrection. And I would not suggest that until all alternative solutions have been examined."

"Mutinous talk, Lieutenant Campbell," Gus muttered.

"Is it mutinous, sir, to place welfare above reputation? Nay, I speak of duty, of carrying out the instructions given the King's regiment. Why are we here? To protect you and your families."

"A fact Major Gladwyn seems little concerned with," Priscilla interjected, to the agreement of all save Gus and Karen.

The farmer named Decker stood and spoke again. "What was this you said of help not being on the way?"

"I doubt there is any. As you know, I escaped a week ago, after being in the savages' hands for eight days. I determined to gather what information I could. You have heard gossip, now listen to the truth. All the outlying forts—east, west, north and south, very possibly even including Schlosser and Niagara—have suffered the same fate as Michilimackinac. Of all the English personnel, military and civilian, that were at one time north of here, I am the only known survivor. Detroit is alone. We are alone."

No one spoke. A sob from one of the women reflected the feelings of all. "Under optimum conditions, and if the French are not actively aiding the Indians, General Amherst will require at least a year—a *full* year—to defeat a rebellion of this magnitude." Patrick's voice dropped ominously. "Ladies and gentlemen, there is no possible way Detroit can hold out for a whole year. We are doomed."

"And what would you suggest we do, Mr. Campbell?" Karen Schraner spoke for the first time, startling the others, who sat in shocked silence.

"I should press my opinion to the commander of this fort. If he continually refuses to consider your grievance . . . The next step will be for you to decide."

"Me, I'm fer goin' on ta the next step," Mr. Barr grumbled, eliciting a general response of assent.

"Surely the good Major will act as you suggest," Patrick remonstrated unctuously. "I would, were I in his place, which, of course, I am not. However, I do wield some power, and recognize that desperate situations sometimes call for drastic remedies. If that should be the case . . ."—he paused and looked about the room, contacting each eye—" . . . perhaps we should meet again and pursue a course more suited to the occasion." With a curt bow toward McBeecher and the rest of the assembly, Patrick left the room.

There was little more of substance to be said. Everyone tried to talk at once, quieted at McBeecher's command. Five minutes later Jess McBeecher and Guthry Decker were authorized to present the settlers' case to Henry. Priscilla Hampton took the floor to assert that their deliberations must be kept from Major Gladwyn until the formal presentation could be arranged by their representatives. Marian McBeecher pointed out the proscription extended to and included Mrs. Gladwyn and Sabrina, a warning directed at the Schraners. The last business concluded, the meeting disbanded and the participants slipped into the night.

Safe within the privacy of their home, Gus and Karen lingered over a final pot of tea and plate of warmed biscuits with honey. They ate in silence, locked the shop, cleared the table and headed for bed. Gus blew out the last candle and the bed groaned beneath his weight.

Neither could sleep. Finally, Gus turned on his side, gathered Karen's full, buxom figure close, kissed her forehead and cheek. "You did not approve of the meeting?" he asked.

"No. This Lieutenant Campbell. I do not trust him. Do you?"

Gus shook his head. "It is hard to tell about men like the Lieutenant. They are dangerous and should be followed only with great care. Yet much that he said is true."

"But this is our home," Karen exclaimed. "Ours."

Gus lay back, blinked away the patterns of night swirling before his eyes and silently cursed the fear that had suddenly surged through his veins. "And we will stay," he replied at last. "We will stay as long as we can."

Two days later Jess McBeecher and Guthry Decker stood nervously outside Henry's office, their resolution melting to uneasiness despite hours spent preparing their demands. The door opened and they were ushered in.

Henry eased back into the chair behind his desk, gestured toward two others. "Please be seated, gentlemen."

Both men continued to stand. Each waited for the other to speak. Decker finally summoned the courage. "Major, the inhabitants of this settlement, our friends an' neighbors, have asked us ta speak ta you on behalf of everybody."

He paused. Henry made a steeple of his index fingers and continued to stare at the men. Decker looked at McBeecher, who cleared his throat and came to the farmer's aid. "Major Gladwyn, we listened to the screams an' seen the bodies, same as you. Our women are scared, an' truth is, we are too. We're of a mind to give Pontiac what he wants."

"You are," Henry said matter-of-factly. He did not seem at all disturbed by the proposition.

"Aye," McBeecher said, breathing a little easier.

Decker's homely face bobbed up and down in agreement. "Open the gates. We'll give the savage his day. Amherst will raise an army, you'll come back and give the heathens a thrashin'. There ain't no sense in us dyin'—not when Pontiac's offerin' ta let us out."

"Have you forgotten Fort Munro, gentlemen?"

McBeecher colored. "Munro? They was massacred. So was a bunch of others. But that was during the war. Hell, this is . . ."

"This is a war!" Henry exclaimed, slamming his fist on the desk top. "Are you blind to what's happening? Homes have been burnt. Families slaughtered. Detroit is the last English stronghold on the Lakes Frontier. If this siege is successful, if we relinquish Detroit, the whole Northwest will be in Indian hands. Lord knows what will happen then. Word will spread like wildfire. How many tribes will follow Pontiac's example? If the English can be driven away from here, why not further south as well? Why not from all the colonies? Why not push us into the sea? If we surrender here, gentlemen, we visit disaster on thousands. Detroit must not fall!"

"Major, those others aren't a thousand miles from nowhere. They can get help. We can't. Your duty is to protect us."

"And so I shall, Mr. McBeecher. I will protect you by keeping Detroit's gates closed against the Indians. I will protect you by refusing to acquiesce to Pontiac's demands. I will protect you, dammit, against yourselves, whether you want protection or not. Detroit will *not* fall."

"Now, see here," Decker started. "We . . ."

"The discussion is ended, gentlemen. I've made myself quite clear. Good day."

"But you can't . . ."

"Good day!"

McBeecher and Decker glanced at one another, then at Henry. Nothing more would be gained. Not with Gladwyn, at any rate. They left without pressing the matter further.

Sunset. All day the din of the falls throbbed in his dreams. Jeremy Turner woke, looked around and finally crawled from under the pile of brush. Quickly he relieved himself, as quickly crept to the edge of the water and drank. Ahead lay Fort Schlosser and the most dangerous four miles of the journey, smack dab through more Indians than he cared to think of, none of whom he dared consider friendly.

The trek had been difficult. He had travelled mostly by night, and had had little to eat save what could be gleaned from the forest. Five times he had been forced to hide from marauding war parties, and each delay had meant another day lost, or more. As many times, Indian camps had meant detours, stretching a journey of a hundred miles to nearly two hundred.

He lost track of time, knew only summer was well on the way. Niagara must have learned of the insurrection by this time, yet without knowing for sure, he had to press on. Across the river on Grand Island, a fire sprang up, lighting the trees. Jeremy crawled back from the water and melted into the shadows.

"Fort Schlosser, here I come," he said to himself, laying the improvised pack aside where it wouldn't be found. The night closed around him like an old, familiar blanket and he moved off confidently. One thing about having to take a trip like this, he thought. A fellow sure learns a lot. A far cry from Portsmouth. Old Jehu'd be proud. Damned near two hundred miles with hostiles at every step. By God, it would be good to talk to real people and hear their voices. A man got tired of talking to himself. Real food, too. Damn, but he was hungry. Another day on the trail and he'd turn into a berry.

Five hours later, Jeremy crested the last rise. Ahead lay Fort Schlosser, quietly asleep in the river breeze. There shouldn't have been any Indians so close, but nearly six weeks of solitary travel had taught him caution. Carefully, he slipped from shadow to shadow, crawled down the slope and bellied across the open ground, finally reaching the wall of raised logs.

A sixth sense tamped the exultation that almost sent him to his feet. Sweat broke out on his forehead and he realized for the thousandth time a man just couldn't be cautious enough. A glance up reinforced the lesson: a musket barrel was silhouetted against the sky. Would have been pure hell to get to the fort just in time to be shot for a fool.

Quietly, he inched along the perimeter until he found the gate, eased to his feet and pressed as close to the wall as possible. Inside, someone moved and metal thudded against wood. "Hello, the fort," he called softly. "I'm a white man. Don't shoot."

"Jesus Christ!" came a muffled oath. "Sergeant! Get the sergeant, somebody."

Silence, and a new voice, deeper and more sure. "Identify yourself."

"Corporal Jeremy Turner, sir, of Detroit. I have dispatches."

"What the hell you doing, coming in the middle of the night?"

"Detroit's under siege, sir. I . . ."

"What? Get that gate open, Private! Now!" A hinge creaked and a hooded lantern showed the way. "Well, what are you waiting for? I'm not going to keep this goddamn gate open all night, you dumb son-of-a bitch!"

Jeremy grinned and hurried in. English, by God! Sure was a beautiful sound.

CHAPTER 24

Their world ended at the gates. The spacious vista from the walls taunted the beleaguered inhabitants, for torture and death waited beyond. Detroit no longer counted the days. The siege had gone on forever, it seemed. Day after boring day passed under a blistering July sun. Occasionally, someone fired a musket, but that was all. The summer's quiet and enervating heat became the fort's worst enemy, for it threatened everyone's sanity.

Amidst these uneasy surroundings, Detroit's newest inhabitant completed her second month of life, and bravely began her third. Tucked into her crib and kissed good night by her mother, Juliet slept, innocently unaware of a none too certain future.

Anne patted the child, then hurried downstairs, ignoring the men in the front room and rushing into the kitchen. If the Langfords could see their daughter now! Sir Spencer would have been appalled to see Anne toiling like a common servant. Well, Papa, I've learned something, Anne thought. Karen—and Sabrina too, now that I think of it—are far from common. Their energy shames me. She poked at a new log just catching fire under the water cauldron and shielded her eyes against the fierce heat rising from the glowing orange coals. Karen came to the door once again. "Are you sure I cannot help?"

"No. Really, I'll manage by myself," Anne replied, secretly wishing for Sabrina's assistance and silently cursing Jehu for taking the woman from the house. A second later she was scolding herself for being so selfish. Sabrina had proved an invaluable assistant to Private McManaway, and the wounded derived a great deal of comfort from the old woman's presence and mothering ways.

Cooking a meal alone imbued Anne with a growing sense of unadmitted pride. The single act gave her an opportunity to show off newly acquired skills and hopefully would help ease the tension that had sprung up between Henry and herself since that horrible day when her affair with Patrick had finally come into the open. Since then, not quite reconciled nor completely at odds, they had been careful to skirt the issue. Anne had tried in a thousand subtle ways to show Henry the affair was an unpleasant and embarrassing incident of the past, forgotten by her and best so by him. To what degree she was succeeding was difficult to tell, for he spent most of his available free time playing with Juliet.

Hot grease popped in the cast iron frypan. Anne hurried to pour in the corn bread batter and dashed off a silent prayer that it wouldn't char this time, before turning to the open door for a breath of badly needed fresh air. Perspiration beaded her forehead and dampened her hair. Another airless July night, much too warm to be struggling in the kitchen, laboring over an open fire. But Henry had wanted to talk to Gus about the morale of the civilians and Anne was determined to prove she could be just as capable a hostess as Karen.

The stew! She hurried to the kettle, called by the dancing, rattling lid which had been forced ajar as broth bubbled over the side and splattered into the flames. She lifted the lid with an iron tong and stirred the heavy mixture of vegetables and chunks of pork. The aroma blended pleasantly with the wafting odor of the corn bread, almost done. "Oh, no you don't!" she exclaimed, swinging the stewpot a little further from the fire, jamming the lid back on and turning to the frying pan to rescue the golden brown bread. "Aha! Perfect!" she said, turning the still-steaming corn bread onto the table and sighing with relief. Corn meal was much too precious to waste. She licked her fingers, broke off a piece and tasted it. A slow smile crossed her face: Sabrina would be proud.

At last, the meal prepared, she filled the serving bowl and carried the stew to the table, returning for the corn bread and the last of the butter. Gus and Henry rose from subdued earnest conversation and approached the table. Karen put down her mending and joined them. "Such a meal," Karen beamed appreciatively, "is it not, husband?"

"Aye, and the way it smells makes a man wish his appetite was bigger than it is," Gus answered with exaggerated cheer, as aware as Karen of the subtle bar of tension separating Henry and Anne.

Henry clapped the cabinetmaker's shoulder. "And were that so, the rest of us would go without."

A resounding chorus of gunfire interrupted Henry's well-meaning attempt to join the levity. A cannon's throaty bellow followed another round of musket shot. Henry strode to the front door and peered out into the night. With the next volley, he crossed rapidly to the fireplace, buckled on belt and saber and thrust a pair of pistols in his belt. "Sounds like the west wall. I'll let you know."

"I'll go along," Gus said, leaving the table.

"No need," Henry replied, advice Gus chose to ignore. Henry turned to Anne. "I'm sorry. There's no need to worry."

Anne followed him to the door, felt cold lips briefly brush her cheek. Another day he would have kissed her more meaningfully. Doused in self-pity, she closed and barred the door, went back to the table and slumped in a chair to stare blankly at the untouched meal. All that work for naught, she thought with a woebegone sigh. "The corn bread will be cold. It doesn't taste good cold."

Karen moved behind Anne, massaged the younger woman's shoulders. "When they get back, they'll be so hungry they won't care. And thirsty, too. How about a nice bottle of rum from the cellar, eh? Anne? Come, *liebchen,* you mustn't sulk."

Anne sighed, then laughed ruefully. "For a few moments, I was really happy, Karen. It was as if we were in another time and place, safe and enjoying one another without the threat of savages or the thought of how empty the house seems without poor Beth. For one, furtive instant . . ."

"Stop it, Anne." Karen moved around the table, sat and shook her head. "We must live where we are. Do you understand? Live and be happy."

"And satisfied too? No, thank you," Anne said bitterly. "With foul corn bread? With greasy *stew?* With Indians? With a husband I hardly see and don't understand? No thank you." Near tears with disappointment, she ran from the table and fled upstairs to the quiet of her room and the soft and gentling beauty of Juliet.

"Better keep the food near the fire," Karen muttered,

shaking her head regretfully and starting for the kitchen.

Searing explosions scattered the darkness, revealing the position of the more daring Indians who had taken advantage of the moonless night to creep close to the wall. The parapet was alive with soldiers, hastily called out to meet the attack. Lieutenant Campbell had deployed them well. Henry noted with professional calm the precise rhythm of men stepping forward to fire as others stepped back to reload. Johnson's fire brigade was out in force. Half-dressed soldiers, helped by all available civilians, rushed hither and yon to douse the lower flames with buckets full of water and pull off burning shingles with long-handled rakes where the fire was too high to be reached by hand. Somehow, in the madhouse of confusion, they kept pace with the profusion of new missiles that arched in from the darkness surrounding the fort.

Henry scrambled up a ladder and ran along the firing platform toward the southwest blockhouse. As he neared the door, a soldier stumbled out. Futilely attempting to staunch the blood flooding from his side, the wounded man tumbled over the railing and dropped to the yard, landing with a sickening thud. Henry grabbed the youth's musket, saw it was primed, leaned through one of the ports and fired at an Indian who was heading for the wall. The flash blinded him momentarily, making it impossible to tell if his aim had been true. No sooner had he ducked below the wall than several balls whistled through the open space where he'd just stood. Gus crawled to Henry's side, stood, fired, and dropped back to the floor. "Perhaps Pontiac has tired of waiting, *ja?*" he asked, reloading.

"No. This isn't a full-scale attack. He'd never try that at night. Probably just a trick to make us stay up all night. Whatever, we'll soon put an end to it."

Ensign Price's head appeared in the trap door. "Saw you come in here, sir. My men are in position to reinforce you."

"Who the hell ordered you to leave your post?"

The ensign blanched. "Sir, the attack . . ."

"Damn it, man, your place is on the east wall. Take your men back there at once."

"They're already deployed, sir. I . . ."

"Goddamn it, Mister Price! I want those men rounded up and gotten the hell back where they belong. Now, move!" he roared over the din of battle. Price disappeared and the trapdoor slammed shut. Henry turned to the three soldiers crouched in the blockhouse, all in various stages of panic. "Where the hell's the gunner?"

"Hit, sir, both of them. Right after the first shot," a private answered.

Henry cursed. "Which one of you men can reload and fire this four-pounder?"

"I can, sir," one of the three answered.

"What's your name?"

"Private Danfield, sir!"

Henry shrugged. It had worked with Turner. "Make that Corporal Danfield, son. Earn it tonight and you'll keep it. Now load that thing with shot and get to work."

"What do I fire at?"

Henry spun Danfield about, grabbed him by the breeches and coat, hoisted the startled youth and shoved his head out one of the upper firing windows. Like brilliant orange flowers, blooming and dying on the instant, gunfire erupted from the base of the wall.

"Them!" he roared, at the same time letting the lad drop. "You understand?!"

"Yes, sir!" Danfield rushed to the cannon and with his two companions hauled it around to the side window to enfilade the wall.

Henry motioned for Gus to follow. One after the other they dropped through the trapdoor and descended the ladder to the ground in time to hear Danfield's first round off. Ensign Price was still trying to pull his men from the wall. One of the fire brigade swerved barely in time to miss him, sloshing water down the ensign's boots in the process.

The back of Henry's neck bristled. His mind raced, sorting unseen factors, analyzing, assessing. The east side of the fort was virtually unguarded.

Damn! Price and his well-meaning inexperience may have cost them their lives. Luckily, he'd yet to hear shots from the *Michigan* covering the east wall, and at any rate, the skeleton guard posted there at all times would have sounded a warning. Still, the intuitive sense of danger was overwhelming.

The cannon above thundered again and was answered by an agonized scream beyond the wall. On the wall, the firing slackened: the brigade had the fires well under control. All senses alert, Henry enclosed himself in a cocoon of contemplation and forced himself to consider the overall picture. As far as could be seen, the attack would be repulsed and the only worry they had was that it might be a feint of some sort.

That was it! Why else the uncharacteristic night attack? The settlement's mysterious betrayer! "Come with me," he shouted to Gus. The powder magazine was on the east side of the fort. So was his home—and Anne and Juliet!

* * *

Action at last, Patrick thought. Duty officer on the early watch, he rushed to the west wall with the sound of the first shot and immediately took over from Ensign Hammon. Runners were sent to Major Gladwyn and the other officers, apprising them of the situation. As the first hostiles reached the wall, he realized that this might be the final attack, and felt a rush of excitement.

He looked around. Johnson's men were functioning well and all fires seemed to be under control. A runner appeared at his side. Without thinking, Patrick spoke quickly. "Northwest Blockhouse. Tell them to put grape in the cannon and enfilade the wall." The runner was off immediately. Patrick glanced around, irritated. The southwest blockhouse was quiet, after a single shot. Where were the damned gunners?

He reached out, grabbed a man who was heading north along the wall. "Corporal Burns, move your squad over the gate. Double time."

"Aye, sir!"

Patrick turned, looking for a runner. One was climbing up the ladder. Beyond, Major Gladwyn stood, assessing the situation, then quickly moving to the southwest blockhouse. No need to send a runner, then. The cannon would be at work shortly. A private appeared at his side. "Sir! Mr. Price advises his men are on the way and asks for orders."

"What the hell is he doing here? Find him and tell him to get back to the east wall where he belongs." The runner disappeared. Good Lord! if this was a diversion . . . ! "Livingston!"

"Sir?" The sergeant bulled his way along the wall, saluted peremptorily.

"Send someone to the east wall and make sure this

isn't a feint. Tell them to get back to me fast. You check the northwest corner and keep them firing. Make sure the hostiles aren't moving against the north wall. I'll be in the southwest blockhouse for a minute."

"Aye, sir!"

The men over the gate were firing well, rising to aim and shoot, then dropping out of sight to reload in orderly waves. They couldn't see what they were shooting at, of course, but mere firepower should slow down the savages. He worked his way along the parapet, ducking from time to time, shouldering past the men. So Pontiac had finally brought the fight to Detroit. The Major was at last being forced into action. No way to avoid it. No excuses. A soldier clambered up a ladder in front of him. One of Price's men! "What are you doing here, Private?"

"Orders, sir!"

"Get the men from your company and head them back to the east wall on the double."

"Sir, we . . ."

"Move! I've sent orders to Ensign Price. Don't make me tell you again." The startled soldier crablegged along the wall, yelling at the members of his squad. A bullet plucked at Patrick's sleeve. Enraged at his own carelessness, he shouted at the nearest soldiers, exhorting them to reload and fire faster. It was important the Indians think there were twice as many men on the wall as there really were, important they be allowed to continue the feint, if that's what it was, and lose as many as possible. God only knew what was in store, only that the fort was sure to be hurt. The attack was certain to increase the discontent and anger of the civilians and those soldiers who would follow him when the time came. Reaching the blockhouse wall, he looked in the window in time to see the first shot fired. "Where's the Major?" he yelled, his ears ringing.

One of the privates pointed to the trapdoor. Patrick cursed and turned back along the wall, heading for the nearest ladder. He'd enjoy watching Gladwyn's face. By the time this was over, Henry would be disgraced, if not dead, and a strategic retreat with the possibility of a rearguard engagement or two along the way would be a distinct opportunity. Not as good as a smashing victory, of course, but sure to bring a commendation from Amherst and perhaps command of a punitive expedition to teach the savages a lesson once and for all.

With a last glance along the wall to make sure all was well, he slid down the ladder. The Major was standing there like a bump on a log, staring around as if he'd never seen real trouble before. Patrick laughed outright. Trouble? He didn't know what trouble was, yet. "Major Gladwyn?" The Lieutenant stopped in his tracks, staring as his commanding officer suddenly took to his heels, heading across the fort for the east wall. Must have had the same thought I did, Patrick thought with grudging admiration. The cannon sounded again, followed by the scream of a wounded warrior. On the wall, the firing slackened. Patrick turned and headed for the gate to check the defenses there, wishing he knew what the hell was happening on the east side of the fort.

The child slept. Anne stroked Juliet's silken locks and felt the quick rush of irritation subside next to such innocence. In the background, gunfire cracked and popped. Karen appeared in the doorway, silhouetted in the flickering candlelight. Neither woman spoke, but watched the babe instead and tried not to think of the rattling gunfire and the throaty roar of the cannon. "I'm sorry, Karen. I didn't mean to be so childish. My outburst should not have been directed at you." Anne leaned over the crib—a lovingly crafted present from the Schraners—and tucked in the light coverlet. The roar of a cannon rolled across the fort. Anne glanced toward the open window, unnerved by the sound.

"Come and have some tea," Karen said. "There's nothing we can do."

"I'll close the shutters first. It might lessen the noise." Anne walked quietly to the window. A slight breeze touched her face. From her vantage point portions of the east wall and the southeast corner were visible. Though most of the sound came from the west, a surprising amount of activity could be seen below. "Karen?"

"Yes?"

"Come here." Figures moved away from the wall, dodging through shadows and coming toward the house. Whatever were they doing?

Something grabbed Anne's shoulders and spun her from the window. A hand clasped over her mouth to stifle a scream. "Not a sound," Karen whispered. "Blow out the candle."

Anne scurried across the floor, complying with the mysterious order. "What are you doing?" she asked, hurrying back.

Karen bobbed up, reached out and swung the shutters nearly closed. "There. Look," she said, gesturing through the narrow crack.

Anne peered over the sill but could see nothing but shadows within shadows. "I don't . . . Oh, my God! Those aren't soldiers!"

"No," Karen answered, closing the shutters the rest of the way and latching them. "The front door. Is it barred?"

"Yes." Anne's fingers dug into Karen's arm. "But the kitchen . . . I think it's open."

The seamstress sped from the room, Anne flying in her wake. Skirts lifted, they swiftly descended the stairs. Karen snatched a fowling piece, a large-barrelled blunderbuss, from beside the fireplace, frantically priming it while Anne continued into the kitchen.

Anne reached the door as the first footsteps sounded outside. She grabbed the bar and tried to shove it in place, but the heavy oak door burst open and threw her back. Hideously painted faces and bodies glistened in the firelight. A shriek turned her blood to ice. A leering face . . . two . . . three . . . Karen shoved her aside as the sharp clap of a musket sent leaden death across the room. The blunderbuss answered in kind, a blossom of flame darting from the fluted barrel. The noise was deafening. The warriors, taken by surprise by the heavy load of shot, stumbled back. The brave who had been directly in the line of fire crumbled, nearly torn in half.

"Hurry!" Karen shouted. "The door!" She dropped the blunderbuss and rushed to swing it shut and bar it before the intruders could regroup. Damp with fear and exertion, the two women leaned against the wall.

A ferocious pounding reverberated through the house and they rushed from the kitchen to see the front door shivering beneath heavy punishment. Mortar fell away from the hinges. There was a scream of terror from upstairs. Juliet had awakened. They had only a few moments.

"The window over the door!" Karen panted. "Quickly. Follow me."

Anne stared at the empty room. Now the shuttered downstairs windows were under attack. Karen grabbed her, spun her toward the kitchen. "Be quick, child," she exclaimed, leading Anne to the kitchen and grabbing the blunderbuss as they entered.

Not yet comprehending, Anne watched as Karen slid the blunderbuss through the metallic handle of the large cauldron half-filled with boiling water. "Help me!" The two women lifted the cauldron from the fire and placed it on the floor. Karen seized the smaller pot of bubbling stew, dumped the contents into the larger cauldron. "Upstairs. Quickly!"

Anne grabbed the barrel end of the blunderbuss and lifted. The muscles along her shoulders and back strained with effort as the pot rose from the floor. "Gently," Karen chided as the handle slid along the smooth barrel and sloshed a few drops of the boiling mixture on her skirts. "Gently but quickly. Upstairs."

Straining, Anne complied. The two women eased sideways through the door, through the lower room and to the stairs, the most difficult part of the trip. Anne, in the lead, had to stoop over and ascend backward. Karen was forced to hold the stock of the blunderbuss high to avoid being covered with the boiling water. How they managed, Anne never knew. She was conscious only of the noise, the deafening pounding, the quivering door about to give way. Sweat stung her eyes, her arms were aching from the bruising weight. Only Juliet's wailing cry, penetrating the madness, gave her the strength to persevere.

They hurried as best they could down the hall to the window. Karen signalled to set the cauldron on the floor, where the wood surface immediately began to smoulder from the heated iron, then opened the shutters. Below, the rampaging Hurons clustered about the door, hammering at it with war clubs and muskets. One had found an axe and began to hew the oak planks. Great, heavy chunks of wood flew away at each blow.

Together, the women lifted the steaming cauldron, raised it to the window sill where it caught on the edge and threatened to spill back into the room. Before Anne could react or protest, Karen dropped the blunderbuss, grabbed the lip of hot metal with her naked hands and shoved the cauldron out the window. The scalding broth showered onto the attacking savages and shrieks of agony split the night.

It had worked! Jubilant, Anne turned from the window in time to see Karen collapse with the pain. Her hands, badly burned, oozed blood where the flesh had been stripped off. "Karen!" Anne dropped to the floor, lifted the Dutch woman's head. Only then did she see the crimson stain blotching the front of Karen's gown.

Shot . . . but how? The kitchen . . . One of the Indians had fired as Karen shoved her aside. "No . . . not Karen! Please, God, not Karen . . . Oh, please . . ." Anne cried aloud, cradling the wounded woman.

Pounding down rue Ste. Anne, Henry stopped only long enough to shout a stream of commands at Jehu, whose men were held in reserve at the intersection. Within seconds, the majority of the rangers were streaming toward the powder magazine. The remaining few, accompanied by Jehu, headed for the parade grounds, then south toward Henry's house.

The parade grounds were aswarm with howling, battle-crazed Indians. Gunfire echoed from the walls in a cacophony of death. A lead ball whistled past Henry's ear. A ranger to his left fired in return. Other muskets spouted flame from all sides, whether from friend or foe was difficult to tell. Henry neared the house in time to see the boiling liquid spew from the upper window and scatter the braves clustered about the front door. Another warrior had beaten open one of the lower windows and was squirming through, still too far away for a pistol shot. Jehu's musket barked and the Indian's body jerked wildly and collapsed, hanging half in and half out of the house.

A warrior stepped out of the shadows, levelled his musket. Henry fired and the brave grunted, dropped his weapon and staggered away. The attacking Indians, unorganized and badly confused, tried to retreat around the side of the house, only to be met with gunfire from the river wall.

The braves reversed direction and charged, having determined they would only be cut down if caught fleeing. Henry, Jehu, and the half-dozen rangers, badly outnumbered, evened the odds with a ragged volley. Henry scooped up the musket dropped by the Indian he had wounded a moment earlier and whirled to snap off a shot at a warrior who had gotten the best of one of the rangers. Before the brave could lift his tomahawk to deliver the *coup de grâce*, Henry's shot caught him in the chest. The Indian slumped forward, dying.

A flash at the window caught his attention. Anne! Juliet! Briefly visible, she suddenly dropped from sight with a cry. The anger and grinding pain of learning of her affair with Patrick forgotten, Henry roared a battle cry and charged into the front yard.

Henry parried a knife thrust, kicked a snarling Huron whose hands grappled for his legs, clubbed another with the heavy brass hilt of his saber. A musket barrel struck the side of his skull, spinning him around, as a third warrior closed in for the kill. Dizzy and half blind, Henry thrust his blade under the bludgeoning musket barrel and into his assailant. The Indian sank to the ground gasping.

Stunned, pain-filled, Henry fell to his knees as two more Hurons screamed and dove at him, pinning his sword arm. He slammed his left fist into a hate-filled, paint-smeared, leering face. A knife gleamed in the air. Henry braced himself, caught the descending wrist and held on with all his waning strength as the brave's companion, weaponless now, pummelled the officer with his fists.

Suddenly the weight on his chest was gone. Gus stood over him, a warrior's neck in the crook of each powerful arm. The Dutchman's hands locked and his muscles bulged with a sickening pop of breaking bones; the struggling Hurons twitched and slumped like lifeless rag dolls. Pleased, Henry fell back, unconscious.

Someone was holding him, slapping his face. Henry forced open his eyes and made out the furry images of Jehu and Gus, both covered with the gruesome stains of the evening's work. "You all right, Major?" The words were far away.

"Yes." He sat up, groaning. In the distance, a few musket shots were followed by silence. "Help me up."

With Jehu on one side, Gus on the other, Henry stood, still weak but regaining strength. "What happened?"

"Just wipin' up the last of 'em. They come through the secret entry in the south wall. The sentry there got hisself killed like Rexrode and Drummond. Price has his men along the wall. Showed up in time ta keep any more from sneakin' in."

Henry looked around. The situation appeared to be well in hand. Soldiers hurried about on a host of errands. A half-dozen Indians lay dead within sight. "The fires?"

"All out. No major damage."

"What about the magazine?"

Jehu grinned. "That's what they were after, but they missed it." He jerked his head toward the front of the house where an Ottawa brave lay with his skull crushed by the iron cooking pot. "Looks like the women done their share."

Henry started. "My God! The women!"

They turned at the sound of a bolt being shoved back and the door scraping open, swinging on only one hinge. Anne stood in the doorway. Sweat-soaked and streaked with blood, she stared blankly in Gus's direction.

The Dutchman's face paled. "Where's Karen?"

Anne felt haggard and drawn and old. "Up . . . upstairs."

Gus read the look in the woman's eyes. "Karen!" He shoved through the knot of silent men, past Anne, calling his wife's name as he hurtled up the stairs.

Henry turned to Jehu. "Send someone for McManaway. Hurry."

Jehu shook his head. "Only reason McManaway got stuck with Drummond's job is he can't see to shoot. I reckon I forgot more about this than that boy ever knowed," he said with quiet determination. "Do it myself, Major." Without waiting for Henry to agree or disagree, he disappeared into the house.

"I bandaged her. There's nothing else I knew to do," Anne said, still numb with shock. "She saved my life,

Henry. She saved . . ." Words, futile mouthed symbols, died. Great sobbing spasms shook Anne's frame. Gently, Henry held her close as she pressed against his shoulder and buried her face in the coarse and tattered fabric of his coat.

CHAPTER 25

Anne quietly closed the door to Karen's room, carried the tray to the kitchen and finished cleaning up before checking on Gus. She paused in the doorway of the carpenter shop. "I'm leaving now, Gus." The stocky artisan sat humped forward in an unfinished chair, forearms on knees, hands loosely clasped. "She drank some soup. There's bread and stew keeping warm, when you want some."

Gus looked up, his face blank. "Thank you, Anne. I will eat soon . . . To keep up my strength."

"I'll be back later. If you want . . ." Gus was staring at the floor again, not listening. Quietly, Anne backed into Karen's shop, eased open the front door and left. Louis Bouvier was waiting on the corner and motioned for her to join him.

"Did the doctor . . . I mean, could McManaway do anything for her?" he inquired anxiously.

"What could he do that Jehu can't?" Anne asked in return, her voice sorrow-soft. "The wound is clean and heals on the surface as best it can. But inside there is infection. Last night she was feverish, today she seems better. Seven days, up and down. Who can tell?"

The portly Frenchman shook his head in dismay. "It is so sad. Poor Gustav."

Anne stared down the center street. She could see

over the south wall, across the river. In the distance,
dark green hills met the sky. Louis followed her gaze.
"It is beautiful, no?"

"I don't know, Louis." She considered the question.
"Perhaps it would be more beautiful without so much
hatred and death all about."

"But does not beauty exist independently of death?"
Bouvier replied, his voice soft and gentle.

The new question brought her back from the distant
vista. Vaguely troubled, she didn't know how to answer, knew only her breasts were full and ached, that
she had no time for philosophy. "I'm sorry, Louis. I
must return home."

"*Mais oui*. I understand."

"Juliet will be waiting . . ."

"Of course. Try not to give up hope. Nothing has
happened for a week!" He patted his face with an
already damp kerchief. "Perhaps the weather is too hot
for Pontiac also. Maybe the sun will drive away the
heathen like the morning does a bad dream, no?" He
bowed, chuckling optimistically, and wandered off to
visit Jess McBeecher. Something was happening among
the English settlers, and though as a Frenchman he
wasn't privy to their plans, he was determined to learn
as much as possible.

Evening. A distant, blood-red ball sank through a
hazy western sky and hovered hesitantly, pricked by
the towering pines. Shadows spread liquid-like from
the palisade, gradually inundating the interior of the
fort. To the south a gathering of clouds promised
rain. An empty promise, thought Anne. Exhausted by
her long day, she turned from the window to a room
filled with memories. It had rained the day she arrived.
A day in July, almost like this one only a year ago.

Juliet cooed and giggled, delighted to discover a foot, which she promptly tried to chew. How lovely to be so delighted with no more than a toe to chew on! The bittersweet smile faded, overcome by dark thoughts. The walls of the house pressed in. Beyond them, the stockade, pressing too. Beyond that, the teeming hordes of savages. And still no relief, for worst of all, the interminable forest that stretched into the unending distance was the ultimate prison. The wilderness . . .

"Anne?"

She spun, startled and crying out. Unable to stand, dizzy from fatigue and the sudden movement, she sank to the bed.

Henry sat next to her, stroked her hair. "You look tired. Are you all right?" he asked solicitously.

"Well enough, thank you. Just tired of waiting, of not knowing what will happen next," she answered dully.

His lips touched her neck. "We have been together hardly at all these past weeks, mistress."

"You have your duty. I've been very busy."

"Yes," he said, the pressure of his arm forcing her to lie back.

Anne stiffened, not certain of her own feelings. "We must talk, Henry."

"Words, words, words. Over and over, the same thing."

"I want to know, Henry. Has Dumas renewed his offer?"

Henry sighed bitterly. "I saw him today. I think he wished to see if the sortie last week did any important damage. He made the usual demands."

"Which you refused."

Henry nodded. "I think he's worried. I think Pontiac is beginning to have problems. They lost too many last week. Indians don't like to die at night and there'll be grumbling and complaints. They'll question why Pontiac hasn't been more successful and taken the fort. Some of the older, wiser heads will begin to get anxious about winter. There's been no time to hunt or gather food. Each day we hold out, we gain an advantage." Idly, his fingers toyed with the lace at her bodice.

"So you're no longer worried. Is that what you've come to tell me?"

Henry frowned, beginning to get angry. "I'm more confident that we'll hold out. But that's not what I came to tell you."

"And what about Beth?" Anne asked, knowing she shouldn't, knowing there was no real answer, but unable to resist asking.

Henry rose abruptly, startling Juliet. "Not a day goes by that I do not think of her." Desire waned in the face of her frigid temperament. He moved to the desk, poured a glass of port. The last bottle; he had been saving it for a suitable moment. Now was as good a time as any.

"And still you do nothing?"

"Anne, over and over the same thing? I am trying to win our safety."

"Dr. Drummond is dead. Eight enlisted men have been buried, another two dozen are wounded. Karen lies burning with fever, perhaps dying. You are overseeing the destruction of us all."

"I am doing what needs to be done."

"No! What needs to be done is to free Beth. What needs to be done, sir, is to see your family back to civilization."

"I will not surrender this fort."

"And your daughter?"

"She will grow strong and happy, right here where we stand."

Anne's face whitened in disbelief. "What?"

"You heard me. By next summer all this will be, if not forgotten, safely in the past. Wounds will heal. Juliet will be safe, will grow . . ."

The man she had loved, followed and clung to! He had betrayed her. He had no intention of taking her home. Reason fled, replaced by a rising tide of uncontrollable animal rage.

"You promised me we would return to England. You wrote to Amherst."

Henry shrugged. "We're under siege, Anne," he explained patiently. "That letter is meaningless now. We'll go back when the time is right. Someday."

"Liar. I will not listen to you."

"This is our home, Anne. I don't intend to leave."

"No!"

"You know it is. My—our place is here. I've thought it all out. We've too much invested. We've fought for this land. With the Gladwyn wealth at my disposal, there's an empire to be won, next to which the petty intrigues of life in England pale in comparison. Our life is here."

"And our death!"

"No," he said, slamming down the glass.

"It's true. You would see us all killed. Me, Beth and Juliet!"

"Stop it!" Henry shouted, shaking her.

Juliet screamed in alarm. Anne tore free. Quivering with fury, she stood between Henry and the crib. "No! I will not abide such talk. Beth's life is held in precarious balance, subject to the whims of a savage, and you talk of 'someday'! Karen Schraner saved my life. Now she lies at the edge of death in recompense for her pains, and you speak of next summer when all is forgotten." Her voice rose, shrill with hysteria. "I have seen men slaughtered, murdered, and you would have me see the same done to my daughter? No. I will not! I refuse! Stay in this cursed land, if you wish, but you stay alone!"

"And what," Henry asked, deadly calm, "am I supposed to take that to mean?"

"If we survive this ordeal," Anne hissed, "at the very first opportunity, I will take my child to England."

"With Patrick Campbell?" Henry said, the words coming of their own volition, unstoppable.

For a moment, Anne appeared as if she had been slapped. Her eyes cooled, became guarded, impenetrable. "With whomever it takes to get us there."

Pontiac grunted, rolled off the pliant flesh, scowling as the woman sighed contentedly. She was his favorite, but had not pleased him this night. Something, some shapeless spirit weighted the darkness, tainted the night with vague misgivings. The woman rubbed the palms of her hands along the smooth, hairless skin of his body, but he was no longer interested. The spending of seed had accomplished no more than quick physical relief. Rising abruptly, he ordered her to stay in the lodge, and ducked through the low opening.

The air was hot and humid against his sleek naked flesh as he strode slowly through the camp. The sun rested. Now was the hour of sleep, the time Pontiac reserved for thought and contemplation. The pleasant, soft sounds of mothers talking to restless children, of men at quiet talk at the end of day, came from the long communal lodges. The sound of flesh against flesh could be heard outside the smaller bark and leather wigwams where youthful braves sported with willing maids. Now and again a dog barked, the sound short and sharp in contrast to the muted voices of the People.

Pontiac sniffed the air, the familiar odors. Fire. Drying meat. Pine, sharp and acrid; cherry wood, pungent and sweet. He smiled. The cleansing smell of cedar was his favorite. At the lodge where the old men sat far into the morning, kinnikinnick smoke wafted from between the slabs of bark, carrying the tales told back to the woods. For a fleeting second, he felt anger. The old men talked of going back to the woods, of leaving Detroit. Pontiac forced away his bitterness: old men would talk. Someday, perhaps, he would take their place while a younger brave walked by in the night, grumbling of old men.

The nightly strolls through the peaceful camp had become a ritual for him. During these few minutes between waking and sleep, he listened to what the People really felt, really thought. The sounds and smells were a book in which he read contentment or discontent, anxiety or peace, happiness or grief. Tonight, though, the sounds were jumbled, the smells disorienting. An unidentifiable tension filled the camp. It wasn't merely the unrest of the younger braves since the ill-conceived night raid a week earlier. That he had known and discounted. It wasn't the muffled grumbling of the elders; he had known and discounted that too. No, something else kept him from sleep.

The faint, keening tap-tap-tap of a drum floated through the sultry air. The sound was low, so closely matched to his heartbeat Pontiac had not noticed it until now. Stick Dancer, medicine man and conjurer, the most aged of all the tribe, was awake in his isolated dwelling.

Suddenly, Pontiac spun. He could see nothing, yet he felt eyes watching him and an icy pressure on his spine. As if seeing what Pontiac could not, Stick Dancer began to chant. His words, too soft to be distinguished, mingled with the tapping drum.

Pontiac whirled at another sound. The forest beckoned. Naked and weaponless, he approached the cluster of trees cautiously, and paused, kneeling to touch the earth. There were no tracks, and yet something had moved through the brush. He entered the path in pursuit. From the far edge of the camp, Stick Dancer's voice rose ever so slightly in the mysterious chant.

"Stand, or I will slay you," Pontiac whispered. Still as a statue, he waited for a response, waited for the telltale answer that would lead him to the enemy.

Laughter floated from ahead like the rustle of wind through spiny winter branches. Pontiac searched the ground for a suitable branch to use as a club. Ahead, a mocking, shifting shadow-shape drifted from behind an oak, sought a new hiding place in a clump of sumac. Pontiac moved swiftly, growing anger mixing with the prickling sensation of fear, the stillness and the drifting song of Stick Dancer making him uneasy. He stopped, thinking he'd heard the night call his name. A ghastly pale moon outlined the trees in an unearthly design, configurations that swayed in the breeze and clicked dry, sere threats of death and desiccation.

A willowy shape emerged from the sumac, stood half hidden in the shadow of an aged and lightning-split pine. Pontiac approached cautiously. "I have found

you, evil one," he whispered more to himself than the
half-glimpsed figure. "Perhaps your magic is the
cause of my distress. Well, no longer. You will die this
night. Pontiac, chief of the Ottawas, will kill you."

A voice answered, as tremulous as the rush of a
night bird sweeping from the sky to waken the unhappy with its swift passage. "What, my brother?
Again?"

Pontiac backed away, heart threatening to burst.
Now he knew. Flower-on-the-Water, pale, hardly
distinguishable from the air, stood before him. "Has
my brother forgotten his sister that he has no words of
comfort for her who was of his blood?"

"You are dead," Pontiac whispered, fear tightening
his chest, choking each labored breath. "You are dead.
The Great Spirit knows . . ."

"Well *I* know, my brother, my murderer . . ." The
final, fragile murmur hung on the voice of wind and
memory. A dying breeze shuffled through the timeless collection of days, of which each man knows only
the briefest afternoon.

She was gone. Pontiac faltered. Had she, in truth,
ever been there? Slowly, he walked back to the camp,
watching closely on every side.

The lodges were quiet. The dogs no longer barked.
No longer did the smell of pine or cherry or cedar
scent the night. Instead, the harsh perfume of fear lay
heavy in the air.

Pontiac shoved aside the flap and entered the medicine man's lodge, squatting by the glowing embers
that bathed the interior with a reddish glow. Stick
Dancer, wrapped in a ragged blanket, his leathery
face split by colorless lips and toothless, discolored
gums, peered through age-dimmed eyes at his visitor.

"The night is too warm for a blanket, Stick Dancer."

The wizened figure shrugged. "An old man gets cold. When others sweat, still he shivers. It is the way with all old men."

"You are sweating."

"Outside, I am hot. Inside, I am cold. This night has been one to make an old man . . ."

"Be still. You talk too much, I think."

The medicine man shrugged. It was very possible. He had never thought so, but admitted it was possible.

Pontiac reached out and picked up the ancient drum. The cracked hide seemed as fragile as Stick Dancer himself. "Why did you play, old one? Have you been up to mischief? First the drum, then the spirit chant . . ."

The medicine man's eyes glittered, emphasizing the hollowness of his face. "Mischief?" he cackled, taking the drum from Pontiac. "Stick Dancer drives away mischief. Blame another for her coming, Pontiac."

"Her?" Pontiac's flesh turned cold in spite of the fire.

Stick Dancer shivered violently. Though the spell eventually passed, he closed his eyes and would speak no further.

Private McManaway stumbled onto the porch and removed the thick wire-framed glasses he had taken from a French officer four years ago at Quebec. His expression bore the deep markings of fatigue time would never erase. Breathing heavily with the heat, he reached into the water bucket with cupped hands, doused his head and face, picked up the dipper and drank deeply, then again and again. His thirst could not be slaked, for it stemmed from spending every waking hour in the impossible confines of the sweat shack that served the fort as a hospital.

Sabrina, still bustling with energy, joined him in the cool shade on the porch, pleasant compared to the sweltering interior. McManaway offered her a dipper of water which she accepted gratefully, peering over the rim at the private as she drank. "You should try smiling, David," she said. "It will help."

"It's no good, Sabrina," he answered. "God, but I rue the day I was ever appointed Dr. Drummond's assistant. All I can do is watch them die."

"That's not true," Sabrina chided. "You've cleaned their wounds and bound them. No one could have done more."

"And Mrs. Schraner?"

"The wound is healing. Her fever is not your doing."

"I don't know. Dr. Drummond could have helped her."

"Dr. Drummond is dead, God rest his soul. The welfare of the sick and wounded has passed into your hands. You must not falter. Whether or not you can do anything," she nodded toward the hospital, "they think you can. If nothing else, the poor lads are comforted."

"I suppose you're right. I'm feeling sorry for myself." He rubbed his red-rimmed, bleary eyes, put on the glasses and sucked in a deep breath. "Thank you, Sabrina. Will you come by this evening?"

"Yes. And try to get some rest between times. It will do no good for our doctor to become a patient as well."

McManaway grinned. "Listen to who's talking. When will you sleep?"

"She's too ornery fer sleep. You can tell that by lookin'."

"Oh, dear lord!" Sabrina jumped with surprise. "Must you always sneak up on a soul, Mr. Hays?"

Jehu grinned. "Some habits is hard ta break, 'specially when they been keepin' me alive these many years. You doin' all right, McManaway?"

"I guess so. Got a new batch of your poultice brewing for Peters. Guess I'd better get to it."

Jehu and Sabrina watched McManaway enter the hospital, turn and walk down the empty street toward the commanding officer's house. "Quiet, ain't it? Trouble with a siege. Nothin' ta do but wait. People get bored, get that faraway empty look in their eyes . . . How is the corporal, anyways?"

"Peters? Better than I thought possible. What's in that horrible smelling mud you put on him?"

"Well, let's see. Mostly bear grease, o' course, an' herbs and a dollop of kinnikinnick, which should be chewed on first. Works better with some boiled dogwood bark, but we ain't got any of that, bein' as we can't get to the dogwood. An old conjurer man showed me how to make that poultice."

Sabrina made a wry face. "I wish you hadn't told me."

"He's healin', ain't he? Yessir. Good for cuts, gouges, jabs, gun wounds—once ya get the powder out, if there's any in there—knife wounds an' broken hearts," Jehu finished with a knowing wink.

Sabrina laughed, sobered immediately. "I wish I knew how to use it for that. There are two I would cover from head to toe if I thought your cure would take."

Jehu shook his head in agreement. "I never seen the like. Two people beatin' each other over the heads like they was Injun an' white man. Take the Major, now," he said, as they started toward the commander's house. "There's been a strange mood on him. I was glad at first, 'cause it was like old times. Less of this redcoat persnickety an' more plain ol' down ta earth fightin' savvy. But he ain't the same—ain't like he used ta be. Infernal waitin' is gettin' ta him, too. Sometimes there's an anger in him that looks like it's fixin' ta bust out. God help the poor soul nearby when he lets go."

"It's the same with Anne," Sabrina confided. "One moment she's warm and friendly, the next a stranger, cold and distant, like a wall come down betwixt me and the girl I helped raise. Maybe it's the waiting like you say, but I think it's more likely her. In love with the man and won't admit it. In love with the place, too, if she'd only let herself. Poor thing has got herself so confused she can't tell what she's about. All love and pleased as punch one day, and spiteful the next; up and down and up and down until my head swims with keeping it all straight. I wish I could see what they'll come to, but I can't," she concluded glumly.

They stopped at the white-washed picket fence, paused at the gate opening onto the parched lawn and axe-marked door. What had once been a lovely flower garden was trampled to dry twigs and stalks, evidence of the attack a week earlier. Jehu, with the true spirit of a man who had seen a lifetime of sorrow and joy and lasted to live with both, took Sabrina's arm. "Of course, you an' me ain't changed. We're just as good as ever. Maybe better." His grin was utterly lascivious.

"Mr. Hays!" Sabrina left him standing there and hurried to the door. She turned before entering. "I'll be at the hospital after supper," she said, just loud

enough for him to hear. "If you're up to it later, we'll
find out just how much better." Before Jehu could
answer, she winked at him and ducked in the door.

Jehu grinned, set his hat at a jaunty angle and strode
off toward the barracks. Come sundown and he'd
sneak out the river gate. He hadn't had a bath in over
a week.

CHAPTER 26

August brought no respite from the enervating heat. The wind abandoned the world to the fierce jurisdiction of the sun. Beth no longer even tried to keep track of the days. Counting had become a pointless exercise. Little more than a common serving woman, no better than the meanest indentured servant, she passed the daylight hours in subservience to Jean Dumas, Thomas St. Aubin and André Charbonneau. At night she was locked in the stifling attic. Isolated and without human companionship, she escaped madness only through prayer and the conviction the English would eventually win and she would be rescued.

Her jailers grew more sullen and meaner each day the siege dragged on, for they were as much its prisoners as those in the fort. Wherever Beth went, their eyes raked her thinning form. Whatever she said or did, salacious suggestions rewarded her. André was the lesser threat. But Thomas St. Aubin was a constant menace, a continuing reminder of the precarious situation into which she had been thrust.

Seldom was there a break in the routine. For three days Beth lay on her pallet, quivering with mortal terror as the shrieks and cries of newly arrived English prisoners rent the air day and night. The next evening at supper, St. Aubin, as usual, waited at the table for his meal. A severed hand, ghost-white and with a ring still on the little finger, rested by his plate. Horror stricken, Beth fled sobbing to the kitchen, chased by St. Aubin's loathsome laughter.

Only once, when Pontiac visited in order to deliver a pair of moccasins and a doeskin smock, was she treated kindly. Accepting the present gratefully, she ran to the attic, tore off the tattered gown held together by crudely fashioned knots, and donned her new clothes. Hair combed out, then neatly replaited in braids that hung to her waist, she reappeared downstairs. Pontiac grunted his approval.

Ever since that day, Beth had found herself wishing Pontiac would visit again. She knew the chieftain participated in unspeakable atrocities, knew white men had died horribly at his hands. Still, Pontiac was different. Unlike Teata, who was merely brutal, the Ottawa bore himself with an air of majesty. He would have been a king, no matter where he lived.

And then one night Beth woke to a series of resounding explosions and scattered musket fire. The noise lasted for a full five minutes and seemed to come from the south. Through the unevenly spaced plank wall, she could see a series of tiny orange flashes along the banks of the Detroit River, the answering crimson blossom of a bellowing cannon. The muggy blanket of night descended once more to smother the land when the interchange ceased.

A short time later, there was a commotion downstairs. The bolt rattled and her door was thrown open. Beth squinted, shielding her eyes as a lamp was thrust into the room and Thomas St. Aubin ordered her downstairs to prepare a meal.

Dumas, André and three other Frenchmen, unknown to her, waited in the main room. Dumas stood by the

sideboard, pouring a drink. One of the other Frenchmen casually dabbed at his arm where grapeshot had
ripped through the sleeve and torn away a chunk of
flesh. The three new men stared at her, and watched
her move toward the kitchen with hungry eyes. The
burly one, a giant *voyageur* named Montbar, rolled
his eyes to the ceiling. "*Mon Dieu,* but who would
have thought . . ."

"Forget her, Montbar," Dumas snapped, lifting a
new cask of rum to the table. "Where the hell were
those fire rafts?"

Dieppe, the scrawny one with the wounded arm,
eyed the cask greedily. "Ningas was supposed to have
his warriors build them, but since the first two failed,
he must have decided not to bother."

"Damn!" Dumas cursed. A key part of the overall
strategy had been to burn the *Michigan* and so gain
control of the river, and the crucial south bank across
from Detroit. Twice, fire rafts had been floated down
the river and twice Captain Smalley, reacting more
quickly than they had thought possible, maneuvered
the *Michigan* away from the fiery vessels, laughing
at the enraged Indians and then ridiculing their failure
with well-placed cannon shots. This night the third attempt should have been made, but the Indians had not
completed their task and Captain Smalley had slipped
downriver and into Lake Erie.

"But who would have thought they would chance
letting the *Michigan* go?" the *voyageur* Montbar
grumbled, draining his tankard and seizing the cask
with both hands to fill the jack a second time.

"I thought of it," Dumas said sourly. "I knew
Gladwyn would have to send Smalley out. That's why
I wanted the damned thing fired. Now, with any luck,
he'll reach Fort Schlosser and carry or escort troops

back here. Dammit, we should have razed Detroit at the first, and been done with it. We have no choice now."

"It will take more than the six of us," Montbar said.

Dumas scowled. "You were supposed to convince Mackinac to our way of thinking."

"He convinced Mackinac of nothing," André chimed in angrily, "and now it's too late. Without Mackinac to hold them together, the Wyandots have pulled out and influenced the Chippewas to do the same. If any more leave, we might as well give up and run."

Montbar frowned. "Easy little one, or Montbar will swat you like a bug, eh?"

André tried to look unconcerned, but swallowed his next remark. Beth entered the room, bringing a platter of pork and bread. Montbar grinned, caught her by the arm. "Thomas, you have not told me the truth. Did you not say you guarded an old hag? I see an English wanton."

Everyone laughed. Beth extricated herself from Montbar's grasp and escaped to the kitchen. "Ah, but Monsieur Dumas will let us have none of her," Thomas sighed.

Dumas shrugged. "It is not my doing, but Pontiac's order."

"*Merde!*" Montbar exclaimed. "Pontiac and *merde*, are they not the same? Do we now take orders from him?" He looked around the room, his eyes stopping at Dumas. "Are we not white men? You, Jean Dumas, are our leader, not Pontiac."

Dumas sat, clicked a fingernail against his teeth. André was losing his spirit, and now there was more pressure from new sources. "Go on, Montbar. Perhaps you say what we have all needed to say for some time."

"Pontiac is a coward. Teata and Ningas are willing to fight. Their braves thirst for action. It is Pontiac, the old woman, who holds back. Maybe someday soon I break him, like this." The *voyageur* slammed his fist on the corner of the oak table, breaking off a chunk in a prodigious show of strength. "I say Pontiac can go straight to hell. It is a long time since I had a white woman."

Dumas shrugged eloquently. The girl just might be the answer. Montbar was an oaf and a lout, but he might be a great deal more useful than he believed, the French leader mused. If, for example, Montbar were let loose like the slavering dog he was, and if Pontiac knew, would not the Indians come running? Certainly. And then what? Be killed by Montbar and the others, of course, leaving Teata in charge. Teata— the malleable one, hungry for action and glory. Dumas smiled, rose lazily to his feet. There would be time to find Pontiac, who would come running to save the *putain*. He, Dumas, would have to return, too. Watching the *coup de grâce* to the Ottawan war chief would make the evening worthwhile.

Casually, he walked across the room, opened the front door and paused in the doorway. "Go ahead," he shrugged. He didn't wait to hear their response.

With a roar of triumph, Montbar erupted from his chair and headed for the kitchen. The others followed, hot on his heels.

Beth heard the uproar, and terrified, ran without thinking, darting around the table, kicking aside a chair and rushing out the back door and into the night air, turning to circle the house and head for the river.

Ahead, the front door flew open and André yelled in triumph. Beth swerved to her left. From inside the

kitchen, a bellow of pain erupted as St. Aubin ran into
the overturned chair. Then the rest of the pack poured
out of the kitchen door.

She ran blindly now, eyes not yet fully accustomed
to the night. A yawning doorway loomed. The barn!
Was there a back door? Yes. With no time to think,
she plunged into the darkness like a hare scurrying for
the safety of its hole. Suddenly, André slammed into
her, knocking her to the ground. "I have her! I have
her!" he screamed.

Beth squirmed, kicked out and clawed her way free.
Groping blindly across the hard dirt floor, she quickly
found the back door, almost cried aloud with disappointment to find it wouldn't open. She spun to the
left and ran back through the barn, past the empty
stalls.

Thomas St. Aubin, Montbar and the others blocked
the single exit. She veered wildly away from them and
nearly fell against a ladder. Without hesitation, she
clambered up, driven by whoops and eager war cries
close behind. A hand grazed one of her ankles but she
kicked free and gained the loft in time to turn and
shove her foot into André's face, as it appeared over
the top rung. The young Frenchman went sailing
back, stopping with a bone-crunching snap when his
foot caught between two rungs, leaving him hanging
upside down and howling for help. The only sympathy
he received was a raucous chorus of laughter.

Panting violently and gasping for breath, Elizabeth
fell to the floor of the loft. She could see four men below in the dim lantern light. One, Montbar, climbed
the ladder, dragged André free and carried him back
down. Beth frantically searched the piled straw and
barren boards for a weapon while the *voyageur* named
Dieppe bounded to the loft with Montbar close be-

hind. Dieppe started for her just as Beth's fingers closed on the wooden haft of a pitchfork. Struggling to her feet, she swung with all her might. Dieppe screamed and leaped away, a bloody furrow sliced across his chest. Brandishing the pitchfork's cruel tines before her, she backed against the wall.

Montbar kept a wary distance. "The little cat has claws, eh?" he laughed. "You should be careful, Dieppe. You have bad luck with cats."

Dieppe scowled at the giant's humor. "I'll have this catamount, I swear," he muttered, fingering the streak of blood on his chest.

"Not 'til I've had her myself," Montbar warned. "Come, *chérie*," he turned in heavily accented English. "You will make Montbar a happy man."

Another head showed above the floor and Montbar aimed a vicious kick which missed. "Stay below and wait, scum. The mademoiselle will join you in a moment. Wait your turn and keep her for me. The man who dabbles before Montbar will lose his winesacks to my skinning knife."

"Who tosses her down has first honors, agreed?" said Dieppe in French.

The huge *voyageur* grinned. "But perhaps the mademoiselle wants *me* first, Dieppe."

"Touch me and I'll kill you," Beth cried shrilly, her voice wavering. She didn't have to know French to understand their intent.

"Fiercesome words, *ma putain*, but I doubt you've the spirit," Dieppe laughed.

Little light filtered into the loft, but Beth could imagine Dieppe's face, hawkish and scarred. The shadow that was Montbar moved to block the light even further. "Now! Take her."

Dieppe leaped, helped along by a tremendous shove

from the rear. Beth butted the handle against the wall,
aimed the prongs at her attacker. Unable to stop,
Dieppe tried to protect his face, only to realize the
rusted iron tines had punctured his belly, piercing
the flesh with a hideous sound. Dieppe groaned and
fell over onto a pile of straw, his weight dragging
the pitchfork from Beth's hands. Montbar lunged in
the same second, and before Beth could even scream,
she was caught in a suffocating embrace, carried across
the loft and dropped over the edge into St. Aubin's
arms. "She's mine," the giant bellowed from above.

In the shadows, Dieppe groaned. "Montbar! Oh,
mon Dieu! Help me, Montbar!"

Montbar knelt at his henchman's side, glanced carelessly down with a practiced eye. Dieppe lay in a pud-
dle of blood that had already drenched the brittle
straw and seeped through to the loft's dusty
planks. There was nothing to be done. "I will ream
her for you, *mon ami*. Adieu." Without a backward
look, Montbar scrambled down the ladder.

If he squinted, Dieppe could make out the long
wooden handle sprouting from his stomach. He tried
to pull it free, but the pain was too great. He tried to
call to his friend, to explain he did not want the
girl. Or the booty from Detroit. He only wanted to
live. "My God, please . . . let . . . me . . . live!" were
the last words on the *voyageur's* lips as he died.

Hands and legs and bruising bodies assaulted her
but she was too dazed to crawl free. She heard Montbar's gleeful roar from above as he skinned down the
ladder. Leering faces shifted in the shadows east by
the orange lantern light.

The buckskin shift was ripped away and Beth's arms
were pinned to her side. Calloused fingers grabbed her

breasts, kneaded fiercely, tugged and poked. Thomas
St. Aubin squatted over her like a carrion bird. He
had kicked aside his breeches and his manhood pressed
spasmodically against her thigh. He ran his fingers
over the white flesh of her abdomen and then eagerly
explored the soft umber triangle. "Somebody beat you
to her, Montbar. You'll not be the first."

The giant shoved through the group. Beth screamed,
closed her eyes against the sight of the hairy naked
beast whose lumbering staff swayed taut and eager before him. "What's this?" he bellowed, pushing St.
Aubin away to investigate for himself. Beth struggled
against the rough touch, shamed but unwilling to surrender to their lust.

Montbar grinned lasciviously. "It's true. Maybe
Gladwyn himself. Wouldn't be the first time an uncle
dipped his wick in the family wax, eh? But she's still
ripe enough."

André and the remaining Frenchmen struggled to
rid themselves of their clothes. Beth cursed, lashed
out, kicking and biting. The blows landed without effect on Montbar's muscled chest. Montbar laughed and
lost his grip. Beth rolled over and tried to crawl away
but the *voyageur*'s fingers dug into the pink flesh of
her buttocks. She screamed as one massive arm circled and lifted her, as his knees forced her legs apart
and she felt the blunt instrument of rape touch her between her buttocks and slide down and forward,
searching.

St. Aubin yanked her head back. "I'll be next, little
one."

Montbar thrust forward, André and his companion
cheering him on, stopping abruptly as the massive
front doors slammed open with tremendous force.

A flaming brand flew through the air into the cluster

of naked and half-dressed men, then a demon of the darkness voiced a marrow-chilling war cry and leaped into the barn. A musket roared, numbing their ears. St. Aubin shrieked in horror and collapsed onto Beth, hands clasped to the remains of his face.

Montbar scurried aside and the nameless Frenchman, clasping breeches in one hand and badly burned buttocks in the other, kicked open the rear door and fled. André recognized Pontiac in the torchlight and groped for the knife he kept in his boot sheath. Pontiac swung the musket barrel, catching the youth flush in the mouth, sending him reeling back, spewing blood and teeth. Whimpering, he crawled toward the rear door, lust forgotten, escape—from the barn, the farm, Dumas, Pontiac and the whole madness of the rebellion—his only thought.

Beth, sick and trembling, shoved Thomas St. Aubin's corpse to one side. "Autumn Woman," Pontiac called, starting for her.

Montbar leaped from the darkness. Beth screamed a tardy warning as Pontiac was flattened by the *voyageur's* enormous weight. The spreading flames rapidly consumed the barn. Beth grabbed the smock to cover her nudity and started at the naked, struggling forms.

Montbar rose, a hulking mass of milk-white flesh tinged by red fire glow, and swept the Indian into a powerful bear hug. Holding the chieftain off the floor, he began to squeeze. Pontiac grimaced in agony, slowly reached up to entwine the fingers of one hand in Montbar's greasy hair. His other palm cocked under the Frenchman's jaw. Montbar's grip tightened. Pontiac wheezed, fighting the terrible, crushing pressure. Slowly, Montbar's head bent further and further back. The veins and muscles in his neck stood out. An awful silence fell, broken only by the crackling laughter of the flames.

Pontiac could take little more. Already the mist floated over his eyes. His breath was gone and liquid fire coursed through his chest, burning his lungs. Calling silently for the strength of the spirits, he tapped the last surge of energy, jerked back with his right hand, up with his left.

Like a great beam breaking, Montbar's neck snapped. The huge arms loosened and the giant staggered back. Pontiac crumbled. Falling to his knees, he toppled the *voyageur's* lifeless body into a flaming pyre.

With blind, aching will, Pontiac refused himself the great gasps of air he needed so badly, scooped Beth into his arms and tottered from the smoky barn even as a super-heated pile of dried straw exploded with a roar and filled the entire structure with flames. Racing far enough away to escape the heat, he set Beth down and collapsed himself, finally allowing his lungs the fresh air they so desperately craved.

When he stood again, it was to face a circle of curious faces. Brusquely, Pontiac ordered his warriors to return to camp. They turned at his command, leaving only Dumas, whose pistol dangled from his hand. A look of consternation masked the Frenchman's face. For the first time, he fully understood why the Ottawas held this chief in such great respect.

Pontiac gestured toward the barn. "Like the wind among the clouds, I have scattered your men," he said in husky, broken French. "It is fortunate for you, my *brother*, that I came in time." Dumas glanced at the pistol at his side and decided not to try. Pontiac was too close. "Go, now," the chief continued, "and bring

Monsieur and Madame Charbonneau back to their house. They will guard Autumn Woman from now on."

Dumas nodded in compliance and hid a scowl of displeasure as he walked away from the burning barn. If I had any sense, he thought, I'd leave. Surely, within two weeks, travelling alone and light, he could be on the Mississippi and heading south. And yet, Gladwyn still lived, and Gladwyn was the only one who had escaped at Fort Munro. Gladwyn was the only man alive who had seen it with his own eyes. Dumas' jaw tightened. And more important, France's position in the Northwest was at stake. The war could still be won. Somehow he would find a way. Detroit *would* fall.

Pontiac carried Beth through the fields to the river's edge, set her down on the still-warm, grassy bank, and dove immediately into the water. A second later he emerged a few yards out, blowing mightily. Beth watched as he swam. Long powerful strokes propelled his compact form easily against the current, and she was reminded of the porpoises in the Hudson River. How sleek and beautiful they were! How like them Pontiac was in his unstudied grace.

Trembling, Beth stood, ran into the cool water, gasping for breath as her feet slipped from under her, and she fell. Five yards upstream the water exploded and Pontiac emerged, coppery skin shining as the water ran off. Laughing, he strode through the water and helped the girl to her feet.

Confused, Beth covered her breasts, reached down and splashed water on herself. Pontiac, finally aware of her embarrassment, turned and dove again, reappearing a moment later in the deeper water, swimming against the strong current.

Suddenly the water felt good, cool and refreshing. For too long she'd been locked in the attic, covered with soot and ashes, dirt and perspiration, and she sensed about herself the odor of fear and barely escaped danger, sharp against the sweet smell of night and the river. Beth waded back to the shore, grabbed a double handful of the sweet grass to scrub herself. Five minutes later, rid of the ravages of the night, she felt cleaner than she could remember, purified, almost.

She'd forgotten Pontiac, and when he broke from the water a few yards upstream she jumped, almost fell again. For a moment they simply stared at each other. Her eyes were used to the faint light now and she noted the rise and fall of his chest as he breathed, the muscles that rippled across his stomach, the movement of his thighs as he strode toward her.

This time she was not embarrassed. His shoulders bunched as he picked her up. Beth relaxed in his arms. The water caught her hair, spreading it downstream in a dark, waving carpet, The swift current flowed effortlessly along her legs, between her thighs, over the young, taut stomach and around the gently swelling breasts, nipples erect and tingling from the swiftly coursing bath.

She was intensely aware of Pontiac. His right arm supported her shoulders effortlessly, his left was caught half way up her thighs. His arms were silk smooth on her skin. His stomach muscles relaxed and the gentle curve of her side fit against him. She was not surprised to feel the burning spot where his manhood rose to touch the small of her back, a tiny pressure, rubbing gently as the water rushed by. Pontiac's gaze was like the water itself, slowly covering her body, flowing over her legs, stopping momentarily at the dark triangle of curls, then fondly touching each breast before meeting her own unfrightened eyes.

He smiled, and Beth sensed the heat coursing through his limbs as he carried her through the water to the shore and laid her on the fragrant mattress of earth. The sloping bank hid them from the garish light of the still-blazing barn. Only the stars and the sliver of moon gave them light. Beth, strangely unfrightened by the figure of primeval energy looming over her, fought with waning strength the urge to bring her arms about his neck and pull him to her. Still, he had saved her life, carried her to the water, held her: with a small cry, she gave up the fight and reached upward to meet and guide him deep into her being. Nothing else mattered. Cleansed of the horrors of the past weeks, the terror of flight and the pawing degradations of the Frenchmen, she wept softly against his shoulder as he entered and filled her, as their bodies blended in that most timeless and powerful of rhythms.

Was she moving? Yes. Like the river, plunging, cascading through the night, heedless of all save the sweeping forces urging her on. As never before, Beth was woman, earth, air, fire and water, at one with the universe, a shameless creature caught in the arms of a man who, ravaging, was consumed.

Suddenly, Pontiac shuddered and stiffened. At the threshold of her own peak, Beth clasped her legs about his waist and cried out as she tightened around him, holding him deep inside, catching the eruption of life. Plunging down the breathless slope of night, the two of them mingled the precious wine of life and rose to meet the stars.

* * *

A gray pre-dawn light flattened the view across the Detroit River. Beth woke outside the stuffy attic for the first time in months. For a moment she lay without moving, simply breathing, tasting the fresh air, testing the clean river smells, luxuriating in the murmur of water and the rustle of leaves. The world was alive.

Pontiac still slept. Beth raised herself on one elbow, gazed down at him, then herself. They had slept naked under the stars, at one with earth, air and the river, naturally and without sin—something that would have been unthinkable in England, or anywhere near civilized men.

How sad, she thought then. How infinitely sad we must disguise ourselves. How ludicrous the restrictions with which we clothe our bodies and souls. What was civilization? Breeches and petticoats? Pontiac looked as noble in his tattoos. She had accepted his flesh willingly, joyously, held his body deep in her own. Where was the shame?

She could see none. The river still ran. The trees did not blush. No bird or beast frowned in censure. She let her head fall back, felt the weight of hair. The sky was blue. She could stay here forever, she realized. Stay and . . .

"What does Autumn Woman see?"

Beth started, turned her head to see Pontiac awake and watching her. He looked different. The tattooed face . . . the flaring sun on his chest . . . She looked back to the sky, confused. "The sky. Empty sky. It is beautiful."

Pontiac grunted, heaved to his feet and plunged into the river. Elizabeth sat up, clasped arms about breasts and waited. He'd moved so quickly. Like a cat. One moment asleep, the next flashing through the air. He dove, disappearing beneath the water, then surfaced and swam swiftly back to shore.

Beth shivered slightly as he approached and knelt at her side, naked and dripping wet. A tattooed hand reached out to touch her breasts, slide down to her stomach, lower still to the reddish gold ringlets, musk-fragrant from the night's lovemaking. "I will take you back."

"To the fort?" Beth asked, smiling awkwardly.

Pontiac frowned. "To the Ottawa camp. When Detroit has been burned and the land is rid of the evil Eng-lesh, then we will leave. Autumn Woman will live in Pontiac's lodge. She will bear fine sons. Our days will be many."

"You hate the English, yet would take me for your . . . your squaw."

"You are Autumn Woman. You are Ottawa."

She wanted to cry out. No! Oh God, she couldn't! The Indian women were said to help with the tortures. Sometimes men were turned over to them alone for killing and . . . Nausea turned her stomach. Somehow, she had to get back, had to convince him to let her go. She had willingly made love with the magnificent man who had saved her life, but she would never be able to live with him.

She turned away from his stare, no longer able to bear its intensity. She took a deep breath. "I am Elizabeth Gladwyn," she said defiantly. "I will never be an Ottawa."

"You are Pontiac's woman."

The night before had been filled with almost unbearable ecstasy, but that moment was gone. She was *English.* "No. I cannot stop Pontiac from taking me away, but I will never give him sons. I will smother them as they come forth."

Pontiac reached down and grabbed her arm, jerked her upright. "Do not say this!"

"I will. I swear it." The tattooed face, inches from her own, was a gruesome, macabre mask. The patterned scars covering his body told a tale of a primitive culture that could not have been more different from hers. She wanted to weep, but could not. "Why did you not leave me to die in the barn?" she asked bitterly.

Pontiac loosed her arms. "Why did you accept me?" he asked in return, indicating the depression where the grass lay crushed.

"Because . . . Because . . ." Beth stammered, trying to put in words the welter of contradictory emotions that raged in her breast. "I . . . don't know," she finally announced, crestfallen.

Pontiac scooped up the soiled doeskin smock, thrust it in her arms. His face was rock-solid, impassive. "Go to the house. I will send for Monsieur and Madame Charbonneau."

"Pontiac . . ."

"Do not try to escape. I cannot always be nearby to save you, Eliza-beth Gladwyn." Neither waiting for a reply nor looking back, Pontiac strode away across the open fields toward the Ottawa camp.

Weary and drained, Beth considered running, considered trying to escape down the river. The attempt would be useless. Near tears, she pulled the smoke-stained garment over her head and started for the Charbonneaus'. She took care to look away from the blackened skeleton of the barn, and the flock of ravens that had come to feast among the ruins.

CHAPTER 27

The men of the King's First sipped mugs of weak tea in disgruntled silence. Only one spoke, a private whose name Henry could not remember. The soldier loudly decried the lack of proper nourishment, namely the rum guaranteed to them that served in His Majesty's army. America was horrible enough, he was saying, without having to go without one's ration of rum while being stuck in an isolated and beleaguered fort with nothing to do but wait for a bunch of stinking redskins to kill a man.

Henry did not blame him really. The tea leaves, boiled to an unfragrant mush, could hardly be expected to produce even a marginally palatable beverage. But there was nothing better to drink and the private knew it. There was more in his complaint than the usual barracks gripes and Henry, poised in the doorway, was uneasily aware of the restless silence in the room.

Having heard enough, he stepped inside the open door. The men sat with hunched shoulders. Those who faced him stared glumly down from under hooded eyelids, surly and uncommunicative. More startling was the presence of Patrick Campbell, lounging against the wall by the opposite door. Detroit had come to a pretty pass indeed when such comments could be made openly in front of an officer.

"Atten-shun!" With the automatic cry from the sergeant, chairs scraped and knives clanked on metal mess tins.

"As you were!" Henry responded quickly. The chairs scraped again and all sat, still at attention, backs stiff, elbows to sides and eyes straight ahead.

Henry strolled at an even pace through the double line of tables, a broad, powerful figure in cotton blouse and buckskin breeches, hair unwigged and hanging mane-like about his neck, the hilt of a broad-bladed knife jutting from his belted waist. No one spoke when he stopped in front of the malcontent, stood without looking down. "Does any man here have a complaint?" he asked quietly.

No one answered. The men stared blankly at their plates and cups.

"Private?" Henry snapped, finally focusing on the offender. "Any complaints?"

The young man withered under the officer's stare. "No, sir," he answered in a sullen, frightened whisper.

"Well, I have. I'm out of port and haven't had a cup of chocolate or coffee in over a week. My wife can't find her favorite perfume and the theater is closed for the duration. I haven't had a decent meal in so long my stomach thinks my throat's been cut. Powder for my wig can't be had at any price, and polish for my buttons is as scarce as hen's teeth. Things are rough all around, gentlemen."

Someone snorted, a laugh quickly cut off. Patrick Campbell watched the quiet confrontation from the door leading to the duty sergeant's office and scowled, realizing that Henry led not so much by Amherst's in-

vestiture as by his own unique force of personality. On
one point he was determined: if and when they ever
got out of Detroit, Amherst most certainly would hear
of Gladwyn's behavior.

Henry noticed Patrick ease out the door. The tension broken, he followed the Lieutenant into the
privacy of Sergeant Livingston's office. "A moment,
please, Mr. Campbell." The sergeant bolted to attention. Patrick was already on the porch. "As you were,
Sergeant," he continued, passing through the office
without stopping and joining Patrick outside. "You
too, Lieutenant. I think we needn't be too concerned
with formalities."

Patrick nodded, walked alongside Henry, from
time to time casting an eye in his commanding officer's
direction. The two men ambled down rue Ste. Anne,
neither speaking. Patrick felt the sweat trickle down
between his shoulder blades and from his armpits.
Gladwyn seemed comfortable in the infernal heat, a
fact the regulation-dressed Lieutenant found galling
in the extreme. They drew abreast of Patrick's quarters. "Well, sir, here I am. If you'll pardon me . . ."

"Not at all, Lieutenant. May I join you for a moment?"

Patrick stiffened perceptibly and gestured toward
the door of the small two-room cabin. "Of course," he
said, voice controlled. Responding to a vague premonition, his hand touched the reassuring stock of the pistol thrust securely in his belt. After all, the Major was
a cuckold, and rightfully entitled to seek redress.

"I'd offer you something to drink, Major, but as you
see, I am a trifle lacking." A sweep of the hand indicated an all but barren shelf over the small fireplace.

"No matter. I am not thirsty."

"How fortunate," Patrick answered drily, rummaging among the few belongings, garnered for the most part from Jess McBeecher's dwindling store. With a grunt of satisfaction, he produced a clay pipe, filled it with tobacco. A coal stolen from the fireplace glowed brightly over the bowl, and within a moment a sluggish cloud of blue-gray smoke hung in the air. Still, Gladwyn had said nothing. Patrick perched on a corner of the table, puffing on his pipe and waiting, a picture of unflappable calm even when Henry started to pull the door closed. "Isn't it a bit warm for that, Major?"

"Yes, it is, but I think neither of us want a dozen prying ears eavesdropping on what should be a private conversation. Unless, of course . . ."

"No! By all means. I wouldn't . . ." He stopped, damning himself for allowing Gladwyn to play him for a fool.

"Yes, Lieutenant?"

"Nothing," Patrick snapped. "Close the door if you wish."

Henry noted the nervous darting of the man's eyes, the unsettling mixture of anxiety and calm. Jehu's howling wilderness at work? "Lieutenant, I have noted a great deal of unrest among the garrison."

Patrick nodded, smiled benignly. "Only the garrison? No others?"

Henry frowned, quickly banished the tortured vision of his wife in Campbell's arms. The impulse was to lash out with fist and knife, but he was damned if he'd let the Lieutenant have the satisfaction. Not yet. Not this time. "Mr. Campbell. You are in many ways a highly commendable officer, capable and brave under fire as I have personally observed. It would be a shame and a loss to this command if I were forced to order you confined to quarters."

Patrick flinched. His eyes narrowed. "May I ask for what cause the Major threatens me with incarceration?"

"Why were you in the mess hall?"

"I . . . Why, I was attempting to observe the morale of the men. Also, as you know, Ensign Price's quarters are nearby. My clothing was lost at Michilimackinac and I was going to ask . . . Well, we're both approximately the same height and build . . ." He puffed nervously on the pipe, found it had gone out. Frowning in dissatisfaction, he tapped the bowl on the heel of his hand, at the same time peering at Henry through slitted eyes.

Henry sighed inwardly, knowing he would get no more. "Very well, Mister Campbell," he said, starting for the door. "However, word has reached me through, as our Indian friends would say, some little bird, that there is a conspiracy afoot to usurp my authority. It seems some of the civilians and certain members of the garrison wish to surrender Detroit to Pontiac."

He paused, stared at Patrick to reinforce the message. "You, sir, have been named as one sympathetic, to put it mildly, to this mutiny. You should know, then, that so long as I live Detroit will not be surrendered."

"Sir! I resent . . ."

Henry waved away Patrick's display of righteous indignation. "If I were totally convinced of the truth of these allegations, I would not be here to talk, but to place you under arrest. Do not doubt my intent, Mr. Campbell. I will consider participation in such a conspiracy prima facie evidence of mutiny and treason, to be punished by hanging."

Patrick rose stiffly, his face reddening. "And you'd like nothing better than to see me dance a jig from the gallows branch?"

"Not at all. I came only to caution you. We both know what I'm talking about, and you have been duly warned. Do not force me to take an action only I will survive to regret."

Neither spoke. Henry watched the younger man's face, noted the pistol in Patrick's belt and the hand even now firmly grasping the wooden stock. His eyes rose to meet Patrick's. His voice was soft. "I do not wish to make an issue of this, sir. A simple declaration will suffice. With whom does your allegiance lie, Lieutenant?"

Patrick's gaze grew distant but his features betrayed no emotion. His fingers tightened on the flintlock but he made no move to bring it forth. "With the King," he finally replied in a near whisper, leaving Henry to judge the true meaning of the answer.

Henry nodded, glanced one last time at the belted pistol, then offered his back to Patrick and left, leaving the door open.

The hot, stagnant time of day had passed. Long tendrils of under-lit clouds streaked the sky. An evening breeze, cool at last, escorted Henry to the east wall near his home. He joined Jehu on the ramparts. Neither spoke during the first moments of their vigil.

"Plenty of powder and shot," Henry finally said, as if talking to himself. "Enough food, however plain, to keep body and soul together. Water in plenty so long as the river runs."

"They're still unhappy," Jehu replied, indicating the homes of the civilians. "They ain't come right out an' done anything, but I'd not turn my back on 'em."

"We'll find out more tonight."

Jehu cast a shrewd glance in Henry's direction. "Still ain't gonna tell me how you heard?"

"I've got my ways," Henry replied, staring out at the campfires and making a mental count.

"There are fewer," Jehu commented, reading his commanding officer's mind. "I been countin' 'em the past week." Jehu's rangers had proved invaluable. Engaging in nightly forays to gather information, they had brought word that Pontiac had divided his camp. This, coupled with the lessening number of fires, boded well for the fort. "Some of 'em have pulled out," Jehu said. "Which figures, with fall comin'. Pontiac's gotta be worried. If some of the tribes have pulled out, others might too. We could lick 'em, Major. If Smalley would only show with reinforcements, we could win this yet."

"Win?" Henry asked grimly. "Not as long as they have Beth."

Jehu coughed. "Sorry. I forgot about her."

"I didn't." Henry turned and started down the steps. "You're invited to supper, if you want."

"In a minute. I want to watch a little longer."

Henry nodded, continued on down from the wall and crossed to his home, pausing to stare forlornly at the unkempt and weedy garden before entering. The place seemed empty. He ascended the steps, hoping Anne and Juliet would be there. But the bedroom was empty. Vaguely irritated, he continued down the hall and into Beth's room, converted to a study so he could work without waking Juliet. Papers littered the desk. Notes and completed dispatches he dared not attempt to send lay in a pile, ready for the time he could spare a man from the defense of the fort. The last such missives had gone with Captain Smalley aboard the *Michigan*. Only two weeks ago? It seemed far longer. All time seemed long. May ninth, the day the siege had begun, was a little less than four months past; it could as easily have been a year.

Henry sat, the dream souring even as he began to envision it. What kind of an empire would there be without Anne? And would she take his—*his*—child away? Back to England? Never! Bitterly, he cursed and swept the pages from his desk, overturning a fortunately empty inkwell. "Never, goddamn it. Never!" A startled gasp drew his attention to the door. Sabrina stood there. "Well, what do you want?"

"I just . . ."

"It's all right, Sabrina. I'm just a bit tired, is all."

"You've a right to be, Master Henry, working so hard . . ." She stopped, flustered. She was upset about something. "It's grim tidings, sir. Karen's taken a turn for the worse, and just when we thought she might get well. Miz Anne's gone to be with her and help Gus."

"And Juliet?"

"She's there, too. I imagine they'll be the night."

Henry nodded. "It's just as well, I suppose." He noticed the old woman's worried expression. "Have you heard anything new?"

"No, sir. They're going to have another meeting sometime soon, but no one will say when." She coughed nervously. "Sir?"

"Yes?"

"If anything . . . happens . . . to Karen, they might . . . That is, it might make things worse."

"Where'd you hear that?"

"At McBeecher's. They guarded their tongues, but I caught the meaning well."

"Was anything said about Lieutenant Campbell?"

"No, sir. Just implied. But he's in it, sir, I'm sure."

"So am I, dammit." Henry rose to pace the room.

"If I leave him alone, there's no telling what foolishness they'll try. If I arrest him, Anne will never believe I had good cause." He caught himself. There were no secrets where Sabrina was concerned, but still, a man could admit only so much, aloud. "Thank you, Sabrina. Don't worry. We'll have this business settled soon. Is there any tea left?"

"Some that pretends to be."

"It will do. Make enough for Jehu as well. He'll be along shortly. And something to eat, if you don't mind. We'll need it before the night is through."

Her breath came raggedly, as if shredded by the fever. Shallow breaths, light as a sparrow's, rapid fluttering breaths that barely lifted her chest.

How chilly it is, Karen thought. Strange that beads of sweat should run down her neck, tickle her sides. The covers were too heavy; they were smothering her. "Take them off," she mumbled, the sound loud in her ears but a whisper to the white faces peering from above. "Take them off."

She opened her eyes to a shimmering aqueous veil behind which phantom-like figures swam. "Gustav?" A ragged breath rattled off the walls of her chest. "Gustav?"

Why didn't he answer? Perhaps he was sad. Or tired. How long has he watched, she wondered. How long had she been in the bed, cold and burning at the same time? "I'm burning in the snow, Gustav." Something wet touched her forehead, then her lips. A hollow, far-away voice said something about water and a trickle wet her tongue before she managed to shake away the hand.

"I want the children!"

The hollow voice again. Was it true? Were the children really gone? If she could only remember. Yes. Of course. Their graves were in Holland. That's why they had left, wasn't it? That's why they had come to the bright glowing new world. She hadn't wanted to come at all. "Gustav? I'm sorry . . ."

"No, Karen. You don't . . ."

"I'm sorry I cried. But our house was so beautiful. Do you remember?" A silk-soft answer descended but she didn't hear it for the images were flooding back, rushed by the fever. There was the beautiful stained-glass window in the front door . . . the marble balustrade down which little Gustav had loved to slide . . . the long green lawn cut with walks and beds of bright tulips, through which they'd walked arm in arm. She'd had a light blue gown.

Karen's eyes squinted closed, and she shook her head back and forth. The light blue gown was gone and the house had disappeared. "Where are my children? What have they done to my children?"

Again the moistness touched her forehead and a cool palm smoothed back her matted hair, calming her. The seething, turbulent discord faded and the flat, verdant tableland of Holland populated with troubles and hate raced away, receding into the past as the colonies worked their magic, the wilderness spun its web. There was room, endless vistas in which a person could thrive and grow and be alive, and always, there was Gustav. The hand on her forehead was heavy with grief, hard with the calluses of loving labor. Gustav was near.

"Gustav? Is that you?" she murmured, the words husky and rasping.

"*Ja*, Karen. It is I."

"Dear . . . Gustav . . ." A long pause. The shallow breaths, collecting energy. "Do you remember . . . the storm? Tell me . . ."

"The storm?" Gus sat on the edge of the bed, holding her hand. Tears streamed down his face and he started to talk, the words halting, coming between silent sobs. Anne bit her knuckles to keep from weeping aloud. "It was the first spring, no? You cried during the winter . . . said you wanted to go back . . . no matter what waited . . . And then, one day, the snow stopped and rain fell. The snow began to melt. The forest was black . . . and muddy . . . and ugly. You were so sad . . ."

"Go on . . ." A smile. Her eyes were open, staring into the past.

"In the night, the wind stopped. It was very cold. When we woke, I stirred the fire, but there was not enough wood. I opened the door to go out and get more. 'Karen!' I called. 'Come see!'

" 'There is nothing to see,' you said.

" 'No. You must come see!'

"You stepped from the bed and pulled on the old coat—you remember the coat your mama gave you— and came to the door."

"What did I see, Gustav?" Karen whispered, her face radiant.

"You saw . . ." Gus stopped, cleared his throat. "You . . . we . . . saw . . . the most beautiful sight. During the night the sky had cleared and the rain had frozen. Everything—trees, rocks, ground, the woodpile —was covered with ice. The sun . . . was bright . . . and everything looked like . . ."

"Diamonds, Gustav. Do you remember?"

". . . diamonds . . ."

"Glittering . . ."

"Glittering in the sun . . . like the whole world was on fire . . . and shining. New . . . bright and shining . . ."

"Gustav! Gustav!"

It was over. Karen lay motionless and at peace. For a long moment, Gus sat without moving. The tears had stopped. Slowly, he bent to the lifeless face, kissed Karen on the forehead once, tenderly, and sat back up, gazing at the wife who had fled to a land of ice and fire, a land of remembrance and distant diamonds.

Finally he rose, pulled the cover to her chin, and with trembling fingertips, gently closed the unseeing eyes. Anne wept uncontrollably. She felt Gus's hands on her shoulders. "Do not cry, Anne. Do not cry, little one. She is gone, but I think she will be happy."

"Gus, I . . ."

"No. Go to your baby." From the living room, Juliet's wail of dismay at being neglected could be heard. "Go. She never could stand to see a hungry baby. I will sit with Karen for a little while longer."

"Gus . . . ?"

He shook his head gently, insistently. "Go, *liebchen*. We would be alone together for a moment. Go."

Anne left them, went into the shop where Juliet lay in a blanket-lined box. The child bawled, her face contorted with rage. Anne moved quickly, picking up her baby and freeing one milk-swollen breast.

Karen lay dead in one room: at the same moment a child took sustenance and reaffirmed life in another. Juliet murmured, butted and tugged. Anne walked back and forth, felt the tiny toothless gums against her breast. A soft, tingling, warm feeling spread up her back and across her shoulders, and spread to envelop her and the child in a protective cocoon of love.

Karen's diamonds sparkled in her imagination. The

simple story Karen had remembered at the last blossomed into meaning for her. Diamonds were everywhere: simple joys. A flower. A sunset. A slow spring rain; even a dewdrop. A task completed.

How many times had someone tried to tell her? Henry had. Louis Bouvier had. Karen certainly had. Even Catherine, in the woods that day when she gestured to the trees. Was she talking of beauty, too?

The past months had twisted Anne's world beyond recognition. England and London, courts and balls and fetes and masques . . . Had she, simply, been unable to see past them? For a time in the winter, yes. For a time on the cliff facing the roaring falls, yes. But at the same time, no, for she had never accepted the new world on its own terms. For her it had been an illusion; only the old country and the old ways were real. Suddenly, for the first time, she understood that the old country and old ways were the illusions. Here, in the wilderness of bright and shining diamonds, was the real world.

Unaware, she had begun to cry again. Anne wept for the woman she had grown to love. She wept for the great gift of awakening, bequeathed at such unthinking cost. She wept, too, for her own obstinacy, and the time wasted.

Gus entered the shop sometime later. Moonlight streamed through the unshuttered window. Anne sat in the rocking chair, Juliet asleep at her breast. "Anne?"

She sat up, guilty for having dozed off. "I'm sorry, Gus, I . . ."

He shook his head. "No. I understand. You were her friend. She loved you. For her, I thank you more . . ." Words failed him. Gus stood motionless, as if stunned by a physical blow. The tears had stopped and his face was immobile and betrayed no emotion. The door to the shop creaked open. Neither Gus nor Anne noticed.

"Meetin's about to commence at the school." The hoarse whisper startled them. "You comin'?"

Gus turned slowly. "No. I have work that must be done."

"My God, man. This is important. Can't it wait?"

"No. It cannot." Without further explanation, Gus closed the door in the man's face and plodded toward his shop.

"Meeting?" Anne asked, puzzled.

"*Ja*." He stopped. "You do not know?"

"Know what?"

"They want to leave. Does not Henry know of this?"

Anne shook her head. "He's never said. Who wants to leave? Why?"

"McBeecher. The others. Some of the army. The Lieutenant will lead them in accord with the Frenchman Dumas' offer." He paused, shook his head. "I do not think I like the Lieutenant."

"Campbell?" Anne asked, not wanting to be told.

"Yes. That one. I am sorry. I will build the box now. You will stay here, no?"

Anne nodded without thinking. Gus left the room and a moment later she could hear the clink of tools being taken from their place and the scrape of wood against wood. Patrick Campbell was going to lead the civilians out of the fort? But he couldn't! The very idea was insane. Dumas would see them all killed.

For weeks she had longed for such an exodus, to leave the beleaguered fort by any means, to go home, to England. Now she saw it more plainly: if she left, if they abandoned Detroit, it would make meaningless Karen's sacrifice and dream. They were fools! They could not be allowed to leave, not after so many had fought so long, held on against such odds. Moving quietly and quickly, Anne buttoned her blouse, bundled Juliet in a blanket and hurried from the house.

Amber light trickled around the weathered shutters of the schoolhouse. Pausing on the porch to catch her breath, Anne squared her shoulders and rapped softly, struggling to retain her composure when the door opened almost immediately. She slipped in before the surprised doorkeeper could sound a warning.

A majority of the English settlers crowded the small schoolroom. Anne laid the sleeping Juliet on a rear bench and made her way to the front of the room, pretending not to notice Patrick, who stood to the left of the teacher's desk. The news of her arrival swept through the gathering in a swell of angry conversation. Jess McBeecher managed to still it with several raps of his pistol butt on the desk top. When the meeting finally regained some semblance of order, McBeecher fixed Anne with an angry stare. "How you learned of this meeting I don't know, but your presence here changes nothing, lass. There's work afoot and best you be off while we see to it."

"I hardly think Mrs. Gladwyn will cause us undue alarm," Patrick broke in. "If there's any in favor of what we propose, it is she. In truth, she is more eager to return to England than any of us."

Anne blushed to think her private matters public knowledge. But Patrick's statement had given her their attention, so she kept her peace. "Work?" she asked, pleasantly enough. "Foolishness, I think."

McBeecher cast an angry glance at Patrick, who shrugged in surprise. "Now see here, Mrs. Gladwyn." The storekeeper pounded on the desk again and the rising hum abated. "You've no right . . ." He stopped, suddenly suspicious. "Who told you we'd be here?"

"I'll bet I know," Jacob Barr interrupted. "Where's Gus Schraner? Why isn't he here?"

"He told me he had work to do," another chimed in. "Then it was he," Patrick concluded.

"And who else has he told?" Barr asked ominously.

"I don't think it matters," the Lieutenant replied. "Most of the men will follow me in any case. I've talked to them myself."

Priscilla Hampton stood abruptly. "What I want to know is, where is Gus Schraner now? He could be summoning the Major and his guard, for all we know." The gathering echoed her strident sentiments.

"You needn't worry about that," Anne said bitterly.

"Where is he then?" Priscilla screeched.

"Building Karen's coffin."

Each face registered sudden shock. Only hours before Karen Schraner had been stable and they had all supposed she was recovering. For a long moment no one spoke. Priscilla Hampton broke the spell. Her face contorted by sudden grief, she rose and headed for the door without saying another word.

Patrick stirred uneasily as the focus of attention shifted. "All the more reason for you to continue on this course of action," he began, moving to the front of the desk. "The same fate awaits all your wives and children. The same or worse. Henry Gladwyn must be removed from command and this settlement quitted at once. You must decide, and decide now. I cannot legally initiate such an act; I can only accede to the will of those whom our General and King have sent me to protect."

"Aye! What say you lads?" McBeecher asked.

"I will speak," Anne said, pushing to the desk.

"You have no cause. This is none of your concern."

"As much as yours, sir. I will speak."

"Of valor?" Patrick mocked.

"Of cowardice, Mr. Campbell."

Patrick flushed angrily. McBeecher scowled, as did many of the others. "We don't have to listen to this," he raged to the assembly.

Anne waved him to silence. "What else would you call those who shirk their duty and submit the innocent and helpless to the deprivations of the savages?"

"We're trying to save them!" Decker shouted.

"By running from your land and your homes? What is worth fighting for if not these?"

"You sang a different tune once," Patrick accused, white-faced with anger.

"As did we all. I considered you one of the most valiant of the King's officers once, but that estimation has proved false." She turned from Patrick to face the silent men and women. "I don't know what Lieutenant Campbell has told you, but I would have you understand this: if every man and woman here flees Detroit on the morrow, if not one has the courage to stay, my husband will remain—alone if necessary—to the end, faithful not only to King and duty, but to himself."

"Now see here!" Decker called angrily. "I'll not be called a coward by one such as yourself. You've been here but a year. I've seen five Detroit winters. I've raised my family and cared for them well. Every man here knows the mettle of Guthry Decker. What do we know of you?"

"That I have been foolish." The admission stilled the crowd completely. Nearly whispering she went on in the hushed room. "I have been vain . . . frightened . . . alone . . . Yearning for what I once knew, I could not accept the beauty that surrounded me, could not accept the people who . . ." She paused, near tears. No one interrupted. She breathed deeply, regaining control of voice and emotions. "But was it any different with you when first you came here? Granted, I have kept aloof, but in truth, who among you has even tried to accept me? Who beside the dead helped me find my way?"

Anne laughed softly. "Believe me, ladies and gentlemen, I have at last found my place. You . . . have lost yours. You, Mr. McBeecher, and you, gentlemen, have chosen to place faith and trust in the heathen whose atrocities have been demonstrated at every turn, in a Frenchman whose true history none of you know, and a fanatic . . ."—she pointed at Patrick—"whose only acquaintance with valor is the loss of Michilimackinac, who fled captivity leaving my niece behind, and now proposes to lead you defenseless into the warm and forgiving embrace of those whose sole ambition is the destruction of Detroit and the English. If you believe *that* . . . !"

"Enough!" Patrick lunged, infuriated beyond reason.

Jess McBeecher, not so confused that he'd let a woman be set upon, rounded the desk to step between Anne and Patrick. "I'll not stand for that, Lieutenant," he said roughly, shoving Patrick into a chair.

McBeecher turned to Anne, a flint-eyed, calculating expression on his face. "So the Major will stay all by his lonesome. Then what exactly is your place, lass?"

"With my husband," said Anne. "I don't know what I can do, but I shall be with him."

For a long, long moment, no one spoke. Patrick stared blankly at the men and women in front of him. Someone coughed. Another shifted uneasily in her chair. Guthry Decker cleared his throat, half rose and sat down again.

Few realized when McBeecher started talking, his voice was so soft. "You spoke of vanity. The Good Book does, too, and I reckon we all been acquainted with that sin." His voice was stronger now, carrying through the crowded room. "I been sitting here and listening. For over a month now we've been talking about leavin'. We've had meetings 'til we're talked blue in the face, I'm thinkin'. If we'd wanted to leave, we would have long ago."

An odd gentleness crossed the moody Scot's features. No longer hesitating, he took two steps to stand at Anne's side. "The Major's staying, she's staying. I'm staying, too."

"But, Jess!" Marian cried.

"Hush, wife," the storekeeper retorted. "That'll make three of us."

"Aw, hell!" Decker exclaimed gruffly, rising to his feet. "There ain't no sense in three fools goin' down when there's another handy. I'm stayin', too."

As if a dam had broken, the room filled with uneasy laughter as others chimed in their decisions to stay. "The hell with Pontiac."

"Dumas, too."

"By God, I'll set a mark to any heathen come to burn *my* home."

Everyone forgot Patrick in the excitement. Knots of angry men and women formed, broke up, coalesced again as opinion hardened. Within the quarter hour there was no question but that the settlers would stay and fight to the bitter end.

A cry from the back of the room halted the buzzing voices. Amy Barr picked up Juliet and carried her to Anne. The crowd watched appreciatively as the baby snuggled up to her mother and stopped crying.

"Best be goin', I reckon," a voice said quietly.

"John? Come by in the mornin'."

"Right, Abner. I'll bring the boy."

"Good night, Miz Gladwyn."

"You tell your husband. We're behind him."

"That's right. Bloody redsticks!"

The room emptied. Only Anne, McBeecher and Patrick were left, alone with the sputtering candle. "I'll walk ye home, ma'am," Jess offered in contrition.

"Thank you, Mr. McBeecher, but Gus may need some help. I can manage by myself."

McBeecher nodded. "Yes'm. I reckon you can."

Together, the two walked to the door, leaving Patrick behind.

In the darkness around the corner, Henry and Jehu watched the exodus without comment. Only when Anne and McBeecher appeared did Henry start and almost speak. The incongruous pair split, Jess heading for his store and Anne for the Schraners'. A moment later, Patrick emerged. The Lieutenant paused on the porch, and then vanished, gliding into the night.

When the street was finally empty, Henry and Jehu stepped from the shadows. "I never would have believed it, Jehu."

The woodsman fidgeted. "Well, now, Major, you never can tell. Might be more than meets the eye."

Henry stood gazing down the street where Anne had disappeared. His voice was low, weighted by the discovery of his wife's treachery. "My own wife, Jehu. My own wife." Jehu didn't answer. "Makes a man wonder." Slowly, he turned from the school and trudged along rue St. Joseph, back to his office.

CHAPTER 28

The stars burned brightly against the subdued light of dusk. Weary from a particularly trying day that had seen five of the settlement's inhabitants and nine of his command wracked with fever and chills, Henry was forced at last to accept the possibility that Detroit would indeed have to be abandoned. The epidemic that had broken out four days earlier had become an even greater threat than the besieging Indians. Just the night before, Jehu had led a burial detail outside the walls and laid to rest two more of the King's soldiers, marking their graves with a deceptive arrangement of stones until Detroit might be permitted to erect more suitable headstones without fear of the Indians exhuming and mutilating their dead.

Henry picked up a quill pen and drew an X through another day. September ninth. Four months to the day since the beginning of the siege. A Friday. Friday's child is loving and giving. Child? On what day had his own child been born? His mind fought to recall it. At last, he admitted failure.

Failure. The word stuck in his mind, would not leave. Twelve days had passed since he had been stunned by the sight of Anne leaving the schoolhouse in the company of a traitor and followed by Patrick, her lover. Karen's death had cast him into despondency. There could be no doubt the leaders of the conspiracy would use her demise for their own purposes. As commandant, he presided at her funeral, reading a passage from Malachi which expressed both sorrow and rage. ". . . and I will rebuke the devourer for your sakes, and he shall not destroy the fruit of your ground . . ."

Since Karen's death and his terrible discovery, Henry had clung to sanity by adhering to a rigidly prescribed daily routine which allowed little time for thought. Grimly determined the fort would not fall, he ignored his personal life until the present crisis should end and immersed himself in detailed planning for the welfare of the settlement.

Driven by a tight-lipped commanding officer, soldiers and rangers trudged back and forth to the river by night, filling every available receptacle with water. Dirt was thrown on all the roofs to minimize the effectiveness of fire arrows and free some of the fire brigade for duty on the walls.

Posts normally held by three or four men were broken up to separate the regulars. For the first time since Henry's tenure as commandant, a ranger guard was posted at various strategic points. The native Americans were the only members of his command he could trust. When all was done, he sat back and waited.

And when the mutiny failed to come he was confused. Henry listened to reports from Jehu, Sabrina and one or two of the older rangers without quite believing all he heard. The secretive meetings at the school had ceased. McBeecher had become positively generous and, though not yet seen smiling, had ceased to rail about the two dozen French still left in the fort.

McBeecher wasn't the only one to change. A half

dozen women had taken to helping McManaway with the myriad chores in the small hospital. As for Patrick Campbell, there was simply no telling. The Lieutenant attended the daily staff meetings, sat glumly and offered no comment except when asked a direct question. Reports indicated he spent his off-duty hours alone in his quarters.

Anne remained an enigma. Outwardly, she had changed, but Henry saw her sudden and unexpected display of warmth as a ploy to disguise her true feelings. He could not understand what she hoped to gain. His blessings, in spite of the fact she had joined a mutinous conspiracy? His benign indulgence as she cuckolded him with a subordinate? Each smile, every pleasant word infuriated him more. Yet facing her with the charges was so onerous a prospect he could not bring himself to do it. So, he turned away from her and did nothing.

A drum roll sounded. Henry checked Davers' watch. Eight o'clock. The guard would be changing. It was getting dark. Time to get home. And what then? To bed with a deceptive wife? He grimaced, folded hands over face and massaged his weary brow. Something had to happen soon. Dangerously low morale, the onslaught of sickness, the threat of revolt, an unfaithful wife . . . Any day now, he repeated for the hundredth time. Any day now Smalley would return with a relief force. Any day now the attack would come. Any day now . . .

Jehu burst into the room. Henry had rarely seen the frontiersman so flushed with surprise. Music—how could there be music?—filtered through the open door. "Major! Come quick. You ain't gonna believe this."

"What?"

"Come and see for yerself. It's the goddamnest thing . . ."

Henry followed Jehu out the door. The street was alive with off-duty soldiers heading toward the parade grounds, from which a harpsichord's lively melody could be heard. Jehu grinned and hurried on. Henry matched the ranger step for running step.

Anne beamed with no small amount of satisfaction. At first the women had balked at the incredible suggestion, but persistence and persuasion had forced them to reconsider. A party! In the midst of illness, grief, danger and tension, Anne turned her hand to what she knew best, to the one activity she determined might raise morale and so help the fort and settlement wait out the siege. A party? Why not? The women plotted, connived, planned—and succeeded. Startled soldiers were requisitioned to carry planks to the parade ground. Husbands found themselves toting cauldrons and platters. A pair of privates hauled Bouvier's harpsichord down the street. Women, dressed in their best clothes, emerged from houses and descended on the parade grounds. They carried torches, poles, and baskets full of decorations, made of whatever was at hand. Before anyone could collect his thoughts, the party was underway.

Soldiers not on the wall or otherwise occupied thronged the streets, heading for the light and music. Every civilian female, married or maid, waited to be asked to dance. Even the French settlers had been invited. Most stood nervously to one side until the Faurots, an elderly couple, led the way to the dancing. Louis Bouvier sat at the harpsichord, fingers lightly eliciting an effervescent strain from the delicately

tuned instrument. Candles quivered in the evening
river breeze. A colorful array of pennants and long
ribbons fluttered from slender poles, giving testimony
to the efforts of the younger girls under Beatrice
Hampton's guidance.

Food! The best tablecloths had been brought from
storage to decorate the trestle tables heavy with pots
of robustly seasoned beans and salt pork and platters
of trout and bass, caught the night before and fried in
corn meal and oil. Best of all was the makeshift plank
laden with cleverly concocted desserts. Mock apple
pies made from soda crackers cooked in cinnamon
water and sweetened with honey fresh from the settlement's straw skeps were the mainstay. Surrounding
the pies were bowl upon bowl of thick custard
made of cream, molasses, honey and eggs hoarded
for the last week. The few chickens that remained
in the fort belonged to a French farmer and his
family. Anne reflected on the loss of a jeweled
necklace with which she had paid for the eggs.

McBeecher was in the midst of explaining how each
man could eat only so much in order to save a share
for the men on duty when Anne saw Henry and Jehu
on the fringe of the dancing area, already alive with
whirling couples. She started to wave but was interrupted when Ensign Johnson bowed and asked her to
dance. Making do with a smile, Anne curtsied and
whisked away with the young officer. Johnson would
spend the remainder of the night reliving the wonderful way in which Anne's voluptuous figure had filled
his arms and sent his heart pounding in his throat.

Henry stared in amazement. Laughter, almost unheard for the past four months, filled the air, wafted
upward, beyond the walls to the ears of the Indians
and French waiting in the woods.

The harpsichord broke into a new tune and the dancing continued. "The men, Jehu," Henry said, awed. "Yesterday everyone was dismally sober. Tonight . . . Well, by God just look at them! I'll be damned if they look beat. Whoever contrived this deserves a medal."

Ensign Price, decked out in parade best, strode up and saluted his commanding officer. "Marvelous remedy, Major Gladwyn. My compliments to your wife."

"Thank you, Mr. Price," Henry responded, his face reddening because he hadn't the slightest idea what the young man was talking about.

Price looked down, remembered the bowl of custard in his left hand and laughed. "Unmilitary, sir, but damned good. Damned good! Certainly beats the drab offerings we're used to. I don't even mind not having a tot of rum to wash it down."

"I'll see if the cook can't be persuaded to exert a little more effort, Ensign."

The dry retort dampened the ensign's ebullience. "Yes, sir. Well, if you'll excuse me?" He grinned in spite of himself. "Miss Hampton has promised me the next dance."

"By all means, Mr. Price."

"Good evening, sir." Custard bowl hidden behind his back, Ensign Price saluted smartly and pivoted away.

Henry stared as the ensign deftly cut in on a corporal, and custard bowl held high, danced off with Beatrice Hampton. What was that he'd said? Compliments to Anne? What in God's name was going on? He spotted Sabrina sitting off to one side guarding Juliet's cradle. Jehu was already nearby, leaning down to catch a whispered comment. He rose with a barely controlled laugh as Henry approached.

Juliet seemed altogether happy at being included in the proceedings. She cooed and giggled as Henry reached down to straighten her covers. Jehu winked at Sabrina, reached into the cradle and tugged at the infant's nose. "Redsticks do this so's the nose'll grow proud and long," he said in defiant answer to Henry's stare.

"That's ridiculous," Sabrina scolded.

"It works for them."

Henry eyed the old woman speculatively. "Sabrina, is this Anne's doing?" he asked, waving a hand to indicate the entire party. Sabrina nodded. "But how? Why?"

"Master Henry," Sabrina snapped exasperatedly, "if you don't know or can't see, there's little good my tellin' you will do." With that, the spry servant scooped Juliet from the cradle and handed her to Henry.

"Now, what . . . ?" Too late. Jehu had grabbed Sabrina and spun away into the stream of dancers.

The party continued. The guard was switched at ten so the men on the wall would have a chance at the food and dancing. Arriving with whoops of joy, they begged the exhausted women to join the music and dance. Though their feet were sore, the girls smiled and acquiesced. Worried, Henry gave Juliet back to Sabrina, and toured the fort. The men seemed to be more alert than usual: the walls were secure and the night quiet. Shadowy figures could be seen with the aid of a spy glass, but none ventured much further than the edge of the woods. They were curious, Henry supposed, probably wondering if the English had gone mad at last. There was no indication, though, that the Indians would take advantage of the merriment and launch an attack.

Midnight came and the watch changed again. Henry

had remained aloof from the dancing, taking satisfaction in the smiles on the men's faces and the closeness of Juliet. He was more puzzled than proud of Anne's accomplishment and dreaded the moment when they would at last be left alone. Whatever good purpose the night's exercise had filled, Anne's renewed affair with Patrick Campbell was unforgivable. Worse, he could not forget the sound of her voice as she threatened to leave with Juliet, nor the shock of recognition as she left the schoolhouse in the company of the ringleader, McBeecher.

Yet, there was the storekeeper, actually smiling between scowls. Priscilla Hampton—not much better than McBeecher—had danced with just about everyone and was looking about for those she'd missed. And when Bouvier held up his weary fingers and cried "enough," Anne took over at the harpsichord, that the night's revel might continue. At one point she even sang. Her high, sweet, lilting voice alternately lifted the spirits and tinged the merrymaking with exquisite melancholy before finishing on a bright note. Were these the doings of conspirators? Nothing made sense.

Food finished, the happily satiated soldiers and townspeople lingered about the parade grounds to enjoy the soft fragrant September wind that had driven away the intense summer heat. Anne finally sought out Henry, saw Juliet asleep in his arms and smiled. Since the night of Karen's death she had yearned for her husband's trust and love, but, preoccupied with the defense of the fort, he'd come home late and left early. She'd tried to talk to him the day after the funeral, but he'd excused himself abruptly and stalked out the door, leaving her alone, frustrated and in tears. Though they shared the same household, the awful barrier that kept them apart had still stood.

The next days had been worse. Tension in the fort rose to the breaking point. Isolated and uncommunicative, Henry admitted into his circle no one save the rangers. McBeecher had tried to talk to him twice, and failed. The rest of the English settlers were afraid of the fever and kept to their houses and out of sight. Detroit was on the verge of self-destruction.

The party had been an inspiration born of desperation. Luckily, it had worked, for the charged, sullen atmosphere was broken. Men told jokes and laughed. The look on Henry's face was warm and gave her hope. Perhaps they would be able to talk at last, Anne thought, as she approached Henry.

Gunfire crackled along the river wall. Cries and shouts interrupted the merriment. Henry shoved the infant Juliet into his wife's arms. "Get to the house. Hurry!" he ordered shortly, breaking into a run.

Seized by panic, Anne found herself caught in the rush as men and women hurried to post and home. Juliet started to cry. Sabrina shoved through the crowd. The two women escaped the parade ground and made a headlong rush for the house. "The back door," Anne gasped, setting Juliet down and reaching for the front door bar. Juliet squawled as the hickory bar slammed into place, echoed a moment later from the kitchen, and then in quick succession around the house as the lower shutters were closed and barred.

The gunfire continued, and rose in volume until the house seemed to shake. Anne stood in the middle of the floor, frozen with fear. "Stop it!" she finally screamed. "Stop it. Stop it. Stop it!"

"Anne!" Sabrina's voice lashed across the room, slicing through panic and mindless terror. Anne looked about frantically, ran to pick up Juliet from the chair where she lay howling. "No, baby, don't cry. Don't cry, my darling . . ." Weeping with shame, she cuddled Juliet to her breast.

"Hush, child," Sabrina soothed, leading the way upstairs. "We'll be safe enough . . ."

"The cradle!" Anne halted, seemed to want to turn back.

"We'll get it later. Let her sleep in the big bed." Coaxing and cajoling, Sabrina led Anne into the bedroom, sat her in a chair and carried Juliet to the bed. Sabrina sat on the arm of Anne's chair, holding the younger woman's hand.

As Juliet's cries became sniffles and finally a contented sigh, Anne relaxed. "I'm sorry, Sabrina."

"No need to be."

"I was so happy, I thought things had changed. All of a sudden everyone was running and yelling . . . It was just too much."

"Nothing learned quickly lasts to be of any use. It's the slow, stop-and-make-a-mistake-and-keep-on-going knowledge that endures to the end."

Anne smiled, color gradually returning to her cheeks. "What would I do without you, Sabrina?"

The old servant blushed. "Not my words, mum. Something Karen said."

Both women grew silent as a gentle, friendly memory filled the room. "Listen," Anne whispered after a few minutes. "It's stopped. The firing has ceased." In response, someone hammered at the front door. Anne jumped in surprise and quickly left the bedroom when she heard Henry's call. The downstairs was oppressively dark, and she realized there was only an hour left until dawn.

"Anne!" Henry called again as the bar was raised

and the bolt shot back. The door swung open and Henry burst into the room half supporting an oddly familiar wounded man in bloodstained buckskins.

"Morning, Mrs. Gladwyn."

Anne held her hand to her mouth. "Jeremy! My God. It's Jeremy Turner!"

Henry helped the youth to a chair at the table as Sabrina brought a lantern. "McManaway has more patients than he can handle," he said. "You all right, son?"

"Yes, sir. I'll be fine." Jeremy grimaced, fighting the pain.

Jehu entered, a beaded deerskin war bag in hand. "We'll need water and bandages," he announced, already starting to remove the torn, bloodstained shirt.

"Sabrina, tear up that cotton sleeping gown of mine," Anne ordered without thinking as she started for the kitchen. "I'll get the water."

"Yes, mum," Sabrina replied, on her way.

His shirt stripped away, Jeremy winced as Jehu applied a steaming cloth to a bleeding shoulder wound. Anne averted her eyes at the sight of the ugly red hole surrounded by puffed and torn flesh. "Lucky for you that redstick got close," Jehu announced. "If he was any farther off, that lead ball woulda stuck inside instead of goin' clear on through. Then we'd be diggin' it out with a knife." He dabbed again at the wound, grunted with satisfaction and poured in a dollop of grain alcohol to sterilize it.

"Lucky for me I'm so lucky," Jeremy managed through gritted teeth.

Anne arranged the bandages, wrinkled her nose in distaste as Jehu dug a wad of foul-smelling glop from a pouch taken from the war bag and smeared the greasy substance over the lacerated flesh. Sabrina brought in a huge mug of weak, honey-sweetened tea which Jeremy gratefully accepted.

"Now, boy. Tell us the news. How did you get here? Where's Smalley and the *Michigan?* What happened to the *Huron?*"

Jeremy proceeded to recount his adventures and hardships since leaving the fort. He told of shipwreck and tragic massacre, of wandering half lost through the woods and remembering the lore learned at Jehu's side, how to live off the land by eating berries and roots and such small animals as could be trapped. He recounted with pride how he hid from war parties and circumnavigated the Indian villages, finally arriving at Fort Schlosser. A day later the exhausting trek caught up with him. No sooner had he delivered the dispatches and told his tale, including a full description of the troubled Detroit, than he was delirious with fever. Upon recovering, he learned the whole of the Northwest was aflame. Relief could not be expected for some time. Amherst had vacillated too long, losing the opportunity to move quickly to suppress the rebellion before it grew, and was forced to fight everywhere at once, and never with enough men.

Turner was ordered to remain at Schlosser until a suitable expedition could be formed to raise the siege at Detroit. There he whiled away the time until Captain Smalley finally arrived on the eighteenth of August. Ten days later reinforcements from New York reached Niagara. An expedition comprised of the *Michigan* and two dozen *batteaux* sailed for Detroit on the first of September and had anchored at the mouth of the Detroit the night before.

"How many?" Henry asked anxiously.

"Two hundred and fifty, sir, complete with food,

guns and ammunition. They're just sitting there on the lake, cussin' and waiting for the wind. The Indians paddled out looking for a fight, but turned back before they got in firing distance. Of course, they got close enough to me, as you heard." He touched the bandage on his arm and grimaced, "and saw."

"Did Captain Smalley give any indication when he thought he'd get here?"

Jeremy shook his head. "Maybe this morning, maybe tomorrow, depending on the weather. If there's a breeze, we'll see him."

"And the *batteaux?*"

"Captain Vestal and Captain Smalley both felt they should wait and come with the *Michigan.* The boats would never make it past Turkey Island without the ship's cannons."

Henry swore. "Damn. Pontiac knows they're there. If he ever expects to take us, it will have to be soon."

"That's why I came ahead, sir. Figured it might help if you knew."

Henry rose and went to the door, where an orderly waited. "I want a close watch kept on the river for the *Michigan.* I want every post double guarded, with a keen eye kept on the woods in case of an attack. I want to be kept informed of the weather. If there's wind on the river, I want to be told immediately."

"Yes, sir," the orderly replied, saluting and moving off smartly.

Jehu waited until Henry returned. "You thinkin' what I am, Major?"

Henry nodded. "They have two choices . . ."

Jehu completed the thought: "Call off the siege an' lose face, or wipe us out. Now."

The room was silent. Anne shuddered. Henry crossed the room, donned saber and thrust a brace of pistols in his belt. "Corporal Turner, stay here and get some rest. Sabrina, feed him plenty of soup and hot tea."

He turned to the ranger Captain. "Jehu, have your men bring all the weapons in the fort to the wall. Tell them I want a quarter of them loaded and primed, the rest loaded only. I want the heaviest concentration along the east and north walls, with definite assignments given to those who'll man the west wall, in case we're hit there. Everyone will be tired. Let them rest, but along the wall and with at least a quarter of them awake at all times. I'll make rounds and then be in my office. I'll want reports from you, Campbell, Busby and Melton within the hour."

Anne's longing gaze stopped him at the door. There was so much to say and so hopelessly little time left. "I'll be back. Keep everything locked," he said.

Anne did not trust herself to read his words or expression with any degree of accuracy. "Be careful," she answered with a tiny, weak smile meant to appear brave. Henry nodded and was gone. His duty was with the entire settlement. She understood that now. "I'll be all right," she added, more to herself than the empty doorway.

Morning light streamed cheerlessly into the room. Sabrina blew out the lantern. It would be another hot day. "Have . . . have you news of Beth?" Jeremy said from the table.

Anne gathered straying thoughts, shook her head. "Henry thinks she's still at the Charbonneaus'."

Jeremy's brows knotted in worry. "I wish . . ."

"You don't wish anything right now, young man,"

Sabrina said, helping him to his feet. "You'll feel better after you drink some soup and sleep for awhile. We can talk about Elizabeth then."

"Jeremy?"

The lad stopped, turned to look at Mrs. Gladwyn. She was holding his musket and her voice was far away and yet determined. She sounded like a stranger. "Ma'am?"

"After you've rested, would you teach me to load this?"

Afternoon. The sun trudged across the sky, burned down on the besieged fort. To the casual observer, Detroit looked innocently lazy, a town insulated from the surrounding world. The initiated knew better: the forted settlement was charged with readiness, alert though resting momentarily, poised for action. Every able-bodied man was within ten seconds' distance of the firing platform.

With the exception of only a few sentries, the soldiers found shade under the shooting walkway and slept or talked in desultory whispers of home or women or rum. Few talked of fighting. Detroit's English settlers waited behind closed doors, ready for the sound of the first shot or the ominous growl of a drum roll signalling an attack. No one found much comfort in the knowledge a relief force lay close by. The arrival of help could be a prelude to disaster, for it might well set off the attack that hadn't come all summer. Relief could mean death. Everything depended on Pontiac's reaction. Would he attack or simply give up and disappear into the woods? No one could answer.

Anne walked down rue St. Louis. Several of the soldiers turned and waved. Some cheered as she passed. Anne returned the greetings and continued on her way to Bouvier's, the last of several stops.

The Frenchman, his cheeks puffy and eyes bloodshot, admitted her with a noticeable absence of courtesy. The odor of brandy was on Bouvier's breath and the house smelled musty, old and uncared for. No one had cleaned for some time. Books, papers, glasses and even apparel lay scattered about in disarray. "Ah, Madame Gladwyn. A most appropriate time. I had thought to come looking for you." He offered Anne a drink from a dust-covered brown bottle. When she declined, he poured himself another gobletful. "This is the last. I had three. I hid them, as you can see. You are displeased, no?"

"You have a right to whatever is yours, Louis." Anne couldn't help but think of McManaway and his patients, and how useful those spirits might have been.

"And you?" Bouvier asked a little drunkenly. "To what do you have a right? To death in this filthy settlement?"

"I think not. After all . . ."

"But you will die, you know. Dumas and Pontiac will never give up Detroit. They are determined to eradicate the last trace of English influence in the Northwest."

"They have not conquered us yet, Louis. We are equally determined to defend our homes."

"Your determination is admirable. But why do you come to see Louis Bouvier, eh?" Not waiting for an answer, the Frenchman sank into a chair, motioned for Anne to do likewise. A languid left hand caught the chesspieces in mid-gesture, scattering them from the board on the table next to him. The black pieces clattered to the floor. Louis turned a sour eye to the few ebony pawns left facing a superior force of precisely aligned ranks of white, and turned a bemused eye back to Anne. Fate would be tempted.

"Louis, I've come to talk to you about the French families," she began. "There aren't that many, but we need all the active support we can get. I know they're not sympathetic to English rule, but that war has been fought and won. We will win here, too. Detroit, in the meantime, is their home. They might as well . . ." Louis Bouvier was laughing. Anne frowned, displeased. "I thought I could count on you. After all, you played for us last night."

"Ah, my dear Anne. I was afraid not to. Everyone knows how much Louis enjoys his own playing and an appreciative audience. Of course I played. But now you ask this?" He laughed again, harder. Brandy sloshed from the goblet and splattered a once-handsome waistcoat.

Anne stood, more shocked than angry. "I'll come back later, Louis. This is a bad time."

Louis' entreaty halted her short of the door. "Anne, hand me my cane. Please?" He struggled to rise, groaned and sat back. Anne took an ivory-handled cane from against the wall and returned to his side. She had never known him to need a cane. "Ah, *merci*, madame." Awkwardly, he rose, made his way across the room, innocently placing himself between Anne and the door.

When he turned, his face had hardened into somber lines. The cane separated with a single, deft motion, the crook remaining in his grasp while the wooden shaft clattered to the floor. A half yard of slim, gleaming steel jutted from the grip, the point directly in line with Anne's breast. "Do not move, *ma chérie*. My blade is sharp, and I am quite adept."

The wavering blade sparkled in the dimly lit room. Bouvier smiled. The sword, held in front of him, looked like an evil, gleaming fang. A slashed throat . . . a blade of steel. Drummond's tortured countenance flooded into memory. "You!" she said, horrified. "Drummond, the others . . ."

Bouvier grimaced. "Why could you not let McBeecher's conspiracy continue? You might have been on a ship to England. Now there is nothing left but to accomplish this one final deed. Why?"

"Louis! Drummond was your friend."

"I know. Do not think I have escaped punishment. His spectre haunts me yet." He sighed, shrugged apologetically. "But am I not French, and so bound in loyalty to my sovereign? Dumas presented me with instructions at the party for Elizabeth. I did not think it would come to this, but one night, when I had stepped from the room, I returned to find Amideus reading the dispatch. I watched in secret and saw the tormented question in his eyes, saw he would do as he must and inform on his friend, who then would be shot as a spy. I had no choice, I followed and . . . killed him. And now . . ."

"Now me?" Anne backed away, shocked by the revelation, not yet fully comprehending the enormity of her discovery.

"Do not try to run," Louis said, standing easily. The lethal sword held to prevent her escape, he walked to a nearby desk and brought forth a pistol. Within seconds he had loaded the piece and cast the sword to one side. He removed his waistcoat, donned a buckskin jacket. "The Major would not trade the fort for his niece, but perhaps he will for the mother of his child. You are very dear to our cause. I will not kill you if you do not try to run."

"I won't . . ."

"Anne, dear, you really must be quiet. Now. We shall stroll to the blockhouse at the northeast corner of the fort. Please, do not make a sound." He motioned for her to step outside.

Anne subdued the urge to run, thought instead of Juliet. She desperately wanted to hold her baby once again, wanted to feel the tiny lips tugging at her breast, the miniscule fingers around her own.

Louis held a gun. He had killed, and would again. She stumbled out the door and down the steps. No one called out to stop them. Louis Bouvier and Anne Gladwyn were friends, after all. There was no cause for alarm. Arm in arm they walked slowly past silent houses and through the empty streets. Shadows crept around them like an oncoming tide: Anne was sure she could see them move.

The corner of the stockade loomed ahead. Men lay about asleep or resting. Others had wandered off to eat. A few greeted her and Anne made empty excuses to them as she and Bouvier climbed the ladder into the blockhouse. The one soldier on duty inside was engrossed in watching the line of trees through a glass. He lowered the telescope as Anne entered. "Mrs. Gladwyn. 'Scuse me, ma'am, but . . ."

Bouvier rose from the trapdoor and pulled the pistol from below the buckskin. "Not one word, soldier."

The private's face drained. He started to reach for his musket, stopped as Bouvier stepped forward to point-blank range. "Ma'am? I don't under—"

"Close the trapdoor. Quickly."

The private's eyes hardened. "There'll be a dozen men up here if you fire that thing, Frenchman."

Bouvier whirled, jammed the pistol into Anne's side and pushed her forward. "Immediately, Private, or she dies and you can explain why." The private moved quickly, let the door down without a sound. "Good. Now move to your left, turn around and put your hands against the wall. High, so I can see them!"

The soldier obeyed reluctantly, watching Anne with each move, trying to apologize with his eyes. When he could no longer see her, he hung his head in shame, so embarrassed he didn't even hear the pistol butt slide through the air until the sound exploded in his brain and he slumped to the floor.

Bouvier smiled wanly. "I'm really not much for violence, my dear, but necessity sometimes dictates it. Do you understand?" Waving the pistol, he indicated Anne should move to the window. "Monsieur Dumas will be pleased to see you. We should not keep him waiting. If you please . . . ?"

"You know him well?" Anne asked, stalling for time and edging toward the place where the soldier lay.

"We have worked together. Now, madame . . ."

"Henry will never throw open the gate, Louis. Not even to save me."

"Perhaps not, but we must try. There is little time left. This land belongs to France. My people settled here, bled and suffered."

"As have many Englishmen."

"I will not argue numbers. You did not know Montcalm. I loved him. Everyone did. When he died at the fall of Quebec, it was as if the very heart had stopped in all of us. You would have liked him, Anne." Bouvier cast about, located the rope escape ladder on a shelf high on the wall, took it down and hooked it to the iron rings below the wide cannon port. All was ready. "But the time for tears is long past. The heart is gone, but we go on with the struggle that has no end."

Louis scooped up the rope ladder and leaned over the broad portal. In that moment, Anne saw her chance. Hardly thinking, she scooped up the musket and tried to remember Jeremy's brief instructions. The sound of it cocking made Bouvier spin around. Posed in a tense tableau, neither moved for a second.

Slowly, Bouvier extended a hand. "Give me the gun, Anne."

"No," she said, terrified.

"Give me the gun," he repeated hypnotically. "Give me . . ."

He jumped without warning, at the same time reaching to bat aside the barrel. Anne jerked back. Bouvier's hand missed and he ran into the gun. Anne screamed and pulled the trigger without thinking. The musket roared, bucked in her hands and knocked her back against the wall. Her eyes fought to see through the powder smoke. Bouvier was slumped opposite her, a ragged, smouldering hole in his coat and crimson staining his chest.

He glanced down in disbelief. Puzzled, he blinked his eyes and shook his head as comprehension slowly dawned. He was going to die. We are born, we die, nothing else counts. Who said that? Someone long ago when someone else was born. How ironic! Now he thought the words at the moment of . . .

Better not say the word. Bad enough to face the fact without drawing attention . . . Damned black pieces anyway. An omen. A symbol. Amideus had white the last time they played. He'd died, too. Symbols weren't worth a damn. Not a damn . . .

A wall rose in front of him. The trapdoor. Anne was leaving. He could hear her calling, and through the roar of rushing time, increased activity below. Should have . . . Should have . . .

The wall disappeared. There was nothing ahead, now. Nothing but air, nothing but sadness and an ending to the dark deeds that had so tortured him.

"We go on, Montcalm!" he whispered, dying. "We go on!"

Someone was there, helping her down the ladder from the blockhouse. Men crowded around, asking questions. Numbly, she recounted what had happened, but her words came out in incoherent phrases. Then Henry was there, asking again . . .

She remembered saying, "I want my baby," over and over, and then being escorted to the house and taken to her room and given Juliet. Dry-eyed but in a state of shock, she sat and rocked her child, her sweet Juliet.

Henry took the report from the injured sentry and then kept a vigil next to his silent wife. He had searched for words of comfort, knowing there was little to say. Finally, he kissed her on the forehead and left. Sabrina waited outside the door. "Just leave her alone for awhile," Henry instructed. "She has to find her own way."

He left then. In the night street, he looked back. The glow of a lamp filled the bedroom window. The soft amber light was a tenuous bulwark against the growing darkness that surrounded them all.

CHAPTER 29

Shifting volumes of gathering fog alternately obscured and revealed a gibbous moon hanging low in the night sky and filling the west with a pale ghost-white light. High above, fairy-tale cloudscapes tumbled past blue-white star points, magic scalding eyes forever alert in the deepening void.

Dumas wrapped the blanket about his shoulders and wished for the coat he'd left behind at the Charbonneaus'. It was unusually chilly for mid-September, colder than he had expected. A dram of rum would have helped. He cursed the rising fog and the soft, incessant tapping of a drum. For what seemed the hundredth time, he considered taking to the woods.

It wasn't time yet. There was work to be done, orders to be carried out. Detroit waited, and must fall. A thousand gold sovereigns and the blessing of His Majesty's government had not been promised for failure. The arrival of reinforcements changed nothing. If the fort were reduced, the newcomers would be slaughtered to a man and the tribes that had departed might be persuaded to renew their efforts against the British.

More important, Henry Gladwyn waited. The Major was the only one alive. The others at Munro had found an earthy bed before they could talk, but Gladwyn had escaped to spread the tale of ignominy and cold-blooded massacre. Gladwyn had to die. Only then could Dumas rest, when the last pair of eyes that had seen were sightless.

If Pontiac had only attacked at the first when the advantage was all theirs! Failing that, if he'd allowed Teata to have his way with the girl, to torture her in full view of the fort. The Major would have thrown open the gates then, would have thrown open the gates and walked out to pay in full for the dishonor heaped on Dumas' head.

Little matter now. There was still time. The calm that allowed the fog to accumulate kept the *Michigan* on the lake. Why was Pontiac waiting? Why did he waste valuable time with that foolish old medicine man? The mist brushed a clammy finger against Dumas' cheek. From his vantage point at the edge of the forest he could see the long cloud marking the Detroit River and the ghostly tendrils spilling over the banks to inundate the empty land around the fort. Of course, he grinned. Pontiac had anticipated the mist. Or caused it, Dumas thought with a shiver. The ground fog would be heaviest at dawn. The attacking forces would enjoy an incredible advantage. The fort's armament would be hampered, the soldiers unable to see. Once the walls were breached, Munro's fate would . . .

Munro? No. Detroit. He had to remember. Detroit. Past threatened to smother present with misty visions of carnage. A heady fragrance of burning pine weighted the night, clouded the deeds of yesterday in confused time. Once again Dumas heard the anguished pleas for mercy, the shrieks of the damned, the tortured cries of the innocents.

"No!" His own voice was a surprise. Dumas peered

through the fog, afraid someone had heard. In any case, the dead were not "innocent." They too had fought and killed. War allowed no innocence.

"Dumas!"

The Frenchman spun around. Teata stepped from a clump of night-blackened sumac. The Huron seemed pleased to have startled Dumas' reverie. "You must be more careful, monsieur. There are those among the Eng-lesh who move as quietly as the Huron. The rangers have taken many scalps and are an honored enemy."

Dumas chose to ignore the Huron's smugness. "I *am* careful," he replied, lifting a corner of the blanket. Teata glimpsed the heavy barrel of a pistol aimed directly at his breechclout. He scowled, then managed a wide grin. "It is good. I would not wish my French brother to be taken unawares. Tomorrow we will taste much Eng-lesh blood."

"And the Potawatami?"

Teata spat. "Ningas scurries from the Eng-lesh ship-of-many-thunders as a rabbit from the hawk. We will have no need of rabbits when we strike our enemy. Only men." With that, the Indian vanished into the darkness, leaving the Frenchman to his lonely vigil.

Dumas shivered again and recalled an old wives' tale. Overhead, dry branches rattled like bones dancing on a grave.

Pierre and Evangeline Charbonneau sat in somber quiet. Roused from sleep, Beth surveyed them from the doorway, and wondered if she looked as haggard as the elderly couple. She had lost weight, she knew. Her cheeks were hollow, her shoulders angular beneath the soiled doeskin shift. "What is it?" she asked. "Has something happened?"

Neither answered, instead looked down to the table.

Beth could feel the tension bunching her shoulders. She wanted to scream, "What's happened? Tell me!"

"Autumn Woman."

Her flesh numbed. Pontiac stood outside the back door, a few feet from the porch. "He would speak with you, child," Evangeline said.

Beth paused, then stepped outside. "Oh!" she exclaimed as the Indian moved into the shadows, away from the light spilling from the kitchen lantern.

"You are afraid?"

Beth wagged her head from side to side. In truth, his appearance was startling. Dressed in full war regalia, he wore buckskin leggings, beaded moccasins, and a coarse breech clout. His chest was naked, the tattooed sun outlined in black. His face was more fearsome than she had ever seen it: the left half had been painted ochre, the right a vibrant white.

"Autumn Woman. When the sun ceases to sleep, I will burn the fort. Major Henri has refused my demands. The fate of Detroit is on his head."

"You can't. The soldiers will come . . ." She stopped, but too late.

Pontiac glared past the open door. "Old people will tell stories."

"But it is true."

"Yes. Many Eng-lesh come. But not yet. There is time, and they will not keep me from this. Without Detroit, they will die as they step onto the land."

"More will come next year. And then more again. Many of your warriors will be killed."

"Only if the Master-of-all-Breaths wishes. I do not think he will abandon his children."

"Why do you tell me this?" Beth asked.

"So you will know, and be ready when I return. I shall come for you and you will be ready."

Beth retreated a step. "We have talked of this before. It cannot be. I will not go."

Pontiac did not move, instead stared intently, his eyes riveted on hers. "Go back inside and prepare," he said suddenly. "I will come for you." He turned and left her standing in the yard. The encroaching fog soon concealed her, and when Pontiac looked back, all he could see was a shadow in an amber mist.

Near dawn, Patrick applied the last hoarded residue of powder to his wig and secured the single black bow. A brief examination showed the sleeves of the borrowed coat to be woefully long. "I should have liked a better fit," he muttered, brushing a trace of powder from the scarlet fabric. At least the buttons were bright. The tricorn hat fit well, for which he was thankful.

A small piece of mirror bought from McBeecher lay propped on the mantel. Patrick squinted, inspecting himself. Not quite dashing, but it would have to do under the circumstances. He had appeared much this way when first he'd met Anne. Odd how he continued to desire her, though she was hopelessly lost. Lost? Everything was lost.

Everyone conspired against him. Only the night before he'd heard the soldiers imitating him and laughing. The settlers—the same barking fools who had wanted to escape—were no better. They'd repudiated his leadership. The Major thought him a fool and ignored his very command. Even Anne—worst of all, Anne, who still loved him even if she wouldn't admit it—had turned on him in front of the whole meeting and called him a coward.

Coward? Patrick Campbell could tell them all a thing or two. So could Oliver Page. But Brohan's Mound was long ago. No matter. They'd learn. He'd show them. He chuckled softly, then shivered. The rasp of rapier sliding into scabbard helped ease the shame. He'd show them all.

Henry rubbed red-rimmed, sleepless eyes as he strolled the length of the river wall toward the southeast blockhouse, cursing the fog with each step. The sun would eventually burn it off, of course, but eventually would be too late. Apart from an occasional rock, shrub or high piece of ground jutting island-like in the gray mist, the fog covered the open plain in a flat featureless blanket deep enough for a whole army to crawl within reach of the walls without being seen.

Jehu appeared at his side. "You been home?" Henry shook his head "no." "Man lucky enough to have a home ought to visit there from time to time."

"I catnapped in the blockhouse," Henry answered waspishly, splashing his face with water from a nearby bucket.

"How much? An hour? Two at the most? Pacing these walls like an old hound smellin' fer . . ."

"I can't leave. Not now. There'll be time for home when the *Michigan* and the *batteaux* arrive. Time for a great many things," he added pensively.

"Wind ought to come up a little later. Hope there's enough for Smalley to make his run. Don't like this fog. Damn place could be crawlin' with Injuns an' we'd never know it."

"The thought crossed my mind," came the sarcastic answer.

Jehu shrugged, changed the subject. "There's another had as little rest," he said, indicating Gus

Schraner. The carpenter lay dozing on the walkway, legs thrust out and back against the blockhouse wall.

Henry was paying no attention. He stood peering into the fog, straining every sense. Something . . . was getting ready to happen down there. "Drummer!" The youth slept soundly, slumped at the base of the two-pounder swivel gun taken from the *Huron.* "Drummer!" The soldier jumped awake. "Call the men to arms. Be quick, man!"

The soldiers to either side burst into furious activity. The drum roll, like thunder in the heart, brought the settlement to life. "Mister Price!"

The officer hurried to Henry's side. "Sir?"

"Pass the word. Dry all weapons. Prime two pieces per man and stand by. Send a runner to fetch Lieutenant Busby's men from the west wall. He's to keep the ten assigned him and no more. I want a rocket if he comes under direct attack. Is that clear?"

"Yes, sir!"

Henry gave his attention to where the sun hung below the lip of the earth. "It has to be now," the thought screamed. "It has to be now!"

Waiting . . . A morning without the cheerful distant melody of birds. Only the muffled, sluggish dirge of the fog-shrouded river broke the silence. The men were staring to the east, willing the sun to rise. The same sun that had been the object of curses for the past months, the same blinding, swollen sun that had risen day after day to parch the earth and dry mouths and skin now waited behind the misty curtains of fog which surely held the enemy. Henry reached behind him for a gun and grasped without thinking the stock that was slapped into his hand. "Thanks."

"You're welcome."

He spun in amazement. Anne, garbed in homespun, was drying off the dew-dampened weapons, blowing out the damp priming powder and dribbling new in the pans. A glance showed other civilians, men and women alike, ranging the walls and attending to the same task as Anne. Some of the less severely wounded soldiers, Jeremy among them, helped. Many of the men, after finishing the loading, took places at the wall with the soldiers.

Henry grinned. So much for the conspiracy. Why and how the change of heart had come about he didn't know, nor did he care: they needed every man they could muster and he'd not argue with the extra firepower. The women were different, though. They should be down below, out of danger. He caught Anne's arm. "What are you doing here?" he asked in a voice both urgent and subdued.

"Seeing to my duty," Anne replied firmly.

Henry searched her face and at last saw . . . the truth. He had almost lost her, not only to Bouvier's treachery but through the jealous, harried workings of a heart too proud and a mind too suspicious. In no way had he suspected the depth of her transformation. "Juliet?"

"Safe with Sabrina."

He gripped her hand, gazed into her eyes. Anne exulted in that look, yearning to speak but unable to find words deep enough to capture her joy. Words would only shatter the beauty of the moment. She smiled in response and returned to her work.

"Major!"

Henry quickly returned to the wall. Anne, at his side, caught her breath. "What the devil . . . ?" he muttered.

"Secure that gate on the double!" Sergeant Living-

ston bellowed from below. Pounding feet, the slam
of wood on wood and the solid "chunk" of iron
sounded as the door swung shut and was barred.

Anne's heart felt about to burst, as she recognized
the scarlet-coated figure who had slipped from the
fort.

"It's Patrick," she whispered, throat dry with fear.

"My God!" Jehu echoed softly.

Lieutenant Patrick Campbell walked at a steady
pace, his bearing erect. Though it was difficult to
see, he moved with the surety of vision. Patrick did
not hear the cries from the fort; Henry ordering him
to return; Anne's impassioned plea. They were lost
in the din raging in his own head:

Cannonades. The cries of men. The steady tramp of
feet. He marched at the head of a noble regiment,
the bravest of the brave, in time to the rolling beat
of the drums. A single fife shrilled a keen and anxious
tune. Just behind, he could hear the snapping of the
wind-rippled flag. Blue. Red. White. England. Bri-
tannia. The verdant isle that ruled the civilized world.

"Forward, lads!" The steel blade slid free. "Advance." A shot sounded but he paid little heed. "Heads
up, lads. Take their fire. Steady as you go!"

He was a third of the way across the rolling field.
The fog rose to cover him entirely as he traversed the
low ground. The dark tricorn appeared. For a long
moment a disembodied head floated on the surface.
A dozen yards later, shoulders emerged, followed by
the whole man rising spectrally from the mist until
only his feet remained concealed. The ground dipped
again and he swam along waist deep, sword held high.
The warriors lurking in the mist watched in muted
wonder. They respected courage . . . and madness.

A shot rang out. Another. Still Patrick marched,

oblivious to danger. Another shot, and a volley. Was he charmed, impervious? A lone shot. Anne stifled a scream as Patrick staggered, then resumed his solitary march.

"Close up, men. Show them your bayonets! Hear the music of the drums. We'll take our glory this day!"

Two more shots exploded. Something hammered his leg, kicked his chest. Patrick fell to his knees, lost in the covering fog. He was midway across the field. Anne no longer called, could no longer hold back the tears. In another time and another place she had been another woman and taken a gay and reckless lover. They had played that game so well together. Poor Patrick, she thought as she watched his scarlet coat reappear out of the gray fog.

Patrick cursed the dampness, spat crimson bile. He did not know he was dying, only urged the imagined skirmish line forward, as had many a gallant officer before him. "First rank, fire! Fall back. Second to the fore, and fire! We have them, lads! See them scatter? Showing us their backsides, they are. The day is ours!"

A volley crackled. Hit from every side, the patch of scarlet danced and spun and crumpled, sank into the mist and disappeared. The flat blanket eddied and lay still, featureless once again, covering the crumpled remains of Patrick Campbell.

Anne buried her face in Henry's encircling arm. To their right, Jehu sighed wearily. "He'll rest easy. They respect that, you know, walkin' through the fog like a ghost. By an Injun's lights, there's somethin' holy 'bout a madman. They'll kill 'im, but they won't cut 'em up. One thing for sure. We know they're out there. Campbell give us that."

Anne sobbed and Henry, groping for words of comfort, found himself repeating her name over and over again. Finally, he motioned to Jeremy. "Corporal Turner, please escort my wife back to our house."

Anne broke from his grasp. "No!"

"But, Anne . . ."

"No," she exclaimed defiantly, drying her eyes. "My place is here. I'll help load like anyone else."

"They're comin', Major," Jehu said, in a voice placid as a pond. Anne was shocked to see the old man smile in devilish glee. He looked for all the world like a malevolent sprite. Suddenly he howled, the cry echoing through the fort. "Here they come, boys! Goddamn! We got us a fight!"

Warlike whoops responded, rose to a deafening pitch. Anne covered her ears. The English soldiers stared dumbfounded, grinned nervously at their American counterparts. "Mother of Christ! They're looking forward to it!" one startled corporal gasped.

"They're mad, mad. Mad as hatters."

"Stand steady, men!" Henry called. "Pass the word! Be ready!" Anne stared at him, shocked to see the same wild joy mirrored in Henry's gleaming eyes. Transformed by the light of battle, his handsome features had become almost inhumanly cruel. "We'll settle this at last, damn them!"

The walkway on which they stood was eight feet deep and provided ample room for soldiers to rush past those who had assumed the task of keeping the weapons loaded. Heavy wooden ladders provided access to the ground fifteen feet below. A rail afforded some security to those on the wall, and to this rail were nailed racks and bracings in which muskets and pistols were placed to be loaded after firing. Officers and noncoms moved back and forth behind the men, issuing orders, readying them for the fight to come.

The heavy concentration of fire on Patrick confirmed that the east wall would bear the brunt of the attack. Anne looked along the walls. One hundred and sixty-eight regulars and rangers; two hundred and thirteen, including women, civilians and wounded. They seemed so pitifully few to stand against the horde creeping beneath the malevolent grayness. The wall of tree trunks thrust into the earth and the wood planking beneath her feet were all the world remaining.

She crept forward, drawn to look down in morbid fascination at the ghost blanket. What could Henry and Jehu see that she could not? She listened, heard nothing. Peered into the heart of silence, saw nothing.

And then she knew. As if she had become one with the fort, with the earth and humid, pregnant silence she could feel the padded tremor of moccasined feet, hear the soft, sibilant breathing of men. The smell and taste of fear sent the blood pulsing through her veins. An inexplicable surge of wild exhilaration swept over her. The moist, fibrous wood beneath her hand, the chill damp of metal, the smell of men and wet earth. Eyes, ears, nose, throat, arms, legs . . . All senses, each muscle and nerve end, were keyed in anticipation.

Thoughts raced pell mell. What I have is mine. I have lived and loved and suffered and now I shall fight for all that has become mine. She glanced at Henry in that moment, memorizing the strong forceful contours of his face, the rough-textured shadow of beard that outlined his stubborn jaw. His was that strange mixture of savagery and civilization. His was the kind that would last. If she never saw him again, she would have possessed him completely, would retain the wild love he had offered, the calm acceptance of his dream. It was her dream now. Their dream.

A drumbeat in the distance. Detroit's defenders

stood stock still, listening. The beat grew, swelled, came from all sides to envelop the fort in a crescendo of throbbing sound that railed against the blood and froze the muscles. If the drums weren't enough, an eerie, chanting cry rose from the invisible ground. A thousand unseen throats chanted cutting war cries, sent the voice over the drums, over the walls. Henry stood motionless, waiting. Jehu spat over the wall, checked his priming and cocked the musket. The metallic click went unheard in the rising din. Anne shivered, wished for it to begin, for something, anything, to happen . . .

Movement in the mist! The war cries stopped. Silence, deafening quiet. Suddenly the mist broke, pierced by a hundred leafless trees rising out of the gray concealment. Sturdy, slender poles of birch, branches lopped off to handhold length, stood poised and motionless, a fearful skeleton forest.

"Fire!" The fort exploded with gunshots. Pealing whoops and war cries ranged the length of the east and north walls. The birch poles swung forward, landed against the logs. A splinter jabbed into Anne's cheek as lead shot struck the palisade. She staggered back as the defenders answered with their own outcries. The cannons in the blockhouses bellowed at the painted figures rising from the mist, scrambling in ever-increasing numbers up the makeshift ladders. Anne, momentarily startled by the murderous din, grabbed the nearest smoking musket, thrust a ramrod down the barrel to extinguish any burning residue, quickly withdrew the rod and thrust a torn paper cartridge into the barrel, added ball and patch and rammed them into place. A trickle of gunpowder in the pan and the weapon was reloaded, ready to be re-

placed within easy reach of her husband. Two more
waited.

Time disappeared as she fell into an unconscious
rhythm, repeating over and over the simple steps
Jeremy had taught her, ignoring the pain in her cheek.
Fighting ranged the circumference of the fort now.
The men on the west and south walls, though not under immediate assault, received a steady harassing
fire designed to keep the defending forces spread out
and unable to concentrate on the main attack from
north and east.

Men pushed off the birch poles as they landed on the
edge of the wall, but there were too many and they
could not keep up. This was the critical moment.
Henry motioned for Ensign Price, shouted in the ensign's ear. The men parted, racing off to the opposing
blockhouses. Other soldiers moved to fill the gaps left
by the officers' departure. There was no time to sustain
the brief panic when Henry disappeared. Anne gritted
her teeth and worked even faster, loading and placing weapons in the nearest outstretched hand.

The number of poles jutting over the wall increased.
The soldiers were hard pressed to concentrate their
fire on the braves scrambling up because of the heavy
fire from the warriors scattered on the ground, who
kept rising in deadly waves from the covering fog,
firing, then dipping back to roll to a new position, reload and repeat the tactic. Jehu was a fury. Face distorted, he screamed imprecations at the Indians, ex-
horted the defenders with a never-ending stream of
oaths and curses. A demon defying the searching
muskets of the foe, he leaped up, fired a brace of
pistols into the rising ranks of redmen clinging to the
birch trees, whirled, grabbed two more and fired again.

Other soldiers had less luck. Already, many had been wounded, some badly. Anne gasped as one bleeding soldier fell against her then crumbled, slipped under the frail railing and plummeted to the ground. Another young private turned to reach for a weapon. Jeremy handed him a loaded musket, but the youth sagged forward, a tomahawk lodged deep in the base of his skull. Anne looked away and into the painted face of a snarling warrior just gaining the wall. Jeremy struggled to free the musket from the dying soldier's grip. The Indian raised his own flintlock. On reflex, Anne lifted the pistol she had just loaded and squeezed the trigger. Smoke jutted upward from the striking flint. Flame and black smoke leaped from the barrel. The Indian jerked as the ball took him in the chest. His musket discharged, but aimed toward the heavens. Blood spurted from the redman's chest, showering the air as he fell backward.

Another scream. More warriors surged over the stockade. Soldiers grabbed muskets with bayonets already fixed and joined in the hand-to-hand fray. Ottawa and Huron alike wielded knives and tomahawks. God only knew what was happening along the north wall, but the bayonets held against the shorter weapons drove the Indians back against the parapet they'd just surmounted.

Jeremy fought his way to one of the swivel guns, a heavy bore musket lighter than a cannon but requiring an iron tripod mounting. He rammed home a charge, and as a new group of braves swept over the wall, swung the gun about and fired. The warriors flew backward, head over heels.

Frozen with fear and horror, Anne watched as men lost their balance on the slippery planking, screamed in pain, were trampled and died while others climbed over their corpses. Jeremy was overpowered by one warrior. Weak from the two-day-old wound which had opened and was bleeding again, he fell onto the ground, escaping death only when a ranger appeared from nowhere, drove a knife into the warrior and heaved him over the palisade, using the corpse as a weapon to knock other climbing Indians from a ladder.

But the wall was breached in too many places. Indians and whites mixed in bloody fray. Cowering, Anne clutched the railing, afraid to jump, afraid to dare the walkway. A hand grabbed at her arm, pulling her aside. She tried to fight, stopping only when she realized it was a white man. He pointed to the ladder, pulled her through the melee and screamed for her to climb down and get out of the way. "No!"

"Yes, damn it! Move!" A Huron was on his back, and he was fighting for his life.

Henry leaped into the blockhouse at the junction of the east and river walls. Three soldiers lay sprawled in death. A fourth and fifth wheeled a cannon forward to blast the dissipating fog. "Bring that gun to this port!" Henry screamed over the din.

The men turned at the sound of his voice. Startled, they helped drag the six-pounder to the side window so the barrel would discharge its load of grape along and into the east wall. One of the privates blanched as he saw how dangerously close Henry would come to raking his own men. The fort was reduced to firing on itself.

Across the way, the northeast blockhouse cannon had likewise aimed along the wall. Cannon faced cannon. In the middle, a ragged line of birch ladders leaned at precarious angles, rocked and bounced with the weight of the climbing, half-naked, painted Hurons and Ottawas. Oblivious to whirring balls of lead, Henry leaned out the firing port, a kerchief tied to the tip of his sword. A white blur answered from Ensign Price, barely visible through the smoke of battle. Each second saw more savages gain the walkway. He forced back the thought of Anne standing so close to the line of fire and, bending, sighted along the barrel. It would be close, very close. Flame touched the priming powder. A puff of smoke . . . the flame ran through the hole in the breech . . . caught . . . The cannon blast shook the floor beneath their feet. "Duck!"

Ensign Price returned the fire. The shot failed to reach them, rather chewed the birch ladders and bored through the ranks of hapless targets in between. Shredded flesh and wood flew through the air, splattered the walls and punctured the roiling mist. Another round clawed the wall that was their very protection. Though he knew some of his own men would die, Henry swabbed the bore, helped reload and wheel the cannon into place, fired again. The Indians' ladders collapsed, spilling ruined bodies.

Price answered in kind. The blockhouse disappeared in clouds of black powder smoke which made it more difficult to aim. But they had to take the chance. "Load! Aim! Fire!"

Screams of blind agony shrieked through the air. The same tactic was working as well along the north wall. Cannons roared, bodies tumbled and crawled amid a wreckage of timber. One section of the east wall shuddered, sagged. The carnage continued on the walkway where those braves who had gained the wall were now isolated. Deprived of retreat or support, they were on the defensive, badly outnumbered and fighting for their lives. A final cannonade, two explosions so close together they sounded like a double blow, signalled the Indians' knell along the north wall.

Gunfire still crackled, diminished now. The shrill war cries from below were gone, replaced by eerie, rising death chants as warrior after warrior sang for his ebbing spirit, sang to the world he was leaving. Henry charged from the blockhouse, searching for Anne, madly shouting her name, and listened for her answering call.

"Continue firing!" he yelled over his shoulder. Sword in hand, he fought through the struggling fighters, shouting "Anne" over and over as he cuffed, stabbed and sliced his way to where he had left her. A warrior lunged, knife in hand. Henry swerved to one side. The brave impaled himself on the sword. Henry yanked the blade free in time to bludgeon another with the dull brass basket hilt.

Where was Anne? A tomahawk slashed past his face, cutting his cheek. A soldier screamed and knocked Henry off balance as he fell. A Huron gave a cry of victory, but Henry recovered in time to parry the tomahawk, grab the warrior by the throat and hurl him through the balustrade. The Indian landed with a bone-snapping crunch on the packed earth, there to die at the hand of a wounded but still game soldier.

Gus Schraner, swinging his musket like a club, cleared a path to Henry's side. Jehu came scrambling up a ladder, a bloodied hunting knife in either hand. "Where's Anne?" Henry shouted.

Jehu pointed toward the Gladwyn house. "Sent her there when I saw what you was up to. She didn't want to go, but I made her an' the other women he'p with the wounded. Jesus, but we got a mess of 'em."

Henry wiped the sweat from his forehead. The breeze felt good. Breeze? He rushed to the wall. The fog was breaking apart, pushed by the wind and burned by the sun, already well up. Had time passed that quickly? Below, tendrils thinned, cloudy vapors parted. A shot whistled past. Jehu grabbed a musket and fired back. An Indian ducked, turned and ran.

Fighting had ceased along the north wall. The Indians left on the field to the east stared mutely at the stockade, grabbed fallen companions and retreated out of range. "They're beat! Goddamn it, they're beat! Look at 'em!" Jehu yelled exuberantly. "They're taking to their heels, boys!"

"There's the reason," Henry replied, pointing farther to their left. A lone birch tree ladder had survived the withering crossfire. Teata dangled in view of the whole battleground, his ankle caught in the V of a stubby branch, one arm blown off at the elbow. A leg was missing. The corpse was a grotesque crimson banner rocking to and fro above the mutilated remains of the warriors who had died in the deadly crossfire. The Hurons would fight no more. Their chief was dead.

The Ottawas remained where they were, scattered about the fort. Exhausted, the few remaining soldiers on the walkway held their fire. Men slumped against the walls. Some moaned for water, others stared blankly into space or down at the equally exhausted Indians. A black haze of powder smoke drifted in the air. The ground fog was evaporating rapidly, leaving behind only token wisps in the hollows.

Below, Anne and the other women had started for the walls, this time carrying buckets of water for the beleaguered combatants. Anne stopped at Henry's side. She was exhausted, haggard, covered with smoke and sweat, stained with blood. Henry thought she had never seemed so beautiful. He drank greedily from the dipper she extended to him, sighing with contentment as the cool water soothed his throat.

"I don't know which is worse," Anne whispered. "The clamor and explosions or this quiet. What are they waiting for?"

"Pontiac."

The war chief watched without speaking as the Hurons left the field. He had refrained from the immediate fighting in order to better oversee the whole attack. Now the braves left alive around the fort awaited his signal. The Ottawas would continue the struggle alone.

Pontiac looked up at Teata's body. Foolish Huron! In his haste to take an English scalp he had been killed, leaving his warriors leaderless. They would fight no more. To either side the two hundred warriors he had held in reserve waited for his command. He considered well. They would fight if he wished. But there would already be weeping in the villages. Winter, when the earth slept, was not far off. Defiantly, Detroit still stood.

He knew in his soul Henry Gladwyn had won. His sister's killer had won. He had only two alternatives—continue to sacrifice the warriors who followed him, or submit to the disgrace. The Gods were arrayed against him. Even the breath of the Great Spirit had returned to blow the mist away, leaving his warriors without cover, standing amid the gruesome harvest of death reaped from the fecund field.

You have beaten me, Major Henri, Pontiac thought to himself. But I will yet have my revenge.

From the wall, all could see Pontiac raise his musket

overhead, then point it muzzle first to the earth. Jehu expelled a long sigh. "He's callin' it off. By God, he's callin' it off."

Below, the warriors cast one lingering look of animal hatred toward the stockade, then sullenly followed the already departed Hurons' lead. The day was lost. Silently, with the help of the two hundred in reserve, they collected their wounded and dead. The siege of Detroit had been broken.

Cries of triumph rang through the fort. Men and women wept openly. Only Henry seemed not to share in the euphoria. Anne knew why. She touched his arm. "What will he do now?"

Henry searched the western bend of the river, hoping to catch sight of a sail. The river was empty. His fists clenched helplessly and he searched the far forest. Pontiac was no longer visible. "Jehu."

"Yes, sir, Major."

"I need ten men. Ten of your best, if you still have them. It's all we can spare."

Jehu shook his head. "We're askin' for it, Major, walkin' out there before they clear out," he said, then suddenly realized the cause of Henry's concern. "Damn me for a fool! I forgot. Ten of my best." He hurried away.

Anne's grip tightened on Henry's arm. Henry wished he could reassure her.

The attic was empty. Pontiac bounded down the steps. Pierre and Evangeline sat in the living room. "Where is the girl, old man?" The Charbonneaus remained silent. Pontiac drew his knife, held the blade to Evangeline's throat. "I have no time, Frenchman. Where is Autumn Woman?"

"No!" Evangeline said. "Do not tell him!"

Pierre Charbonneau lowered his head. "She is down by the river," he said softly. "Where we keep the canoe."

The light birchbark craft bobbed up and down in the tiny cove. Beth cursed the leather thong. The knot was wet and tight and she could not loosen it. Grasping the knife taken from the Charbonneaus' kitchen, she hacked at the leather until the line parted and fell into the water.

"Autumn Woman!"

Beth screamed, forgot the canoe and hurtled down the sandy river bank in a desperate bid for freedom that ended abruptly when the warrior buffeted her to the ground. The knife slid from her hand. If she could only get to the water . . .

Too late! Pontiac dropped his musket, caught her ankle and pulled her back. Dragged up the bank, her smock slid up to reveal slender, pale thighs. Pontiac grabbed an arm, flipped her over, straddled her and pinned her arms with his knees. Eyes wide with terror, Beth watched as the strong, red-brown fingers descended to close about her throat.

Pontiac's mind filled with a thousand fleeting images. Soon she would be dead. As Henry had killed Flower-on-the-Water, he would kill Autumn Woman. Death for death. He would kill the girl. Autumn Woman. Eliza-beth Flower . . . Kill her! Kill her as Henri . . . as *Pontiac* had killed Flower-on-the-Water!

Beth felt the pressure on her neck ease. For long moments she lay gasping and choking, heaving for breath. Curtains of red mist distorted the face peering into hers. Suddenly the figure receded and the heavy weight lifted from her arms and stomach. "Go. Return to your people, Eliza-beth." The voice was far away, barely audible. "Go back now."

Beth could see him, far above. She wanted to say something, but a booming voice interrupted. "I think she will stay, *mon ami*. I think she will stay here forever."

Dumas stepped into the open. He had known of the Charbonneaus' canoe, had sought the river as a means to escape. The Frenchman levelled a pistol at Beth. Pontiac's musket lay too far away for use. "My Indian brother has forgotten the dead."

"My French brother mistakes. I remember well the dead."

"And you would set the sorry *putain* free? We should have killed her long ago. The fort would have been ours."

"I do not think so, Dumas. It does not matter now."

Dumas sneered. "Doesn't matter?"

"No."

"Your braves no longer follow you."

"So be it."

Dumas stepped closer, his eyes narrow and filled with hate. "Pontiac has no stomach for revenge," he hissed, "but I have. I owe Major Gladwyn too much. The revenge of Jean Dumas."

Pontiac shrugged. "Do what you will. As for me, I have spoken. It is done."

Dumas levelled the pistol again. Beth held up her hands as if to ward off the killing explosion. Pontiac turned as if to leave, then spun about, his right arm sweeping over and down. Dumas jerked away the pistol. Too late! In the still point of fractured time, he saw the tomahawk, hinged unmoving in space.

The hatchet blade bit into Dumas' chest and the

pistol discharged into the ground. The Frenchman screamed and ran, panic-stricken, into the water. He tried to gain solid footing but the bottom was slippery with smooth rocks. His arms flailed the water, churned the crimson-clouding surface to a froth.

The blade in his chest . . . ! He clawed at the wooden shaft, but the pain was too terrible. Gawking faces stared gleefully. Eyes wide, his mouth opened in a continuous, soundless shriek. The strength ran from his chest. Slowly, Dumas' head sank into the water. The faces followed, circling, gurgling and blowing tiny bubbles. Laughing and pointing, they swam out the open gate to welcome treacherous death. Time was askew. Did Munro still stand? Swimming, fighting the river, he struggled through the gates. Fort Munro was empty. He was alone. The dark gates closed.

Pontiac stepped over the dead man and caught the drifting canoe. Grasping the sides, he leaped into the birchbark craft and grabbed the paddle.

"Pontiac!" Beth called. "Wait, you're hurt."

Pontiac glanced at the crease of blood streaking his shoulder, the tiny rivulet running down his arm. "Hand me the musket, Eliza-beth."

Obeying without question, Beth picked up the weapon, stepped into the shallow water, avoiding Dumas' corpse. "Pontiac?"

The Indian laid the musket on the floor of the canoe. Swiftly, he maneuvered the boat into deeper water.

"Where will you go?" Beth called, in tears now, weeping because she would never see him again.

"Tell Henri . . ." He stopped, a puzzled look on his face. Suddenly he laughed. There was nothing to say to the one who had been his brother. "Goodbye, Eliza-beth. Goodbye, woman-of-my-heart."

The paddle dug into the water and the canoe pushed forward into the current, heading upriver. Beth watched as a group of men came running along the water's edge. Henry was in the lead, Jehu and Jeremy only a pace behind. Pontiac's canoe was heading east and slightly north. In an hour he would be in Lake Saint Clair, before nightfall on the open reaches of Lake Huron. He was gone forever.

Beth cupped her hands to her mouth.

"Pontiac!" she shouted. "Pontiac! Autumn Woman will not forget!"

Her voice resounded through the wilderness. Distant echoes returned, faded quickly.

She thought she saw him wave.

CHAPTER 30

Like kindled fires, the glory of fall swept the woods with a lavish palette. Golden aspen and brick-red cut-leaf maple glowed against the deep emerald of cedar, juniper and pine. September's grief had passed, put aside to make room for the living.

There was time at last. Time enough. Anne walked alone in the soft autumn hours, enjoying the last fluted bouquets of wild rose and black-eyed susans. A squirrel chattered lazily overhead, pelted her with the torn husk of an acorn. A contentious blue jay argued long and loud, protesting in vain the ownership of the tree in which the squirrel sat. Anne heard laughter. Her own.

She had been out every day since a week after the *Michigan*'s arrival. The tribes had melted into the woods after their stunning defeat. They would not return until spring, and then as if nothing had happened, or so Jehu predicted. For the moment, the forest was her own private garden, housing mystery and wild, reckless bounty.

There had been work. Many had been wounded and needed care. Many had died and needed burying. Many were left alone and needed love and compassion. Anne lost herself in labor. The house was a shambles after having been filled with wounded men.

Marian McBeecher had been wounded badly. Worse, Jess had been killed. Time held the only balm for such a sadness as that.

The new soldiers helped take up much of the slack, but there were tasks only a woman could do well. For the most part, Anne forgot her dream of England. When she did remember, it was usually in the middle of some menial chore she would never even have contemplated a year earlier. At those moments, Anne smiled and pushed on, happy enough to be where she was, doing what she was doing.

Henry's time had been occupied with reestablishing the outposts lost during the rebellion. Leaving before dawn each morning, he worked long hours and stumbled home to fall asleep in her arms. Once, he tried to change Juliet, but the hands that fought so competently were no match for the challenge. Face red, he muttered dire imprecations and gave up. The next morning, the obligations of command beckoned him to Michilimackinac: he had been gone ever since.

Anne sighed, shook her head. Henry Gladwyn was a man destined to be busy forever, and his wife might as well get used to the idea. Somehow though, duty seemed not so terrible now. She had responsibilities too, after all. The *Michigan* was due back any day, full of new settlers who would make Detroit their home. They would need help, and Anne had resolved to make their transition to frontier life easier. There were sufficient hardships in the howling wilderness, and not so much perfection, without having to face a Detroit winter without friendship and what little civilization those who knew the ways of the wild could offer. Of course, she wouldn't overdo it. This wasn't England.

Once in the deep woods, Anne wandered toward the pond she had discovered so long ago; where she had slept, confronted Catherine and her own unhappiness. The clearing was empty. With a pang of remorse, she realized the fawn was probably dead, taken for food by the Indians who had camped so near and in such great numbers. At least the beaver mound stood untouched, the mud and twigs impervious to the swiftly passing days.

Anne unwrapped the packet she had carried from the fort and removed a beautifully beaded doeskin shift given her by Henry before he left on his inspection tour. Unused to what would be considered "native" wear, Anne had not been able to reconcile herself to wearing the shift in the fort until she realized how completely the dresses she had brought from England were worn. There would be little room aboard the *Michigan* for luxuries like cloth until the more essential articles used up during the siege could be replaced.

The doeskin certainly felt like it would last. Perhaps she would even look good in it. Hurriedly undoing buttons before her nerve failed, she stepped out of her dress and quickly slipped into the soft garment, surprised and pleased at the way it caressed her flesh.

"It looks beautiful on you."

Anne gave a startled scream and whirled about. Grinning, Henry stepped into the clearing, dropped a pack and propped his musket on a fallen tree trunk.

"But I liked what was underneath better."

"Sir . . ."

The sentence died with the first word as Henry swept her into a crushing embrace. Anne tilted back her head. The sun on her eyelids was warm, but his lips warmer. Afire with hunger, she clung to him and returned the kiss.

Still holding her shoulders, Henry stepped back. "Did you miss me?"

"You were gone thirteen days and . . ."—she glanced at the sun—". . . approximately four and a half hours." His shirt was undone to the waist. Anne's fingers strayed to his chest, dropped to the wide leather belt around his waist. "I missed you," she muttered huskily.

Henry caught the short sleeves of the new shift and pulled upward. Anne raised her arms, felt the soft, tanned skin slide over her stomach and breasts. The cool October breeze caressed her thighs, buttocks and back. The shift fell to the ground and she stood proudly unclothed, breasts held high, legs slightly spread. Henry's eyes travelled the length of her body, slowly rising from the ground to her face, stopping now and again, pausing. When their eyes met, his hands moved to his belt, slowly undid the buckle. He shrugged his shoulders and the shirt fell. One quick movement and the leather breeches followed and were kicked aside. Naked, they stood motionless as statues, as much of nature as the woods themselves.

The breeze died and the forest fell silent in expectation. Slowly, Anne moved into his arms, sucking in a great breath as their bodies touched. Thigh met thigh. His swelling manhood pressed against her belly. Her breasts met his chest, crushed against the ridged muscles. Without a word, they sank to the waiting bed of grass and there lay joined as one, a marvellous panting, thrashing creature of love and passion which froze in attitudes of ecstasy, sculpted by the sweet pain of consummation.

❄   ❄   ❄

The sun crept overhead, passing into the azure eternity of the western sky. They lay back, Henry on his side, Anne nestled in the crook of his arm, both covered by the kicking breeze. Henry lifted a single auburn curl from the still swollen crown of her breast. "I would have nothing conceal you, my darling."

Anne trembled at the pressure of his manhood lying across her thigh. She smiled impishly. "Not even you?"

Henry grinned. "You have named the sole exception."

"You take advantage, sir."

"Advantage? Not at all. I cover you, you imprison me. We are both the loser—and in losing, are both the winner."

Anne laughed. "You play well with words."

"Aye. And elsewhere as well." Leaning over, he sought her breasts, gently kissed them, lingered to tease with tongue and lips.

"So soon?" she whispered. Her hand crept down, stroked and pressed his manhood to her thigh.

Henry sat up unexpectedly. "You, madam, are incorrigibly voracious. I am thirsty. Come." Heaving to his feet, he pulled her by the hand and headed for the pond. They walked slowly, arm in arm. At the water's edge they lay down, cupped the cold water and drank. The pond was clear. Beneath the still surface minnows darted back and forth, playing tag with the shadows and the sun.

Satisfied for the moment, they relaxed, drowsy with the sun and happy to be near each other. "I think I could stay here forever," Henry finally said, a little wistfully.

"And what would they do at the fort without you there to guide their course?"

"Why, drift helplessly, of course. I grant them a merry journey." He grinned. "For one day, at any rate."

Anne lay with cheek on hand, reached out to write Henry's name on the water. "What about Beth?"

Henry nodded. "Safe enough with Jeremy. Michilimackinac will suit them, I believe. There's a sadness in her eyes from time to time, but the lad loves her deeply. The last thing she needs is the watchful eye of an old uncle." He chuckled.

"Sir?"

Henry laughed, rolled to his side and pulled her to him. "Forget Beth. It's you I'm interested in."

"Really?" She snuggled against his chest, breathing the heady fragrance of pine and earth as his arms closed around her, enfolding her with his warmth and stillness. Her contentment was complete. She sighed and closed her eyes.

When she opened them, stars glimmered like icy fires on the velvet sky. "Are you asleep?" Anne asked.

"No."

"Thinking?"

"Yes."

"Of what?"

Henry turned on his side, stroked her face. Her lips were moist, eager for another kiss. He complied, then pulled the blanket around them. "A time . . . a gaming table. The most beautiful woman I had ever seen. I could not rest until she was mine. We played at cards."

"How romantic."

"You don't know the story?"

"Oh, no. Tell it to me."

"I searched the deck for one card, to win or lose forever. I wondered if she knew."

"I think so."

"Yours, I said, playing the first card. Mine, another card. And so it went."

"Until . . . thine . . ." said Anne.

"You know, sweet liar."

Anne giggled, kissed him on the chest. "I wished to hear the tale again. It's the story closest to my heart."

"The queen of hearts," Henry said, startled by the tears his lips found on her cheek. But Anne was smiling, and her face was radiant in the moonlight.

On the forest floor, a man and a woman lay lost to their own sweet mingling, caught in the rhythm of whispered endearments, held in the magical awareness of union and release.

"A truer game we never played, my dearest love," Anne said at last. The night wind whispered to the sleeping flowers ". . . nor truer love lived."

The first novel in the spectacular new
Heiress series

The English Heiress

Roberta Gellis

Leonie De Conyers—beautiful, aristocratic, she lived in the
shadow of the guillotine, stripped of everything she held
dear. Roger St. Eyre—an English nobleman, he set out to save
Leonie in a world gone mad.

They would be kidnapped, denounced and brutally separated. Driven by passion, they would escape France, return
to England, fulfill their glorious destiny and seize a lofty
dream.

A Dell Book $2.50 (12141-8)

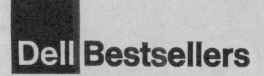